Raves for SHARON WEBB

". . . Does a marvelous job of keeping the action swift and unexpected while developing the characters . . . (in) an entertaining and intelligent novel of suspense. Her medical knowledge and research are evident throughout the book. . . . a page-turning tale of international intrigue."

—*Atlanta Journal*

". . . A better writer than most . . ."

—*The New York Times*

PESTIS 18

"Ironic plot twists. . . . With brief but sound character profiles, colorful environmental descriptions, and plenty of action . . ."

—*Library Journal*

"Hair-raising clinical detail."

—*Kirkus Reviews*

PESTIS 18

SHARON WEBB

TOR

A TOM DOHERTY ASSOCIATES BOOK

PESTIS 18

Copyright © 1987 by Sharon Webb

First printing: March 1987
First Mass Market printing: March 1988

A TOR Book

Published by Tom Doherty Associates, Inc.
49 West 24 Street
New York, N.Y. 10010

Map by Tom Deitz

ISBN: 0-812-51066-6
CAN. NO.: 0-812-51067-4

Library of Congress Catalog Card Number: 86-50958

Printed in the United States of America

For Harriet McDougal

Acknowledgments

A book like this is not possible without expert help. I would like to thank the following people who gave their time and shared their knowledge so graciously:

Fellow writers John M. Ford and Robert Jordan for their help with demolitions, procedures, and materiel. Gerald W. Page for his encouragement and support. Doris Buchanan Smith for specialized island lore.

Steve Nesheim, M.D., and Michael J. White, Major, USAF, MC(FS), for our many discussions about plague, bioengineering, isolation, and hypothermia.

Wendy Nesheim, R.N., M.Ed., Jerri Thompson, R.N., and Carmen Fitton, R.N. and nursing school buddy, for their special input.

Woody Bell for media information.

Tracey Kolbinger for the music of St. Cyrils Island.

The late Lieutenant General Mitchell Livingston Werbel III for his insight into the terrorist mind and for information about terrorists, defense, and materiel.

R. J. Harris, Special Agent in Charge, Region 8, Georgia Bureau of Investigation, for his help with GBI, sheriff's office, and police procedure and for his advice on evacuation procedures.

Randy Thompson, R.Ph., for detailed information about antibiotics.

Lieutenant Colonel Gerald Wannarka, R.Ph., Ph.D, Medical Chemical Defense R&D Program, Fort Detrick, for dissecting my scenarios and for pharmacological advice.

Charles W. Hinkle, Director, Freedom of Information

and Security Review, Office of the Assistant Secretary of Defense; John E. Bacon, Information and Privacy Coordinator, Central Intelligence Agency; Captain Pat K. Bowen, Post Judge Advocate, U.S. Army Dugway Proving Ground; Colonel Harry G. Dangerfield, M.D., U.S. Army Medical Research and Development Command, Fort Detrick; Major General Niles J. Fulwyler, Director of Nuclear and Chemical, Office of the Deputy Chief of Staff for Operations and Plans, Department of the Army, for their cooperation under the Freedom of Information Act.

Bryan Webb for everything else.

I would like to emphasize that I am solely responsible for any errors in this book.

Sharon Webb

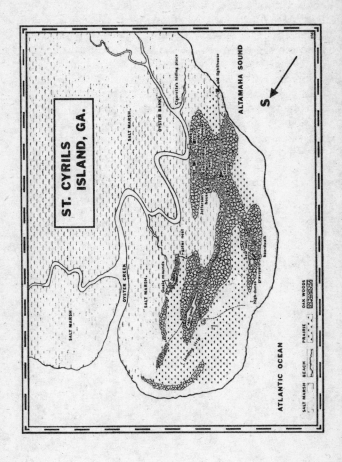

ST. CYRILS ISLAND, GA.

ALTAMAHA SOUND

Cigarette's hiding place

old lighthouse

OYSTER BANKS

SALT MARSH

S

SALT MARSH

OYSTER CREEK

Jefferson house

Easter mist

SALT MARSH

Gun mount

high dunes graveyard boardwalk

Sand Dune

Hell Hole

hunting strip

SALT MARSH

ATLANTIC OCEAN

SALT MARSH BEACH PRAIRIE OAK WOODS

Ring around a rosy,
Pocket full of posy,
Ashes, ashes,
All fall down . . .

Prologue

THE APE HAD TWENTY-EIGHT MINUTES LEFT TO LIVE. SHE lay in the sealed isolation room while cameras recorded her agony on videotape, and air samplers caught her ragged expirations and shunted them to remote biological LIDAR detection systems.

Ostensibly, the building housed a small pharmaceutical company; in fact, the company did produce a limited amount of commercial generic drugs. Most of the employees knew nothing about the freight elevator in the storage room behind the double doors stenciled AUTHORIZED PERSONNEL ONLY.

Inside the elevator the division officer stabbed the button marked BASEMENT, reached into a pocket of his rumpled gray suit, and drew out a plastic badge marked with a series of vertical bars. When the elevator door wheezed open to a fluorescent-lighted area filled with steel shelving and cardboard cartons, he pressed the badge to a small rectangle on the control panel. A green light flashed, the doors closed, and the elevator began to drop again.

On the lower level an armed guard in a bulletproof booth examined his credentials minutely before letting him pass. At the end of the featureless white-walled hall he came to a doorway. Red lights gleamed from it; another blinked on, flashing the words RESTRICTED AREA. Again he reached for the badge. When he pushed it into a slot to the right of the doorway, he was answered by a faint hum. The door slid open.

A man in a white lab coat looked up. Above the breast

pocket of his coat the name "Sanders" was embroidered in red. He extended a hand to the man in the suit. "I was told to expect you. Come with me, please."

The division officer followed Sanders into another white corridor studded with matching closed doors. Refrigerated air bearing the faint, sharp scent of disinfectant whispered through filtered ducts.

They came to a double door. To its right a white keyboard sat tucked in a shallow niche. Sanders tapped out a code and the doors swung open. They stepped inside. The officer turned with a start as the doors, with a sudden swishing sound, closed behind them and locked.

They stood in an anteroom now. Ahead, a red light above an oval air lock flashed PROCEDURE 4 AREA. "We change here," said Sanders. He took off the lab coat and hung it on a stainless-steel hook. From a metal cabinet against one wall, he pulled out two folded yellow jumpsuits and handed one to the other man. "Take off your jacket."

The division officer did as he was told. He put on the jumpsuit. Its sleeves ended in gloves, its legs in oversized shoe covers. Awkwardly imitating the movements of Sanders, he pressed Velcro tabs, sealing the garment, and pulled on the attached helmet, leaving only his eyes exposed behind curved goggles.

Sanders pressed a lever, and the air lock swung open. They stepped through, and as the officer stared uneasily, Sanders sealed the lock. The motion activated another warning flash: IN EVENT OF SYSTEMS FAILURE, CHAMBER WILL NOT OPEN.

With a hiss the far door opened and they stepped out. The room was little more than a corridor. Along one wall at waist height, a dark window palely reflected the two helmeted figures. Sanders faced the window and thrust his hands into a pair of limp black gloves attached to a panel. With a slight motion of his fingers he pressed a control and lights sprang on behind the windows. Both hands moved now—delicate, caressing movements. On the other side of the window, remote-controlled Waldos responded. He stared intently through the thick glass as the metal clamps moved, paused, moved again.

A clamp swung toward a series of sealed glass tubes of culture media. Sander's hand moved almost imperceptibly. As it did, the clamp gripped the thin glass cylinder. The metal arm swung toward them and stopped.

Through the window the division officer could see quite clearly the words on the tube's surface: YERSINIA PESTIS 18.

"We used plasmid R factors to alter the bacteria," said Sanders. "You're looking at a plague bacillus resistant to every antibiotic you could name."

The officer's pupils dilated slightly as he stared at the culture. Within its glass prison, fluffs of sediment, innocently white, bristled with living stilettos. The man let out a held breath that sighed against the window.

"Penicillin, chloramphenicol, and streptomycins are destroyed outright," said Sanders. "Tetracycline is kept out by plasmid-encoded modifications of the cell envelope." He went on: "The sulfas and trimethoprim are bypassed—" But the division man had ceased to hear Sanders. The technical jargon was beyond him; it was the preliminary report that he was remembering now, the terse sentences that had stuck with him ever since: *The first authentic pandemic in the sixth century is estimated to have claimed one hundred million victims. . . . The second pandemic in the fourteenth century was known as the Black Death.*

Dealing with the operation on paper had been an exercise, an intellectual game—knight to king's bishop four; checkmate. He had worked on that part of NKWILY that dealt with dissemination of a hypothetical BW agent: the foreign port; the planting of one or two victims of traditional bubonic plague; the aerosol device that would spray a tiny corner of the world with an altered bacillus designed to spread an incurable, pneumonic form of the disease.

It was a sound scheme; it would look like a natural outbreak of the disease in a part of the world where plague still lurked in vermin-ridden docks. Only when its resistance was discovered would the enemy suspect. Suspect, but never prove.

The division officer looked at Sanders, then back at the thin glass tube that hung delicately from the claws of the Waldo. "Can you kill this thing?"

"Give us time," said Sanders. "We have a small amount of experimental antibiotic. We're some way off from considering production. Antibiotics aren't the answer, though. Our real defense lies in an immunizing vaccine."

"How far off is that?"

"At least two months' more work," said Sanders. "Then we're talking about four to six months on a priority basis to produce enough commercially to protect the populace."

The officer nodded. He hoped Pestis 18 would never be used. If it were, the infection would inevitably spread back to the U.S. mainland. But if it came to that, they would be ready. Stockpiling of the vaccine could begin in a few months.

It had worked before, he thought. When intelligence obtained the Soviet-designed Swine Flu virus, they discovered it was close enough to our own for cross-immunity. Millions of Americans had been immunized, defanging the Red threat and aborting their planned attack. Of course, there had been the expected credibility loss when the Swine Flu epidemic didn't materialize. The selling job to the public was going to be harder next time.

The officer stared through the window at the suspended tube. "How do you handle that stuff? Outside the lab, I mean."

"I'll show you." Sanders touched the controls and the Waldos moved, this time toward a silvery metal cylinder. The culture tube hung poised for a moment over the open canister, then slowly lowered inside. Another clamp grasped the lid, turning it. At the faint click of the locking mechanism, Sanders's hands moved again and the Waldo's guided the container onto a conveyor.

Watching closely, the division man followed its progress to a small compartment. Suddenly white flames surrounded the canister. As quickly as it came, the fire vanished and a muffled hissing sound began—air evacuating the chamber. With a change of atmospheres the canister moved again through a fog of gas. Another flash of fire, another evacuation of air, and then the container popped into a glass-doored box next to them.

"Open it." Sanders indicated the small door.

The officer's hand moved toward the port, then shrank back.

Sanders laughed. "It's perfectly safe. The surface is decontaminated." He pushed the door open, picked up the canister, and held it out to the other man. "As long as it's sealed, there's no danger."

The officer made no move to touch the cylinder. "How can it survive the heating?"

"Insulation," said Sanders. "The flames are followed by immediate cooling. Pestis 18 doesn't even know it's been moved." He turned the canister in his hand and looked at the bright metal. "Put this in an aerosol and it's lively enough to infect an area the size of Manhattan." Sanders reinserted the cylinder, pressed a button, and watched as the canister traveled back to its original position. As he touched the controls a final time, the lights went out and blackness hung behind the windows.

He turned then and headed farther down the corridor. The division officer followed through a rat's maze of windowed passages.

They came to a wider area banked with electronic equipment. A man clad in yellow protective clothing sat at the console and watched a group of monitors. He looked up as they entered. "She's pulled off an electrode," he said to Sanders. "It was sutured, but she got it, anyway." He indicated the green phosphor tracing of the cardiac monitor to his right. "I've switched to an MV1 lead."

Sanders nodded. "This way," he said to the officer.

They stepped into a chamber which held three white contoured chairs that faced a heavy glass cage.

The orangutan was dying now. She lay on the floor with

her back to them. Quick, gasping breaths shuddered through her body. Her reddish fur was matted with excrement.

A video screen on the wall above them flashed green:

```
EXPOSURE TIME PLUS 18 HOURS, 23 MINUTES
EKG—SINUS TACHYCARDIA; INTERPOLATED
         VENTRICULAR BEATS
RESPIRATIONS—36
PULSE—130
SPUTUM—LUMINESCING. 4.0 RT SCALE
```

A clear plastic cone dropped from the ceiling of the cage and hovered a few inches above the animal's head. Within thirty seconds a slim tube near the ceiling began to glow faintly.

"What's that?"

"Chemiluminescent reaction," said Sanders. "It's measuring expired live bacillus in real time."

"She's contagious, then?" asked the officer uncertainly.

"Contagious as hell."

```
EXPOSURE TIME PLUS 18 HOURS, 25 MINUTES
EKG—SINUS TACHYCARDIA, FREQUENT PVCS
RESPIRATIONS—36
PULSE—138
SPUTUM—LUMINESCING. 4.2 RT SCALE
```

With a shudder, the ape flopped on her back, her sternum retracting now with every gasp, her ribs flexing as if they would snap. At her right shoulder, where she had clawed at the EKG electrode, a dribble of congealing blood streaked dark against her fur. She turned her face toward them. Her large brown eyes stared blindly. They were filmed with matter. A spasm of coughing shook her body, and white froth flecked with blood bubbled at her lips.

Avoiding the glazing brown eyes, the division officer focused on her hand. It lay palm up, half open, fingers curled. How human it looked. He suddenly felt quite ill. He turned away and stared at the floor, and with deep breaths tried to control his nausea.

>   EXPOSURE TIME PLUS 18 HOURS, 27 MINUTES
>   EKG—VENTRICULAR FIBRILLATION
>   RESPIRATIONS—AGONAL
>
>   EXPOSURE TIME PLUS 18 HOURS, 28 MINUTES
>   EKG—DYING HEART
>   RESPIRATIONS—CEASED

The two men walked back toward the air lock. "It's too bad we had to sacrifice her," said Sanders. "Expensive animal."

They were back in the original corridor now. The officer felt shaky. He put out a hand to steady himself. Just beyond, behind the thick, dark windows, hung the tubes of milky broth that nurtured Pestis 18.

He had no idea, of course, that two of the sealed test tubes contained a harmless culture; he had no way of knowing that two tubes of Pestis 18, trapped in silvery sleeves of metal, were gone.

WEDNESDAY

MUTATION

Chapter 1

THE GRIZZLED MEDICAL EXAMINER LOOKED UP IN ANNOY-
ance at the nondescript man in the rumpled gray suit.

Jack Hubert extracted a flat I.D. folder from an inner
pocket of his jacket. "I'm here about Sanders."

The M.E. laid down the Dictaphone mike, clamped his
Danish briar pipe in his mouth, and examined the man's
credentials. Raising an inquiring eyebrow, he asked, "One
of your boys?"

The division officer looked at him evenly. "Just someone we're interested in."

The medical examiner stared at him for a moment and
then, sucking at his pipe, rose. Hubert followed him into a
white-tiled room that echoed their footsteps.

"Dr. Parker's doing him now." The M.E. nodded
toward one of the tables where another man was handing an
assistant a yellowish piece of tissue clipped from the gap-
ing body.

The medical examiner reached into a battered wire basket and pulled out an envelope. "Looks like your boy was
going on a trip. The police found an up-to-date passport on
him and an airline ticket to Argentina. One way. One
o'clock flight, I believe." He handed the sheaf of photo-
graphs to Hubert.

The first picture showed the sprawling body with its
right hand outstretched on a patch of grass. The lines of a
barbed-wire fence trailed away in the background. The
second, a close-up, showed the Aerolineas Argentinas ticket
firmly grasped in his hand.

11

"Just like he was standing at the ticket counter," observed the medical examiner. "Looks like somebody wanted to know about that flight."

Hubert looked at the pictures for a moment longer and then handed them back. His expression was impassive, but a dozen thoughts cluttered his head. Sanders's body had been arranged carefully. The message was unmistakable: a sellout. He was afraid he knew what the merchandise was. Taking a step closer to the table, he looked down at the body. "Have you got the cause of death yet?"

Dr. Parker reached into the abdominal cavity and caught a loop of intestine with a gloved hand. The bowel was engorged with dark blood. He squeezed the loop of intestine, blanching it. At the answering cramp in his own gut, Hubert took a slow and silent breath.

"As you can see, marked visceral congestion," observed the medical examiner. "When we're finished testing, I don't think there'll be any doubt. Your boy was poisoned. Organic nicotine."

Dr. Parker released the loop of bowel and nodded in agreement. "He was dead before he knew what hit him."

The dark glitter of anger grew in Hubert's eyes. It would have been easy to put down Sanders so that it looked like an accident. Instead, they broadcast it. NKWILY was compromised. There was no doubt now about what Sanders had sold—none at all. And it wasn't a covert weaponry buy; they were flaunting the sellout, proving beyond doubt that they had Pestis 18. That left one of two options: ransom or a strike. But when? Where?

Jack Hubert stood by the table and looked down, this time at Sanders's face. Glazed and dilated eyes stared back at him from a gray-white face with its black stubble of beard. You bastard, he thought. You fucking bastard.

Chapter 2

DR. DANIEL ELTON GLARED AS THE PONTIAC SWERVED, overcorrected, and missed him by inches. Outmaneuvering a Bronco for the last parking space, he cut the wheel and pulled into a slot beneath a shedding oak tree. The Camaro lost traction on the slick pavement and slid into the curb. Elton grimaced. He'd been in Atlanta too long. Couldn't even drive on a wet leaf anymore.

The heater was blowing chilly air again. "Wonderful," he said out loud. And what did it plan for an encore when the cold front got here? Disgusted, he clicked off the ignition and the Camaro's frayed wiper blades gave a final groaning swipe. Slamming the car door harder than necessary, he turned up his collar and sprinted toward the Ethiopian restaurant across the street. As he reached for the door, a cold stream of rain slid down the waxy leaves of a tubbed magnolia and spattered the back of his neck.

Through fogged horn-rims Elton scanned the tables. He spotted Bru Farrier at once—and so, apparently, had several others who caught Bru's quick wave and stared with open curiosity. Feeling a little self-conscious, he slid into a chair.

"I've already ordered for us," Bru said with a glance toward the waitress.

"Fine." Elton pulled out a wadded handkerchief and began to polish his glasses. "You got my message?"

Bru nodded.

"I'm really sorry to bail out of the trip at the last minute." Elton stared owlishly at the lunch platter the

13

saffron-clad black woman set between them. He had never eaten Ethiopian before and he wasn't entirely sure that he wanted to now.

"What happened?"

"Well, Congressman"—Elton held the glasses up to the light, squinted, and slid them back on—"you're not the only one who works for the government. I got the news an hour ago: all day today, all day Friday, and no promises for Thanksgiving." He watched doubtfully as the waitress ladled large, dark blobs from half a dozen bowls onto what looked like raw pizza dough. Another raw pizza, this one small, was arranged in napkin folds on his plate. "We'll need silverware," he said to the woman.

"No, we won't." Bru gave the waitress a conspiratorial grin. "We use this." He tore off a fold of the moist, spongy bread and scooped up a bite. "Bread and your fingers, just like your mamma taught you never to do. Therapy for your inhibitions."

Hesitating, Elton stared at the platter. "It looks a lot like camel droppings."

Bru threw back his head and laughed. "I thought all these years in Atlanta would urbanize you."

"Still the Lumpkin County boy, I guess." Elton tore off a couple of inches of bread, peered at the platter, and snared a dab of what he hoped was meat. Holding it to his nose, he gave a cautious sniff.

"So why did they cancel your vacation? Do we have a new epidemic somewhere?"

Elton shook his head. "They've got a scenario they want to run by us. Something about a genetically altered bacillus. Plague." Then waving a dabbed forefinger at the platter, he said, "This stuff isn't bad."

Bru Farrier paused in mid-bite and raised a dark eyebrow. "Sometimes I wonder what you boys are up to over there. You're supposed to control disease, aren't you? Not invent it."

Elton glanced up sharply. "Is that what you think?"

Bru gave him an even look. "I was thinking about the source of your funding."

A startled expression crossed Elton's face; he had never really thought about precisely where the department's money came from. He started to ask and then thought better of it.

Bru scooped up another mouthful and said lightly, "So you're really going to let me spend Thanksgiving on a desert island without a doc? No one to pull the thorns out of my paw, Dr. Daniel?"

"I think you'll survive. Sorry I can't fly you down. Can you get a commercial flight in the morning?"

"Not in time to catch the boat. The puddle jumper gets there too late. I'll have to get up early and drive." He narrowed his eyes and stabbed a finger at Elton. "Up in the middle of the night, and all because of you. It's just as well, though," he added with a quick grin. "I don't think I'm ready for a mad pilot and an aircraft hung together with bailing wire, anyway."

"My car should be in such good shape."

"Too bad about you. You're going to miss out." Bru gave an exaggerated cluck and shook his head. "You'd love St. Cyrils, too. All that sun and sand—in late November."

A rueful smile quirked Elton's lips. "I hope you freeze down there." It was a long time since he had hit a beach with Bru. Not since college. "Ginny's pissed," he said. "She figured this was her last chance to get out of the house before the baby comes. Guess I'll have to take her out for Thanksgiving dinner. She's in no mood to cook on top of missing the trip."

"I'll take her with me. I'll even pass the young'n off as my own."

Elton shook his head. "She won't do it. But thanks." He knew Ginny would never agree. To her, three was not only a crowd, it was an unspeakable intrusion—especially at this stage of Bru and Sally's relationship. He wondered how long Bru was going to keep one foot planted in the past. Why didn't he take the next step? he thought. Get the damned divorce and get on with it. Did he think a girl like Sally was going to wait forever? None of your business, Danny boy, he told himself sternly, and looked away. He glanced toward an elderly woman perched at a corner table. "Friend of yours? She's been trying to catch your eye."

Bru swung toward her.

The woman got up and came over. "Aren't you Bruton Laird Farrier? I've seen you on T.V."

"Yes, I am." Bru smiled warmly and stood. "And you?"

"I'm Cora Dyer and I want you to know I voted for you."

Bru clasped her hand. He was leaning forward now, listening intently in that way he had—charming her socks off, thought Elton. There was something about Bru Farrier that made people see him as taller than he really was, better looking than he really was, smarter than he really was, as if each of them held out an image that was bigger than life and said, "Now, fill it." It was the image they wanted, he thought, not the private guy inside.

The woman hesitated and then said something in a low voice. A moment later Bru reached into his pocket and pulled out a well-worn notepad. Elton remembered when it was new. The leather cover was stamped in gold with the single word "Ubiquitous."

Bru had been in a rare, confiding mood that night on Lake Lanier: "I want them to associate this with me—Bru Farrier and his ever-present notebook. The guy who cares enough to write things down and get things done." He had searched Elton's face for a reaction. "You think it's a gimmick, don't you? You'll go far, young man; just speak softly and carry a big shtik."

The pun distanced them. Bru looked out at the dark water beyond the deck, staring, as if he could read his fortune in the moon-specked ripples. A minute passed, then two, before he said, "You know, one of the Greeks—I think it was Aristotle—said, the best man, the one most

qualified to lead, never does; he would never seek office."
He was silent for a moment, looking down at the little
leather pad, stroking it with his thumb. Then he had
grinned. "So when you're number two, you try a little
harder."

The old lady, flushed and obviously pleased, gave Bru a
parting smile and left.

"Goes with the job," he said to Elton with a nod in the
woman's direction. "Just like your fictitious plague bug."

The doctor nodded. "All in a day's work." But there
was an unusual urgency attached to this particular scenario—
an urgency the department hadn't felt since the outbreak of
AIDS.

Elton glanced at the check. "Think you'll still be able to
make it Saturday? Or shall I hawk your tickets?"

A look of feigned horror crossed Bru's face. "Have you
ever known me to miss the Georgia-Georgia Tech game?
We'll be back in Atlanta before the kickoff. Neither rain,
nor dark of night, nor nasty germ . . ."

Elton smiled, but the nagging in his mind wouldn't go
away: Not since AIDS, he thought. But AIDS had been real.

Chapter 3

THERE HAD BEEN NO ANSWER FROM THE BRANCH CHIEF YET.
Jack Hubert swigged down the last of his coffee and
glanced with distaste at the grounds clinging to the inside
of the cup. Then his eye went back to the preliminary
report:

    . . . Two canisters of Yersinia pestis 18 are believed miss-

ing according to gross examination of the cultures. Lab confirmation will take longer.

Laying it down, Hubert took up the document coded NKWILY—SUBPROJECT 6. After an eclipse beginning in the late sixties, Subproject 6 had regained priority in recent months. Before that, research had concentrated on the viruses: Lassa fever, Rift Valley, the Ebola virus, the hemorrhagic fevers. Most of the work on bacteria was confined to Legionnaires' or to the spore-producing bacteria, while the truckloads of reports and documents on *Yersinia pestis* gathered dust. But when intelligence reports began to indicate renewed Soviet interest in plague research, Subproject 6 sprang back to life. *Yersinia pestis* was far too dangerous to allow unilateral genetic tinkering.

Hubert poured himself another cup of coffee, his fifth today, and glanced at his watch. The coffee was bitter and sat uneasily in his stomach. The cup rattled down, sloshing, bleeding brown fluid into its saucer.

He stared uneasily at the document, not wanting to think too intensively about the implications of this thing. But it wasn't going to go away. If he was right—and the prelim said he was—Pestis 18 was in the hands of terrorists.

Better the KGB. Far better. With them, probability said that it would be no more than an attempt to even the odds. If the KGB had it, by now it would be out of the country. Hubert tried to focus his thoughts on the oddly comforting thought, but he found it jostled away by the image of the two missing canisters: They could be anywhere. And each was enough to infect an area the size of Manhattan, Sanders had said. Funny how Manhattan Island was always the hypothetical yardstick. It was somehow easier to deal with, to depersonalize. A mythical Manhattan with people no more real than dots on a computer graph.

He had never thought about Subproject 6 in more than statistical terms before. He stared at the little oval picture on his desk, at Marta, lips quirked in a bright paper smile, at Jamie wearing the miniature tie "like Daddy's" that he was so proud of. Manhattan, he thought. Let it be Manhat-

tan. Not a real place. Not Alexandria. The thought was a
shield, a talisman that captured Pestis 18 on paper and held
it well away from the rambling old Victorian house that
yielded its past to Marta's paintbrush and scraper, far away
from its weedy yard and its doltish Irish setter who still
thought he was a pup, safely away from the treelined street
and the Anderson Preschool a block away.

Hubert reached for a cigarette, lit it, and felt the smoke
grate against his throat. A minute late he stabbed it out,
knowing that he smoked too much, that it was bad for his
lungs. He thought of the dying ape then. He thought of her
ribs moving in and out as she tried to breathe through
lungs clogged with bacteria. He pushed the thought away
as the phone shrilled and summoned him to the branch
chief's office.

On the way, he felt relief. It was out of his hands now.
There would be directives, action, a job to be done.

Jack Hubert automatically reached for a cigarette before
he remembered the supergrade's aversion to tobacco. Coffee, too, for that matter, although the branch chief's reli-
gious principles didn't seem to extend to the caffeine in
Coke. The branch chief clutched one now. Draining it, he
set it down next to the report and fixed the others with a
look. "Put that in English," he said to the thin man next
to Hubert.

"In English? Sex." Dr. Flagg leaned back and tented
his fingers. "Conjugation is the equivalent—to a bacteria.
During conjugation, plasmids are passed to, uh, what you
might call the female. A plasmid is simply a ring of
nucleic acid, usually DNA, outside the chromosome. That's
the key to understanding Pestis 18.

"Plasmids are a protein code for R factors—resistance
factors. R factors disable antibiotics. Since they lie outside
of the chromosome, it's not too hard to introduce plasmids
from a combination of other bacteria with natural or ac-
quired resistance to a wide array of antibiotics."

"And the effects," prompted the branch chief.

"Aerosols would spread the pneumonic form." The doctor spread the fingers of his left hand and began to enumerate with the index finger of his right: "Prostration, pyrexia, dyspnea—" At the branch chief's look he gave a faint smile. "English, then: first collapse. There's fever, cough, shortness of breath. Later cyanosis—the skin turns dark blue, because of the lack of oxygen. That's how it got its old name, the Black Death."

Hubert stared at the thin upturned hand and remembered the curved human-looking fingers of the ape. The doctor droned on, but only the tone of his voice, not his words, came through to Hubert now. How calm his voice was. How very confident. He cast a sidelong look at the doctor and wondered how he could talk about people as if they were no more than statistics. But that's all it meant to him, of course. He didn't know about the missing canisters.

The branch chief fingered the document on his desk. "This morbidity thing—it says one hundred percent."

"That means everyone exposed comes down with it," said the doctor. "The mortality rate is closer to seventy percent."

"In other words, seventy percent would die."

"No. Not really. Not everyone would be exposed. Realistically, we could expect a general mortality of, say, no more than forty to fifty percent. Enough to totally incapacitate any civilization as we know it today." The doctor gave a short laugh. "Pretty grim, gentlemen. Be glad Pestis 18 is on our side."

The branch chief sat alone in his office staring at the report, turning over and over in his mind its ramifications. Then he began to compose his memo to the chief of Technical Services Division:

TSD/BB 183-87

MEMORANDUM FOR: Chief, TSD
SUBJECT: NKWILY, Subproject 6

1. With a mortality in excess of 70 percent
and a morbidity of 100 percent, the biological *Yersinia pestis 18*, if introduced covertly
by hostiles, would result in total incapacita-
tion of the nation.

2. Infection would be of a fulminant pneumonic form with initially infected individu-
als providing the starting point for a man-to-
man epidemic cycle.

3. A vaccine, now in preparation, will not
be available for general use for at least six to
eight months from this date. Effective antibiotic
exists only in R&D quantities with no possibility of stockpiling sufficient amounts; therefore, it is recommended that in the event of
covert introduction of the biological, stringent
containment of the outbreak by any and every means available be considered the only
way possible of preventing a continent-wide
epidemic.

                                    Chief
                                    TSD/Biological Branch

Distribution:
   1—C/TSD

When the knock came, the deputy director of security
glanced in irritation at the door, then at his watch. Christ.
It was one o'clock already. All morning it had been one
damned interruption after the other.

He looked up as the secretary came in. The new girl this
time—what was her name? He nodded and took the Manila
envelope she handed him. As she walked toward the door,
he watched the way her buttocks moved under her dress.
Nice ass. A speculative look came over his face for a

moment. Then it faded and he opened the envelope and began to read the message from counterintelligence:

DC/CI 428-87

MEMORANDUM FOR: Director, Office of Security
ATTENTION: Deputy Director of Security
(Investigations and
Operational Support)
SUBJECT: NKWILY, Subproject 6

1. Charges of violation of the Geneva Protocols and the Biological Weapons Convention of 1972 are expected as a consequence of agency contract biologist Sanders's compromise.

a. At the outset of this project the calculated risk associated with participation in this type of activity was carefully considered, and the operational decision was made that the effort was worth the risk.

b. Since no good purpose can be served by an official admission of the violation, and existing federal statutes preclude the concoction of any legal excuse for the violation, it must be recognized that no cover story is available to any government agency. Therefore, it is most important that all U.S. intelligence agencies vigorously deny any association, direct or indirect, with any such activity as charged.

c. In the event of the introduction on U.S. soil of *Yersinia pestis 18*, it might become necessary, under the worst circumstances, to find a scapegoat.

2. In conclusion, therefore, it is stated that in the event of public compromise of the project, NKWILY will enter a general denial to any and all charges, as may be necessary.

Deputy Chief
Counterintelligence Staff

Distribution:
1—DDS/DOS

The deputy director of operations was disturbed when he came out of the hastily convened meeting with counter-intelligence. He didn't like involving security, but what choice did they have? The shit couldn't be deeper, he thought. Disaster, unless they acted immediately.

The gnawing in his stomach took precedence. He pulled out a roll of Tums from his shirt pocket and peeled back the wrapper. He had eaten too fast, wolfing a sandwich during the meeting. Should have left the mustard alone, he thought. Maybe he ought to go on the bland diet again. Get himself back in shape. He chewed the Tums and followed it with another, swallowing hard to make the fragments go down. Then he went back to his memorandum to the director:

DD/O 298-87

MEMORANDUM FOR: DCI
SUBJECT: NKWILY, Subproject 6

1. Confirmation of the disappearance of the two (2) canisters of the genetically altered biological *Yersinia pestis 18* from an agency proprietary leads to these conclusions:

a. Agency contract biologist Sanders was overtly compromised in an attempt to demonstrate opposition control of the substance.

b. Opposition is expected to take the form of ransom demands and/or a terrorist strike.

2. The "flap potential" of this project cannot be overestimated. A "flap" will put us "out of business" immediately and may give rise to grave charges of violation of the Geneva Protocols and the Biological Weapons Convention of 1972.

3. A determination as to whether the compromise has been such as to preclude continuation of the project will have to await the outcome of the compromise.

4. In this extremely sensitive matter it is suggested that if the director wishes to continue the project, a special-category file be established and all existing records of Project 6 be excised from NKWILY files for immediate relocation.

5. In the opinion of the CI staff, this project could "blow" at any time. It is suggested that in this event, the biological *Yersinia pestis 18* be proven to be of foreign origin. Therefore, documents or other evidence incriminating Libyan nationals must be planted as a means of redirecting attention from this agency.

Deputy Director/Operations

Distribution:
1—DCI

Jack Hubert crumpled the empty Winston package and reached for another. Not even three o'clock yet, he thought, and he was already into pack number three. He tore off the cellophane, squeezed out a cigarette, and lit it. Need to cut down, he thought. He was getting a morning cough from the damned things.

He picked up the paper and read it for the second time:

MEMORANDUM FOR THE RECORD
SUBJECT: NKWILY

1. In accordance with a new policy confirmed this day by CI/EXO and C/CIOP, Project NKWILY will handle henceforth as follows all items originated by or addressed to Subproject 6:

a. All items will be placed in a separate file titled "SPECIAL-CATEGORY ITEMS," which will be kept in C/CI/Project's safe. This file will also contain a log indicating dissemination, if any directed, return of items by cleared customers, etc. This file will of course be available

to analysts requiring it for any research that
may be necessary.

   b. No special-category items shall be entered into the NKWILY Machine Records System.

   c. <u>Dissemination of special-category items</u>
<u>will be at the discretion of DC/CI (and/or C/CI)</u>
<u>ONLY</u>.

<u>No copies shall be made of summaries on</u>
<u>special-category items for either the analyst's</u>
<u>file or the reading file.</u>

   <u>No references shall be made in regular</u>
<u>summaries to any special-category items.</u>

                    <u>Read and Understood:</u>
                    <u>Date:</u>

Taking a last drag from his cigarette, Hubert stubbed
it out, reached for his pen, and signed and dated the sheet.

THURSDAY

PRODROME

Chapter 4

THE FADED SIGN OVER THE LINTEL READ:

TEC WOOD AP S.
BLD . C

A one-eyed tricolor cat slunk away at the stranger's approach. Turning up the collar of his blue down jacket, the man leaned into the north wind that moaned through the bare oaks and skittered brown leaves across the uneven concrete walkway. A torn sheet of *The Atlanta Constitution* sailed on a gust and caught against the rough bricks of the building. Impaled for a moment, it hummed in the wind like an angry insect until it fluttered to the ground at his feet, flapping its message: BULLDOGS FAVORED OVER YELLOW JACKETS.

The wind fought for supremacy against the bleat of horns and the rumble of traffic on I-85. With cold-stiffened fingers the man shifted his briefcase from right to left hand and opened the door to the small entry hall. On the second floor he turned left down the dim hallway that bled the remnants of stale breakfast smells and decay from its transoms.

He fumbled for a key and opened the door marked 209. Inside, an iron bed with a stained, striped mattress squatted against one wall. Hoisting the briefcase carefully, he laid it on the bed.

Below the single window on a scarred table of indeterminate vintage perched a telephone next to two shiny new

Atlanta telephone directories. The man looked at the number of the Touch-Tone phone, memorizing it, reinforcing his memory with quick movements of his fingers, stabbing out the final four digits with his right hand: twice with the index finger, then the ring finger, then the thumb—7796.

In a few moments he nodded and then pulled off his jacket, tossing it onto the bare mattress next to the briefcase. Without its bulk he was thin, almost slight. His navy turtleneck outlined shoulder blades and spine and spread its cloth ribs over his with every breath he took. To a casual glance he looked like any of the Georgia Tech students who infiltrated the shabby apartments each year. Only his eyes made him seem older. They were black and opaque and curiously expressionless.

He opened the closet. A single wire hanger, bent and rusty, hung from the bowed rod. Two new sealed cartons sat on the floor. He stared at the boxes minutely, as if to assure himself that they had not been tampered with before he pulled them out of the closet. He knelt beside the larger one. SEARS was printed in large black letters on the box. Below that, PAINT TANK, then in smaller print, 30G 14459C.

He reached into a pocket and brought out what looked like a silver ballpoint pen. He pressed the pocket clip, and a stiletto sprang from its tip. With a low ripping sound the sealing tape gave way to the thrust of the blade. At its release the carton top sprang open, and he lifted out a galvanized steel tank. The other box held a portable air tank. He ran his fingers over it, then stood.

The briefcase was next. Thumbing its combination lock, he snapped it open and took out two brown-wrapped packages. The one to the right, the thinner of the two, gave under his fingers as he grasped it. He pulled off the wrapping paper and began to unfold a double-walled silver bag made of Mylar.

He held it up and examined it critically. The bag was rectangular, flawless, and exactly the same size as the room's single window.

Laying it down, he opened the other package and took

out a squat, sealed container. Next to it, in a nest of wire and plastic tubing, lay a telephone tone decoder. As he stared at it thoughtfully, his fingers began their memory-reinforcing movements again: first the left hand, then the right—index finger twice, ring finger, thumb—7796.

He turned back to the briefcase and pulled out a cylinder wrapped in a thick pink sheet of foam. His thin tan fingers worked loose the fastenings and unrolled the cushioning sheet.

Sunlight from the dingy window played on the slim metal canister. He looked at it for a long moment before raising his eyes with their measured stare to the window—the window with its unobstructed view of Georgia Tech's Grant Field.

Chapter 5

THE GEORGIA SEA ISLANDS STALKED THE COAST LIKE blurred green footprints. On the outskirts of Brunswick, Bru Farrier turned off Highway 17 and eased onto Torras Causeway. The low November sun raking across the salt marsh struck him in the face and he flipped the sun visor down. He squinted at the clock: 8:28. Time enough for breakfast before the boat left.

At the tollbooth the attendant gave him a quizzical "Don't I know you?" look, but Bru was staring in the rearview mirror at the light blue Chevy Citation closing behind him. As it swung into the next lane, he saw that it was a different model from the one he expected. He gave the attendant a quick wave and drove over the first of the arching bridges toward St. Simons Island.

Across the Frederica River, marsh grass gave way to old live oaks that filtered the morning sun through dark green leaves and silver curls of Spanish moss. Soon the road was no more than a tunnel through the trees. The islanders, fiercely proud of their centuries-old oaks, guarded them from any incursion bearing the name of progress. It reminded Bru of an aging spinster protecting her hymen: God put it there, and there, by God, it would stay, come hell or hurricane.

He turned off King's Way toward the village and pulled into Pier Alley. He stood by the car for a moment and stared at the ocean. It always made him feel good to come back to this place. For a fleeting moment he was a small boy again, helping his grandfather pull in a net of crabs, squealing as a waving claw threatened a small finger. A north wind ruffled his dark hair and bit through the thin wool of his sweater. The tide was going out, leaving the smell of salt and oysters behind.

He turned toward the old frame restaurant that faced the water. As he crossed the wooden porch and opened the door, Higdon's gave off its own morning scent of sizzling bacon and coffee. A half-dozen customers looked up over eggs and biscuits as Bru walked in. He scanned the faces.

"Out of your district, aren't you, Congressman?" said a crushed-gravel voice at his elbow as a ruler-thin man unfolded from a chair and extended a hand.

Bru clasped it with a grin. "Wally." He slid into the seat across from the man. "It's been a long time." He peered into a lined face set with steel-gray eyes and tried to remember if he had always looked this way. He decided that he had. Wally Carruthers was one of those people who had looked fifty-five years old back in the forties and no more than sixty now. Still, he did not remember the pale cast around Wally's lips and the slight hunch to his shoulders. "What brings you down to Glynn County for Thanksgiving breakfast? Out of uniform, too—and on a holiday. Playing hooky?''

"Earned a day's vacation.'' Wally took a swallow of coffee, then leaned back. "Me and two deputies cleaned up a sweet little cocaine operation last week. With a little help from the GBI,'' he added. "Biggest in this part of the coast. They'd been slipping up the waterway and unloading up Darien Creek. This time we were waiting.'' The gray eyes twinkled. "Came off slicker than snot on a doorknob.''

Bru shook his head in amazement. Most guys who retired from the highway patrol looked forward to getting a little fishing in; Wally had run for McIntosh County sheriff. "When are you going to slow down?''

"When I stiffen up for the last time.''

"Did you call in the Coast Guard for the bust?'' asked Bru with his best wide-eyed innocent look. Then he chuckled at the outrage that tracked over Wally's face.

"Put those blue boys on to that?'' Carruthers snorted. "Would you put a fox in your henhouse? They've still got a few in the brig from that pot diversion a couple of years ago. Besides,'' he added, waggling a hand at the waitress who emerged with a steaming coffeepot, "by the time those boys found their charts, we'd of been there and gone.''

The waitress stared at Bru, smiled, and with a half turn moved to a wall rack covered with dangling brown mugs marked with the names of Higdon's regulars and visiting notables. Hooking a finger through a handle, she pulled off the mug inscribed BRUTON LAIRD FARRIER, U.S. CONGRESS, placed it in front of Bru, and filled it with coffee.

He remembered the girl from his last trip down. She had a pleasant open face and too-blue eyes from her tinted contact lenses. Giving her his sexiest wink, he parted his lips, and in a husky whisper said, "Mary Jim''—retrieving her name from the tag she wore—"you remembered.''

"Of course.'' She laughed. "Black. One sugar.''

Bru liked her laugh. It was rich and completely unaffected. "This lovely girl replaced the computer," he said to Carruthers. He caught her eye again. "Tell me about your eggs."

"What would you like to know?"

He flashed an imp's grin at her and stared at her breasts. "Are they large and smooth and pale as the moon on a summer night?"

A smile twitched at the corner of her mouth. "Larger and smoother and paler than you will ever know."

He nodded solemnly. "I'll have both . . . uh, two. Over light. Ham, biscuits, and obligatory grits."

It was her turn to raise an eyebrow.

He gave her a wicked small-boy wink. "That's Yankee talk, sugar. I've been corrupted by the buggers."

When she was gone, Carruthers industriously sopped half a biscuit into what was left of his egg yolk. "Feisty as ever, Bru."

"Feeling mean." He grinned. "And you, Wally? You're craggy as an oyster these days."

The biscuit, dripping with yellow, stopped short of Carruthers's mouth. The gray eyes above narrowed in mock serenity. "An oyster, eh? You keep a civil tongue, young'n. You're still not too big for me to whip up on."

"My other daddy." Bru stared fondly at the older man. "You did whip me once, remember?" He had been spending the summer in Darien with his grandparents, or summer nights at least. Dawn to dark he spent on the salt marsh near the Carruthers's isolated house or on breathless races with Jimmy down shaded dirt roads to the water's edge. Only the need for nourishment forced them inside, barefoot and wet or covered with varying thicknesses of sand or mud and drying salt.

Early one evening, faces streaked with the remains of Martha Carruthers's Dickensian "highly geological home-made cake," they found Wally still in uniform, dozing in front of the TV, his .38 gleaming at his side.

Without knowing why he did it, Bru slipped the gun out of its holster. Wide-eyed, he felt its heft, its slickness

against his sweaty palm as he and Jimmy sneaked out into
the yard through the wheezing kitchen door.

"Maybe you better put Daddy's gun back now," said
Jimmy with a nervous sidelong look at it.

"You chicken or something?" he whispered, when suddenly an iron hand swooped down from above and behind
and closed over his wrist. . . .

"You nearly stopped my heart when you grabbed that
gun, Wally."

"Nearly stopped mine when I knew you two had it."

"I was a good kid. The Devil must have whispered in
my ear."

"As I recall, you didn't need the Devil's help. But no,
you weren't a bad young'n"—the gray eyes twinkled—
"for a rich kid."

"That was a long time ago, Wally." A long time, he
thought. And Jimmy, MIA, lost somewhere in Nam over
fifteen years ago.

"And how has it been for you, Bru?" The loose-gravel
voice softened as it spoke.

Wally's question carried the weight of a dozen others
with it. Bru stared down at his hands for a moment without
seeing them. On the third finger of his left hand a band of
skin showed pale against his tan. He had put away the ring
six months after Laird died, a year after the weight of their
dying child had tattered the fragile silk of his marriage to
Kathlyn. He had put away the ring carefully, as if it could
be taken out again and worn, but he knew it never could
be. Their marriage was over now, dead as their little boy,
and yet they had never taken the final step to dissolve it.
Instead, they had set it on the shelf like a worn and ragged
garment, knowing that it was useless, knowing that it
would never fit again, yet hesitating to throw it away.

Bru touched his fingers together and looked up at Wally.
Two dozen years rolled away again and he could see him
sitting in his battered easy chair with an enormous book
open on his lap. Wally read to Jimmy and Bru every
evening because it was good for children to be read to,

because his daddy had read to him from these same books—the heavy four-volume set of Dickens with black leather covers rusty with age and Bible-paper pages blotched with yellow—the only books that Wally owned.

Bru could hear him reading in a voice that seemed to come from a throat paved with chuck-holed asphalt: *"There are strings,"* said Mr. Tappertit, *"in the human heart that had better not be vibrated."*

Wally's question hung between them. Bru felt the tug of those clear gray eyes, and he felt the concern that lay behind them. "Great expectations, Wally," he said lightly, pushing the question away. He added a grin, a raised eyebrow, and a ribald joke about a deaf, nearsighted senator, and using the shield of humor, deftly turned the conversation toward neutral ground.

The door with its red, backwards HIGDON'S rattled shut at the passing of another customer. Wally Carruthers sipped the last of his coffee and set down his cup. Bru glanced at his watch, stood, and threw down a tip. "I've got to see a man about a boat."

"Going over to St. Cyrils?"

Bru nodded and scooped up his check. "Lillian's been after me for years to spend Thanksgiving on St. Cyrils. This time, I took her up on it." With a wave he turned and headed toward the cash register. On the way an outthrust hand caught his and pulled him into a conversation.

That's what being in the public eye did for you, thought Wally. Couldn't get across a room without somebody wanting something. The sheriff unfolded from his chair, reached into his pocket, and drew out a handful of change. He selected a quarter and placed it beside his plate. After a moment's hesitation, he fished another quarter from his palm and set it next to the first.

He paid the bill, drawing crumpled dollar bills from a wallet stained black on mahogany from years of use, and walked briskly against the wind to his car. Inside, he steadied his forearms on the steering wheel, clutching it as the pain caught him. It traveled up his left arm and nested in his jaw, taking his breath with it. Each time the pain had come, he had quickly called it indigestion or tooth-ache, but underneath his pat reassurances he heard the harsh whisper of his own mortality.

Sixty-two, he thought. But he'd kept in shape, hadn't he? Sixty-two wasn't old these days. Not even retirement age for most jobs. The pain pitched him forward. Fore-head against the wheel, panting, he focused on the gas gauge. Low. He was low. Had to fill up. Get filled up.

The car door swung open; a hand gripped his shoulder. Wally sucked in a long, shuddering breath and looked up, slowly, at Bru Farrier. "Little indigestion," he managed to say.

Bru narrowed his eyes. "Bullshit."

The pain eased its grip and slowly the numbness began to leave his hands. Cushioning his palms against the wheel, he stretched out his fingers. "It's okay. Better now." He reached for the ignition. "See you."

Bru grabbed the keys. "I'm the driver. Move over."

The pain was fading quickly now. Probably a tooth, he thought, and shook his head, but he slid over as Bru took the driver's seat. "Probably a tooth. Just a bad tooth." Probably that molar he'd chipped a while back.

"We'll let the doctor decide that." With a crunch of gears, Bru turned onto Pier Alley.

"It's too far to Darien," said Wally. He should have gone to Doc two days ago when it all started. Doc would have taken him in right away. Right away—through a waiting room full of gossips: *Poor old Wally. Looks bad to me. He's getting on, you know. Strain of the job. Maybe a younger man.* . . . . "It's too far. You'll miss your boat."

"We're not going to Darien. We're going to Brunswick—to the emergency room." And over Wally's protests, Bru swung the car onto King's Way and headed toward the mainland and Glynn-Brunswick Memorial Hospital.

Chapter 6

IN A SMALL FRAME HOUSE ON THE OUTSKIRTS OF BRUNSWICK, Georgia, the man known to the others by the code name Iguana looked up from the kitchen table. Narrowing his eyes against the glare of the morning sun, he scanned the salt marsh stretching toward St. Simons and the Atlantic. As he stared, the fingers of his left hand caressed the chain that circled his waist.

Taking up his tiny cup, he sipped what was left of his coffee. The brew was black, its bitterness mitigated by enough sugar to give it the consistency of syrup. He took a final swallow, set the cup down on the chipped enameled kitchen table, and began to study the map again.

With eyes as black as the dregs of his cup, he stared at each twisting trail, each curve of shore on St. Cyrils Island. Elbows on the table, he leaned forward, closed his eyes, and began to visualize the map. The fingers of his right hand caressed his brow as if he tried to draw the information from his brain with them; the thumb pressed into his temple just above the dark mole that rode high on his cheekbone. He frowned and the motion drew his thick eyebrows together so that they seemed like one. Then his brow relaxed and his hand fell away. Like the faint lines of a television picture sharpening as the set warms up, the map of St. Cyrils came into his mind—indelible now.

Tearing the map into narrow strips, he burned it in the large cracked ashtray on the table; he had no further need of it.

He reached for another paper on the table and shredded

it into the ashtray. As flames consumed it, he saw it again in his mind—the St. Cyrils Lodge guest list, handed over so cheaply by the whey-faced day maid:

> *Dr. and Mrs. David Cole*
> *Miranda Gervin*
> *Cass Tompkins*
> *The Alex Borden family*
> *Sir William Talbott*
> *Sally Strickland*
> *Bruton Laird Farrier*

One name was pivotal: Talbott—the United Kingdom's ambassador plenipotentiary to the United Nations.

Sir William Talbott had visited the island before. His office had made reservations for this trip months ago, but reservations were easily canceled. The guest list was verification, but it was not enough. Only the ambassador's arrival on St. Cyrils Island would give them real confirmation.

Without Talbott they would abort.

A smile played over Iguana's thin lips and flickered in his eyes as he contemplated the last—the unexpected— name on his list: Bruton Laird Farrier.

A United States congressman had swum into his net.

We have fish for dinner, he thought. *Pescados grandes.* Very big fish indeed.

He picked up the ashtray, rose, and walked toward the sink. With each step the slim metal canister chained to his waist bumped against his thigh. Turning on the tap, he watched the gray-black rivulet of ash swirl down the drain.

Chapter 7

THE DRIVER THRUST OUT A GNARLED HAND AND SWITCHED
on a CB microphone. "Green Jeep to base. Hoby, here.
Heading home." With a crunch of gears the St. Cyrils
Island guest tram pulled away from the floating dock and
began a joggling assault on the crushed-shell road that led
toward the Atlantic.

Sally Strickland wrapped her arms across her chest as
the chill wind bit through her new cashmere—the only one
she owned. The Sea Islands were supposed to be warm,
weren't they? Not like the rest of Georgia in November.
She cast a half-envious glance at the white peekapoo standing on the lap of the woman in the seat ahead of her. He
looked warm enough. He was encased from neck to tail in
an Icelandic wool turtleneck that probably cost more than
her entire outfit.

The little beast bared minuscule teeth and curled its
upper lip in her direction. Snubbed by a peekapoo. By a
filthy-rich peekapoo, she amended. And what was she doing
here, anyway? A shiver trembled across her shoulders, but
the chilly feeling wasn't altogether from the cold. Damn it,
Bru Farrier, where are you? It's Thanksgiving. She had
hesitated at the landing back on St. Simons as long as she
could, looking back, listening for his car, until the old man
took her by the arm and guided her onto the launch. She
found a seat and stared back across the fanning wake of
the launch until the wooded landing was out of sight and
there was nothing to see but the dark creek gliding through
fissured grass flats and an occasional glimpse of open water.

His plans must have changed again, she told herself. She had spent the first three days of her vacation with her sister in Savannah. Last night while Sally was in the shower, Barb had taken the call: Bru was driving, not flying. He would meet her on St. Simons. But maybe Barb had scrambled the message. It wouldn't be the first time.

The tram rattled past the ancient skeleton of a rowboat beneath a gaunt oak. Leaves covered the spine of its keel and fluttered in the wind against its naked, gray ribs. Beyond it, Oyster Creek slithered through the cord grass like a dark snake.

She had not expected the island to be so wild. To the west of the creek and the anchored motor launch, a green carpet of salt marsh stretched as far as she could see. To the east, past the little cluster of buildings, there was nothing but dark woods straight out of *The Wizard of Oz*. If the trees start throwing things, she thought, we're in real trouble.

Sally shivered again. Just worried about Bru, she told herself. And yet even as she thought it, she knew there was something else—something that had stalked her dreams the last two nights and woke her with a chill. The dream had faded almost at once, leaving in its wake a foreboding that reason hadn't budged. Cry of the banshee, and all that. She felt a grin creep over her face. That's what came of superstition, and yet it couldn't be helped. Fate. Didn't every redhead have the inevitable Irish grandmother? At work it was an occupational hazard. They were all trained in science and observation—doctors, nurses, lab personnel— yet everybody got "feelings" about the patients; everybody knew that drunks and emergency appendectomies came in threes; everybody skittered on edge at full moons and "quiet" nights.

The Jeep with its rattling train of cars wound past an old two-story frame house and began to climb toward the crest of an oak-covered dune. Giant live oaks, gray spines tortured with the curve of age, bent low and shook their dark heads in the wind. The sharp breeze caught at unkempt beards of Spanish moss, goading gray curling tendrils into a ragged dance.

A branch trailing a long strand of moss caught at the edge of the tram and snapped loose. Sally ducked involuntarily. At the movement the peekapoo growled deep in its throat and tried to launch himself over the back of the seat.

"Stop it, Caligula." The woman plucked up her pet in mid-lunge and turned half around in her seat. "Behave." Round blue eyes lidded with purple shadow met Sally's. "He's just trying to protect me. But, maybe you don't like dogs."

Sally aimed an uncertain smile at the dog's owner. "I love them," she said, not sure that Caligula qualified.

A thrust-out hand enclosed hers in plump fingers. "I'm Cass Tompkins. And you're—" The blue eyes widened; the hand clasped hers moistly. "You're perfect. I do hope you'll let me use you."

Sally stared blankly at the woman. The sheer white wool of her pantsuit accentuated the plump curves of her breasts and hips. She was about fifty, and pretty in an overdone way.

The woman gazed at Sally intently and then said to the square-faced younger woman on the tram bench next to her, "Isn't she perfect, Miranda?"

Miranda looked up from her paperback and nodded absently.

"You're exactly right for *Dark Frenzy, Dark Desire*," said Cass. "You have just the right shade of auburn hair. I hope you don't mind if I use you. I can't get going on a book until I have my heroine exactly right."

Sally stared at her, unable to decide whether she was repelled or attracted by the effusive little woman who smelled of Joy and crackled with energy, and who spoke with the thick slur of the southern lowlands. It seemed to her that something sly was hiding behind those ingenuous eyes. "I really don't know what you're talking about."

The blue eyes widened again. "Why, of course you don't honey. How silly of me. I write romances."

"Her pen name is Cassandra Temple," said Miranda.

Cassandra Temple. Suddenly Sally realized that she was looking at one of the most prolific writers in the country. Hot romances, too. Hanging on the cusp between flattery and unease, she said, "You want to put me in your next book?"

"Not the next. There are three before *Dark Frenzy*—or is it four, Miranda?"

"Four," said the younger woman, "not counting the reissue of *Seething Ecstasy*."

"My secretary, Miranda Gervin," Cass said to Sally. "Without her help I couldn't manage at all." Miranda thrust a stubby hand over her shoulder. When Sally grasped it, Caligula, taking offense, quivered his lip, exposed his tiny teeth, and raked her arm with his claws.

Cass snatched up the dog and thrust him at Miranda. "Here. See if you can control him." She patted the sleeve of Sally's sweater, ignoring the snag Caligula had left there. "You should always wear that color, sugar. It's perfect with your hair."

Sally stared at the damage and tried to smile. "That's what my mother always said." Pink is your best color, was the litany. It makes my Sally rosy. And never, ever, wear yellow. It makes redheads sallow. Sallow Sally? Never, Mother. Her hair was the color of old mahogany when she felt good about it; when she didn't, it metamorphosed into Lancers rosé bottle rust, or worse. Open Pit barbecue sauce this morning, she thought darkly. So here she was, Rosy Sally, in a new pink cashmere she could ill afford with a dog snag on the sleeve. So much for elegance.

The tram dipped into a hollow between two dunes and began to climb again. As it reached the top she caught her breath. Just below the crest, a white four-point buck stood next to the broad trunk of an old black gum. He froze for a moment and then with a bound disappeared into a thicket of palmetto and holly.

Holding the Jeep wheel with one hand, Hoby looked back over his shoulder. "That's a fallow deer. The woods are full of 'em. Some of them swam over from Little St. Simons about twelve years ago, and now they're giving the native whitetails a run for their money."

"Beautiful," said Cass. But Sally didn't hear. She was clinging to the side of the tram, staring back at the shallow ravine behind them, crying, "I think I see another one down there!"

The girl stared up at the road as the tram rattled past. "Someone's coming." Catching the edges of her flannel shirt together, she pulled away from the boy's embrace.

Nathan Katz caught his breath and stared at the rustling underbush. Then he laughed. "That's the 'someone.'" The white buck leaped past them in two bounds and disappeared in a stand of cedar. He reached for her again, but she struggled to her feet. "Not now, Nathan."

He scrambled after her, taking her shoulders in his hands. She shook her head and stared toward the woods where the deer had vanished. She felt shaky, as if her blood sugar had plunged.

Nathan moaned and buried his face in the hollow of her throat. A tickling wave of nausea suddenly struck her. "No," she said sharply, pushing him away. Then with a whimper, "I'm going to be sick."

He was instantly contrite. "What can I do? Is it your sugar?"

She was on her knees now, feeling the damp ground press coldly through her jeans. The nausea, stronger now, slithered in her belly.

Nathan fumbled in a back pocket and pulled out a partially melted Hershey bar. He tore it open. The white inner wrapper was dotted with dabs of brown. "Here." He held it to her lips.

She moaned and shook her head. A cold sweat beaded her upper lip. She stared at the chocolate bar he held. With a sudden tunneling of vision, she could see nothing else except his square hand, fingers streaked with brown, thrusting the candy toward her mouth. She wavered, wanting the relief it offered, but the thought of sugared chocolate, slimy in her mouth, caused her stomach to twist. Her hands trembled and clutched at her knees.

She twisted away from the insistent hand and felt the dark rags of unconsciousness begin to wrap around her mind. Couldn't he see she was sick? Why didn't he go away and leave her alone?

He grasped the back of her neck roughly. "You've got to eat it."

With a sudden blaze of anger she slapped at his hand, catching him on the wrist. "Fuck off."

As she spoke, he crammed the chocolate into her mouth. "I said, 'eat it.' "

She hated him just then. And, hating him, she began to chew as if it were an act of retaliation, as if each sobbing bite tore into his flesh. Then exhausted, she sank to the ground, one hand clamped over her mouth, the other reaching toward him.

He ran his fingers over her dark hair, tracing it as it fell in long waves over her shoulders. "You'll be okay in a minute." He sounded like he was trying to convince himself.

She lay on the ground with her eyes closed. With an effort of will, she tried to make the sickness stop.

The fingers paused. "Ashley?"

The nausea ebbed a little.

"Ashley! You all right?"

She managed to nod. Gradually the bone-melting weakness slid away and she turned on her side and looked at him. Relief flooded his face. She reached out and grazed his cheek with a touch. Remorse stung her. "I was a bitch." She stared at the arch of live-oak branches that filtered the sun. "I ought to die. I ought to be dead."

"What did you eat this morning?"

She flung a hand over her eyes.

"What did you have for breakfast?" When she didn't answer, he said, "You didn't have anything, did you?"

"I had coffee," she said in a small voice. "With cream."

"Wonderful. Coffee and insulin. No wonder you got sick."

Ashley tried a smile. "Cause of death: eight units of regular insulin and thirty-two of NPH."

"It's not funny." He folded his arms around his knees and stared at her. "Do you think it's funny?"

She rolled away. "I don't think anything's funny."

"Are you trying to kill yourself?"

"Why not?"

He tugged at her shoulder, rolling her back toward him. "How about me? Don't I count for 'why not'?" He reached out and gently wiped a smear of chocolate from her mouth.

"You don't know me at all." She stared at him, at the look of puzzled hurt that began to track across his face.

"I thought I did."

"You've known me for six days. That makes you an expert? A specialist in Ashley Borden, girl disease?" The echo of her words struck her as overly dramatic, like something on a TV soap. She set her chin, and anticipating his response, headed it off with a sharp "You make me sick."

He didn't answer. She stole a glance at him and then looked quickly away, studying the crotch of an old oak, thinking how it looked nearly human—standing on its head, grotesque gray-barked legs spraddled in the air. She was trying to hurt him and she didn't know why. Perversely she wanted him to make her stop. If he really cared about her, he would. Instead, he sat staring at her in silence.

She whipped a glance at him. "So I don't eat breakfast. That makes me a suicide?"

"Maybe."

"What the hell do you know about it? Did you have to shoot up every day since you were four years old?" When he didn't answer, she said, "Try it on for twelve years and see how it fits. See how you like the idea of maybe going blind or having your feet rot off by the time you're twenty-five, or having a stroke." She thrust out her chin. "See, I don't have to kill myself. I've got an old friend that'll do it for me.''

She tented her fingers, staring at them as if they were infinitely fascinating. Finally he said, ''I don't think it matters how long I've known you. I know enough. I know how I feel.'' He reached out and touched her hand, running his fingers over the delicate little bones of her wrist. ''You're smart. You're beautiful—'' Suddenly inarticulate, he stopped.

''Sure,'' she said ruefully. ''The bright, beautiful genetic defect—lighting up everybody's life. Adored by her little brother, favorite of her mother, apple of her father's eye. Sure.''

Nathan glanced at his watch.

''Don't let me keep you.''

''I'm late for rehearsal.''

''That's me. Second fiddle to an oboe again.''

''Look. I'm really late, okay? I mean, I want to be with you, but it's my job. I'll see you tonight after dinner. All right?'' He got to his feet and pulled her up with a steadying hand. ''You need to go eat something. Will you?''

''I guess.'' She began to brush off the oak leaves clinging to her jeans. ''I look like somebody's compost pile.''

He plucked a twig from her hair. ''Promise?''

Her lips twitched in a faint echo of his smile. ''Okay.''

He gave her a quick, rough kiss and then they turned away from each other and began to walk in opposite directions through the woods.

The tram came to a clattering stop. The loop of shell road here near the front of St. Cyrils Lodge was little more than a tunnel cutting through the woods. When Hoby shut off the Jeep's engine, the only sound was the wind shrilling through dark green leaves and the low counterpoint of the surf.

They were in a narrow trough between two lines of old dunes. The tram lay cupped in a curving palm of green that rose gently on either side. Sally caught the damp odor of humus mingled with the salt smell of the sea. Toward the east and the measured sound of the ocean, a rough cedar boardwalk climbed through somber oaks and glossy magnolias. Pausing at a tall stand of whistling bamboo, the walkway turned and climbed again until it was lost behind thick gray oak trunks and sharp fans of palmetto.

Toward the west, terraced steps led up to a three-story cedar building that seemed to have grown from its gray shell-studded foundation as naturally as the old live oaks and pines that whispered around it. The scent of hickory smoke puffed from its many chimneys, and sun glinted on its tall mullioned windows.

With much clattering of the hinged wooden tram seats, the three passengers got out. When Sally reached for her suitcase, Hoby took it gently but firmly out of her hand. "Just you let me do that for you, miss." He smiled, but his faded blue eyes were determined; there were some things that a guest just did not do. Gaffe number one, she thought.

As he swung her suitcase to the ground, Caligula, with a low, throaty growl, yanked away from Miranda Gervin's grasp, and trailing his leash, launched himself at the old man. Hoby looked down at the dog and said deliberately, "Be a good idea to keep him tied up while you're here."

Wrapping the leash around a square hand, Miranda plucked her employer's pet from Hoby's pants leg with a tug. "Are you afraid of an ambush?" she said with a tight smile.

Hoby raised his chin and leveled a gaze at her. "We lost a dog here a few weeks back."

Miranda arched an eyebrow. "Lost?"

"Gator got him."

"An alligator?" Cass Tompkins wheeled toward Hoby in disbelief. "You mean it ate a dog?"

"They generally do, ma'am. When they can get one."

"God." She waved a plump hand toward the lodge. "They don't come right up here, do they?"

"Your little dog'll be safe enough. On a leash."

Somewhat reassured, Cass turned and glanced toward the third-floor dormers. "Would you look at this place? Amazing. What a combination of styles: *Elephant Walk* out of the abbey in *The Sound of Music*." A distant grunting sound followed by the shriek of a wild bird caused her to cast startled blue eyes in the direction of the sound. A half smile wavered on her face. "—And the hills are alive." She marched toward Miranda. "I'll take Caligula. You go get some pictures." Grasping the leash with chubby fingers, Cass hiked toward the veranda in a swaying walk that was wonderfully like the curly-tailed trot of the peekapoo.

Miranda dug into the depths of her bag and extracted a Minolta. She flipped off the lens cap and began to snap pictures of the building.

Sun drenched the sixteen-light window above the door and glinted on the old Chinese gong in the wainscoted entry hall. An oak serving cart pushed by a lean ebony woman rattled across the parquet floor and clattered to a stop as the woman paused to give the gong two reverberating blows with a felted mallet and then trundled the cart through a pair of dark doors.

"Coffee bell," said Hoby, hoisting Sally's suitcase and heading for the stairs. "This way, Miss Strickland. You're on the third floor."

"The man I was supposed to meet back at the dock—" Sally began.

Hoby paused and looked down at her. "Mr. Farrier, you said."

"Would you check and see if he's arrived?"

"I did, Miss Strickland. He isn't here yet."

"Was there a message?"

"No. No message."

She followed the old man up the curving stairs and turned right through dark-paneled double doors. They passed through a wide alcove lined with books and leather armchairs and came to a door marked B.

As he reached for the knob, an explosion of sneezes from the door labeled HONEYMOON SUITE across the hall were followed by an aggrieved female voice: "I don't care whether it's ready or not. Five more minutes in here and I'll be dead." Another volley of sneezes ended in a despairing "Oh" and a prolonged sniff. "I've got to get out of here." The door swung open and a slim snub-nosed girl in an emerald-green bathrobe stepped out. She seemed startled to find Sally and the old man there, and quickly smoothed her short, tousled hair. "Is our room ready yet? They said they could put us in there." She nodded toward room B.

Hoby glanced at Sally, then back at the girl. "Who did?"

"The maid." The girl fished a wadded Kleenex out of her pocket. "She's in there now."

With an apologetic look at Sally and a muttered "Let me check," Hoby disappeared into the room.

"I don't think it's the llama." A bearded young man lugging two blue American Tourister suitcases and a canvas tote inelegantly patched with AC tape appeared at the door of the honeymoon suite. "You said yourself you were never around llamas before."

"I was around it all night, Dave—while you slept." It was an accusation. "I didn't get to sleep 'til six." She blew her nose and muttered, "Happy Thanksgiving."

He stepped into the hall, snagged the tote on the door, and groaned as the handle ripped loose. "Jeez." He plopped the suitcases in the hall and probed at the damage with an index finger. "Guess I need to get new luggage."

"First we pay for the honeymoon," said the girl. Another sneeze exploded. "And allergy tests. Oh, damn."

"Do you have something to take for that?" asked Sally. "I've got some Benadryl."

"Thank God." Then to him: "Why don't we have Benadryl? You're the doctor."

"It's in my suitcase," said Sally. "When I get in my

room—'' She glanced toward room B, then back at the girl.

The girl followed her gaze. "Oh," she said slowly, "that was supposed to be your room." She plopped down on one of the suitcases and stuck out a hand. "We might as well get acquainted while they sort us out. I'm Paige Cartwright . . . uh, Paige Cole," she amended with a grin, "and this is my husband, Dave."

"I'm Sally Strickland." Even with the red nose and puffy eyelids, Paige was attractive. Sally stared at the girl's velvety robe in admiration, wishing she could wear that shade of green without looking like a Christmas tree. "You're a doctor?" she asked Dave.

He nodded and brushed a thick lock of hair from his forehead. "Third-year resident in pediatrics."

"I used to work in pedie. I'm a nurse. In ICU now." She turned to Paige. "Are you a nurse, too?"

She shook her head. "Everybody expects doctors to be married to nurses. I'm working on a master's in biology. Next fall I start vet school."

Dave clamped a hand around Paige's shoulder and brushed her ear with a kiss. "In a few years when the phone rings and someone asks for Dr. Cole, we'll have to say, 'Was that about your daughter or your goat, Mrs. Jones?' " Then as a thought struck, he said to Paige, "What are you going to do if you have a llama for a patient?"

Paige groaned and blew her nose.

"What's this about a llama?" asked Sally.

"It's on the wall," said Paige. "This huge llama skin. And believe me, I've memorized every hair on his miserable hide." She glanced at Sally's suitcase. "Do you think you could find that Benadryl pretty quick?"

"Sure." Sally snapped open her suitcase and fished inside an inner pocket. "Here you go." She handed the little bottle to Paige. "Can you swallow it without water?"

"I'd swallow a dry rock if it would help."

The door to room B opened and Hoby came out, followed by a pale-eyed woman in a maid's uniform. "We need to swap your room with Mr. and Mrs. Cole, if that's all right.'' At Sally's nod he said, ''Why don't you go down for coffee and we'll have you in there in about half an hour.''

''Thanks for changing with us,'' said Paige. Just inside the door, she added, ''And watch out for the llama.''

''We'll get along just fine,'' said Sally. Then as the door closed behind the newlyweds, she thought, at least he'll be company.

When Sally came down the stairs, the double doors to the great room were open. Sunlight streamed through the tall windows leading onto the veranda and glistened on the silver coffee urn tucked between two facing leather couches. Next to the cart, Caligula, free of his leash, sat in the classic begging position. Cass Tompkins divided the last of her muffin, popped part into her mouth, and held up the other half. ''Dance.'' Eyes never leaving his mistress's hand, the little dog rose on his hind legs and turned solemnly in a small circle. Miranda Gervin, perched on a narrow chair beneath an imposing set of antlers, balanced her saucer on her knee and opened her book.

From the balcony above, a door opened and a beefy man with deep-set, dissipated eyes stepped into the hall-way and looked down at Sally for a long moment before moving on.

Cass tucked a muffin onto her saucer, reached for another one, and waggled it at Sally. ''You've got to try one of these. They're wonderful. Sweet potato, I think. Whatever they are, they're addictive. I can't stop eating them.''

''They look good.'' Sally poured a cup of coffee, started to drink it black, then hesitated and added cream.

''And who are you?'' asked a man reaching around Sally for a pot of honey.

''Sally Strickland,'' she said, recognizing the man from the balcony.

Lacing his coffee with a liberal dollop of honey, he took

a gulp and reduced a croissant to crumbs in two bites before saying, "Alex Borden, C and N, Houston," as if expecting her to understand his meaning.

"Oh," she said brightly, wondering if she should have introduced herself as Sally Strickland, R.N., ICU, Atlanta.

He looked at her appraisingly. "Alone?"

"Not really." But from the way things looked so far, maybe she was.

Borden reached for a cheese biscuit, popped it into his mouth, and chewed, all the while eyeing her in a way that seemed calculated to make her ill at ease. He was about fifty, she decided. Good-looking once, before the lines of his jaw blurred with fat. With each chewing motion the pouches under his eyes wobbled as if they were filled with fluid. "Your first trip here?" Without waiting for her to answer, he said, "You should see the old lighthouse. I'll take you there."

Just like that. No room for argument. She stared at him, at the yellowish fatty plaques that dotted the thin skin beneath his eyes.

He took her elbow in his hand and leaned against her, kneading her arm with insistent fingers. "You'll love it."

A smile began to twitch at the corner of her mouth. There to have his way with me, she thought. On the windswept moor. "I don't think so," she said, turning briskly away.

Across the room, a young girl in faded jeans and a flannel shirt was watching them. With a carefully bland look, the girl walked toward the serving cart, reached for a croissant, and with a sidelong look at Borden began to heap it with guava jelly.

"Is that for you, Ashley?" he asked with a disapproving look.

In answer, she took a huge bite and began to chew insolently, as if daring him to stop her.

"Is that smart?"

She looked at him evenly and took another bite.

"I asked you a question, miss."

With a quick narrowing of her eyes, she reached for another croissant and the jelly pot.

He grabbed her wrist. "I asked you a question."

With a condescending cluck of her tongue, she shook her head. "Remember your ulcer. You shouldn't get excited." As his hand tightened on her wrist, she twisted out of his grip and yelled, "Why don't you take a Tagamet, Daddy. Before you die." She spun away, ran out of the room, and with a clatter of the front door, was gone.

Chapter 8

AT THE SOUND OF FOOTSTEPS IN THE HALLWAY OUTSIDE THE Techwood apartment, the thin young man paused and stared toward the door. Then as the steps faded away and were lost in the continuous rumble of Atlanta's traffic, he turned back to his work.

Brown wrapping paper lay wadded on the grayed linoleum. And though the sun shone bright outside, the overhead light was turned on, its yellow glare harsh in the room; the single window was sealed off now. The deflated silver Mylar bag snugged against it in a perfect fit.

He reached for the last package and then hesitated. Instead, he turned to the bed and the jacket he had tossed there and pulled out a package of cheese crackers and two Slim Jims from an inner pocket. He sat on the floor, shoulder blades cushioned by the edge of the mattress, and skinned off the wrappings. As he ate his breakfast, he gazed thoughtfully at the window, scanning the Mylar again for any defect.

When he finished, he got to his feet and opened the last

package. Tossing its wrapping onto the floor, he carefully added the primacord inside to the little pile of wires and tubing on the table and went back to work. Within moments his concentration had narrowed to laser width.

Finally, he stood and surveyed his work. At the center of the Mylar bag hugging the window hung a battery-operated blasting cap. Primacord detonator ran like rays from the blasting cap to the edges of the bag and its plastic explosive, so that the whole resembled a silver alien eye.

A clear plastic tube looped from a corner of the Mylar bag to the Sears paint tank. Another tube connected the paint tank to a separate air tank. A thin wire snaked from the air tank's solenoid valve to the telephone decoder on the scarred table. Two more wires emerged from the converted pressure gauge of the paint tank and connected with the decoder.

Checking connections and airtight seals, he reviewed the sequence carefully: In response to a remote signal, the decoder would detonate the two bursting charges on the canister sealed inside the paint tank. He stared at the tank, imagining the silvery cylinder hidden inside. The bursting charges he had attached to the canister were tiny—not enough to explode the paint tank. Tampers directed the charges inward—just enough energy to rupture the canister, just enough to spray liquid bacterial broth inside the paint tank when the charge went off.

He touched the other wire, checking its connection from the phone decoder to the air tank. As the canister bursting charges detonated, the decoder would open the solenoid valve on the air tank and start the delay timer on the blasting-cap igniter in the center of the Mylar bag.

It would take six minutes for the bag to fill, six minutes for it to bulge with its swarming mixture of air and bacteria. Then it would blow.

He stretched his slight body, relieving the strain of tight muscles. Through the thin glass of the window, through its silvery Mylar covering, came the sound of male voices shouting rhythmically in response to an unheard command.

The man raised his eyes as if he could see through the silver barrier to Grant Field, where the Georgia Tech football team moved in ordered bull-muscled exercises.

His mind's eye moved ahead in time and he could see the stadium: Saturday—the first of the crowd trickling in, then the gush of people moving in a human river, clotting the stands, staining the University of Georgia side with the bloodred colors of an old rivalry. And across the field thousands more bleeding into the stadium, spilling the yellow banners of Georgia Tech against gray benches. Nearly sixty thousand fans converging from every section of the country.

A brimming bowl waiting for his touch.

His fingers moved again, tapping out the phone number in almost imperceptible movements against his thigh. His lids slid shut and he could see the explosion: the flash, the invisible cloud boiling toward the stadium. He could hear the gasp of the crowd, its reflexive intake of breath sucking at death, drawing it deep into the moist lining of throat and lung.

Like the altered bacteria it harbored, the crowd would divide and grow into sixty thousand separate vectors. Sixty thousand moving through the city, infecting its hotels, its streets, its airport; sixty thousand scattering across the country, going home: a teacher to her civics class in Charleston, an electrical engineer to his colleagues at Bell Labs, a young computer technologist to Silicon Valley. A graying architect heading back to his Chicago high rise, a retired couple joining the Airstream caravan to Disney World, a salesman—an army of salesmen. . . .

And there would be no place to hide from them. No corner of the country. Nowhere.

The man stood for a moment, his strange gaze fixed on the shimmering covered window, his face impassive. Then he retrieved his jacket from the bed, put it on, and moved to the door. He stopped then and, turning, scooped up the wadded wrapping paper, the cellophane torn from the cheese crackers, the oily plastic Slim Jim casings, and deposited them carefully into the wastebasket.

With one hand on the light switch, he turned and gave a final look. The bacterial aerosol was ready. He flipped off the light, locked the door carefully behind him, and was gone.

In the old house outside of Brunswick, the phone shrilled from the kitchen wall. The man called Iguana reached out and caught it. His cautious "Yes?" was faintly accented.

"Your order is ready." The voice on the long-distance line spoke rapidly in Spanish. "It will go airmail."

"*Muy bien.*" He replaced the receiver and nodded to himself. The fail-safe was ready. Soon he would be able to sleep for a while. But not yet. Not until the nesting of the hawk.

He stood by the window and looked out over the dark green salt marsh stretching toward the east. Closing his eyes, he visualized the map again: St. Cyrils Island, fractured by the tortuous meanderings of the creeks and rivulets that cut through the marshes on its lee side. The tide was low now, running many feet below the cord grass that lined the creek banks. Low enough to conceal the sleek white boat hidden there and the men aboard who watched and waited.

Chapter 9

BRU FARRIER TURNED ONTO A RUTTED SHELL ROAD THAT angled toward the east where McIntosh County met the water. He stole a quick glance at the old sheriff on the bench seat next to him.

Wally was staring out of the window as if the view absorbed him, but his lips were pressed together and his chin jutted out with more than a touch of belligerence. Stubborn, thought Bru. In Wally's own words, "just plain cussed." He belonged in the hospital, not stuck out here on the edge of nowhere by himself. The cardiologist had insisted that he stay for observation, but when Wally set his jaw, the doctor knew he had met his match and gave in reluctantly after exacting a promise from Wally to come back the next day—or sooner if the pain got worse. "You still planning on going in for those tests tomorrow?"

Wally's voice was harsher than usual. "I said I would."

The Ford scraped bottom as it negotiated a sharp right past a cluster of mailboxes and turned onto an oak-lined stretch paralleling a dark waterway. Beyond it, the cord grass of the salt flats rippled in the wind.

Wally shifted in the passenger seat, rattling the bag of Purina Dog Chow pressed against his knee. His thumb and forefinger ran absently along the crease of the white prescription bag on his lap, squeezing, releasing, squeezing again. Not a word. He hadn't volunteered a word for the last two miles.

Bru turned into the scuffed drive that curved through a grove of live oaks and switched off the engine. Mr. B,

Wally's aged basset hound, raised a silver muzzle and peered mournfully over the edge of the hole he had excavated below a sprawling crepe myrtle. Sighing, he struggled up on stubby legs and slowly wagged his tail as Wally swung open the car door.

Bru scooped up the dog-food bag before Wally could lift it, and carried it to the house. The screened porch wheezed open and Mr. B pressed past, toenails clicking across the gray enamel. He waddled over to his dog bowl, lowered his massive haunches, and raised expectant eyes to Bru. "It's a dog's life, isn't it, Mr. B?" Ripping open the bag, he poured food into the battered red bowl and grinned as the basset sank slowly onto his belly in his customary dining position and cradled the bowl with his paws.

Clutching the prescription bag in one hand, Wally felt his pocket, then looked at Bru. "You've got the keys."

The brass doorknob, long ago bronzed by the salt air, wobbled in Bru's hand and turned.

"Used not to have to lock it," said Wally. The door rattled shut behind them.

"It's still the same," said Bru, looking around. The couch still wore lace antimacassars on each arm and the mahogany secretary still displayed the iridescent carnival glass bowl that had been there for as long as Bru could remember. Nothing was different, really, but with Martha gone the house had changed somehow. He wasn't sure why. And then it came to him: He had never known the place without the smell of a cake baking, or fresh-ground coffee, or morning bacon—and it was Thanksgiving. "Have you got anything to eat?"

Wally nodded.

Bru gave him a sharp glance. "Tell you what. Why don't you ride with me over to St. Cyrils. I could run you back tonight after dinner. Have you back here by nine or ten o'clock."

"I'll be fine right here."

"You know Lillian would be pleased if you came."

He shook his head. "Got too much to do here."

Bru was sure that was a lie. "Feeling all right?"

"I told you I'm fine." For a minute they stood looking at each other until Wally said, "You'd better get going. You're late enough."

Bru started to say, "I'll stay here," but something in Wally's face made him think better of it; he had seen that look before, and he knew that if he were to stay, it would somehow be an unconscionable intrusion. Instead, he put on a smile and said, "Are you sure you trust me with the boat? It's been a long time."

"Take the boat. That was the deal."

The condition, thought Bru—the only way he had been able to persuade Wally to let him drive him home.

They walked through the kitchen, past the battered citizens band station that monitored channel 9, past the old white stove and the drainboard with the half-moon chip, and went outside. The little outboard rode the lowering tide far below the floating dock. It was moored next to a twenty-four-foot Chris-Craft twin V-8 with MCINTOSH COUNTY SHERIFF'S DEPARTMENT on the bow. "Sure you don't want to give me that one?" Bru said with a straight face. "It looks like a new trophy."

This time, it was Wally who smiled. "We've had that one awhile. Government seizure. But we picked up another one last week in that cocaine raid I told you about."

"Already painted, I'll bet, and pressed into service in the McIntosh Armada."

Wally grinned slowly. "Maybe so. Now get going." He tossed the key.

Bru caught it with one hand and ran nimbly down the sloping ramp to the water's edge. The outboard coughed once and then fired. As he pulled away from the dock he yelled over his shoulder, "Call St. Cyrils for me, will you? Tell Lillian I'll be there in twenty minutes."

Upstream from the St. Cyrils Island dock, in a narrow tributary of Oyster Creek, the white ocean racer snugged the bank. The sleek Cigarette rode low on the tide; oyster banks thatched with cord grass loomed above her. To anyone standing at the dock, that section of the marsh would appear quite deserted.

The Cigarette and its crew had entered Oyster Creek in the night, gliding toward St. Cyrils dock at a quarter throttle, then poling silently past.

The predawn high tide found the Cigarette a half mile upstream and deep in the island's interior. As the day came on and the tide fell, the rising banks obscured her movements and she began to creep downstream, closer to the main channel of Oyster Creek. The next high tide would bring the cover of darkness.

At a bend in the creek, midway between the dock and the hidden boat, something moved in the marsh and startled a wading bird. Concealed by the wind-rippled grass, clothed in camouflaging browns and drab greens, the man lay on his belly far above the lowering water. Holding an FM transceiver to his lips, he spoke in a low voice, listened, spoke again. A moment more and he returned the transceiver to his belt.

The spongy ground was cold under his body. Dampness penetrated his clothes. Ignoring the wind, he concentrated on the warmth of the sun on his back and the chill passed. When high tide came again, the grasses that concealed him would drown in the dark inrush of the sea, but by then his job here would be done.

He scanned the stream and the higher ground beyond it. Below its fixed platform, the dock, on its bed of white-washed floats, angled sharply downward to meet the water. Bowing slightly in the wind, the anchored motor launch rocked in its berth; a brace of rowboats bobbed and tugged at their moorings.

Beyond the dock in a copse of oak trees stood the old house that had once been the main lodge. Now vacant of guests, it housed the musicians who provided the island's evening entertainment. Their rehearsal had started, and the distant reedy sound of woodwinds mingled with the wind singing through the grasses.

He scanned the other buildings. Next to the old house stood a smaller one—the black couple lived there and the grandson. The house closer to the dock was where the old man stayed. Both were empty now. Quiet. Satisfied, he turned his gaze upstream. In the distance he could see the narrow mouth of the tributary. Beyond it, out of sight, the Cigarette was waiting.

Still and alert, he lay on his belly in the tall marsh grass and kept his vigil: La Culebra—The Snake—cold eyes hooded against the glare of the sun that warmed his back and glinted darkly from the weapon he held.

Sally Strickland took her coffee and muffin to the relative seclusion of an alcove below the Great Room's balcony. To her relief, the C & N man, Alex Borden, did not follow. It was a little too early in the day to have to fend off advances.

At the cart, a boy—about nine years old, she decided—was stuffing sweet-potato muffins into his mouth as if he had not eaten in a week. When he reached his capacity, two more went into his pants pocket and a third was about to follow when a woman came into the room. At the sight of her, the boy laid the muffin back on the plate and darted away.

The woman was about sixty—a slim, athletic sixty. She was dressed in tan slacks and a tan jacket, her white blouse open at the throat. She stood between the double doors for a moment, scanning the room. Then she spotted Sally's hiding place and came up to her. "You're Sally Strickland, aren't you?" Without waiting for an answer, the woman said, "I'd like you to come with me."

"Oh, is my room ready?"

The woman shook her head. "Not yet. I just got a call from Bru Farrier. He's on his way here by boat." The woman extended a slim hand and took hers. "I'm Lillian Sniveley. I own St. Cyrils Island."

Sally followed her outside and, at Lillian's nod, got into the CJ5's passenger seat.

As they pulled away with the empty tram rattling behind them, Lillian turned on the CB radio and keyed the mike switch. "I'm taking the green Jeep to the dock." Then she said to Sally, "We like to keep track of our vehicles. St. Cyrils is over five miles long, so we need to do a good bit of shuttling." She smiled. "I'm sure Bru will give you the guided tour this afternoon. You'll have plenty of time. We don't serve Thanksgiving dinner until evening. That way, our guests have a chance to explore in the daytime."

"I'd like that," Sally began. "I guess it's quite a job, running the lodge." She gave Lillian a sidelong look. The woman seemed pleasant enough, yet there was a distance about her. There was something else, too: something in the look Lillian had given her, as if she didn't quite approve of what she saw.

"I've never done anything else," said Lillian. "I've always lived here. I was born on St. Cyrils. I grew up in the old lodge—the one by the dock." She downshifted, and the burdened Jeep began to climb a long, low hill. "I was supposed to be born in Savannah at my grandmother's house, but it didn't work out. A hurricane was on the way and Mama was near term. Before Daddy could get her to the mainland, she went into labor. You'd know all about that, though; you're a nurse—but back then nobody knew that low barometric pressure brought babies. So Daddy delivered me, and I came during the eye of the storm.

"He always used to tease me about that. He used to say, 'The circumstances of Lillian's birth marked the child. She may seem calm, but she keeps things stirred up all around her.' "

And do you? thought Sally. She said, "How did you know I was a nurse?"

"Why, Bru told me, I think. He must have."

"Have you known him long?"

"Long enough. His granddaddy and I were first cousins. Bru used to spend every summer down here after his mama died. His new mother—well, she had other things she thought she had to do."

The Jeep stopped near the dock and Lillian switched off the engine. At first, Sally could hear only the wind shrilling through the cord grass. Then a faint buzzing like a distant honeybee grew into the angry hum of an outboard. It's about time, she thought. And then aloud: "Bru was supposed to meet me at St. Simons this morning."

Lillian gave a short laugh. "I remember when he and Kathlyn were here on their honeymoon. Why, Kathlyn thought that. . . ." Her words faded to nothing. Then with a quick glance at Sally, she said, "What I meant to say was, Bru has always been unpredictable."

Sally returned Lillian's look with a faint smile, but she was thinking, What you meant to say was exactly what you did say. Every syllable weighed on a jeweler's scale. That type always did.

And what did that mean? Ever since she was a freshman in nursing school she had heard the refrain "Don't be judgmental." And yet, people were types sometimes, weren't they? Not stereotypes, she hastened to tell herself— just types. Lillian Sniveley and Warren's mother could have come from the same mold: slim, cool, with that way of making other people feel . . . out of place.

She was just nineteen when she met Warren's mother and became the "little student nurse" without a name. She had never really experienced until then the rigid caste system that some sons and daughters of the Old South still clung to. For the first time she realized that the profession she had chosen was faintly distasteful to certain people. To them, nursing was a type of servitude—employment for the lower classes, begun with a sordid hospital apprenticeship straight out of the eighteenth century.

Sally looked at the woman behind the wheel of the Jeep. Come on, she said to herself. You don't even know her. It was just that Lillian was so much like Warren's mother: so cool, and proper, so correctly polite and yet so distant to the girl her son had attached himself to: *"Your father drives a bus, dear? How intriguing."* Her tight little smile was followed by a dismissing pat on the hand. Two weeks later, Warren was unexpectedly summoned to his uncle's export house in Frankfurt to "learn the business," and that had been that.

As the hornet's buzz of the outboard grew louder, Sally threw open the Jeep's door and headed for the dock. Lillian followed. In a moment the white boat rounded a curve in Oyster Creek. Sally thrust a hand in the air in greeting. Bru waved back and headed toward her. Then suddenly gunning the motor, he swerved away from the dock and roared past at top speed.

Lillian raised a delicate eyebrow. "What does he think he's doing?"

Sally gave her a sly, sidelong look. "Being unpredictable." Then with a grin, "He always was, you know."

The smell of salt and decay was strong in La Culebra's nostrils. Belly pressed to the wet, spongy ground, he slowly shifted position. Rough blades of cord grass ripped over his hiding place.

Across the creek, the Jeep and its rattling train of cars came to a stop and two women got out. He recognized the younger one; he had watched her disembark that morning.

The sound of the outboard was closer now. Much closer. He stared downstream as the boat sped around a curve in Oyster Creek and came into view. Only one man on board. His black eyes narrowed under thick lids. The ambassador? No, he thought. Impossible. He was to come by air.

The boat slowed as it approached the dock. Then with sudden speed it headed upstream. Toward the hidden Cigarette.

A rush of adrenaline quickened his heart. A deep breath. Another. The pulse pounding in his throat slowed; his hands steadied on the SIG automatic rifle. Finger cradling the trigger, La Culebra fixed Bru Farrier in his sights.

His mind raced: Stop him. He had to be stopped. But the women— The outboard roared directly below him. Sunlight flashed from its rippling wake. —All of them, then.

As his finger tightened on the trigger, he remembered the musicians. There were three of them. Too close. They could see the dock. They'd hear.

The alternative was to abort. As quickly as the thought came he rejected it. Too late for that. Too late.

The outboard closed on the hiding place. Now. It had to be now.

The wake curved. The boat began to turn.

La Culebra released the trigger. Breath held, he stared as the outboard circled and headed back toward the dock.

Bru Farrier secured the outboard to the dock with a twist of line and ran up the ramp toward the platform. Catching Sally's hands in his, he leaned toward her. She expected a kiss. Instead, his lips brushed her ear and he said in a low voice, "I think I lost them."

A smile teased the corner of her mouth. "Should I ask who 'they' are?"

"The revenuers. But I got 'em with a bootlegger's turn. They'll never catch me now."

"Where have you been?"

"Attending to business." He waggled his thumb toward the boat. "Coke shipment."

"Coke," she repeated, giving in to the game.

He nodded gravely. "Old Coke. In the six-ounce bottles. Worth its weight—"

"And was it the revenuers who took your luggage? Or do you always travel light?"

"Always. But I keep a few things at the lodge. That is, if Miss Lily here hasn't tossed them into the trash." Bru threw an arm around Lillian and gave her a kiss.

"You know I wouldn't toss my boy's clothes," said Lillian with a fond glance. "Oh, Bru, I'm so glad you could come. I've got a real treat for you tonight. It's coming in by plane this afternoon."

He nodded gravely. "A dozen Egyptian dancing girls?"

"Better. A case of Beaujolais nouveau. And it's a vintage year."

"Turkey and Beaujolais," he said with approval. "Now, that's what I call something to give thanks for."

"I'm afraid we can't have it with dinner. Leroy can't bring the barge back until high tide, and that's not until seven. We'll have it later, after the concert."

"Sally's going to love that," he said with a glance at the girl. "I see you two have already met. Have you been showing her around?"

"Not really," said Lillian. "She hasn't even seen the beach yet, I'm afraid."

"But what I have seen is beautiful." Sally looked out over the marsh that stretched for miles to the west. Overhead, a great blue heron took the air with slow, heavy wing beats. "It's magnificent."

Bru followed her gaze. "I used to play out there when I was a kid."

"There?" She was startled. "It looks so snaky."

He grinned. "No snakes. They're on higher ground. Just a few alligators—and, of course, the 'quicksand.' Perfectly safe if you know what you're doing. That is," he amended, "fairly safe."

She gave a little shudder. "Not for me."

"Not for me, either. It's been a long time. Besides, it's November. The water can get good and cold."

"I'm not sure what I expected," said Sally, "but I certainly didn't think it would be so wild here."

"Oh, goodness." Lillian swept a hand toward the handful of buildings tucked in the woods. "This is the developed part of the island. It's the rest of it that's wild. My daddy raised cattle here, but that was years ago. It's all gone back to wilderness now."

"It's like a national park, then."

"Better, we think. National parks are run over by hordes of people. Less than five percent of St. Cyrils is developed, including the roads." Then to Bru: "I'm not counting the airstrip, though. Would you call that developed?"

"Absolutely." He looked at her solemnly. "A strip of mowed prairie and a wind sock. I call that high tech."

Sally laughed, and then with a sudden glance toward the old lodge said, "Oh, listen!" The haunting sound of a single flute throbbed against the air.

Lillian smiled. "Debussy. *Syrinx*. It's lovely, isn't it?"

"Beautiful."

"Miss Lily imprisons young musicians on St. Cyrils," said Bru in a low voice against Sally's ear. "Makes them sing for their supper of bread and water." Then to Lillian: "How many this time?"

"Three. A woodwind and guitar trio. And wait until you hear Nathan Katz play the oboe." Lillian's eyes shone. "He's just nineteen and brilliant. He went to Juilliard when he was barely fifteen." She turned to Sally. "You'll hear them tonight. After dinner. And now it's time to get you two settled. I'm sure your rooms are ready by now."

Sally caught the plural, and an eyebrow rose. Rooms, she thought. So that's the way it was going to be.

Lillian pulled up in front of the lodge and shut off the Jeep. "You really should see the beach now," she said to Sally. "It's just past the boardwalk." She nodded toward the gray cedar walkway angling upward through the trees across the way.

Bru smiled at Lillian, but his voice was firm. "She'd like that. After she sees her room."

Lillian blinked and said, "Of course." She was a little stung at the tone of his voice. He can't wait to get her alone, she thought. He was looking at her the way he used to look at Kathlyn.

The sun gave golden highlights to the dark red of Sally's hair. The girl was pretty enough, Lillian conceded. Fresh as a dish of pink and white mints. She could imagine her in a crisp white nurse's uniform, standing by a little boy's hospital crib, offering quick sympathy to a man whose child and whose marriage were dying. Janie-on-the-spot.

As quickly as the thought was born, Lillian chided herself. She didn't even know the girl. It's age showing, she thought. Hardening of the attitudes. But things were so different now, so . . . casual.

A smile began to play at the corner of Bru's mouth as if something funny had just occurred to him. With a look at Sally, he said, "On second thought, you're right. Why don't the two of you take a look at the ocean?" He gave Sally a quick kiss. "I just remembered something I have to do. I'll be back in a few minutes."

Lillian watched him stride briskly toward the lodge, and for the first time in years wondered what it would be like to be young again. The trace of a speculative smile touched her lips. If she were that age today and someone like Bru came along—well, who was to say? She nodded to Sally, and the two of them moved toward the broad wooden steps of the rising boardwalk.

A gray squirrel gnawing an acorn stopped at their approach and stared, frozen except for nervous quiverings of its thistledown tail. When they reached the first step, it leaped up the curving trunk of an oak and chittered at them from the haven of a high branch.

"It smells good here," said Sally, running her palm along the rough-cut railing of the walkway. "Woodsmoke and the sea." She sniffed again. "And there's that sharp smell—it's almost a taste—of winter air coming." A sudden rustle from a clump of palmettos drew her attention and she cried out in delight as a young white-tailed deer boldly stepped out and gazed at her with liquid brown eyes. One side of his two-point antlers was bent incongruously as if it had melted and then hardened again; the other sported a dangling curl of Spanish moss.

"That's Me," said Lillian with a smile.

"What?"

"One of our orphans, Deer Me. The other one is Oh Deer. She's sweet, but I'll have to admit he's my favorite. I raised them both on a bottle." She looked back at Sally. The girl's eyes were glowing with excitement. "You've never been around wild things much, have you?"

Sally shook her head. "It's a little frightening here, and

yet I feel drawn to it.'' She looked back at the lodge as if to assure herself that it was still there. ''I guess that doesn't make any sense.''

''It does to me,'' said Lillian. St. Cyrils was beginning to work its magic. She had seen it happen many times before. ''We've all grown so civilized that wild places seem alien at first.'' People need the wild places, she thought. They need to know they're there even if they never see them. She remembered the opportunist developers who had swarmed over the island after her father died. They had come back again last year when the faltering economy threatened to make it impossible for her to meet St. Cyrils's increasing taxes. Her eyes narrowed at the thought of them, at how they scoffed at the idea of a lodge for only fifteen guests when rooms for fifty—for five hundred— would be more like it, at how they spoke of leveling the sand hills to give everyone an ocean view.

They reached the crest of the dune and followed the boardwalk through the trees for a way. Then suspended over a dip of wooded land, the rough walk swung east until it reached another sand hill, and the trees thinned and shrank to gnomelike dwarfs. Here and there the leaf mold disappeared, revealing patches of white sand. At the end of the trees, palmettos held their sharp pleats to the sun, and low shrubs and ground cover crawled over the dune. Ahead, a tall, roofed cedar platform perched at the top of the hill.

Wind whipped their hair into disarray as they reached the platform. To the east the dune, fuzzy with pale sea oats, plunged alongside wooden stairs to a wide beach marked with the dark, curving line of the tide's debris. The Atlantic glittered in the sun as far as they could see.

They climbed to a higher level of the tower. From here, Sally could see the beach narrow, then widen again into a curving spit of sand where brown pelicans fished the surf. Turning, she looked back toward the west at the lodge tucked deep in its sheltering valley. They stood in silence for a moment, then Sally pointed to a fenced clearing where an ancient oak wrapped moss-draped limbs around a small white building. "What's that?"

Lillian looked down at the little cemetery and said, "My family. They're buried there." Her brother had been the first: Jason, fresh from the Citadel, proud and strutting as a young bull. He had fallen from the sky in flames and shards of metal somewhere over France in 1943. Shortly afterward, her father joined him. Her mother had lived until 1970, and when she died, Lillian wondered whether to put her there next to the others. Letty had never adjusted to the island. Her only solace had been her old piano with the sticking F-sharp key that so distressed her, and later, the little musicales she gave for her childhood friends from Savannah.

Now only Lillian was left—sixty and a spinster—nun to her sainted island and to the lodge; mother only to the sons and daughters of the aristocrats of government and industry who came to St. Cyrils because they had always done so.

She intended to live here until she died. She intended to be buried under the two-hundred-year-old oak next to Willard and Letty and what was left of Jason. She turned away from Sally then and looked out over the glittering ocean. Please, God, she thought, don't take it away from me. She wanted to stay here, to die here, on her island. And afterward—the thought quirked into a wistful smile— afterward, God willing, she would haunt it as a thin, gray wraith blowing in the sea winds.

"And is it haunted?" Sally asked, looking up at the vaulted ceiling and dark beams of the third-floor hallway.

Bru's eyebrows climbed and he said in a Boris Karloff voice, "Ghoulies and ghosties and long-legged beasties. And after midnight the Guales come out."

"The Wallys?"

"The ghosts of the Guale Indians, m'dear." Bru pointed to the door at his left. "They cluster most hideously in the honeymoon suite. But never fear; I'll protect you."

Sally glanced at the door to the honeymoon suite and wondered if that was where Bru had stayed. Bru and Kathlyn—maybe old ghosts did walk in this place. She stole a look at him as he opened the door. Why had he brought her here? To this old-shoe place where Lillian had filed her discreetly away in a separate room. All she needed was a brass plaque on the door: WOMAN, OTHER.

The door fell open to a bright room with a quilt-topped double bed. At the foot, her suitcase and tote sat on an old Chinese chest. An eclectic collection of antique oak and walnut furniture stood against the rough, white plaster walls. Ruffled curtains sprigged with yellow flowers hung at the twin dormers, and someone—she suspected it was Bru—had lighted a fire in the tiny wood stove between the windows. On the table next to the bed a pile of books lay under an old brass student lamp. "It's charming." Then she began to laugh.

Bru raised an eyebrow. "Something I did?"

She pointed to the wall near the door and the llama skin spread-eagled there. "My roommate."

"Oh," he said. "That's new."

So he did stay here before, she thought. With Kathlyn. Sally turned away and looked through the window. Oak leaves fluttered in the wind, and greenery tumbling down the slopes of the old dune rose again on the next. From here she could see the boardwalk tower and a sparkling patch of ocean beyond it.

"Do you like St. Cyrils?" he asked.

"It's beautiful."

"So are you."

She felt his hands on her shoulders turning her gently toward him. Stiffening at this touch, she thought again of Kathlyn.

His hands dropped away and a sudden smile played at the corner of his mouth. "You haven't seen it all yet." He nodded toward a tall door next to a walnut dressing table. "M'lady's bath. Complete with claw-footed tub."

When Sally opened the door, she stared at the floor and began to giggle.

The giggle turned into a laugh that grew until tears came to her eyes. Her sheer pink negligee lay carefully spread on the floor, its filmy arms locked around an embracing pair of blue-striped pajamas. Laughing, clinging to Bru for support, she was finally able to say, "Shall we leave them there?"

With one hand holding her, he quietly shut the bathroom door with the other and nodded. "They need their privacy. They need it bad."

Crisp, cool sheets grew warm against their skin. The thick quilt writhed and crumpled and the sweet smell of her crept into his nostrils. Tight, curling hair softened, opening to moist velvet. "There?"

A faint, gasping answer.

Sunlight glowed red behind his closed eyelids as he felt her thrust against him. The smell of her, the taste, the stroke of warm, wet flesh climaxed in battering waves— quieter, quieter now until only the salt musk smell of the sea was left, only the wind of her breath against his throat and the hammering surf of pulse to break the stillness.

She lay touching him, long hair glowing copper red against warm skin, a strand shining against the soft pink of a nipple. He touched it lightly with a kiss.

She opened clear green eyes and looked at him. "You've been here before—"

"Since I was a boy."

"—with Kathlyn."

He looked at her for a moment, then rolled over on his back and stared at the ceiling, his hand tracing the damp silk curve of her thigh. He lay there, silent, and though she did not ask, her "Why?" hung in the air between them: Why had he brought her here? He considered the unasked question, and sorting through the glib remarks that sprang into his head, found that he had no answer.

Chapter 10

ASHLEY BORDEN THRUST HER CHIN TOWARD HER BROTHER and narrowed her eyes in disdain. "Crawl away, roach."

Calvin stood blocking the path, grubby hands in the back pockets of his jeans. "Bug off your own self. You don't own the woods."

Ashley shoved past him and stalked a few paces away toward a fork in the path.

He followed. "Bet you had another fight with Daddy. Prob'ly about your *boy*-friend," he drawled.

She gave him a pinch-lipped smile. "Wipe your nose, roach. You've got snot."

"Yeah? Well you oughta look at your own face. *You* got jelly all over." He pointed at her, guffawing with nine-year-old humor and at the same time taking a swipe at his nose with a streaked thumb.

"You ought to be locked up," she said savagely. "In a cage." She whirled away and started walking down the left fork toward the dock and the old lodge.

Calvin watched his sister's stiff-backed exit. Scooping a damp clod of earth from the path, he lobbed it at her blue-jeaned bottom and watched it splat there for a soul-satisfying moment. Then he sprinted down the right fork toward the old lighthouse.

After a minute's breathless run in which he imagined wild bears and panthers were after him, he flung himself off the path and lay on his belly behind a thicket of palmetto. Parting the fronds to an eye-sized slit, he stared down the path. With mingled regret and relief, he realized

that he was not being pursued. He scrambled up, and in
his best Daniel Boone fashion, sneakers cautiously placed
so as not to alert the Indians with a broken twig, he set out
cross-country toward the beach.

The dune dipped slightly just ahead: the Cumberland
Gap. On the lookout for an ambush, he slid beneath a tree.
He could hear the faint boom of the surf now, muttering
over and over, "Dark and bloody ground."

With infinite caution he crept toward the top of the
wooded dune. Another lay ahead, this one higher and
treeless, covered in pale sea oats that rippled in the breeze.
With a sudden shift of scenario Calvin seized a half-rotten
branch that became a sword in his talented hands, and
brandishing it in triumph, he ran to the top of the dune:
Balboa discovering the Pacific.

Fifteen minutes later, a half-dozen sand dollars crum-
bling in his pockets, he spotted the old lighthouse that
once had marked the channel of Altamaha Sound.

The door at its base stood ajar. He stepped inside with a
wary glance at the rusty stairs that spiraled above him. He
sprang up the steps, taking them two at a time, fleeing the
horde of rats that could attack him at any moment. At the
top he clung to the wall, and clawing at the stitch in his
side, stared anxiously down the empty shaft that yawned
below him. No sign of the rats, they were sly and devil-
ishly clever.

A narrow door at the top gave way to his touch, and
Calvin stepped onto the bridge of the Starship Enterprise.
"Warp factor two, Mr. Sulu."

As he turned slowly, the Atlantic gave way to the alien
landscape of St. Cyrils salt marsh stretching away to the
west.

He peered through the streaked glass of the lighthouse
windows, narrowing his eyes at the green expanse bisected
by the silver curve of Oyster Creek and one of its tributar-
ies. In the distance, half hidden by the bank, he spotted a
glint of white in the narrow stream branching off the

creek. Squinting, he saw a movement, then another. "Spock, give me a reading."

"My sensors indicate alien life forms, Captain."

He stared at the slim white boat that was partly concealed by the low tide and the rising oyster banks. Three aliens. Maybe four.

A sudden rumble of his stomach caused him to check his watch. It was time for lunch. And after, Miss Lillian had promised to show him a gator nest. Shoving open the door, Calvin Borden grabbed the rusty railing, ran down the steps, and set off for the lodge at a dead run.

Lena Jefferson shucked off her blue sweater, draped it over the ladder back of the kitchen desk chair, and went back to the worktable. Into the baskets marked COLE and FARRIER she tucked iced containers of shrimp salad, cheese, and a loaf of her French bread, then added red bandanna napkins and a crisp white picnic cloth.

Crossing the room, she opened the large refrigerator, drew out two half bottles of chilled Soave and tucked one into the wicker wine cylinder on each basket. The cold of the salads and the wine throbbed in the small joints of her hands. No time to get stiff, she thought with a glance at the two large turkeys on the countertop. She couldn't afford to give in to the pain; there was too much to do. Stepping to the sink, she ran hot water over her hands, working gnarled black fingers together under the stream until the deep aching subsided.

At the shrill ring of the telephone, she dried her hands and trudged into the dining room. "Rural six," she said in response to the radio operator. Flipping on a house intercom to 2B, she said, "Miz Tompkins."

"What is it?"

"Phone call."

"—Get down, Caligula." Then: "I'll be down in a minute."

"You don't get but three minutes. This be a radiotelephone." And leaving the receiver dangling from the hook, Lena went back to her kitchen.

Miranda Gervin was transforming her dresser into an impromptu desk. To the left of the portable typewriter lay tapes that needed transcribing: chapters three through seven of *Dark Frenzy, Dark Desire*, rife with the adventures of Camilla Stuyvesant, a red-haired heroine with features charmingly ambiguous enough to make each of at least two dozen redheads of Cass's acquaintance believe that she, and she alone, was Camilla's inspiration. But as Cass always said, "It's good for business. And where's the harm?" Every fourth Cassandra Temple romance featured a redhead as part of the cycle: blonde, brunette, brownette, redhead—and there were literally thousands of women ranging in age from fourteen to forty who believed that they were the model for one of the eighty-four heroines.

Desk in order, Miranda began to unpack, sandwiching a mud-colored pantsuit between a murky green polyester and a navy double knit in the narrow closet. Stern white underwear went into the curly-maple dresser. Turning again to the half-emptied suitcase, she added a blue flannel nightgown to the drawer, followed by a white with brown piping.

In the folds of a third lay a small .380 automatic, its dull black angles harsh against its soft beige nest. She looked at the Walther PPK thoughtfully for a moment. Cass had always laughed about it, calling her paranoid, saying, "I thought I hired a secretary, not a bodyguard." But Miranda had carried the gun for twelve years—ever since she had been cornered late at night in the apartment elevator. She could not remember the man's face now, but at times his animal odor came back and brought with it a quick nausea. Laying the gun in the drawer, she covered it with two more gowns and flanked it with a box of Stayfree Maxi Pads and a small cosmetics bag.

Across the hall the intercom in Cass's room clicked once, then summoned her to the phone. Through the half-open door Miranda watched, noting with a quick glance when Cass emerged and headed for the stairs with Caligula in tow. Miranda's hands moved in and out of the suitcase, folding, sorting, putting away, until the hollow tap of footsteps faded and was gone.

She moved to the door and looked out into the empty hallway. Crossing quickly, she entered Cass's room and closed the door.

A small suitcase spilled its cornucopia of frothy underwear in a clutter on the bed. Half hidden beneath a silver-gray peignoir lay Cass's leather handbag, soft as butter in Miranda's hands. She snapped it open and fished through its contents, holding its matching wallet for a moment, letting it go, searching again until she drew out a letter written in a bold, masculine hand.

As she read, sunlight outlined her fingers through the thin aerogram with its foreign stamp. When she finished, she thrust the letter back into the bag and hurried to her own room.

The unmistakable crash of breaking glass came from the dining room. The new girl was at it again. Setting her jaw, Lena Jefferson shut the oven door and went to investigate.

Amelia stood over the shards of a half-dozen water tumblers. "It wasn't my fault." Her pale, almost lashless eyes stared belligerently at Lena. "Somebody left a puddle on the floor." She gave a quick jerk of her head toward the slim, brown-skinned girl swishing a mop over the dark tile.

Consuela, bristling at the attack, spat out an obscenity. "Maybe if you could figure which is your elbow and which is your ass, you not smash everything." She followed this with an impassioned tirade in Spanish punctuated with stabs of the mop into the dripping bucket. "You want puddle? I give you puddle." With a final thrust of her mop, Consuela launched the contents of the bucket toward Amelia's feet.

Lena quickly dispatched Amelia to the third floor, sending her with enough cleaning instructions to keep her occupied there until the five o'clock boat home. When Amelia was out of earshot, Lena drew herself up and stared at Consuela. "She be gone soon."

Her tone implied much to the girl. Lena could hire and fire any of the household help with no more than a nod to Miss Lillian. Amelia was out, and Lena's scowl indicated that she could be next. Without a word, Consuela wrung out her mop and began to clean up the mess.

Lena watched her for a moment, then nodded and went back to the kitchen. Consuela was a good worker. Worth three of Amelia. She wished Consuela would stay over to help with dinner. Holidays were always hard on Lena; with Leroy gone for supplies, she needed the help. He couldn't bring the barge back until high tide, and that wouldn't come till after seven tonight. Leroy was usually here to help on Thanksgiving. If it weren't for Miss Lillian being so set on that French wine, he'd be here now. She sniffed at the thought of flying in wine all the way from France when the lodge already had a cellar full of it. But this was supposed to be different. It had to be fresh, Lillian had said. Lena frowned. It probably tasted like all the rest of it. To her, wine tasted off. If she had her druthers, she'd rather have grape juice any day.

Lena glanced toward the dining room and decided not to ask Consuela to stay. She'd rather go home to Brunswick and her man than get the overtime. Besides, there wouldn't be room enough to put her up in the cottage with Tim in the spare room.

At the thought of her tall, good-looking grandson, Lena gave a quick smile. For the last five months, Tim had been living with them, working the barge with Leroy, doing the innumerable tasks that needed doing on the island, and saving nearly all his pay. Lena had hoped he was saving toward learning a trade. Secretly she wished that he would make a funeral director who would drive a fine car and wear dark striped suits every day. Instead, he told her his plans for college.

"What you gonna learn to do?" she had asked, amazed when he told her that he didn't know yet. "Maybe medicine. Maybe I'll be a doctor someday, if I can save enough for med school later." It seemed like a mighty big "if" to her. She had never had much use for school. After six years of it, she had gone to work in Brunswick, cleaning other people's houses, washing other people's clothes, cooking their food. At sixteen she married Leroy Jefferson and came to St. Cyrils Island, where she bore twin sons. The older one, Tim's father, rode the boat to school every day until he grew into a tall, straight marine who filled her with pride. The younger she laid away in a small white casket covered with roses. It took them nine years to pay for the funeral, but it had been worth it. Each year on his birthday she brought out the yellowing pictures, and laying them on the table one by one, remembered how fine it had been.

As Lena loaded a tray with more water tumblers, she heard the familiar roar of a low-flying plane—the Air Island shuttle from Glynco Jetport. Today they were bringing in the ambassador. Balancing the tray on one angular hip, she stepped to the blackboard in the center of the kitchen. Under THURSDAY ARRIVALS she chalked an X by "Sir William Talbott."

The CB radio crackled. "Green Jeep to base," said Hoby's voice.

Lena pressed the mike switch. "Base."

"Heading for the landing strip. Back in ten minutes."

She nodded, satisfied that lunch would not be delayed too long, and began to distribute the water glasses around the oval oak table set with Blue Onion dishes on white woven mats. Sun from the tall windows glinted on the big copper salad bowl in the center of the table. Lena tucked a basket of fresh bread next to the bowl and turned to poke the fire in the old Franklin stove, causing a spray of sparks to leap up the chimney.

At the bow of the hidden ocean racer the subleader, known to his men as El Ojo, scanned the horizon with powerful field glasses. The driver of the Cigarette, a skilled navigator, dozed, pillowing his head against a dark green canvas pack, while the third man, leaning back in a cushioned seat, sucked an orange and balanced a 7.62-caliber automatic rifle across his thighs.

The Cigarette, loaded with weapons and supplies for nine men, rocked gently as El Ojo turned toward the swelling sound of a low-flying plane. An egret standing motionless in the cord grass gave a low, heavy croak at its approach and took to the air with slow wing beats. For a moment the two glided overhead in parallel, the white egret's spreading wings a reflection of the silver plane's as it neared St. Cyrils's grassy airstrip.

El Ojo stood for a moment, watching. Then he unhooked the FM transceiver from his belt and held it to his lips.

In the frame house outside of Brunswick, the FM transceiver crackled. The man called Iguana reached for it and acknowledged.

The low voice said in Spanish, "The hawk is nesting."

"I would like very much to see that," he answered carefully. "Soon perhaps." He thumbed off the transceiver, laid it on the kitchen table, and stood. He would rest now, sleep awhile. Then it would be time to wake the others.

He walked into the small living room and stretched out on the faded green couch. Through the thin walls he could hear the creak of mattress as one man turned in his sleep and another muttered softly in reply.

He would awaken at 4:00 P.M.—precisely at 4:00—in response to an inner alarm which never failed. Turning on his side, he fell asleep instantly, one hand cradling his cheek, the other curved around the silvery metal canister chained to his waist.

Chapter 11

THE SUN FELT WARM ON ASHLEY BORDEN'S BACK. SHE LAY on her stomach on the crest of a dune and stared out across the ocean. At the horizon a gray speck of a ship crept north.

She had been driven from her refuge in the cedar observation tower by the sound of voices and the clatter of footsteps on the lodge's boardwalk. Wanting to be alone, she walked southeast on the curving beach, past the woods, until she reached the high dunes. Behind her lay an expanse of yellow prairie, a valley of wire grass and cactus, studded here and there with palmettos. Below her perch of sand and translucent sea oats, the beach, widened by the low tide, had captured greenish pools that glittered in the sun.

With raucous cries, a flock of gulls exploded into flight as two people appeared on the beach in the distance. Ashley watched their approach with resentment. Of all the miles of beach, why did they have to come here? Squinting, she tried to make out who they were, but they were still too far away, walking along the dark curving strip left by the last high tide, stopping here and there to sift through the seaweed and shells tossed at the foot of the dunes.

After the first flash of anger at their invasion, Ashley began to enjoy the situation. She was hidden among the sea oats that swayed with her breath and the remnants of the wind; she could watch unobserved.

The couple came closer, zigzagging from tide pool to tide line. Ashley could hear their laughter now, joining with the cry of the gulls. The girl was the redhead she had seen that morning in the lodge—the one Daddy had come on to. She clamped her lips together; she could still see his hand creeping up the girl's arm, could still see the look in his eyes as he leaned toward her and spoke against her ear. "You just can't leave it alone, can you, Daddy?" she said aloud.

Her mother had denied it for years, making excuses for him, covering for him: "Your father has to put in such long hours, Ashley. We have to understand how particular he is about his work." And then Elizabeth Borden would stir a spoonful of sugar into the thin cup that always smelled of tea and Bourbon, and give another fragile smile that was never quite reflected in her eyes.

Something came into Daddy's eyes, too, something that glittered like fear. He covered it with bluster. Ashley tried to talk with her mother about it. For answer she heard the clink of a silver spoon in a thin cup and then the faint voice saying, "Everything is fine, Ashley. Just a few changes in the corporation. Something structural. I don't really understand it all, but everything is fine."

Fine. Sure. Everything is great. Fine to feel your mother's hands tugging at your shoulder at four in the morning. "Ashley, help me." Half asleep, she had followed her mother to the big white bathroom where Alex Borden clung to the toilet and vomited, flecks of bright red blood spotting his undershirt and dribbling on the white porcelain.

It was Ashley who called the ambulance; Ashley who held her father's head during the spasms of nausea—Ashley dabbing at bloody streaks with a green washcloth that turned brown in her hands; Ashley straining to hear the sound of a siren while Elizabeth Borden sat in a darkened bedroom and sipped from a thin white cup.

Calvin slept through it all. Ashley wanted to wake him when the ambulance came and the two men strapped her father into a narrow white stretcher. She stood over the sleeping boy, wanting to wake him, wanting him to help, but he seemed so little then, so much like a baby with his round face nestled in his palm, that she couldn't. She crept back to the bedroom. "Mama, they're going now."

There was a silence, and then: "You ride with him, Ashley. Won't you? I just can't."

A week later, Alex Borden had gone back to his office with a hundred pale gray Tagamet tablets in his briefcase. Elizabeth stayed more and more in her room—holding a cup that trembled in her slim fingers, staring at Ashley with eyes strangely dark and slanting. Elizabeth's clothes were rumpled now, her hair limp and streaked with oil.

Then ten days ago, Alex had picked Ashley up at school early, and as the car slid away down the oak-lined drive, said, "We'll be going on a little trip. You, Calvin, and me. We're going to St. Cyrils for a couple of weeks."

"And Mama?"

"She won't be going with us. Grandma's not been so well, you know. Your mother left today to stay with her for a while." He flashed a quick smile at Ashley and she read it as a lie.

He had been thinking, he said, about her school. Country Day was good, of course, but not top-notch. He was thinking of a girl's academy in New Orleans. "You can start after the Thanksgiving holidays. You'll love it, Ashley," he said, talking too fast. "We'll go to St. Cyrils for a couple of weeks, and then drop Cal at Southern Military—"

She felt her insides grow cold as she looked at him. "I don't suppose I have a choice."

He glanced at her and then back at the road. "No, you don't, Ashley."

She wasn't going to cry. She wasn't going to let him see her cry. While the car prowled the curving streets toward Calvin's school, she leaned against the door and stared at the pile of books in her lap. Thrown away. The discard pile. She clamped her teeth together. She would not cry. She'd never let him see her cry.

She looked out from the dune, past the couple on the beach below, and stared blankly at the ocean. "Why,

Daddy? Why?'' she whispered. "I could have helped you.''
She felt the anger grow again and clenched her fingers in
the soft sand. She was an inconvenience—she and Calvin—
something to put away out of sight.

Calvin didn't quite understand what was going on. She
tried to imagine him in a military school. Nine years old
and playing soldier. He could probably handle that part,
but what about the rest of it? The regimentation? The
discipline? They'd cut off his hair. She thought of how he
had been this week on St. Cyrils—tagging after Hoby,
bugging him about everything, asking how the radios
worked, the generators, until the old man in exasperation
told him to go off and play somewhere else. Poor little
mutt. All by himself. And now they were going to cut off
his hair, and dress him in a uniform, and step on his soul.
The sudden, stabbing guilt made her wince. Why was he
so damn lovable sometimes and such a roach at others?
Lately, every time they were together he was so madden-
ing she wanted to wring his neck.

It wasn't right. He couldn't handle things like she could;
he was just nine. "He needs his daddy," she said aloud.
"Daddy—" she rolled over on her back in the soft sand
with her face to the sun and the salt tears stinging her eyes.

"Bru, look." Sally was on her knees by a pile of debris
left by the tide. "I wish I had a camera."

He squatted beside her, steadying himself by taking her
shoulders in his hands. A bow-shaped piece of driftwood
lay in the sand in a tangle of purple whip coral. A gray
feather teetered on the silver of the wood. "Still life with
boomerang," he said.

She shook her head. "Have you no poetry in your soul,
Bru Farrier? It's a saga out of the Old West." Her fingers
skimmed the lines of the driftwood: "The bow." Then the
feather: "The broken arrow. Abandoned in the desert in a
patch of purple sagebrush."

He grinned at the fantasy and pointed over her shoulder
to a dead starfish two feet away. "And there's the vic-

tim.'' As she raised an eyebrow, he went on. "The sheriff—poor devil. Covered by the shifting sands. Nothing left of him but his star.''

Sally groaned appropriately and added the piece of driftwood and the feather to the store of whelk shells, yellow whip coral, and angel wings now filling the picnic basket. ''There's a touch more wine,'' she said, drawing the half-buried green bottle out of the cooling sand. ''Want some?'' When he nodded, she poured what was left into their glasses—an inch for Bru, a tablespoon for her, and leaned back against his shoulder.

She had changed into jeans and sneakers, pushing her pale blue sweatshirt sleeves above her elbows. Now with the sun warm on her arms she pulled the sleeves down to her wrist as a safeguard against freckles, and narrowed her eyes to subdue the brilliant cut-glass sparkle of the ocean. The wine and the hypnotic pulse of the surf had made her drowsy. Stretching out, cradling her head on Bru's shoulder, she stared up at a flock of white gulls circling overhead, banking against the wind, scolding for a handout from the picnic basket. She felt her eyes drag shut, and within moments she was asleep.

The dream slipped through a crevice of her brain as if it had always been hidden there, biding its time, waiting for the right moment to emerge:

It was night. It was the thick, blurred night of a city that wore the shroud of fog. A torch smelling of rancid oil flickered from a stone niche, its misty reflection dancing on the narrow, rain-slick street. Her shoes were thin, the worn soles scant protection against the cobblestones beneath her feet. Shivering with a chill that penetrated bone, she pulled the ragged shawl tighter around her narrow shoulders. She had to hurry . . . hurry . . . hurry. . . . She was not sure just why. . . .

Running now, running through a thick, encompassing mist, she sped through the twisting streets. Hurry . . . hurry . . . hurry. . . . The pain in her head and eyes was indistinct, as if the night fog had penetrated her flesh, as if the cold river from which it rose lapped against her skull in slow, pulsing waves.

Ahead, glowering over a squat, ugly building, orange light flamed against the sky. It was there she must go. There. . . .

She raced on, feet padding against the pavement, one hand clutching the shawl to her throat, the other catching up her long skirt. She could see the flames now, leaping through the mist, sending blackened shadows to play in grotesque shapes against building stone and wavy panes of glass.

The child was suddenly there, blocking her way, his weasel face breaking into a gargoyle's grin. Another slid from the shadows. Another . . . another . . . Confused, she spun away. Behind her, a ragged line of children pressed in, linking hands, surrounding her, circling in a taunting, raucous dance. Their starved faces contorted. Shadows blackened their eyes to pits, their mouths to yawning holes.

Suddenly they fell back, forming an aisle, pushing her toward the flames that leaped and fell in the darkness.

Hurry . . . hurry . . . hurry. . . .

The wheels of the dead cart creaked to a stop. She heard each muffled thud as the shrouded cargo met the pyre. For a moment the fire died. Then with a hiss, steam and oily smoke billowed, and the hungry flames sent a crackling stream of sparks to meet the angry sky.

Sally woke with a start, the taunts of ragged children echoing in her head. But it was only the mocking cry of sea gulls that she heard, fat white sea gulls circling over-head. She shivered involuntarily.

"Cold?" asked Bru.

Disoriented, she stared up at him. "Yes . . . no." The sun felt warm on her face, yet the chill of the dream still touched her bones. Struggling up on one elbow, she fought against a sudden impulse to cling to him. It was just a dream, she told herself. It was fading rapidly to mists and tatters. A silly dream.

She shaded her eyes against the sun. "I should have worn a hat," she muttered. "Freckles. . . ."

"Then let's take you back"—Bru's voice dropped into a Boris Karloff impersonation—"into the dark woods."

Awake now, she tilted a look at him and grinned. "There to see Madame Ouspenskaya, who will read my palm?"

"The very same, m'dear." He drained his glass, tucked it into the basket, and rising, pulled Sally to her feet.

He clamped an arm around her shoulder as they walked back toward the boardwalk, feet squeaking in the sand. "I think I'll take you to the Guale mounds. We can saddle a couple of the horses."

"I don't know," she said doubtfully. "I'm not much for horses unless they're old and lame and have a name like Dobbin."

"We have nothing to fear but fear," said Bru with a laugh.

Twenty minutes later he held the reins of the small black filly he had picked out for her.

One hand on the saddle horn, she turned to Bru. "It's not that I'm frightened, you understand. It's just that I'm really not at ease."

He patted the filly's sleek neck, causing her to nuzzle his chest. "Look into her eyes. Do you see evil intent?"

"I can only see one of her eyes. The other one's on the opposite side of her head, Bru."

"I'll check it out," he said solemnly. He ducked his face behind the little horse's head. In a moment his hand rose slowly, thumb and forefinger meeting in a circle.

"I give up," she laughed. Thrusting one foot into the stirrup, she swung up on the rock-steady filly. Bru handed her the reins and then mounted a young bay gelding. "This way," he said, and went off at a trot toward a shell-lined path leading into the woods.

"Wait for me," Sally yelled, and gave a hesitant kick at the filly's ribs. The horse minced into a sedate walk toward the bay. In a few minutes it was obvious that she had just one speed forward. "You've got the ten-speed and I've got the training wheels. But I'm not complaining," she added quickly.

They rode in silence down a shaded trail that led through water oaks interspersed with stands of rustling pine and cedar. A brown doe leaped across the path in a frantic, zigzagging escape through the adjacent brush. Startled, Sally snatched at the reins. Bru watched her as she sat unsteadily in the saddle. Unbidden, the image of Kathlyn came to him: Kathlyn on the back of her Saddle Bred, taking the hurdles with her black hair flying behind in a tail that matched the color of her beloved Raven Son.

Eight years ago they had taken this same path, she galloping astride the most spirited of Lillian's trail horses, laughing as she urged the gelding on, scolding him for not being Saddle Bred and patrician.

Eight years ago. Their honeymoon.

The woods thinned. Sally and Bru were at the edge of the salt marsh. They threaded their way single file along a narrow elevated path flanked wtih cord grass until they came to a merging of marsh with higher ground. An island of woods lay ahead.

The path was wide enough now for two abreast. "Look over there," Bru said, pointing. A young alligator sunned itself on the crushed shell.

Sally snatched the reins as the alligator rose abruptly and scurried toward the marsh where it disappeared into a narrow rivulet with a splash. "I never knew they could move so fast."

"They can haul hide when they want to," said Bru, pointing toward a tangled mound of brown grass near a clump of palmettos. "He probably hatched in that nest."

They followed the path upward and to the left as it climbed an old dune into dark magnolia woods. "There are two Gaule mounds here," said Bru. "The Smithsonian excavated one on St. Simons back in the thirties. They were interested in the St. Cyrils mounds, but the Sniveleys refused. Romance of buried treasure, I guess.''

A slim silver-haired man dressed in boots and khakis looked up with a wave and climbed out of an excavation perhaps two feet deep. He carried something in his hand. ''I'd appreciate an opinion,'' he said in a clipped British accent. ''I've gone round and about with this one. I'm not sure whether I've got a mink or a young otter.'' He came toward them with a halting stride that seemed to indicate that the toes of his right foot were missing. He held a thin plastic box toward Bru. ''What do you say?''

Bru dismounted and examined the box. A small jawbone with several teeth gone lay inside. He shook his head and handed it back. ''I'm not sure.''

''Well, I'll send it along to Winslow. He'll know. I'm better at shards than bones, I'm afraid.''

''You're an archaeologist?'' asked Sally.

''Amateur. Although it *has* been a consuming interest. That and motor cars. But then I haven't gone motor racing in years.'' He beamed at them both. A silver, neatly trimmed moustache bristled above the thin lips. His eyebrows, perched above clear gray eyes, were as silver as the moustache. ''I should introduce myself,'' he said.

''Let me guess,'' said Bru. ''Sir William Talbott?''

The United Kingdom's ambassador plenipotentiary to the U.N. smiled.

''It's a pleasure to meet you, Mr. Ambassador. I'm Bruton Farrier.''

Sally grabbed the saddle horn with one hand and thrust the other toward the ambassador. ''And I'm Sally.''

Sir William took Sally's hand and then said to Bru, ''I know your name.'' He frowned, then said, ''Senate, is it? Foreign Relations Committee?''

''The House,'' said Bru. ''Armed Services Committee and Foreign Affairs.''

The ambassador raised a forefinger. ''Human Rights. I read your report on the situation in San Vicente.'' He turned to Sally. "You must be quite proud of your husband."

"Sally's a friend," said Bru quickly. "My wife and I are separated." My wife, he thought, catching the quick embarrassed look in the ambassador's eyes and the heightened color in Sally's cheeks—Kathlyn Layton Farrier.

After the first few heart-twisting days of Laird's illness, she had begun to withdraw from Bru. They had brought their little boy home in remission and that night she dragged the folding cot from the front closet and set it up by his crib. Bru lay awake in the dark, alone in the king-sized bed with its crisp, cool sheets, and heard the cot creak as she rose off and on throughout the night to check on Laird. Three times he got up and stood at her side as she watched the sleeping child. Her face was shadowy above the dim, yellowish cast of the night-light she had bought for Laird—a unicorn with a glowing horn.

When the first relapse came and they rushed him to Egleston hospital, she told Bru that they had to take him to Mexico. He needed amygdalin treatments, diet therapy. As gently as they could, he and the doctors told her no. Everything was being done. They could hope for another remission, even a cure, but only through traditional medicine.

The fight they had that night was vicious—all the more so for the lowness of their voices volleying over the boy, who had gone back to sleep in spite of them. Finally she began to sob—painful, racking sobs that shuddered through her body like convulsions.

The night of Laird's second relapse, Bru hunched over the wheel as they drove through rain-slick streets to the hospital. He could hardly bear to look at his son now. After the first shocking realization, an icy, numbing impotence filled him. Laird looked like a battered child. The disease had struck with mighty fists that left huge, purpling bruises on his body. Pale blood swarming with leukemic cells ran from his mouth and nose. His dark eyes were shadowed with pain and still the fists hammered, damaging internal organs, slowly battering away the life of a little boy. Bru could do no more than stand and watch, and then he found he could not do even that anymore.

He only half listened to Kathlyn as she sat huddled next to him, cradling Laird in her arms. When he did not respond to her accusations, they rose in pitch accented by the staccato clip-clop of the windshield wipers. "I'm not God," he said at last.

"Oh, aren't you, Bru? I thought you were. The omniscient Bruton Farrier—wheel and deal while your son dies. Another human sacrifice to the great god."

Without looking at her he said, "Her voice was ever gentle, soft, low—an excellent thing in women," repelling her with glibness, denigrating her with Shakespeare. A hard smile crept onto his lips—a smile meant to dismiss.

She stared at him. "Damn you, Bru Farrier." Her hand lashed out, stinging his cheek, her hand outlined by the streaming reflection of the oncoming headlights. "God damn you to hell," she screamed over the squeal of tires as he battled the wheel and somehow got the car back in control.

At the hospital, he called his friend Daniel Elton, who had to visit Kathlyn at Laird's bedside because she would not leave it. "I'm afraid it was a half-assed evaluation," he told Bru later. "I'm no psychiatrist, but I think it's time to get one in. Mack Ogletree's good," he said. "He's an old med school buddy. I'll call him for you, or anyone else you want."

Bru spread his hands in a hopeless gesture. "It's all going down the drain, Dan."

Elton looked at him with sharp yet kind eyes framed with owlish horn-rims. "I'll give you some statistics, Bru. They won't change anything, but maybe they'll help you understand. Eighty-seven percent of the families hit with this sort of thing just can't cope with it. Over fifty percent need psychiatric help." His voice softened. "Nearly three quarters of the marriages break up, and there's not a hell of a lot anyone can do about it."

Bru stared at him silently.

"You try to work around it," said Elton. "You sweep up the pieces and then build with what's left."

And what was left? Bru stared at the red-haired girl who held the black filly's reins so awkwardly. Her very awkwardness was endearing somehow. And then as he watched her he knew why he had brought her to St. Cyrils: He was building a stage set out of the shards and splinters of something that once seemed solid. He was playing at commitment, and he knew he lacked the nerve to make it real.

Chapter 12

THE LATE AFTERNOON SUN ANGLING LOW THROUGH ST. Simons's oak trees cast bushy shadows on the pavement. Leaving the business district behind, the rented Dodge sped north on Lawrence Road. It had not passed another car for several miles.

As it came within view of a fork in the road, the Dodge pulled over and stopped. The doors opened and five men got out. One of them reached for the hood and raised it in the universal sign for car trouble. Another, a muscular olive-skinned man with a dark mole high on his right cheekbone, gave a quick motion of his hand. At his signal the other four men swung easily over a low wire fence that separated road from woods. The man with the mole followed. Taking the lead, he walked alone a short distance ahead.

At the sounding of an approaching car, the man gave another hand motion and all five instantly hit the ground, their dark clothing blending with the gray and brown of the shadowed forest floor.

The man watched and listened intently. When he was sure the car was gone, he got up slowly and raised an arm to signal the others. The motion caused the heavy olive-drab shirt he wore as a jacket to flap open for a moment, exposing the lines of a shoulder holster and the slim silvery metal canister chained to his waist.

In response to his signal the others rose. Hidden by the masking oaks and palmettos, the five men made their careful way toward the northernmost tip of the island and the peeled cypress gate that marked St. Cyrils Landing.

Chapter 13

NATHAN KATZ PUT DOWN THE OBOE REED HE WAS MAKING and stared out of the top-floor window of the old lodge. He orchestrated the sunset in his head, blending the brilliant pinks and oranges with brass, the graying purples with somber kettledrums that foreshadowed night on the darkening salt marsh.

The adjacent bathroom door opened, and the trio's guitarist, Tony Herrera, strolled out, toweling his thick curly hair dry. He wore half the uniform that Lillian Sniveley insisted on when they played—the white pants to be topped with a black blazer. He pulled his shirt on, collapsed into an armchair next to the bed, and rolled himself a smoke. With a quick baby-faced grin that made him look younger than twenty-two, Tony held out his hand to Nathan. "Toke?"

Nathan shook his head and set the reed to dry on a thin shaft of metal. Outside in the deepening twilight, the launch pulled up to the dock—back from its five o'clock run to St. Simons to drop off the day staff.

"I thought I smelled something cooking." Tuck Perry walked in, slipped one hand on Tony's shoulder, and leaned over, brushing his face with a strand of straight blond hair. "Sharing?" Her eyes were green and slanted in a delicate catlike face. Tony stared at her through half-lidded eyes and handed her the joint. Taking it, she perched on the arm of his chair. Her skirt moved in a cascade of silky white pleats as she stretched her legs, sliding one slowly across the other.

"There goes Hoby—back to the lodge," said Nathan, watching the old man get into the Jeep.

"He's all the help Lena has tonight until Leroy and Tim get back with the barge," said Tuck. "He'd better hustle, or she'll scratch hide."

Nathan glanced at his watch. "So had we. I'm ready for turkey."

They gathered music and instruments and went inside. Clutching her flute case with one hand, Tuck swung open the door to the old pickup truck the trio used for transportation. "Somebody left the windows open last night. There's a puddle on the seat."

Tony took a look. "Why don't we walk."

"I'd have to change shoes," said Tuck doubtfully.

"Not if we stay on the path," said Nathan. "I'll get a light." He ducked back inside and in a minute reappeared with two large flashlights. Handing one to Tony, he flicked the other on and picked up his oboe case.

Little pools of light bobbed on the path as the group started their half-mile walk to the main lodge.

In the darkness that closed like black velvet over the Cigarette, El Ojo looked at his watch. It had been a long vigil. Now the launch was back for the night, and this final report, La Culebra, moving just ahead of the incoming tide, had rejoined the others.

Nineteen hundred hours, thought El Ojo. The musicians would be driving to the lodge now, leaving the leeward side of the island deserted.

The Cigarette rode high on the full tide in a sea of drowned cord grass. The subleader pulled on a pair of Oldelft night-vision goggles that transformed him into a shadowy Cyclops. He stood and scanned the southeastern horizon. The shades of gray resolved to an outline of the deserted launch snugged to the floating dock. He gave a signal to the driver, and the Cigarette's stern drive engine started.

The boat glided down Oyster Creek and stopped at a spit of higher ground just short of the dock. The others had donned night goggles now. El Ojo turned toward them, his Oldelfts clearly revealing the driver and the other two who were laden with ammunition belts and packs, one studded with the stubby outlines of Mecar BT rifle grenades. At his signal the two men scrambled to shore and set out cross-country.

He looked at his watch again and nodded. The rendezvous was set for 2015. Leaning back in the cushioned seat, he watched the two shadowy figures moving east toward the boardwalk tower that overlooked St. Cyrils Lodge.

The trio moved down the black path, twin pools of light bobbing sedately, when suddenly Tuck whispered, "Stop. I hear something."

"I don't," said Nathan.

"Listen." They stood on the inky path and strained to hear. A faint rustle came from a clump of needle-leafed holly behind them; a faint snap of a dry twig breaking. After that, nothing more except the hum of night insects and the whisper of the surf.

"Something's following us," Tuck said in a low voice. "I know it."

Tony swung his light toward the marsh that stretched beyond a break in the woods. "Maybe it's just an alligator."

"No." Tuck shook her head. "There's someone out there. A person."

"A were-gator," said Nathan.

The laugh that followed broke the tension, and the musicians moved on toward the lodge's lights that glimmered faintly through the trees at the end of the path.

Chapter 14

THE NORTH END OF SIMONS ISLAND WAS NEARLY DESERTED. As the truck with ST. CYRILS LODGE painted on its sides rounded a bend on Lawrence Road, its headlights shone on a car with its hood up.

"Slow down," said the old black man in the passenger seat. "Somebody got car trouble."

The headlights swept the interior as they approached. "It's empty, Grandpa," said Tim Jefferson, leaning forward over the wheel. "I guess they got a ride back to town." He swung the truck onto the right fork of the road and came to a stop at the cedar gate of St. Cyrils Landing.

Leroy got out and opened the gate wide enough to let Tim drive through. With a creak the gate closed behind the truck. Leroy fumbled in the dark for the plank that fastened it. With a shudder of wood on wood, the plank slid in his grip and latched the gate.

"It be dark as the Devil's bowels," he said, climbing back into the truck.

The headlights, rebounding off the dense woods that choked the road, somehow accentuated the darkness. At the clearing Tim turned the truck in a sweeping arc and backed toward the dock and the waiting barge. When he was close, he shut off the ignition. Leaving his lights on, he opened the door.

"Careful you don't come up on a snake," said Leroy, opening the passenger door and scanning the ground that lay in the puddle of light. "Old moccasin got me once. Up by the rain pond south of the big house. It be on a night like this they out."

"Sure, Grandpa," said Tim automatically. He had heard this story many times before. Circling to the back of the truck, he crawled up and began to hand out cartons to Leroy.

"Old cottonmouth got me good," repeated the old man, heaving a case of Beaujolais nouveau to the dock. "Yessir, got me on the fo-arm good. I be shining frogs that night and I reach out and all a sudden I seen this old white mouth open up and—whop—he pop me on the fo-arm. He be a big 'un, too. I got me a chunk of wood and I bash his head in."

The cartons moved from truck to dock in rhythmic swings. "Sick," Leroy went on, "Lord, I was sick to die. That old snake, he be six foot long and thick as you arm. And where he pop me, it blow up and then it begin to slough." Leroy shook his head. "Old cottonmouth got me good."

Tim passed the last carton to Leroy and jumped off the back of the truck. He swung into the cab, and turning the truck, aimed its headlight toward the dock floating high on the tide.

Insects hovered in the beam of the lights, and somewhere in the blackness an owl hooted. Leroy started at the sound. "Some say that be death calling."

Tim clattered onto the dock and hoisted a carton. "That's just superstition, Grandpa. It's nothing but an owl calling for its mate." He passed the carton easily to Leroy, who stood on the barge. The old man caught the box and swung it to the dock next to the gasoline drums they had winched on board earlier that day.

Leroy leaned over, one hand on the carton, and tried to catch his breath—quietly, so Tim wouldn't hear, wouldn't know an old man was winded.

The owl called again. Tim swung another box to Leroy. "Nothing but a lonesome old owl."

When they finished, Tim headed for the truck to park it out of the way. Leroy leaned against a gas drum and stared out across the dark creek that faded to black beyond the truck's headlights.

From the inky shadows by the truck came a scuffling sound and then a yell that cut off with a strangled guttural. In the split second of dead silence that followed, Leroy felt his heart stop, then start again, and pound in his ears. "A snake! I knowed it!" His feet hammered the dock as he ran toward Tim.

He stopped short. Tim stood in the beam of the headlights. His eyes were wide and terrified; his hands were pressed to his throat. A step, a horrible scuttling step, and Leroy saw the man behind Tim—the man holding the garrote around the boy's throat.

Then there were four other men stepping into the light— four men holding guns. At a nod from one, the other released the pressure from Tim's throat and his breath came back in a rattling gasp.

The man who had nodded spoke to Leroy: "You are going to take us to St. Cyrils Island." His voice was crisp and accented. A silvery metal canister dangled from his waist.

Leroy stared at the man, then back at Tim. He shook his head; he had no voice.

The man spoke again: "I am Iguana. You will do as I tell you. You will take us to St. Cyrils. Now—or after you see the boy slowly strangle to death."

The garrote tightened again.

Mute, the old man looked at Tim. With legs of ice he turned toward the barge; with hands that trembled he switched on the running lights. Just as he fired the engine to life, he heard the owl cry once again.

Chapter 15

SALLY STRICKLAND BRUSHED A FINAL STROKE OF BLUSH just under her cheekbones and surveyed the result in the old curved mirror. Her dress was simple, with soft feminine lines; its subtle pink muted her hair to a rosewood glow in the light from the brass student lamp.

A faint tap at the door.

"Come in," she said. When the tap repeated, she reached for the doorknob and turned it. Bru stood in the hall, a wineglass in each hand and a knuckle cocked to tap again. "Aperitif, mademoiselle?" Pressing a glass into her hand, he reached into his jacket pocket and pulled out a wadded cocktail napkin stuffed with salted almonds.

Amber light from the old wood stove danced on the wine as she sipped. "Good," she said as she tasted. "What is it?"

"Amontillado. Got it from an old barkeep in the dungeon. Bit of a loner. He hides behind a brick wall. I couldn't see anything of him but a bloodshot eye with a withered hand passing out the glasses through a missing brick."

She munched an almond and sipped again. "These nuts do something wonderful to the wine. Or maybe it's the other way around."

Bru looked her over appreciatively and nibbled her earlobe. "Goes well with this, too." He gave her a lingering kiss, and then holding her shoulder, he fell into his Charles Dickens mode: "Wery good power o' suction. You'd ha' made an uncommon fine oyster."

100

"That proves it's feeding time." She accepted the almond he popped into her mouth, and they walked down the stairs to the Great Room.

A fragrant oak and hickory fire flickered in the wide stone fireplace. Lillian, dressed in a silver gray that matched her hair, greeted them. "I see you're sampling the Amontillado. I'm glad. Anything harder paralyzes the taste buds." She gave a faintly disapproving look toward the bar, where Hoby, stiff in a red jacket, mixed a Seven and Seven for Alex Borden.

Bru followed her glance and said to Sally, "Brutal case. Paraplegia of the palate. Nothing left for him now but tacos and cigar-flavored chili."

In one corner of the room next to the Steinway grand, three young people dressed in black blazers arranged music on stands and deposited instrument cases. "When will they play?" asked Sally.

"After dinner," said Lillian. "I'm anxious for you to hear them. They're playing an Ibert and then we'll have a premiere: a piece Nathan Katz wrote. I haven't heard it yet, but I suspect it will be terribly avant-garde." She smiled fondly across the room at Nathan. "At first, young composers seem to be all sharp edges and experiment. They mellow later," she said, looking over the top of her wineglass at the boy, then tipping the glass slightly and gazing into the light amber wine as if to suggest that, like the Amontillado, Nathan would improve with maturity. She hurried away then, to "see how Lena is doing in the kitchen," and in a few minutes the old Chinese gong muttered its call to dinner.

Sally found herself seated between Sir William to her right and Alex Borden to her left. Bru sat across the table next to Cass Tompkins, who had contrived to match her eyelids to the lavender chiffon of her dress. In deference to the honeymooners, Lillian had placed Paige and Dave Cole together, and Sally noticed that aside from a slightly reddened nose, Paige seemed to have recovered from her llama attack. From the sounds of laughter and the clink of silverware emanating from behind closed doors, Sally guessed that the musicians were dining early in the kitchen.

The table was transformed from its daytime Blue Onion settings of thin bone china. Swedish crystal gleamed on the white damask cloth. The fire in the Franklin stove across the room cast warm, moving lights onto the dark tile floor.

"I'm afraid I've been a bit antisocial," said Sir William, introducing himself to Miranda Gervin, who sat on his right. "Directly after I arrived, I made for the Guale mounds. Have you been there yet?"

Miranda unfolded a napkin and laid it across her burnt-umber lap. "No, I haven't." She began on her soup in a way designed to discourage further conversation.

"I saw a gator mound today," said Calvin Borden. "It had an old egg in there about this long—" He held up his spoon, indicating half its length. The motion flung half a dozen drops of soup onto the tablecloth. Alex Borden frowned at his son and took another swallow of Seven and Seven.

Lillian smiled fondly at the boy. "Calvin is very interested in natural science, Sir William. I'm sure he'd like to see the Indian mounds."

Calvin stared suspiciously at the Chinese mushroom floating in his soup. He fished it out and dropped it into his bread dish.

Curling her lip, Ashley leaned toward him and whispered, "That's crude."

The ambassador spoke to Calvin. "Perhaps you'd like to go along with me tomorrow."

"Yeah. That'll be neat. We could find Indian feathers and stuff."

"Well," Sir William said, "I'm not sure about the feathers, but certainly . . . 'stuff.' "

"The Indians had Thanksgiving with the Pilgrims, you know," Calvin informed Sir William.

"Not the Guale Indians, nerd," said Ashley.

Pointedly ignoring his sister, the boy planted an elbow on the table and stared speculatively at the ambassador. "How come you limp?"

"Calvin!" rumbled Alex Borden across the table, while the Coles exchanged half-amused, half-embarrassed glances.

"It's quite all right," said Sir William. "I was in a motor racing accident, Calvin. At Le Mans in 1954. I'm afraid my Jaguar and I came to grief at the Mulsanne corner. I lost part of my right foot."

"Your toes even?" Calvin seemed immensely impressed.

"Every one," said Sir William.

"Golly." Then on reflection, "Gross."

Alex Bordon shot his son a murderous look.

"This is a marvelous wine," Sally said quickly. "What is it?"

"Bordeaux," said Lillian, lifting her glass. "Château Margaux."

As soup bowls were replaced with parsleyed ham and turkey stuffed with oysters, Bru turned to Sir William. "How did you get interested in the Guale Indians?"

"Actually, I don't know a great deal about them yet. That's why I came down on holiday—to learn more. It always seemed to me that the more one knew about primitives, the more one would understand modern society."

Cass Tompkins fixed a pair of round blue eyes on Sir William. "What happened to them? The Guales, I mean."

"No one seems to be completely sure," he said, "but there's evidence they might have been victims of biological warfare."

The blue eyes gave a lavender-tinged blink.

Dave Cole leaned forward in interest. "You mean the Spaniards and the blankets?" As Sir William nodded, Dave said to Cass, "The Spanish conquerors introduced smallpox to the Indians by giving them blankets and clothes that were contaminated by the pustules of victims."

"Dreadful," said Cass.

Lillian looked up. "Heavens. What a topic for a Thanksgiving dinner conversation."

Bru grinned wickedly. "I think it's very appropriate. We can all be thankful we don't have smallpox." He winked at Sally and she smiled at what it implied: Dave Cole had aimed the conversation into clinical detail, and Bru had often accused her of doing the same thing. Occupational hazard, she thought.

"Ever use smallpox in your books?" Bru asked Cass with a mischievous if-you-can't-beat-'em-join-'em glance at Sally.

"Oh, God, no," said Cass. "Pockmarks." She drained her third glass of wine.

Bru reached for the Bordeaux bottle and poured her another. "I'm disappointed. I thought there was always a deathbed scene or two in romances."

"Oh, there are," she said, and took another swallow. "Consumption is good. It's feminine and very romantic. Childbed fever is good, too. It makes for a beautiful opening scene: the young girl standing by the deathbed. Nothing but laudanum will ease her mother's pain now." Cass poked at the shrimp mousse with her fork and took another hefty swallow of the Bordeaux. "And so the oldest daughter must make her own way. She becomes a governess in the house of a strange, darkly handsome man . . ."

"Who has a secret and shocking vice," said Lillian, leaning slightly forward in her chair.

"Damn right," said Cass a shade thickly, "but never pockmarks."

"Pizarro was the first," said Dave Cole.

Cass looked at him. "The first what?"

"The first to introduce smallpox that way."

"So we have Pizarro to thank for biological warfare," she observed.

"Not really," said Dave. "It goes back further than that for other diseases."

"Back to the fourteenth century," said Sir William. "The Tartars had besieged the city of Kaffa. When plague broke out, the Tartars threw the corpses of victims over the city walls and caused an epidemic."

"They think that was the beginning of the bubonic plague epidemic that decimated Europe," added Dave.

"The Black Death," said Sally. "Then people were as much to blame as the rats in the harbors." The thought dismayed her.

"*Rattus norvegicus*," said Paige Cole, finishing off her oyster dressing.

And *Rattus homo sapiens*, thought Sally.

"There's a subject for a romance novel," said Bru to Cass. "*Black Death, Black Desire*."

She looked at him speculatively. "I could make you the hero."

"No pockmarks." Bru smiled disarmingly.

"Plague has been a pervasive literary device," observed Sir William. "Dionysius. Camus. Even our nursery rhymes."

"Nursery rhymes?" said Sally, surprised.

"Our 'Ring Around a Rosy,' " said the ambassador. "The 'rosy' was a victim with the characteristic flush of plague."

Ashley looked up. "What does the rest mean?"

"The 'pocket full of posy' referred to the herbs people carried in the hope of warding off the plague," said Sir William. "One version of the third line is 'atishue, atishue': the sound of a sneeze. Another is 'ashes, ashes': the bonfires—the bone fires—that disposed of the victims."

The bone fires, thought Sally. She stared into the glass she held, feeling the chill of it, feeling the chill that somehow crept deep inside her. Like the remnants of a dream, she could see the haunted face of a woman as she stood in a narrow cobblestoned street and shivered in the orange glow of the fires. Rags-and-tatter children surrounded her. *Ring around a rosy*. . . . Circling children, closing in a ritual dance. Malignant, taunting children grinning in the face of death. *Ring around a rosy . . . Rosy . . .* "All fall down," she whispered.

"Exactly," said Sir William.

Chapter 16

THE FLATTENED DISC OF THE MOON ROSE FROM THE OCEAN. White froth boiled from the black water; inkblot shadows lay behind the pale dunes. On the boardwalk tower two men stood with their backs to the sea, their night-bleaching goggles fixed on the lodge below.

On the lee side of the island where angling moonlight glimmered on Oyster Creek, two more men turned their Cyclops stare on the dark-furred marsh and the shadowy barge creeping toward the dock.

Calvin Borden bolted out of the dining room and up the stairs, not pausing until he had reached the sanctuary of the second floor. He knew from experience that if he stayed one moment past dessert, Miss Lillian would grab him in her bony arms and march him in to another concert.

She was a neat old lady in the daytime, but at night she was somebody to stay away from. Every night a dumb concert, and no TV anywhere. Calvin ran his hand over the balcony railing and looked down at the empty Great Room. A large light fixture in the shape of a wagon wheel hung from the beamed ceiling. He threw back his shoulders in the manner of Wyatt Earp: "I reckon you got until sundown to clear outa Dodge City."

In response to his imagined adversary, Calvin's hand hovered over his six-gun. They didn't call him Quick Draw for nothing. He stood wide-legged, pelvis thrust out in accepted form, and narrowed his eyes at the villains. Suddenly he drew, cocked his thumb, and fired.

He blew triumphantly on the smoking barrel of his index finger, but his victory was short-lived. As the doors swung open and the musicians entered the Great Room, he scurried down the hall to the relative safety of the north end of the house.

He went into his own room, flung himself on the bed, and fell into instant boredom. He didn't even have anything left to read. He played with the notion of going up to the third-floor library again. With a sigh he gave up the idea; everything up there was dumb grown-up stuff. He stared at the book he had finished last night: *Slan*. Fascinated by the story of a mutant boy who had telepathic tendrils on his head, Calvin considered reading it again. Fingering the pages with one hand, with the other he felt for tendrils of his own. He found none, but what did that prove? You could be a Slan and not even have tendrils.

The telepathic thought arose that Lena and Hoby would be clearing in the dining room now, and what was left of dessert would be untended in the kitchen. The thought propelled him to the door leading to the narrow back stairs.

The two men on the dock caught the thick white ropes snaking from the barge, and with quick twists, secured the craft. As the men on the barge came ashore, the first two jumped into the Cigarette and began to relay packs and weapons to the others.

One shadowy figure stood apart from the rest, moonlight reflecting coldly from the metal cylinder dangling at his waist. He caught the tossed SIG automatic rifle easily with one hand; with the other he pulled on goggles and scanned the shore. His gaze rested on the pickup truck by the old lodge. Beyond it, another truck was parked by a smaller house.

He closed his eyes for a moment, recalling with minute accuracy the map of St. Cyrils Island: the old lodge. The smaller house beyond it was a staff house; the black man with the barge lived there and the cook. Across from the lodge was a scattering of outbuildings and the island's power generators. He scanned the area north of the dock for another house. Spotting it, he nodded. The handyman lived there.

Iguana was completely oriented now. The new lodge lay east. He unclipped the FM transceiver from his belt and held it to his lips. The response came at once: Lookout One, secure—the boardwalk tower with its unobstructed view of the Atlantic to the east and the lodge to the west.

Lookout Two lay north: the lighthouse, surveillance point for Altamaha Sound and the western end of the island.

Lookout Three was the old lodge. He stared at the dim lines of its roof and the picket surrounding its widow's walk. It was the highest point to leeward—control of the marsh and Oyster Creek.

He looked at his watch: 2015. In less than an hour, Lookouts Two and Three would secure. But now he needed the manpower. Turning, he surveyed the two prisoners. Neither had tried to speak. The boy was frightened, but defiance showed in the lift of his jaw. The drooping lines of the old man's body showed complete demoralization.

Iguana had planned the psychology of the strike well—an initial show of overwhelming force. Only Lookout One would be manned now. When Base was secure, he would disperse his men to Lookouts Two and Three.

It was time now. They would take the barge man's truck as planned. Iguana stepped forward, raised an arm, and motioned twice with clenched fist. *La guerra—ahora empieza.*

The back stairs led down to a door that opened into the kitchen. Calvin peered cautiously around it. Nobody in sight. Sundry clinking sounds from the dining room told him that Lena and Hoby were still clearing the table.

A large aluminum tray held the remnants of dessert. He had no interest in the mince and pumpkin pies, but there was some rum cake left. He eyed it speculatively. He could probably eat a ton of cake, he thought. But the sauce was yuck. Seizing a piece of cake, he scraped off the amber rum sauce with his forefinger. He stuffed a chunk into his mouth and surveyed the little blob of sauce he had left on the tray. Reasoning that someone might find the remains suspicious, he scooped it up and deposited it on another square of cake.

The blinking red dot on the CB base radio drew his attention next. He knew the radio was never turned off; it was used to keep track of the island's vehicles. "*Dispatch*," Hoby had called it. The CB's LED channel display showed a glowing red 16.

Calvin shoved the last of the cake in his mouth and stared at the radio. He wanted to try it out, but he hesitated. Lena and Hoby would be really hacked if they found him there. He remembered the radio in the Jeep. All he wanted to do was just look at it. It wasn't like he was going to mess with it or anything.

Armed with this rationale, he opened the back door and went outside.

The roofed utility porch held an array of wire and wicker baskets that took on monstrous shapes in the night. The moon creeping over the dunes outlined the pale shell path with ragged black. The left fork led to an ancient incinerator that Calvin found fascinating, but now he took the right fork. The Jeep CJ5 was parked next to it. Its tram, detached now, was tucked away in the dark shed beyond.

The sound of music came faintly from the lodge. With a quick glance at the kitchen door, Calvin went to the driver's side of the CJ5 and jumped in. There was no light in the Jeep, and its rag top cast an ink-black shadow over the driver's seat and dash. It was nearly a minute before his eyes adjusted to the faint moonlight penetrating the plastic side window, before he could see the microphone hanging on its metal clip next to the silent radio.

He stretched his body into a reclining position, feet tucked between gas pedal and clutch, neck cocked between steering wheel and seat. Holding the dead microphone to his lips, he pressed the button. "Mission Control, this is Mars Lander One. My sensors indicate life forms. I'm going to investigate."

Reaching for the little knob that glimmered in the moonlight, Calvin turned it on and patched in his brain to the CB.

The green display light showed channel 16. Silence. The life forms were hiding. He'd have to track them down. His fingers moved to the dial; the green light showed 15, then 14. The life forms were on 12. Carefully—ever so carefully—he turned up the volume. Too much and they would zap him.

"—Ten-four on that Southern Comfort. I got me a sweet little jug and some cold Kentucky Colonel. Come on—"

Calvin's eyes narrowed. They were feeding. And he could be next. Lying in the proper astronaut position, he stared at the green number on the dial as the men's voices droned softly in the darkness. His concentration was so intense, he did not hear the distant music. He did not notice how it spoke against the cadence of the surf and the low mutter of an approaching engine.

Chapter 17

As THE TRIO PLAYED THE LAST MOVEMENT OF THE IBERT, Sally stole a glance at Alex Borden, who sat in an easy chair by the little couch she shared with Bru. Borden clutched an elbow with one hand and propped his chin with the other, triangulating himself so that while his eyelids might droop, his face, however vacant, was firmly aimed toward the musicians. At every breath the corner of his mouth puffed open and sent sour little jets in her direction. Borden's empty brandy snifter stood on the end table where he had placed it after two quick gulps.

Sally sipped at hers and wished for coffee. She felt stuffed from dinner, and the low light and the warm, flickering fires were making her drowsy. The couch they sat on held the left flank of the fireplace. At right flank, on a brown leather love seat shared with Sir William, Cass Tompkins stared raptly at the blond girl playing the flute and absently stroked a sleeping Caligula curled in her lap. Cass's head swayed in synchrony with the more pronounced movements of the flautist, and when they both fell into a bobbing figure eight, Sally felt the corner of her lips twitch.

Cass leaned toward Sir William and said something Sally couldn't hear. In response he handed her a pen. Using Caligula's sweatered shoulder for a lap desk, she jotted something on the inside cover of a matchbook. Handing the pen back, she tore off the cover, rolled it into a cylinder, and tucked it between her lace-and-lavender-clad breasts as the Ibert came to an end and the audience broke into applause.

As Alex Borden blinked and began to clap vigorously, Bru leaned toward Sally. "Enjoying it?"

She nodded. In truth, the music was very pleasant to her unpracticed ear, but the people-watching was the best of it.

As the instrumentalists shuffled sheets of music, Hoby, stiff with age and the splendor of his red jacket, renewed the brandy—mostly for Cass Tompkins and Alex Borden. Lillian, after a puzzled glance at the double doors, rose, saying something about checking on the coffee.

Ashley Borden, ignoring the chairs clustered around the room, sat on the floor by the fireplace, watching Nathan Katz thumb through a handwritten score. His detached oboe reed was tucked in his mouth with only its shank protruding. The girl stared at him as if he were the most desirable creature on earth.

They'd make pretty babies together, Sally thought. Babies with brown curly hair and slanting dark eyes.

Retrieving his reed from between pressed lips, Nathan attached it to his oboe and stood. "We'd like to do for you the premiere performance of *Conservatory Suite* by, uh"—a quick grin—"N. Katz. It's in three movements: 'Audition,' 'Practice,' and 'Juries.' " He held his oboe to his lips, gave a nod, and the piece began with a rollicking scale. The flute was answering with an arpeggio when the double doors to the entry hall opened abruptly. Nathan looked up. Suddenly the music lurched to a stop.

Lillian was standing just inside the room. Her hand was raised, fingers stiff as if to ward off something. With a voice as thin as stretched wire she said, "Ladies and gentlemen, I need your attention."

Lena stepped through the door. She clutched the arm of an old black man at her side. A much younger man was just behind her. Sally did not recognize either of the men. Lena's family?

The overhead lights blazed on. Startled, Sally looked up.

Two men stook on the balcony. Their rifles angled downward—trained, it seemed, on her heart.

Bru's hand pressed hers. She caught her breath as the frantic thought fluttered in her head: Don't move, don't move, you mustn't move. She wanted to run. She heard a click, unnaturally loud. Involuntarily she turned toward it. Two more men armed with rifles and handguns stood at the door.

A horrible cold prickling crawled at the nape of her neck. Slowly, very slowly, she looked over her shoulder. The veranda lights glowed yellow as sulfur through the tall, narrow windows. An armed man stood at each.

Her pulse swelled painfully in her throat. Fingers of ice twisted her belly.

From the door a man dressed in fatigues stepped forward. The barrel of his rifle tracked with his stare at each of them in turn. The silence was so complete that each crackling spark from the fireplace exploded in her ears.

Then he spoke: "I am Iguana. You are my prisoners." Suddenly the rifle barrel swung toward Sir William. "You will come with me, Your Excellency." It swung again toward Bru. "And you, Mr. Farrier. Our hostess will come, too." And then a slow, closed-lip smile. "We have a statement to make."

Blevin was the combo man on the evening shift. He eyed the blinking phone and picked up. "WGIR, Golden Isles Radio. May I help you?"

An accented voice came on the line. "Stand by to copy a message of national importance."

Christ. "Sure, buddy. I'll bet I just won a trip to Golden Acres, right?"

There was a pause. Then a woman's voice. "This is Lillian Sniveley of St. Cyrils Lodge. There are—" Her voice faltered, then came back lower, "There are men here with guns. Please—do as he says. Please—" Her voice broke off.

Blevin felt a chill ripple up his spine. Again the male voice, this time heavy with sarcasm: "You will record this message. Then you will relay it to your network news center and to the President of the United States. Indicate when you are ready."

This couldn't be real. It had to be a hoax. A practical joke. But the tension in the woman's voice— He patched in the Ampex and the tape began to turn. "Ready."

The voice began: "I am Iguana. The Organization of the People in Arms now occupies St. Cyrils Island, Georgia, off the United States coast. Two of our prisoners will identify themselves." A pause, a nervous clearing of the throat, and a clipped voice said: "Sir William Talbott here. United Kingdom. Ambassador to the United Nations." Another pause and then a different voice: "Bruton Laird Farrier, United States Congress."

The man who called himself Iguana came back on the line. This time he seemed to be reading a statement: "The United States will deliver five hundred million dollars gold to the Organization of the People in Arms as partial compensation for imperialist aggression, overt and covert, against the liberation army of Guatemala.

"The United States will further cause the nations of the world to hear our manifesto tomorrow at twelve hundred hours. This address will be broadcast on all radio and television networks nationwide and is to be relayed by satellite to all United Nation countries.

"Any incursion of St. Cyrils Island airspace, prisoners will be executed one by one. Any approach by sea, prisoners will be executed one by one.

"Do not believe you can defeat us. We will counter military force with absolute weapons. The Organization of the People in Arms control the fate of North America and ultimately the world.

"Any imperialist invasion, and we unleash a biological weapon on the prisoners of St. Cyrils Island. A second biological aerosol will then detonate within the United States mainland.

"The aerosol will spread pneumonic plague, genetically altered, throughout your people—plague with a mortality of seventy percent. No medicine, no vaccine can protect you." The voice paused, and then with a chilling touch of amusement, began again. "Where is Wily, amigos?"

Abruptly the connection broke off.

Blevin's hand trembled as he reached for the dial. He had to call someone. The police. The Glynn County Police. He dialed and the phone rang once, then twice. He stared at the large clock on the wall. The minute hand clicked—8:40. The disjointed thought came: prime time. They were going for prime time.

On the third ring he got police headquarters.

Chapter 18

CALVIN BORDEN HUDDLED IN THE JEEP AND STARED WIDE-eyed at the lodge. The CB radio was silent. He had switched it off when he heard the truck drive up.

An inky shadow jittered at the edge of the shell path. Don't move, he thought. Don't move. The path, bone pale in the moonlight, lay empty. Black ragged bushes flanked it. There might be more of them.

He blinked and in his mind's eye saw the old black man again: Leroy, climbing down from the back of the pickup, moving like a puppet on a stick, rolling his eyes as if he could see the men and the guns behind him; Leroy, shambling toward the Jeep, then veering in a broken step toward the kitchen door.

Barely moving, Calvin looked over his shoulder. He could just make out the dark lines of the lodge's veranda. Some of them had gone that way. The rest were inside.

Suddenly the music from the lodge stopped. The boy strained to hear, but he heard only the wind and the distant pounding of the surf. Lights flashed, and a mustard-yellow glare angled from the front of the lodge.

Armed robbers, he thought. Or kidnapers. Maybe even murderers. Ice fingers slithered up his spine and raised the hair on the back of his neck. Daddy was in there. And Ashley. Somebody had to rescue them.

The roofed kitchen porch was a dark blot splashed with moonlight. Eyeing it, Calvin began to slide out of the Jeep. As he did, a branch trembled in the wind and dead leaves scurried like mice across the path. He shrank back.

Don't move. Pupils dilated, he scanned the shadows. There might be more of them out there. Dozens even.

Then the thought came: the CB. He could use the radio.

He switched it on. The red LED showed 12. Slowly he turned up the volume. . . .

". . . had him a blue-tick bitch that'd drop ten, twelve pups at a pop. . . ."

The boy clutched the microphone and thumbed it on. "Breaker, breaker one-two." He tried to remember the 10-code for emergency. Failing, he said, "Mayday. This is a Mayday. Do you read me?"

Silence for a moment, then a voice: "Come on back."

"There's these men here with guns. They're murderers, probably. You gotta do something quick. Ten-four."

"Back 'em off, kid," came a second voice. "This channel's for base stations. We're not playing games."

"It's not a game—"

"Butt out."

"Hold it," said the first. "Where are you, boy?"

"St. Cyrils," Calvin whispered. "Outside the lodge."

A faint clicking sound came over the speaker.

Calvin clutched at the mike. "The men—they went inside. My daddy's in there."

"Who do you think you're shittin'?" said the second man.

"I'm not."

"Sure—"

"Wait up, Hoyt. He's due east of here."

"On the island?"

"Signal finder says he is. That, or he's up to his eyes in salt water."

"How'd you like me to call over to the lodge, kid?" said the second man. "Tell 'em you're screwing around with the radios."

"But they're really here. Guys with guns. Please. I'm not lying."

"Well, boy"—a pause—"you damn well better not be."

* * *

Wally Carruthers felt the familiar tightening in his chest that signaled the onset of pain. It'll go away, he thought. He stared at the TV, but its blue-white flickering image did not register. It would probably go away in a minute.

The old sheriff sank back on the couch. His fingers spidered across his chest, tracing the spreading course of the pain. It echoed from his childhood: He was seven when he wound a rubber band in thinning loops around his index finger until the cold, dead-white flesh throbbed with an ache that took away his breath. "Ischemia," the doc had said this morning. "Oxygen starvation. That's what brings on the pain of angina."

He picked up the brown prescription bottle and maneuvered it away until the label, curled inside, came into focus: "Place one tablet under tongue as needed for pain." That's how your number comes up, he thought—typed after your name on a plastic pill bottle. It had been that way for Martha: a number, then another. Two dozen more before the end came.

He stared at the label again, at his name blurring in the dim lamplight, and tried to will away the bands of pain constricting his chest. No good. It wasn't any good. The lid popped off in his palm and a tiny white tablet disappeared between his thumb and forefinger. He winced at the taste. The pills were a compromise, a bargain cautiously struck this morning. No hospital, not today, not yet. Just tests, okay? Friday, for sure.

The pain was easing when the citizen's band base radio crackled. Wally went into the kitchen and thumbed the switch. "Emergency channel. Go ahead." As he waited for the reply, he stared at the yellow plastic trash can next to the wall. He needed to empty it. The edge of a Swanson's Turkey Dinner box and a wad of streaked paper towels were poking out from under the lid. He needed to carry it out before he had trash all over the floor.

The voice on the other end was hesitant. "Maybe this is nothing at all, but there's a kid over on St. Cyrils. Nine or

ten years old, I'd say. He came on the radio and said there
were armed men over there. Said they went inside the
lodge. He sounded scared to me, so I checked his location
with my signal finder. He's on the island, all right, but it
could be he's just playing games."

"Where's the boy now?"

"I don't know. He said he was outside the lodge. He
came in pretty faint so I'd guess he was on a mobile
radio."

"What channel?"

"Twelve."

Wally wrote down the man's name and phone number.
"We'll check it out." He signed off and stared at the
phone for a moment. It was probably nothing more than a
little boy's active imagination, he thought, but maybe he'd
better give Lillian Sniveley a call. He was reaching for the
phone when it rang. "Carruthers here."

It was the Glynn County Police chief: "Sorry to mess
up your Thanksgiving, Wally, but this one's in your jurisdiction. And it sounds like big trouble. The engineer over
at WGIR just called and played me the damnedest tape you
ever heard. He's running it now for the FBI. . . ."

As Wally listened, he felt the steel bands clutch his
chest again. All of them, he thought: Lillian. And those
kids from the music school. And Bru, who was almost a
son to him—the only son that he had left. Hostages, all of
them . . . except for one. Except for a scared little boy
alone in the dark.

Calvin stared at the CB. The red LED 12 seemed to
glow in the blackness with the brilliance of a searchlight.
An ominous quiet had come with the radio's silence.

A harsh voice came suddenly over the radio: "Can you
hear me?"

Startled, the boy caught his breath. Then he pressed the
microphone switch. "Who's this?"

"My name is Wally. I'm going to help you, son. Do
you know how to work that radio?"

"Yeah."

"Go to nine. Go to channel nine. Do you know how to do that?"

"I turn the dial."

"That's right. Do it now."

Calvin reached for the knob. The LED blinked: 11, 10, 9.

The gravelly voice came back. "Are you there?" A pause. Then urgently, "Are you there, boy?"

"Yeah. I can hear you."

"Tell me your name."

"Calvin. I'm Calvin."

"All right. Now, Calvin, tell me what you see right now."

He looked out. "Not much. It's dark. The lights are on inside, but it's dark here."

"Where are you? In one of the pickup trucks?"

"No. I'm in the Jeep."

"Is it parked by the kitchen door?"

"Uh-huh."

"Listen carefully, son. Don't go back in the lodge. Do you understand me?"

Eyes wide, Calvin stared at the building, then back at the LED.

Wally's voice was low, but intense: "Do you understand me?"

"You said, 'Don't go back in.' "

"That's right. It's important. Don't go back into the lodge no matter what happens." A pause. "How many men did you see?"

Calvin blinked. "A lot. They had Leroy and Tim. And they had something around Tim's throat."

"How many men did you see?"

"A lot. Six or seven maybe. But I think there's more. More on the porch, I think." Suddenly a hard lump knotted his throat. "My daddy's in there. And my sister."

"Now, Calvin, listen to me. Do just what I tell you, son." A pause. "We're going to help your daddy and your sister. But first, we're going to get you out of there.

Do you know where the old lodge is? The one by the creek?''

He nodded. "I know where it is. I've been all over.''

"Do you think you can get down there by yourself?''

Calvin looked out at the shell road that led to the old lodge and Oyster Creek. In the moonlight the road was a gray snake slithering into blackness. "It's dark," he whispered.

"Can you do it?''

But the boy didn't answer. Instead, his head jerked toward the lodge and the yellow glare that streamed from the open kitchen door.

Four armed men emerged and moved deliberately toward the Jeep.

Chapter 19

BRU FELT A SHIVER RUN THROUGH SALLY'S BODY. HIS fingers tightened on her hand. The Great Room was unnaturally quiet, the silence heightened by the nervous panting of Cass Tompkins's dog.

Bru eyed the man on the balcony. El Poeta, the others had called him: the poet. His head was shaved, and when he turned to scan the room, Bru could make out a dark sickle-shaped scar that curved across his scalp. He was thin, almost gaunt; his fatigues hung on his body as if they were two sizes too large, and he crackled with a nervous energy that translated into quick twitching movements of his hands and head. One to watch, Bru thought. He was about as stable as old nitro.

Another armed man stood with his feet apart, his back

to the double doors. This one was younger, no more than twenty. He was called Cuclillo.

There were only three men left now, three men armed with rifle grenades and automatic weapons. The other four had gone. But there was at least one more; the leader had spoken to someone else by transceiver.

Bru stared across the room at the man who called himself Iguana and tried to read his face. He was afraid he knew what the expression meant: The bastard was very sure of himself. Everything about the man said it: his look, his posture. He was leaning against the shell-studded wall that flanked the fireplace, eyes half closed, body relaxed, rifle held casually. He reminded Bru of a cat ready to pounce. As if reading his mind, Iguana fixed Bru with a mocking, insolent stare.

The man had to know the odds were against him. St. Cyrils was under the nose of the Fort Steward Ranger base. The Rapid Deployment Force was only fifteen minutes away. Then there was the Federal Law Enforcement Training Center near Brunswick, and a half-dozen more government installations within a hundred-mile radius. The Georgia coast came as close to being impregnable as any part of the country.

Why, then? Why here?

He stared at the silver cylinder dangling from Iguana's waist. The biological. The equalizer . . .

High stakes, he thought with a chill. He had wanted to believe the canister was a bluff; he was sure it was not. The south Georgia coast wasn't an incidental choice; it was deliberate. It was a way of showing contempt for America's defense system.

Very high stakes indeed, he thought. And the terrorists held the joker: The mainland aerosol was real.

Iguana raised the FM transceiver and flicked it on. Bru tried to remember what little Spanish he knew, and thought he heard the word for "boat," then, "Cigarette." He caught a phrase in English: "Lookout Two," followed by a string of Spanish. Then, ". . . Lookout Three . . ."

Something jabbed Bru's ankle. He shot a look at the musician who sat on the floor next to him, face shadowed by the massive end table. He heard a faint whisper.

Moving almost imperceptibly, Bru leaned toward him.

"Lighthouse," said Tony Herrera in a low voice. "They're moving a boat there. To catch the high tide."

The Lighthouse stood in the mouth of Altamaha Sound. If the boat was up Oyster Creek, they'd have to go by way of the Atlantic. Bru flicked another look at Tony, then back to Iguana.

Tony spoke again, so low that Bru missed half of it: ". . . old lodge . . . three . . ."

Lookout Three? The old building had a widow's walk on the roof. From there, a man could see for miles across the marsh—all the way to the mouth of Oyster Creek and beyond. If Lookout Two was the lighthouse, then Lookout One had to be the tower above the boardwalk; you could cover the lodge from there, and the beach.

Bru glanced quickly around the room. Leroy and Hoby were too old, but Leroy's grandson, Tim, was strong and bright. So was Dave Cole, but they couldn't risk the doctor in a confrontation; if there were injuries, they'd need him later. He eyed the musicians: Nathan and Tony looked scared, but in control; the girl was an unknown quantity. So were the rest of the women, except for Lillian; she'd keep a level head, and she could use a gun.

He caught the eye of Sir William, who sat across from him next to Cass Tompkins. The ambassador wasn't young, but his jaw was set, and the look in his eyes reassured Bru; Sir William was going to be an asset.

Alex Borden was half drunk. His daughter huddled on the floor next to him. After her first anguished cry, Ashley had been silent. Calvin Borden was gone. The men had searched the building and found no one. Bru suspected they didn't know about the boy.

The radiotelephone's shrill ring penetrated the double doors. A dozen heads jerked toward the sound. Cass Tompkins started. "Jesus!" She clutched Caligula as Cuclillo's rifle jerked in her direction.

Baring his teeth, the little dog leaped off her lap and flung himself at the terrorist. Cuclillo's kick caught Caligula squarely in the ribs. One frantic yelp and the dog landed halfway across the room, still and crumpled against the foot of a table.

"Fucker!" Cass leaped up. Rocking like an unstrung puppet, she stared at the dog then back at Cuclillo. "I'll kill you. I'll kill you for that." Shrieking, hands curved into claws, she ran at him.

The automatic rifle swung toward her.

A red-sleeved arm reached out; a hand clamped the barrel. Startled, Cuclillo jerked toward Hoby. The old man's grip tightened. For an instant they stared. Then a burst of fire came from the balcony, and the old man crumpled.

Bubbling red began to pool as if the jacket he wore had turned to liquid. Hoby's eyes widened in surprise for a moment before they began to glaze.

Bru's grip on Sally's hand was tight, but she pulled away. "We've got to help—we've got to help him." She was on her feet now, moving toward the old man, while overhead, El Poeta trained his rifle at her heart.

Chapter 20

CALVIN CLICKED OFF THE CB AS THE FOUR TERRORISTS approached. For a terrible moment the boy could not move. Then in one rush he scrambled out of the Jeep and crouched in the shadows. On the other side of the CJ5 the men's footsteps crunched on the shell path.

They were circling the Jeep, heading toward the driver's side. They'd see him! Head low, Calvin darted behind a clump of palmettos.

A second later, the first man reached the driver's side and stuck a hand inside. The keys jingled in the ignition. The man looked up, said something to the others in Spanish, then slid behind the wheel. The other three turned and headed down the road toward the pickup truck.

Light streamed from the Jeep's headlights. A few moments later, the pickup's lights flared.

The Jeep's rear tires scattered a stinging volley of shell fragments and sand as it pulled away. Calvin held his breath until the lights from the two vehicles vanished behind the wooded dune.

When he was sure they weren't coming back, he scrambled to his feet and stared cautiously toward the back door of the lodge. Hoby's Bronco was parked there. It had a radio, too, but the keys to the Bronco were in the kitchen. Hoby always hung them on the wall by the door.

He remembered Wally's warning: *Don't go inside. No matter what happens, don't go back inside.*

The keys were by the door, he thought. Not very far. Hardly inside at all.

In the light from the kitchen windows, a basket swaying from an overhead porch beam blinked slanted yellow eyes. A floorboard creaked under his foot. The boy froze. Nothing. Nobody had heard. A step. Another. He reached for the doorknob. It clicked and he was inside.

The wide door to the dining room stood open. To his right, the back stairs marched upward into shadows. There was no sound except the hum of the refrigerator and the rhythmic plop from the leaky kitchen faucet.

The boy glanced at the wall by the door. The keys to the Bronco hung high on the wall. He stood on tiptoe and stretched out his fingers. Too high. He needed to stand on something. A half-dozen ladder-back chairs were clustered around the kitchen table in the middle of the room. Just as his hands closed around a chair back, the telephone in the dining room rang.

A pulse of silence, then a high-pitched animal yelp and a shriek . . .

Calvin stared at the door with eyes as round as coins. At the burst of automatic rifle fire, he ran.

The kitchen door clattered shut behind him, and darkness struck. He missed the last step and fell, sprawling, scraping his outstretched hands on the crushed shell. Scrambling to his feet, he darted across the road and dived behind the prickly shelter of a holly bush.

The cheerful glow from the kitchen windows accentuated the blackness. A hard lump that he couldn't swallow grew in this throat. Right then, he wanted to hear Wally's rough voice more than anything else in the world.

There was another pickup truck by the old lodge, he thought: the one the musicians drove. It had a radio; they all did. And Wally had told him to go there. Slowly his eyes began to adjust and he could make out the road's faint gray outline in the moonlight. The wilderness, he thought with a shiver. Dark and bloody ground . . .

He could see the top of the dune now, black against a charcoal sky. Somewhere up there was the Cumberland Gap. He stepped out on the road. Moving quietly, just like Daniel Boone so the Indians wouldn't hear, Calvin began to follow the road toward the old lodge.

Wally Carruthers's house had been transformed into a temporary sheriff's office. For the time being, he saw no other choice. He was going to get that little boy off the island or know why not, and the CB base station in his kitchen was his only link to the faint signal Calvin had sent.

He had felt an unprofessional chill when the Jeep radio went dead. But the kid was probably all right. After all, he had told him to go to the old lodge, hadn't he? The boy had simply done it without signing off, he told himself.

Wally didn't want to think about any other possibility right now.

All off-duty personnel had been pressed into emergency service. The headlights of a patrol car pulling into the drive flashed against the windows. Another was reporting in by radio. More were on the way. Marge Tyson was handling communications. She had responded at once, showing up in jeans and a navy sweatshirt, bringing two pumpkin chiffon pies and a coffeepot big enough to accommodate an all-night stand. While the pot was still perking, Wally lifted the tap and caught an amber stream in a chipped mug. It occurred to him that he probably shouldn't drink it, shouldn't have the caffeine, but he dismissed the thought.

The drone of a distant jet helicopter grew to a roar, and Wally glanced up. One of the Black Hawks from Fort Stewart, he thought. Circling. Ready to move toward the island at a moment's notice.

The Black Hawk meant that Washington was beginning to act. He had to give them credit for that. Local and state law enforcement agencies were still autonomous, but he was sure the feds would try a takeover. The chain of command at this stage was as raveled as an old rope. It was going to take a while to tie up all the loose ends and decide who answered to whom. The Thanksgiving holiday wasn't helping matters.

Wally expected the FBI's South Georgia manpower to quadruple within the hour; give them two, and there would be as many as five hundred agents swarming over the coast, but it would take more than the FBI to consolidate a response. The Emergency Crisis Council would be convening, he thought, dragging out some out-of-date, ten-year-old contingency plan—a horse designed by a committee.

The CIA would know about it by now. They were probably here in force already. Oh, not legally, not officially, he thought. But they'd be here, all right. Covertly. Slipping around, keeping an eye on things.

The governor was getting in on the act, too. Joe Murphy

from the Georgia Bureau of Investigation had just told him that an Atlanta Task Force was probable within the next twenty to thirty minutes.

A Task Force would put the state troopers and the GBI under FBI control—and the McIntosh County Sheriff's Department would be neatly cut out of the picture, Wally thought. But he intended to carry on. Do what he could. His men knew these waterways better than anyone else. Certainly better than the Coast Guard, he thought. The blue boys weren't worth the powder to blow them to hell.

He stared out of the kitchen window. The tide was still up and the Chris-Craft V-8 was visible at the dock, a pale ghost floating in the moonlight. He turned to Marge. "Did Shep get there yet?" The question was rhetorical. Wally's unspoken message was, "Hurry him up."

Marge nodded and turned back to her radio.

Delton Sheppard was on his way to Joe Carter's house, where the sheriff's department's other Chris-Craft was moored. Those two were going to be a little boy's ticket off the island. The boat was beefed up—fast as anything on the water. If Calvin could make it down to the dock, they could scoop him up and be out of there in a wink. Wally shot a glance at the CB. Come on back, he thought. Come on back, son.

Draining the last of his coffee, he set the mug on the drainboard with a clatter and went into the dining room. Pete Wiggins was poring over a cluster of maps and charts of St. Cyrils. Like Wally, Pete was a former state trooper and a south Georgia native. They had met in one of the first State Patrol bomb training sessions and had instantly hit it off. That was almost seventeen years ago. When Wally was elected sheriff, his first official act was to convince Pete Wiggins to join the team.

Pete looked up. "Still going to send John Wayne against the Apaches?" Wiggins's reservations about Wally's rescue operation had been clear from the beginning.

Wally's eyes narrowed slightly. Although they didn't

always agree, he respected Wiggins's opinion. "That's the plan."

"The kid's not the only one on the island."

He nodded sharply. "And right now, there's not a goddamn thing we can do about the rest of them. But we've got a shot with the boy."

"Maybe." Pete pulled out a nearly empty pack of Tareytons, poked an exploring finger inside, and pulled out a bent cigarette. He lit it and turned back to his charts. "According to what the kid saw, we know those dudes took Leroy and his grandson first. It's not likely they were waiting on the island for the barge to show up." He waggled the Tareyton at a section near the bottom of the map. "My guess is, they took them hostage at the St. Simons landing."

"You're probably right. But I'm having trouble with it. If they came over on the barge, how do they plan to get away?"

"Maybe the launch. The launch would be tied up at the St. Cyrils dock."

Wally shook his head. "I don't think so. Not unless they're stupid. The launch is too slow to outrun much of anything."

Pete knitted thick gray brows. "I'm having a little heart-burn with that theory, too," he admitted. "They could have followed in another boat. But the tide's up and the moon's pretty full. You can see clear across the marsh from the landing. Leroy would have spotted them." He paused, then raised a brow. "Maybe not, though. If it was before moonrise, it might have been dark as a tomb."

Wally stared at him for a moment. Then he stuck his head into the living room and said to a young deputy, "Rondall, find out what time the moon came up tonight."

Pete poked at his cigarette with an index finger; the paper was split at the bend. Stubbing it out, he absently reached for another. "So it looks like those dudes have another boat on St. Cyrils. If they do," Pete said deliberately, "it might put a kink in the rescue operation."

Wally's gaze slid toward the silent CB radio in the kitchen. His lips compressed to a thin line: He had told the boy to go to the old lodge near the dock—right into the terrorists' path.

Chapter 21

"UP THERE!"

At the sharp whispered warning, Sally's eyes flicked toward the balcony and the rifle aimed at her heart. "Please—" Her head jerked toward Iguana, then back to Hoby and the widening pool of blood. "Please. Let us help him."

At a quick gesture from Iguana, El Poeta swung the rifle away.

Sally went to her knees beside the old man. "Help me," she called to the doctor. But it was Lillian who was at her side before Dave Cole could cross the room.

Lillian's face was pale and strained, but her voice was calm. "What can I do?"

"Pressure. There."

As Sally grasped Hoby's chin and lifted to open his airway, Lillian peeled back Hoby's blood-soaked coat. Wincing at the sight, she pulled off her own jacket, bundled it, and pressed down at the gushing chest wound.

Sally stared at the old man's face. He was unconscious. A blue tinge circled his lips, and beads of cold sweat glazed his forehead.

Dave Cole knelt beside her. "What have we got?" He pulled a penlight from his shirt pocket and flashed it into Hoby's eyes.

"He's still breathing," Sally said, "but he's not perfusing well." Then to Lillian: "We've got to keep him warm." She slid forefinger and second finger under the angle of his jaw and pressed up. The carotid pulse felt rapid and thready.

"Get us something," Lillian said over her shoulder. "One of the rugs. Anything." With her free hand she reached for the small Oriental rug the ambassador handed her and slid it over Hoby.

Dave ripped the old man's shirt. "Shit. We've got a sucking chest wound."

Sally stared first at Dave, then frantically around the room. They had to seal it. A piece of plastic . . . anything to seal it. Just then, Hoby gave a shuddering gasp and stopped breathing. Moving automatically, Sally pinched his nostrils shut, slid a hand under the back of his neck, lifted, and began to blow into his mouth.

Dave felt for the carotid. "Shit," he said again. He pulled Hoby's lower eyelid down and stared at the pupil. "He's dilated."

Sally caught a quick breath and breathed into Hoby's mouth.

"Let it go. He's dilated."

She didn't seem to hear. Sucking air, she blew into his lungs. Keep him going . . . got to. . . . Gasping, she blew again. Got to . . . got to. . . . If he stayed alive, maybe all of them had a chance. . . .

Dave grabbed her arm.

Blinking, she raised her head and stared at him, then at the old man's eyes. His pupils were black pools that engulfed the iris. Fixed and dilated. Brain death.

"It's no good," Dave whispered. "He's gone."

Someone grasped Sally's shoulders and drew her to her feet. It was Bru.

Lillian's eyes were bleak as she turned to the others in the room and shook her head. For a long moment there was no sound except for the anguished keening of Cass Tompkins huddled over the body of her little dog.

Cass's wails muffled her secretary's whispered words to Bru as he and Sally passed.

"What?" he mouthed. His eyebrow rose in question.

"In my room," Miranda Gervin said. "I've got a gun."

Chapter 22

CALVIN STOPPED TO GET HIS BEARINGS. THE SHELL ROAD ended in a T. A left turn would take him toward the rain pond and the airstrip; right, toward the stables and Oyster Creek. But where was the shortcut? He scanned the far side of the deserted road. Nothing.

He took a step, another, into the intersection. There. He could just make out the faint lines of the footpath stretch-ing ahead.

In the dark the shell path seemed narrower than he remembered. Wind-jittered shadows pressed in on either side. As he carefully skirted the edge of the marsh, the smell of salt water grew stronger. He could hear the lap of the tide just a few feet away. Suddenly a splashing sound came out of the blackness.

He started. Nathan had told him all about a giant alliga-tor night before last. He had been following Nathan and Ashley down the park path, taking care to lag behind, shading his flashlight so they wouldn't see him. Then abruptly their light was gone. Confused, he had hurried ahead when suddenly Nathan grabbed him from behind. "It could've been a gator that got you." Nathan's arms had clamped tighter, squeezing the breath out of him. "You could've been alligator bait." And then the two of them had laughed when he ran away.

It was worse now without a light. There was no way to see the things that crept in the dark beyond the path. Calvin broke into a halting run, pausing after each step to spot the glimmering gray of the path ahead.

A low rumble brought him up short. Holding his breath, he stared into the blackness. Then he knew what it was: the electric generators. That meant he was close to Leroy and Lena's house.

The woods began to thin near the creek. Ahead, the old lodge was a black blotch against the lighter sky. The path disappeared as he made his way toward the building.

The living room light was on. Head low, he passed under the side windows and peered out from the corner of the house. He didn't see the Jeep, but two pickup trucks were parked on the road in front: the old blue one the musicians used, and the white one the men with guns had driven away in. He stared up at the window. They were in there, he thought. Right now.

He looked back at the road. Beyond it the marsh stretched out in the darkness. The motor launch was a pale glimmer at the dock. Next to it was the dark, shadowy barge and another boat that Calvin had never seen before.

He needed a radio. He stared at the pickup trucks. Not the white one, he thought. They might use it again. But the blue one had a radio. And the keys were usually left inside. Calvin gave a last glance at the lighted windows and then ran toward the road.

Circling the old truck, he crouched by the side away from the building and reached up, feeling in the dark for the handle. It was cold. He started to open the door, then he stopped. He remembered the flare of lights when the men had opened the door of the other truck. If the lights came on now, they'd see him.

He straightened and felt for the window. It was open. Clinging to the window frame, he got a toehold, pushed up, and scrambled inside. The seat was still wet from last night's rain. Moonlight bisected the steering wheel; its right-hand side glimmered with pale light, its left hung in blackness. Calvin shrank into the shadows and reached cautiously toward the dark dashboard.

In imitation of Hoby he clicked the ignition key to the right. Just one click, he thought. If he did it more than that, the engine might start. He felt for the radio knob and turned it. The CB light came on—channel 12. He turned the knob to channel 9, pressed the microphone switch, and put it to his lips.

Pete Wiggins stuck his head into the room. "TV news bulletin coming on."

Wally stood in the doorway and stared at the screen:

"—and now that tape." As the voice of the terrorist leader came up, the network newsman stared into the camera and froze. A map of the Georgia coast superimposed on the screen. As Iguana's tirade continued, the map dissolved into a blowup of St. Cyrils Island with an X to mark the location of the lodge.

Off by half a mile, thought Wally. The network had managed to place the lodge squarely in the marsh.

Iguana's voice went on: ". . . approach by sea, prisoners will be executed one by one.

"Do not believe you can defeat us. We will counter military force with absolute weapons. The Organization of the People in Arms control the fate of North America and ultimately the world—"

A harsh crackle of static, and the newsman came back on, with an apologetic, "Due to technical difficulties, we're unable to bring you the rest of that tape."

Wally stared at the screen. Technical trouble? Maybe. And maybe not. The newsman signed off with the promise of ". . . more details as we receive them."

Nothing about the plague germ, he thought. Not a word about the aerosol bomb on the mainland. He'd have to give Washington credit for that; they'd managed to convince the network to muzzle the news. Either that, or they'd relayed an edited version of Iguana's demands. He wasn't particularly surprised. They had enough trouble without having to deal with a panicky public.

Wally hadn't even told his own deputies about the aerosol. No one, that is, but Pete Wiggins. Based on the need to know, no one else qualified. He would have to check back with the Glynn County chief, be sure they were keeping it quiet, too. He headed for the kitchen.

Marge Tyson looked up. "Shep just radioed in. He and Carter are in the boat. They're ready when you are." The telephone rang. She scooped up the receiver, listened for a moment, then said, "GBI. Joe Murphy."

Wally was reaching for the phone when the CB radio, silent for so long, gave out a volley of static. Through the interference he heard the faint voice of a child:

". . . Wally?" Then a pause. "I want to go home. . . ."

Calvin jumped when Wally's voice boomed over the CB. He flipped the volume knob down and stared toward the lighted windows. Maybe they heard.

The sheriff's voice came back, lower this time: "Where are you, son?"

"Down by the dock. In a truck. I'm outside the old lodge."

"What do you see?"

"There's lights on inside. They're in there now."

"Who? Who's in there?"

"The guys with guns. Some of them, anyway. They drove here."

"You mean they left the lodge? They were in the lodge and then they left?"

"Yeah. Four of 'em."

A pause. "What else do you see?"

"I see the pickup truck. And boats. There's a new boat there."

"A new one—" Wally's microphone clicked off for a moment. Then he was back. "Tell me what it looks like."

"It's kind of long. But it's not very high." Calvin squinted at the dock. "It's white, I think."

Another pause, this one longer, then Wally said, "You said you've been all over the island. Is that right, son?"

"Yes."

"Do you know the lighthouse? Have you been there?"

"Uh-huh. I was there today."

"I want you to go there, Calvin, as quick as you can. I'm going to send a boat to get you. It'll pick you up by the lighthouse. Do you understand?"

Calvin stared out at the night. "It's a long way."

"Not that far, son. Not for a big boy like you."

"It's real dark out." He felt the lump growing in his throat again. "Couldn't you just come here?"

"We can't do that, son. We can't take the boat up to the dock."

"I could meet you. I could go down the creek a ways."

"No. You can't do that. The only place Oyster Creek hits high ground is by the dock. The rest of it runs through the marsh."

"Yeah, I could. I could do it."

"Calvin"—Wally's voice was sterner now—"you've got to do what I say. I want you to go to the lighthouse. Right now. Just follow the road and turn by the stables. When you're in the boat, we can talk on the radio again." Then gently: "You can do it, son. Will you do it?"

The boy swallowed hard. "I don't know. I guess so."

"Good boy. Now listen to me. I'm sending a boat right away. So you turn off that CB and get going. And when you get here, I'm buying you the biggest chocolate sundae you ever saw. Okay?"

"I guess so," he whispered. "Okay."

When he shut off the radio, the silence was overwhelming. For a long minute Calvin stared out at the night. There was a little moonlight on the marsh, he thought. But he'd have to go through the woods to get to the lighthouse, and the woods were really dark right now. And there were alligators and stuff. Then blinking back the sudden rush of hot tears that stung his eyes, he scrambled out of the truck window, clung for a moment, and landed on his toes.

He had reached the first of the outbuildings when the door to the old lodge opened.

Calvin ducked behind the generator shed. The engines throbbed like his own heart. Their vibration penetrated the rough boards of the building and shivered through his hands.

Just one man came out of the building. He carried a gun. He stood illuminated in the lights from the lodge for a moment. Then he turned down the path that led to the dock, moving as if he could see in the dark. Fascinated, Calvin stared, until another shadowy moment caused his gaze to dart toward the widow's walk on the roof of the old lodge.

Somebody was up there. Watching.

His first impulse was to run. But his knees suddenly began to melt, and it was all he could do to cling, fingernails digging into rough-cut boards, to the back of the shed.

The man had reached the dock now. He swung easily into the Cigarette anchored there. Silence. Then the engines rumbled and the ocean racer headed downstream toward the mouth of Oyster Creek and the Atlantic beyond.

Calvin caught the warm horse smells as he passed close to the stable. At the fork of the road he turned left and followed the dim shell road until the woods thinned and he found himself on the edge of the prairie.

The moon was lower now. Its light slanted over the flat grassland and turned the isolated palmettos into shaggy black mounds. In the distance he imagined he could see the dark lines of the old lighthouse.

Without the baffle of trees the wind blew sharper here, whistling through the low Muhlenbergia grass, bending the taller clumps of wire grass.

Shivering, he folded his arms over his chest and bent forward. His eyes burned from the wind and it was an effort to hold them open in the dark. Digging both fists in, he scrubbed at them, but it didn't seem to help. He wanted to believe this was a game—a computer game like the ones he had played on his Apple. Even the dark was part of it, he thought. There were lots of dark places in adventure games. And even if you had a lamp, it didn't always work; you had to have a match, too, and other stuff sometimes. He wanted to believe this was all a game because it kept away the other thoughts: the ones about Ashley and his daddy.

A tall clump of palmettos blotted out the road. Sliding one foot forward, he tested his way. A gust of wind rattled throught the fronds. He sucked in his breath at the sound that followed: another rattle—sharper, higher pitched.

You want to watch out at night up on the dunes and on the prairie, Hoby had said.

Watch out, watch out, watch out.

You might come up on a rattler.

Muscles tensed, he leaped away, came down, leaped again.

Snakes are moving this time of year.

Moving. Behind him. Coming after him. He ran, heart pounding, feet kicking up slivers of crushed shell. He ran until his throat was dry and a terrible stitch clawed at his side and doubled him over onto his knees. Clutching his ribs, he stared over his shoulder with eyes as wide as he could open them. He scanned the road he had just covered. Nothing. Diamondbacks, Hoby had said. And water moccasins around the rain pond.

Gradually the pain in his side went away. He licked his lips and scrambled to his feet, listening all the while for the rattling sound to come again, but no sound came except for the wind in the grass, and the surf.

And then a kind of exhilaration came to him. He had made it. He had got past the snake, and he was okay. Just like in *Pitfall*, he thought. You had to shove the joystick up and hit the button at the same time. That way, you jumped over the snake in the road and he couldn't hurt you.

Ignoring the thirst that dried his mouth, Calvin turned

and stared down the road. The old lighthouse was a dark finger pointing toward the sky. The tower, he thought. There was always lots of stuff in towers: messages and treasure; people to be rescued.

The lighthouse cast an inkblot shadow that spilled into a black pool of ragged palmettos. Just beyond, he could hear the tidewater lapping at the inlet. He listened for the boat. Nothing. He stared into the thick darkness at the base of the lighthouse and tried to find the door. If he went in, went up to the top, maybe he could see the boat coming.

Hands held blindly out in front of him, Calvin ran his hands along the face of the curving wall until he felt the splintered planks of the door. He fumbled for the latch, but something caught his eye, something sparkling in the shadows of the wind-tossed palmettos. Squinting, tipping his head, he stared at it. Gone. No, there it was again.

He moved closer, and when a gust of wind whipped away the concealing fronds, he saw what it was: moonlight sparkling on glass, on the windshield of the CJ5.

The man in the Jeep. He was here. Calvin's gaze dragged slowly back to the lighthouse. Up there. A chill trembled through his bones like wind. He was up there. In the tower. Looking out . . .

High in the darkened lighthouse, La Culebra scanned the dark waters of Altamaha Sound.

He was tired from his daylong vigil on the marsh, but the adrenaline left from the strike still held its edge. Soon his relief would come and he could sleep, but now it was time to report. Raising the transceiver to his lips, he thumbed it on and spoke quickly in Spanish. A pause, a hiss of static, then the acknowledgment. He spoke again, signed off.

He turned toward the west, southwest, south, gaze sweeping across the inlet, then the marsh. Nothing there. Nothing since a quick glimpse of the Cigarette turning near the dock. It would be out in the open ocean now, skirting St. Cyrils's shore, closing on the lighthouse. He turned again southeast toward the prairie and the woods beyond, east toward the beach, northeast, north.

Again he turned, slowly: northwest, west toward the sound, southwest—he swung back abruptly and stared at the waterway. Something.

He spotted the wake of the Chris-Craft first, saw the moonlight sparkling on the churning water at its stern. Then he could see the pale lines of the boat itself, gray on grayer water, and the two men inside.

He flipped the transceiver switch, spoke. Eyes fixed on the sound, he spoke again. Then he raised his rifle and carefully aimed the Mecar grenade.

Calvin crouched at the base of the lighthouse and stared toward the water. He could hear a boat engine in the distance. Better get down to the water, he thought, and gave a quick glance upward. He'd have to hurry when the boat got here. He'd have to get on before the guy up in the tower saw.

The beach narrowed sharply by the lighthouse. In the high tide it had shrunk to no more than a thinning stretch of prairie grass edged with sand. The water was no more than five or six yards away. Wait for the boat to come in close, he thought. Then run.

The boat was closer now, coming in fast, swerving from the channel toward the shore.

Now, he thought. Run.

He took two leaping steps, and came down to a clap of thunder.

The speeding Chris-Craft shimmied, rose, bloomed into a raging fireball.

The impact slammed him to the ground. He clung to it with nails and toes as showering water drenched him. Rolling desperately away, he scrambled up and stared half blinded toward the sound.

No boat. Nothing, nothing, nothing.

A heartbeat. He ran toward the beach and skidded to a stop as another boat swung suddenly in from the sea. He swerved away and jumped. The ground blazed behind him.

Then he was running harder than he had ever run before, zigzagging, loping strides punctuated with staccato rifle fire. And as he ran, one thought pulsed in his mind: not a game . . . not a game. It wasn't a game at all.

FRIDAY

SYNDROME

Chapter 23

WALLY CARRUTHERS STARED AT THE WALL CLOCK OVER the stove: 12:07 A.M. He would have to note the time in his report. His fist opened, closed, tightened, as Marge Tyson went on:

"So it's a confirmation of sorts. . . ." Avoiding eye contact, she stared down at her notes. Her voice took on a brisk businesslike tone—the way it always did when she had to be the king's messenger, he thought.

"Of course, it's not infallible," she said. "But the Black Hawk pilot did report an explosion just off the old lighthouse. He wasn't close enough to see anything else. Washington's holding off on any closer surveillance."

He stared at the silent radio. There had been no word from Shep and Joe since a sound like thunder had rattled the speaker. Not a sound. Nothing at all.

Pete Wiggins walked into the kitchen.

Wally looked up. "We've got a confirmation."

Pete's lips compressed to a thin line as he read the notes Marge handed him. Hesitating a long second, then two, he said, "I guess it's time to tell the next of kin. I'll get Rondall. We'll go by."

"No. That's my job." Wally took a slow breath. "Give me a minute." He turned abruptly and, avoiding the little room and the little cluster of deputies there, took the narrow back hall into his bedroom. He stood for a moment in front of the old mahogany dresser and stared at the oval picture of Martha. Her round face was open and smiling, and just then he missed her terribly.

He spread his fingers on the dresser top and squeezed his eyes shut. Fool, he thought. He had tried to be a hero and now two of his men were dead. It should have been him. It should have been him in that boat, not Shep, not Joe Carter. And the little boy—if he was still alive, it was no thanks to him. Down the garden path, every one of them.

A goddamned hero. Wasn't that the motivation? Wasn't that what lay hidden under the notion of plucking the kid off the island? Save the kid and get a medal. Win the ears and the tail, and never give a shit about the bull. All the bull had to do was die.

He pulled off his shirt and, throwing it into the green wicker basket by the closet, changed into uniform. He pinned on his badge, and then squared his chin and stared into the flecked old mirror. It was his job to tell Sheila Carter that she didn't have a husband anymore, that her baby girl didn't have a daddy. It was his job to tell the Sheppards that they'd lost their boy.

He slicked back his hair with two quick swipes of the silver-plated brush from the dresser set Martha had tucked into her hope chest when she was seventeen years old. Then, hesitating, he fished the brown prescription container out of the shirt in the hamper before he turned and left the room.

Hot pain seared through Calvin's lungs and he fell, gasping, at the crest of the dune. Rocking on his knees, he clutched his ribs and stared down at the moonlit prairie through a break in the trees. He strained for a look at the man who pursued him.

Nothing.

Cold fingers clenched his belly. Maybe the man was already in the woods—moving behind the trees, coming closer.

He scrambled up, but his legs trembled and he nearly fell again.

He had to get off the road. Thick shadows blotched the shell path, and to either side he could see nothing at all.

He hesitated only a moment before he dived into a stand of young pines.

The ground dropped suddenly away and he slid into a gully filled with dried leaves. Trying not to rustle them, he picked himself up and found the path again. This time he walked carefully, each step tentative until he was sure of his footing. Keeping the road to his left, he followed it until he came to a fork. If he turned right, the path would take him back to the old lodge and the outbuildings. His mouth was dry. If he went that way, he could find a water tap, get a drink. But somebody was standing in the dark on the widow's walk. He shivered. He couldn't go back there. He couldn't.

Darting across the road, dodging into the shadows of the giant oaks, he picked up the bridle trail and began to follow it toward the stables.

Calvin froze at the edge of the woods and stared across the clearing at the dark barn. He blinked as a black shadow moved at the edge of it. A low snort. Relief flooded him. Just one of the horses. He checked out the clearing with a final look and ran toward the fence. Grabbing a post, he hooked a toe into the wire and swung over the top.

He heard trickling water. It was coming from the old bathtub that served as a trough at the side of the barn. A toilet float mechanism kept it filled as the horses drank. Staying in the shadows, he knelt beside it, cupped his hands, and drank until his thirst was blunted.

The inside of the stable was black as a cave and redolent with leather and manure. In one of the open stalls to the right he could hear Cajun's harsh breathing. Hoby had said his wind was broken. The old horse had been taken off the trail years ago. Now he was simply a pet.

Calvin felt his way until he came to the half door that led into the feed room. The top of the door was only as high as his chest. He pushed it open, went in, and carefully shut the door behind him. Because of what Hoby said, he told himself. Hoby always said to keep the feed room shut so the horses wouldn't get in. But underneath lay the desperate hope that the low door would keep out other things besides. Inside, past the galvanized garbage pails that held grain and sweet feed, he crawled over bales of hay and a pile of smelly blankets until he found a narrow refuge next to the outside wall.

It wasn't until he lay down that the pain of his scratched and bruised body washed over him and mingled with the deeper, colder pain that touched his soul. His face twisted and he covered it with grubby hands as silent, racking sobs shook through him. Finally, huddled next to the rough-hewn wall, fingers curled around a shred of blanket, he slept.

Chapter 24

IT WAS HALF PAST MIDNIGHT. THE LIGHTS WERE LOWERED and the fire had dimmed to glowing coals. On the balcony overhead, El Poeta slept, rifle cradled at his side. Through half-closed eyes Bru watched as Miranda Gervin slowly raised her hand to attract Iguana's attention. "Bathroom," she said. "I have to go."

Iguana nodded and jerked his rifle toward the foyer. Across the room Cuclillo opened the double doors and took two backward steps into the wide entry hall. From there he could cover the small bathroom to the left of the stairs.

The bathroom was less than twenty feet away. Its door stood open, and according to Iguana's rules, it was to stay open. "Close it," he had said, "and we shoot through the door." The only privacy was provided by the vanity that screened the toilet beyond.

Miranda cast an uneasy glance at Cuclillo. He held a SIG automatic rifle, and he had a handgun. Moving slowly, she followed him out of the room.

In the armchair at Bru's right, Alex Borden rubbed his eyes with thumb and forefinger in a gesture that effectively hid his mouth. "Can she get it?" he whispered.

He meant the gun, thought Bru. Several of the others knew about it by now. In defiance of Iguana's orders of no talking, a grapevine had sprung up. As the hours stretched by, the hostages had shifted around the room in a slow dance punctuated by monitored trips to the bathroom and cautious whispers. Bru shook his head. Miranda's gun was in her room; it might as well be on the mainland. He wondered why she had brought it to the island. Why did a secretary find it necessary to travel with a gun? Then the absurdity almost made him laugh; what else should a prospective hostage bring along on her vacation?

Borden slid down in the chair as if to make himself more comfortable. The maneuver put him closer to Bru. "I'm an expert with hand weapons."

Maybe, Bru thought skeptically. He didn't trust him. Nearly everything Borden said struck him as empty bravado. The man seemed to have sobered up in a hurry, but it was going to take a lot more than that to do them any good. Without a gun they didn't have a chance. And if they had one, what then? What was one gun against automatic weapons? Against sidearms and grenades?

There was something else: Iguana and his men didn't seem to fit the usual terrorist profile. They were too cool, too disciplined. And they used simple code names instead of grandiose titles and rank. They just weren't convincing as impassioned radicals, he thought, in spite of their ideological demands. He felt sure the men were mercenaries, and he wondered why. Yet it did make a strange sort of sense for a liberation front to hire professionals; too many strikes had failed because hotheaded fanatics decided to play soldier. Still, there was something about this operation that wasn't falling into place. Something felt wrong, and he wasn't sure just what it was.

Sally stirred and he looked down. She lay stretched out on the floor beside him. Exhausted, she had fallen into a disturbed sleep that creased her brow and caused her to mutter under her breath. Suddenly she flung a hand, palm outward, over her eyes as if to ward off a blow.

"Sh-sh," he whispered, as if she were a restless child. He looked around the room at the musicians huddled near the hearth; at Lillian sitting upright, eyes bleak, hand tight on Lena's arm; at Ashley Borden, whose stricken gaze flicked toward the bloodstained rug that covered the dead man.

Iguana had capitalized on Hoby's death after the fact. He had contacted WGIR again, claiming that the old man was executed because of an "imperialist attack" on the island. In broken whispers Tony Herrera had translated Iguana's quick transceiver interchange with the lighthouse. It was over almost before it began, thought Bru. But it wasn't a complete washout. The lighthouse lookout had fired at someone and missed, so somehow they had managed to land a man on the island. Yet what in hell could one man do against these odds?

Iguana wasn't taking the report lightly. The lights outside the lodge blazed; inside they were dimmed. Pulling on night goggles, the terrorists had carefully moved away from the windows out of the line of fire. Periodic low-volume exchanges crackled over the transceiver as Iguana's men methodically stalked the intruder. At least three of them after him, thought Bru. Without backup, the poor bastard was going to do well to stay alive. And Calvin Borden was out there somewhere, too. A little kid alone in the dark. He didn't want to think about what would happen if the terrorists spotted the boy instead.

Miranda came back into the room. Instead of sitting down, she walked slowly toward Iguana until he gestured for her to stop.

"I need to talk to you," she said. "Alone."

Iguana shook his head and jerked his rifle toward a vacant chair.

"Please. I have to go to my room. There's something I have to have."

"You want to go to your room?" He stared at her in amusement. "Maybe you plan to go out the window? You think you run away, huh?"

Miranda shook her head. She stared at the floor a moment, then raised her eyes. "I need my sanitary napkins."

"You need what?"

"Sanitary napkins." The words seemed to be incomprehensible to him. "Pads. Kotex."

The brand name conveyed a meaning. "You are menstruating?" He drew the word out into its four syllables.

She gave a short nod.

"Did you hear that?" he said to the others. "She is menstruating." Then he grinned at Miranda: "Like a bitch in heat, huh?"

She looked away, then back. This time, anger flashed in her eyes.

"What you say?" He was baiting her for pleasure now. "I don't hear you so good."

Miranda looked him in the eye and stuck out her chin. "I said"—a pause—"I am men-stru-at-ing just like a bitch in heat. Now, can I go to my room?"

Iguana's eyes narrowed. "What are you called?"

Her chin went up higher. "Miranda."

Scowling, he stared at her. She stared back with equal intensity, and suddenly Iguana laughed. "You know, I like you, Miranda," he said, stretching her name into Meer-ann-dah. "You got—how you call it?—spunk." He spoke rapidly to Cuclillo, who grinned in answer. Then he said to her, "Cuclillo, he's afraid of you, but I told him he had to be brave and go with you. Okay?"

Miranda looked at him for a moment, nodded, and turned toward the door.

"One thing more, Miranda. Cuclillo, he's so afraid—so I told him, you do anything funny, he should kill you."

*   *   *

Miranda walked up the stairs without looking back at the man behind her. She walked slowly, deliberately holding her head high, but the back of her neck tingled and she imagined the muzzle of Cuclillo's rifle pointing there, aimed at the base of her skull. The reaction came on abruptly and turned her knees to ice water. She wanted desperately to grab the banister for support, but if she did, he'd see the way her hands were shaking. Sweet Jesus, she thought. Sweet Jesus. Why in the name of God had she defied them? She could have been killed.

The doorknob felt clammy. Inside the room she allowed herself a surreptitious glance at the terrorist. He stood a few paces behind her. She nodded toward the dresser and said unnecessarily, "I'll get them now."

The dresser was near the window. A pine branch, shivering in the wind, moved behind the glass and she started. She slid her damp palms across her skirt and opened the drawer, praying that he wouldn't see what she was doing. She felt the hard angles of the Walther PPK beneath the pile of nightgowns. The box of Maxi Pads was next to it. The top was unsealed, the box half full. Not daring to look back, she pulled out most of the pads and slid them out of sight in the back of the drawer.

To her dismay, Cuclillo took a step toward her. Then another.

Wheeling, box clutched to her chest, she stared at him.

He gestured toward the door.

No choice. She had to leave the gun. Heart pounding, she walked past him toward the hall. Outside the door she turned. "I forgot—panties. I need a pair." She nodded toward the dresser. "Please?"

He shrugged.

She crossed the room and glanced over her shoulder. Cuclillo was still by the door, standing just inside. Please God, let him stay there. She began an inane chatter that started as a ruse, but suddenly slipped the bonds of self-control: "Sometimes I think I'd leave my head." She set

the box in the drawer and slid her hand under the pile of
nightgowns. ". . . That's what my mother always used to
say. She used to say, 'Miranda, I don't see how you could
forget . . .' " The Walther PPK was heavy; she slid it into
the box, praying it wouldn't show. ". . . Mother used to
say, 'If I told you once' "—two pads from the back of the
drawer went into the box to hide the gun—" '. . . I told
you a thousand times . . .' "

She snatched up a pair of white cotton panties, trailing
them across her fingers for a moment so Cuclillo would
see, then stuffing them loosly in with the Maxi Pads.

She didn't dare look down at the box, didn't dare draw
attention to it. Clutching it, supporting it so the Walther
wouldn't bulge through the thin cardboard, Miranda turned
toward the door. All she had to do now was cross the room
and walk down the stairs. Then suddenly, incongruously,
she remembered the tryouts for a high school play when
she was fifteen: She had had to walk across the stage. Just
walk. Naturally. With horror she realized that she had
completely forgotten how.

Chapter 25

DR. DANIEL ELTON GLANCED AT HIS WATCH. CHRIST.
After midnight already. He had appropriated the dining
room for his homework on the scenario, shoving the pot of
bronze chrysanthemums to one end of the narrow teak
table, laying his papers out in soldiers' rows. But enough
was, by God, enough. He leaned back and surveyed the
stack of papers. If the country ever had to face a genetically tinkered plague, they were up shit creek.

The logistics alone were staggering: quarantine enforcement, mobilization of medical personnel, supplies, isolation—the list went on and on. And how about "evacuation of surrounding areas"? It was easy enough to stick in a sentence like that, but what about the real thing? . . . And now folks, we want you to pick up and get out—and never mind the dog, the family silver, crippled old Aunt Hattie, or the traffic. . . . Sure. Curling his lip, he shunted the papers into a battered brown folder.

The house was quiet. Ginny, rolling her eyes in practiced resignation, had crawled into bed with Stephen King over an hour ago.

Flipping on the kitchen lights, Elton rummaged around for something to eat and found a stale pecan Danish—a candidate for the Olympics, discus division. Maybe the microwave, he thought. He was immensely impressed with the ability of a microwave oven to resurrect over-the-hill-and-around-the-bend baked goods. He stabbed out thirty seconds on the control panel and sloshed milk into a glass. With a thoughtful glance at the half inch remaining in the plastic jug, he slugged it down and pitched the empty into the trash.

When the microwave sounded its bell, he scooped up the steaming Danish, now satisfactorily limp, balanced it on the milk glass rim, and headed for the living room. The TV screen rippled for a second before the picture formed. He glanced needlessly at his watch, knowing he had missed the Channel 2 news. His day always seemed unfinished somehow without his eleven o'clock fix. He twiddled buttons and raised CNN Headline.

The anchorwoman's voice was regionless, and essentially sexless, in that style that newswomen everywhere seemed to affect. Another graduate of Famous Anchorwomen's School, he thought. She was wrapping up a segment of what Elton had come to consider the Disease of the Month Club, this one about a new sub-rosa treatment for multiple sclerosis.

"This just in." The newswoman fixed him with an even

stare. "According to eyewitness accounts, Black Hawk helicopters from Fort Stewart, Georgia, are circling St. Cyrils Island, a site of a terrorist attack that took captive a United Nations ambassador and a U.S. congressman. . . ."

Bru.

". . . Just after nine P.M. eastern, terrorists took over a small, exclusive lodge on St. Cyrils Island just off the southeastern coast of Georgia. Although reports are as yet unverified, one source has revealed that at least one hostage is dead, a victim of terrorist bullets. . . ."

Bru Farrier. Friend.

The milk sloshed over the polished teak coffee table, the white streams dribbling onto the carpet. Oblivious, he raced to the bedroom.

The bedside lamp was the only light in the room. Ginny lay propped on two pillows, asleep. The Stephen King paperback, sprawling on its face on her pregnant belly, pitched and yawed with every breath, with every thrust of a tiny foot. He stood at the bedside for a moment, wanting to wake her, to tell her. Instead, he stripped off his clothes, throwing them in a pile on the floor beside him, and crawled in beside her.

He stared at her for a moment, at the way her hand fell across her belly in that protective way she had, at the way her hair, falling free from her face, made her look no more than sixteen. He pulled her to him then and woke her with a kiss.

Their lovemaking, awkward as it was—"a *ménage à trois*," she called it—seemed uncommonly urgent to him. Afterward, he held her close and felt her belly quiver between them with the movements of their child. "I'm glad you're here," he whispered.

"Where else?" Her little laugh breathed into a sigh. Turning on her side, she drifted off again.

He switched off the light and stared into a darkness flaring with afterimages. In time they faded to black, but still he stared into the night, listening to the even sounds of Ginny's breathing.

Finally he rose and, reaching for his robe, walked silently through the house to the living room telephone.

Cordell Holt, the White House chief of staff, stubbed out his Merit and said to the others, "We're ready on that psycholinguistics analysis." Then into the phone: "You're on. Go ahead."

The undercurrent of voices in the situation room faded to silence.

"Yes." Roth Nesheim's voice came back over the speaker. "My first impression of the tape held up when I ran it through the computer. I think these boys mean what they say. I'm not getting a classic picture, though. The classic picture of a terrorist is a weak individual who's pretending to be strong—somebody who's really hurting and wants to hurt back. I'm just not getting that kind of pattern here.

"That makes it tougher to get a psychological lever in negotiations," said Nesheim, "but it's got a positive side: They're going to be more predictable. I think you can take them at their word.

"Something else bothers me—this business about the last line. . . ." A rattle of paper, then, ". . .'Where is Wily, amigos?'"

The director of Central Intelligence shifted uneasily in his seat as Nesheim went on:

"There's the implication here—and we're not just looking at words now; we're looking at context—it's as if we're dealing with an insider, almost as if he's taking an inside joke and using it as a needle."

The DCI's chair creaked as he shifted again. It was a needle, all right. Where was NKWILY? Down the sucker, he thought, and according to the brochure, everything else was about to follow. His mouth felt dry. The sinus pill, he rationalized. He reached for a glass of water, drained it, set it down. Unlike some directors, the DCI was a career man. He had been with the agency for thirty-two years, and in that time he had seen it take one crippling blow after another. Now he was watching it all fall apart. All he could do was try to hold the pieces and hope to God the glue set.

As Nesheim signed off, the Crisis Committee chairman, Andrew Hagen, glanced at the FBI director. "Any further communiqués with the island, Burt?"

Burt Kittredge leaned back, hands clasped over his belly. "Not since the hostage was shot. The only line of communication is by radiotelephone, and they won't pick up on our calls. We've got a man on the switchboard, though. Any call in or out goes through the bureau."

The deputy national security adviser, Harold Walheimer, leaned forward: "I've just received a message here from the President. He's been in touch with the United Kingdom. The prime minister is urging him not to accede to these demands."

Andrew Hagen waggled his hand back and forth as if he were giving a benediction. "The U.K.'s attitude toward terrorists is well known."

"But this is basically our baby," said another voice.

"Our biological time bomb," growled the chairman of the Joint Chiefs of Staff. "We need to assemble teams, military capability. I don't want to be held responsible later for not having put together an effective military operation because we let time run out. I would like authorization for that now. I'm thinking in particular about placing Navy Seal teams on the island." General George Everett's gaze flicked from one to another. "All we need is one terrorist left alive to lead us to that mainland plague aerosol." He pulled out a cigarillo and tamped it vigorously against his thumbnail. "I shouldn't have to mention the threat to national defense here. That aerosol could be anywhere. New York. Chicago. Here in Washington."

Harold Walheimer frowned. "I appreciate your position, George. But the President has made it clear that peaceful negotiations take precedence at this time." The deputy advisor edged forward in his chair. "The military is to remain on standby. We can't risk another abortive attack on the island.''

General Everett bristled. ''I'd like to point out for the record that the incident on St. Cyrils Island tonight was an unauthorized attempt by a county sheriff. It was in no way a military operation. Nor was it condoned by this office.''

Andrew Hagen waggled a dismissing hand. ''I'm concerned about the U.K. situation. A leak to the British press about the biological would be picked up on satellite immediately. We don't want to panic the public.''

''That's right, Mr. Chairman,'' said Cordell Holt. ''If the press gets hold of this mainland threat, it would be disastrous.'' The chief of staff exchanged a glance with the press secretary. ''We have to think about the public. The President is concerned that the American public understand that he is in charge. All information about this situation ought to be coming from the White House.''

Andrew Hagen frowned. ''Statements from the White House might be premature at this point. The public isn't aware of the biological. I'm concerned that too much emphasis from the President might inflate the story with the press. We don't want to start speculation.''

Walheimer edged forward. ''We can issue short, low-key reports. We can use the U.K. ambassador as the main reason for White House concern.''

The press secretary, Carter Booth, clicked open a wintergreen Tic Tac box, and, with a rattle, shook one into his hand. ''This, uh, altered plague germ—how sure can we be that it's real?''

The DCI licked his lips. Real! It was fucking real, all right. ''I think we have to bear in mind what the psycholinguistics report said: These terrorists mean what they say.''

''But we're talking about a Guatemalan operation. Not your most technologically advanced country. What are the chances that a Guatemalan group would have access to a bioengineered plague germ?''

The DCI's stomach clenched. ''We're talking about

international terrorism here," he said abruptly. "We have to consider the possibility of connections with Libya, with Iran. Israel's biological labs are among the most advanced in the world. It could have been smuggled out of Israel. Or even Canada."

"How about the Centers for Disease Control?" someone asked. "What do they say?"

"Atlanta's been alerted," said the White House science adviser, Isaac Benjamin. "But we can't expect too much too soon. Without a sample of the biological, the CDC is operating in the dark." He reseated his glasses on the bridge of his nose. "What we can hope for from them is an estimate of the effects of this thing if it gets loose."

"The back-channel messages—" Andrew Hagen turned to the DCI. "Are we getting anything on the People in Arms? Their M.O.? Background?"

The DCI gave a short nod. "You'll be getting a report in a few minutes from the head of the office of terrorism." He glanced at his watch. By now over thirty of his men should be converging on the Georgia coast. He was expecting a coded report from one of them: Jack Hubert—the only operative there from biological branch, the only one of the thirty who knew about Pestis 18.

Andrew Hagen stared down at the scribbled note he had written to himself. "To reiterate then: Our goal is to end the crisis with the least damage to the national interest. The way to this is negotiation and possibly military action." He looked up at the others. "Intermediate goals are finding and aborting the mainland biological, forestalling public panic, and maintaining credibility with the press. Was there anything more?"

Carter Booth rattled his Tic Tac box and looked around the room. "How about the people on the island?"

A series of blank looks met his gaze. They hadn't gotten around to low-priority items yet. They hadn't really thought about the hostages at all.

Chapter 26

THE THIN YOUNG MAN CARRIED THE HEAVY JACKET HE HAD worn in Atlanta over his arm. It was too warm for it in Miami. The briefcase he had taken to the Techwood apartment building was gone, replaced by a small canvas backpack.

Reaching over his shoulder, he pulled out a one-way airline ticket and, fingering it with quick, nervous movements, checked the departure time again. The ticket was issued in the name of Orlando Dominguez Salazar, of Tampa, born March 22, 1963—dead at the age of three months from an automobile accident that also killed his parents and his five-year-old sister, Clara. The Pan Am flight would not leave for over ten hours, but the long wait was of no consequence to him; he had much to do before then.

The airport was not crowded at this hour. He stopped at a newsstand and squatted by a half-dozen bundles of newspapers. The headline on the *Washington Post* read, "UN Ambassador, US Representative Held Hostage."

A finger prodded his shoulder. "Is that the *Times*?" He looked up sharply at a bronzed fat woman wearing a pink Nike sweat suit and rubber sandals. "The *Times*," she repeated. "Is it in yet?"

He got to his feet, shrugged, turned away. Skirting a woman carrying a sleeping infant on one shoulder and a blue plastic tote over the other, he headed for a bank of vending machines and pulled out a handful of change. He stabbed quarters into slots and extracted two packages of cheese crackers and a Cherry Coke.

He ate slowly, pausing now and then to glance at his watch. When he was finished, he found a trash can, deposited the soda can and the wrappers, and moved toward a row of public telephones.

Waiting until none were in use, he went to the phone on the end and next to a row of lockers. The call took most of his change. Returning the rest of the coins to his pocket, he reached into another and took out a small electronic remote device programmed to control all of the answering machines he had been given. He listened for a moment, then held up the device and pressed its button twice.

In a rented room in Alexandria a computer answered. Responding to the high-frequency signal, it beeped once, paused, beeped again. Then, disconnecting, it began to dial a long-distance number. At the third ring someone answered.

Pausing for a count of two seconds, the computer activated a tape-recorded message and an accented voice began to speak:

"Stand by to copy a message from the Organization of the People in Arms." A two-second pause, then, "I am Iguana. I am speaking to you from St. Cyrils Island, Georgia, off the United States coast. . . ."

Another pause, this one for three seconds.

"The imperialist government of the United States deceives itself as it attempts to deceive its people. The imperialist government believes it can conceal from the American people the message I give to you now:

"You cannot defeat us. The Organization of the People in Arms control the fate of North America and ultimately the world. Our demands will be met. If they are not, we unleash a biological weapon on the prisoners of St. Cyrils Island. A second biological aerosol will then detonate within the United States mainland.

"The bomb will spread pneumonic plague, genetically altered, throughout North America. No vaccine can protect you; no medicine can cure you.

"Defy us, and the Black Death will come again to the world."

The computer disconnected and began to dial again. It would take two hours and twelve minutes to cycle through the telephone numbers on its list, two hours and twelve minutes to send its message to each radio and television network, each wire service, each major newspaper throughout the world.

Chapter 27

JUST INSIDE THE BATHROOM, SALLY GAVE A QUICK GLANCE over her shoulder. Cuclillo was still watching from the entrance hall. Her gaze slid toward the toilet and the open box of Maxi Pads between it and the vanity.

Was the gun there? Miranda had not been able to tell them; Iguana had motioned her back to a couch below the balcony, halfway across the room from Bru and Sir William. Except for an arch of the woman's eyebrow and a glance in the direction of the bathroom, there had been no communication.

The toilet was masked from the terrorist's stare only by the vanity and the six inches of wall that projected beyond it to the doorjamb. Cuclillo was looking at her with open insolence. She shook with a sudden, violent anger. Get an eyeful, asshole, she thought. She wanted to scream it. She wanted to grind his face under her heel. And yet at the same time a horrible consuming fear turned her belly to ice.

Rape victims must feel like this, she thought. It was a rape from across the room, a visual thing, a psychic

assault that was almost physical. Thank God her skirt was
full. Thank God for that. The toilet seat was cold against
her bare thighs. The box—don't think about the other,
think about the box.

Staring straight ahead, she let her hand fall to her side.
The Maxi Pad lid was open. She thrust her hand inside.
With fingers that trembled, she felt the hardness of the gun
beneath the thin white pads. Irrationally, she wanted to
pull it out, aim it at his smirking face. She wanted to see
her fear echoed there for a long, sweet moment before she
blew him to hell. With an effort she got control. Standing,
carefully avoiding looking in Cuclillo's direction, she pulled
up her panties under her skirt and flushed the toilet.

The light from the twin brass wall lamps reflected from
the vanity mirror. It was streaked. She could make out the
faint letters traced by a finger wet with liquid soap: F R E
E D O, the M, if there was one, disappearing into the oak
mirror frame. The crazy impulse to laugh welled up.
FREEDO. She could use some of that herself. Large,
please, and hold the pepperoni. She stared at the streaky
letters until they suddenly blurred and she clutched at the
countertop with curling fingers. FREEDO . . . oh god, oh
god . . .

She turned on the tap and thrust her hands under it.
Taking her time, she splashed water over her face, partly
to relieve the burning in her eyes, partly to avoid facing
the terrorist just yet. When she shut off the tap, the pipes
shuddered in protest. Startled by the sudden noise, she
shot an appeasing look at Cuclillo, hating that she did it,
hating that she felt like a small, guilty child trying to
placate an angry parent.

She gave the man a wide berth and went back to the
Great Room. Just inside, she caught her breath. Iguana
stood only a half-dozen feet away near the double doors.
Not daring to look at Miranda, she moved toward the
middle of the room and sank to the floor beside Bru. He
was pretending sleep. Several minutes passed before she
heard him whisper, "Is it there?"

Her rage melted to a sick fear. This was crazy. One gun against an arsenal. Hesitating, she stared at the patch of rug that lay between them, at the stubble of fibers gray in the dimness. She could say no. She could say Miranda had failed, the gun wasn't there. Her eyes dragged toward him. Please, she thought, don't let him do it. If he failed, they'd kill him. She tried to form the word that would keep him from it, keep him alive. Instead, to her dismay she whispered, "Yes. It's there."

As if in sleep, Bru slid his left hand into the pool of light from the end-table lamp. Opening his eyes to slits, he read the time: 3:40. Almost two hours had passed since Sally made sure the gun was there. It was nearly time.

Both the others were in place. At 1:30 Sir William had gone to the bathroom. On his return he contrived to find a place to lie down near the entry hall doors at the west end of the room only a few yards from Cuclillo. Alex Borden had moved to a small couch a few yards from the door nearly an hour ago. They were the only two hostages in that end of the room.

He felt uneasy about Borden. He had been drinking heavily before and during dinner and he had put away several brandies afterward. Bru suspected the man's macho act might be covering up a case of nerves. But there was no other choice; no one else had ended up close enough for communication. The musicians were at the east end of the room near the fireplace, and Tim Jefferson was huddled with Lillian and the rest of the staff beneath the balcony.

He rolled over and stole a look at the setup: Cuclillo in front of the double doors just inside the room. To his right, about fifteen feet away, Iguana, standing back to the wall, rifle at his hip. Bru's anger surged at the sight of the terrorist leader. Keep it cool, he told himself. Stay in control. Getting uptight wasn't the way to do it.

Bru went over the plan again: His target was Cuclillo. Drop him, then cover Iguana. Sir William had to grab

Cuclillo's rifle and aim for El Poeta on the balcony. Tight. Fortunately, El Poeta was still sleeping. They'd have a second or two. Borden's job was to disarm Iguana and get the canister. Bru had rehearsed the scenario a dozen times in his mind; he hoped the others had, too. They weren't going to get a second wake-up call.

It was 3:45. Time. Bru opened his eyes. He lay there for a few moments, blinking as if he had just wakened, staring at Iguana. The terrorist leader caught the movement. Bru slowly thrust his hand in the air. "Bathroom." Out of the corner of his eye he caught a glimpse of Sir William, who moved slightly as if his sleep had been disturbed.

At Iguana's nod, Bru got to his feet. As he expected, Cuclillo dropped back a few feet into the entry hall and gestured for him to pass.

The air in the bathroom felt chilly. The Maxi Pad box sat to the left of the toilet next to the vanity. He shot a quick glance at Cuclillo as a series of sharp coughs from Sir William diverted the terrorist's attention. It was enough. As Bru leaned forward, his jacket hung open. A moment more and he had the Walther tucked inside his belt. The harsh flush of the toilet masked the click of the safety.

Bru entered the Great Room a few steps ahead of Cuclillo. A quick glance told him Iguana was still standing by the wall about five yards away.

"One thing more—" Bru swung back toward Cuclillo. This time the Walther was in his hand. He fired point-blank and the terrorist spun and fell. As Sir William grabbed the rifle and aimed at the balcony, Bru leveled the gun at Iguana. "Drop it."

At the shot El Poeta scrambled to his feet. A woman's scream wavered and rose. The terrorist's rifle jerked away as a burst of shots from below split his chest.

Iguana's rifle clattered to the floor. Tim Jefferson darted from the shadows, snatched it up, and backed away as if to shield the women huddled below the balcony.

Panting, Alex Borden leaped forward and grabbed Iguana's handgun. His eyes glittered with excitement.

The silver canister glinted in Iguana's hand. He held it out toward Borden like a talisman and backed away. "I open it, you die."

"Get it," yelled Bru.

Iguana steadied the cylinder against his thigh. His hands worked the top.

"The canister!"

Eyes wild, Borden swung the gun toward Iguana's chest. His finger tightened on the trigger.

"The canister," screamed a woman. "Shoot!"

The muzzle of Borden's gun slid reflexively downward . . . toward the glint of silver. . . .

"Jesus!"

Bru saw it in agonizing slow motion: the inexorable movement of Borden's finger as it squeezed the trigger; the flash; the buffeting sound waves. . . .

. . . jesus, jesus, jesus . . .

It took the eternity of a blink for the canister to rupture and the red gush of Iguana's blood to mingle with the milky spatterings of *Yersinia pestis 18*.

Chapter 28

"DON'T MOVE!" THE AUTHORITY IN BRU'S VOICE FROZE everyone, but it was directed at Alex Borden.

Iguana lay crumpled on the floor at Borden's feet. Groaning, the terrorist clawed at his leg. The muscles of his thigh, already in spasm from the wound, bulged in an odd curve over his shattered femur. Bright blood spread through his fingers, pooling on the floor, mingling with the broth from the punctured canister.

Borden looked down at the gun he held. Milky liquid spotted the barrel and his hand. The shock in his eyes turned to horror and he flung the gun onto the floor. Muscles tensed, he stared wildly around the room.

"Don't. Don't run." Bru leveled the Walther at Borden. "If you move, I'll shoot."

Ashley Borden gave an anguished wail. "Daddy!" She tried to dart toward him, but Nathan Katz held her back. "Let me go." She clawed at the boy's hand until crescents of blood spouted, but he held fast. "Let me go, you shit. Daddy—"

Bru's eyes narrowed in pain. "We don't have a choice," he said to the girl. "He's contaminated." Then to the others: "Get back. Everyone. Over there." His chin jerked toward the fireplace.

The group behind Borden shrank back. Staring, hugging the wall, they slid toward the musicians at the east end of the room.

The desperation in Borden's eyes grew. "For God's sake, man."

The fight suddenly went out of Ashley. Moaning, she fell to her knees, and Paige Cole wrapped the girl in her arms.

At the sudden crackle from Iguana's transceiver, Bru and Sir William exchanged startled glances. Outside. They'd heard the shots. . . . "Cover him," Bru yelled. "I'll get the other rifle."

Sir William aimed the SIG at Borden.

Bru grabbed Cuclillo's handgun and threw it to Sir William, who caught it with one hand. A volley of rapid Spanish came over the speaker. Bru ran into the entry hall and sprinted up the stairs to the balcony. Grabbing El Poeta's transceiver, he tossed it down to Tony Herrera. "Talk to them. Try to hold them off." He pitched the Walther PPK to Lillian and threw the terrorist's handgun to Dave Cole. "I'll cover the kitchen door." Snatching up El Poeta's rifle, he ran down the narrow back stairs.

Tony stared blankly at the transceiver for a moment.

Then, switching it on, he muffled his voice and spoke in a credible imitation of Iguana. A pause, a reply, and he switched off. "I think they bought it," he said with a faint grin. "I told them I had to kill one of you motherfuckers."

Sally turned in surprise. "You sounded like him."

Still holding the rifle on Borden, Sir William said, "We can't depend on that. If they suspect, I scarcely think they'd tell us so. We've got to be ready for them." Then to Nathan: "Take this." He held out the handgun. "Walk near the wall. Stay clear of the canister. The rest of you look sharp to the windows."

Nathan moved slowly, muscles tensing as he passed by each of the tall windows that led to the veranda. He reached for the gun as if it were alive.

Dave Cole's voice was urgent: "We've got to get out of here. This part of the building is contaminated." He glanced toward the west end of the room. Iguana, only semiconscious now, sprawled near the double doors; Alex Borden, eyes stricken, stood over him. "We can't go that way. We don't know how far the culture splattered." He stared around the room. "There's no other way out. We'll have to go outside. Leave through a window and circle around to the kitchen."

Tuck Perry spoke up from the knot of musicians. "That's crazy." Her eyes flicked toward the veranda. "The lights are on out there. They'll see us."

Sir William glanced outside. The moon had set and the woods were black beyond the yellow lights. The girl was right; they were going to be an easy mark as long as the lights were on. But staying here might be worse. His eyes met the doctor's. "Have we a choice?"

Dave shook his head. "Not unless they were lying about what was in that canister."

Sir William was silent for a long moment. Then he looked at the window again. "It seems we'll have to have a go."

"But what about them?" Sally's gaze darted toward

Borden and the wounded terrorist. "We can't leave them in here alone. He needs help."

"Help 'Guano'?" came an incredulous voice. It was Tony Herrera. "Piss on him."

"He's still a human being—"

"Bullshit. Where's the evidence?"

Dave Cole broke in. "There's nothing we can do for either one of them. Not until we have some kind of isolation setup."

"She's quite right, though. We can't leave our erstwhile captor here alone." Sir William glanced toward the gun Borden had dropped. "What happens if he comes round and decides to have at us with that pistol."

Lillian took a quick step toward the gun.

"Don't touch it," snapped the ambassador. "Get back."

A voice came from the shadows. "I'll stay." It was Leroy Jefferson.

"Perhaps we should draw lots," said Sir William.

"Nosir." Leroy turned his gaze toward Iguana. "I 'spect it's my job to stay." His eyes were impassive, but a steel edge underlay his soft voice.

Sir William raised an eyebrow. "There's danger."

"I reco'nize that."

Why was the man so determined? Why more than the rest of them? Sir William glanced at Tim Jefferson. Was it because of the boy? As quickly as the thought came, he knew the answer: Leroy had had to choose between sacrificing his grandson or betraying the island, his wife, his home. He stared at the old man for a moment, then nodded. "You'll need a pistol."

"Take mine," said Dave Cole. "I'm no good with those things anyway." As he handed Leroy the gun that Bru had tossed down to him, the quick look of relief on Dave's face gave way to guilt. "We'll be back to help you as soon as we can. Just don't touch anything." Dave looked around the room. "That goes for everybody. Don't touch anything. Don't get it on your hands. That stuff could kill all of us."

A low moan came from Alex Borden. He began to shake, and the shaking grew to a terrible, racking tremor. He stretched out his hands. "Do you see?" He turned from one to the other. "Do you see?" With eyes as wide as a child's he stared at his hands, at his trembling fingers. "It's on my hands. It's on my fucking *hands*."

"Oh, Christ," said Tony. "He's pissed himself."

Nathan Katz stared down at the handgun he held and wondered what he would do if he had to use it. In spite of vicarious forays through Ken Follett novels and daydreams that cast him as a suntanned, rifle-wielding Israeli, he had never held a gun before. He slid an uneasy glance toward the veranda, then back to Dave Cole. "I know you're a doctor, but that stuff in the canister can't fly." He indicated Borden and Iguana. "Why can't we just walk by them. We don't have to touch anything."

"It might as well have wings," said Dave. "If you get it on your shoes, you'll contaminate the floor in the rest of the building. When it dries, it won't take much of an air current to move it. If you walk through that end of the room, you're going to end up breathing the stuff. And what's left is going to settle on your food, and your clothes, and the water you drink."

Lillian's eyes were wide with fear. "Bru—what about him? He went out that way."

The ambassador shook his head. "He was by the door—on the far side of them. He was safe enough there." Sir William looked toward the doctor for confirmation. "Wasn't he?"

Dave avoided his eyes. "No one's safe," he said slowly. "None of us. All we can do is try to lower the odds."

"But we can't just parade out there under their noses," Nathan said. "You can see the windows from the board-walk. I know you can. I was up on the tower a couple of days ago and—"

Tony interrupted. "We don't dare turn off the lights. They won't buy that on top of the gunshots."

"No," said Lillian, "but maybe we could put out one light at the edge of the porch."

"How?" Tim Jefferson's black eyes showed doubt. "They're all on the same circuit."

"Wait." Paige Cole peered up at the porch lamp just outside. Its yellow light threw a fuzzy nimbus around her curly hair. "It's high, but I think I can get to it." She stood and tugged at the latch. With a sound somewhere between a groan and a sigh, the window opened and a cold breeze swept into the room.

"Be careful," Tuck Perry whispered.

"Give me that thing," said Paige.

Tuck touched her music stand. "This?" she asked in surprise.

"Yeah. Give it to me."

Tuck tossed the open sheet music onto her flute case and handed the flimsy metal music stand to Paige, who flipped it shut. Now it looked more like a slim metal broom.

Tony Herrera suddenly realized what Paige was going to do. "No, don't!" But he was too late. With a sudden thrust of her arm, she gave the lamp a whack. The bulb shattered, plunging a segment of the veranda in shadow. "Oh, shit," he said. "They heard that. They had to."

"Not from here," said Nathan. "But maybe they saw." He stared into the night. They could be anywhere, he thought. He was afraid he'd see someone moving out there, but he was more afraid that he might not see until it was too late. The gun was heavy. His finger moved tentatively toward the trigger.

"Go on," said a voice from the entry hall. It was Bru, alerted by the sound of breaking glass. "Don't wait." He motioned Paige on. "I'll cover you from the kitchen side."

"Come on," Paige said. Her thin skirt rippled in the wind as she stepped over the sill. In a moment she was gone.

"You next," Nathan whispered to Tuck Perry.

Clutching her flute case, the girl moved toward the

window, then froze. "I can't." She whirled toward him, her blond hair whipping against her cheeks. "I can't."

Nathan stared at her for a moment and then grabbed Ashley by the hand. "Come on. We'll all go together." With a bravado he did not feel, he added, "I've got a gun." It felt clammy as if it had been greased.

One hand clinging to the sill, Tuck stared out into the dark. Then with a sudden movement she thrust a leg over the sill and was gone. With a last, frantic look across the room at her father, Ashley Borden followed.

As Nathan stepped through the tall window, he heard the crackle of the transceiver and a low-pitched voice. "They *did* buy it," said Tony triumphantly. "They're still looking for the guy that landed at the lighthouse." He listened for a moment. "This one's down at the stable." Then shock entered his voice. "The other one—the one he's talking to—he's by the kitchen shed."

Eyes dilating in the shadows, Nathan stared at the dark corner of the house. "Ashley. Come back." But the wind shredded his urgent whisper. "Come back," he said again, and stretched out his hand in the empty blackness, but no one answered. Ashley was gone.

Heart pounding in his throat, he waited a second more. Then he followed.

At the sound that came through the wall, Calvin grimaced in his sleep and threw a hand over his face. In his dream he clung to the black mane of a galloping horse. Faster. He had to go faster. The monster was right behind him. "Now," he yelled. The horse spread its wings and sailed up on the wind. Suddenly there was an ear-splitting crack. Broken . . . its wing was broken. . . . They spun in narrowing circles until his stomach lurched from dizziness. He couldn't hold on. He couldn't. The black mane turned to grease and slid through his fingers. He fell with the speed of a bullet . . . into the monster's outstretched hand. He heard its stone-cold laugh and then it opened its bulging eye. . . .

The sound came again: a low-pitched crackling. Calvin was suddenly awake, staring blindly in the dark. Again a hiss, a crackling like fire. It was coming from outside. Scrambling to his knees, he ran his fingers over the splintered planks and put his eye to the crack he found. The water trough was a black rectangle against the dark gray of the clearing. The moon had set and dawn was only a whisper.

The hiss again. This time voices came, speaking a language he did not know. He bit his lip. A walkie-talkie. With a walkie-talkie he could call the other bad guys. He shivered, partly from cold, partly from a deeper chill. Suddenly he heard a footstep crunch on the shell. An ink-black silhouette eclipsed his view. He held his breath. Moving with excruciating care, Calvin lay back down in the crevice of hay bales and pressed his check against the rough, dried grass. If he was very still, and very small, they wouldn't find him.

The dusty odor of hay filled his nose and made it itch. Not daring to move a hand to scratch, he twitched his nose in a vain attempt to stop the torment. A footstep again. Another, this one fainter. Was he going away? He wanted to look but he didn't dare. What if the man looked back? What if he could see inside? He concentrated on the sounds: the faint creak of leather, the whisper of cloth on cloth.

A whippoorwill began its night cry, an endless looping call. Why didn't it stop? Why didn't it? He could hear nothing else. Nothing but the bird. The man could be anywhere—in the stable, anywhere—and he wouldn't know. Why didn't it stop?

Abruptly it did. And in the overwhelming silence in its wake, he wanted its noisy voice again. He was going to sneeze.

He had to move, had to do something. He grabbed his nose and pinched. The impulse waned, but came back worse. He buried his nose in his hands, pinching, pressing. Half strangling, he gasped, and gave a muffled sniff.

And for a moment he thought that he had beaten it, defused the awful treachery of his body. In that moment the sneeze came—a shuddering sneeze—loud enough, it seemed, to wake the world.

Silence.

Oh, mommy, mommy.

A shoe swiveled on jagged shards of bone-bleached shell. . . .

Oh, no, oh, please, oh, no.

A click, a hiss, a voice, low and excited . . .

He could hear him moving.

The sound of footsteps was fainter now. Was he going away? Scarcely daring to hope, Calvin pressed his ear close to the crack.

Suddenly he heard it again, louder now: the faint scuffling squeak of a shoe on sand. Calvin's eyes darted toward the sound. He was coming back, coming back, coming into the stable.

There was utter silence in the Great Room where Tony Herrera looked up from the transceiver. "The guy by the kitchen shed—he's leaving. He's heading for the stables on the double."

"Thank God," said Sally. Then, suddenly suspicious, "Why? Why there?"

"One of them heard something. The man they're after. They're going to double-team him, I guess."

She looked away and squeezed her eyes shut. Oh, God. When does it end? she thought. Was it ever going to? She stared around the big room. Pools of blood from the dead men were black in the dimness. Involuntarily she moved closer to the window and drew a long, shuddering breath.

"You could call them off," Miranda said to Tony. She stood with her arm around Cass Tompkins's shoulder, steadying her. Cass, still clutching the body of her little dog, swayed from the aftermath of shock and too much liquor. "They'd listen to you."

"That would be pressing our luck, I'm afraid," said Sir William.

"Call 'em all back here," said Cass thickly. "Blow the fuckers away." With an exaggerated tip of her head, she turned to stare at Iguana. "Do you hear me? You motherfucking gringo."

"He's not a gringo," said Miranda in a low voice.

"Don't tell *me*." Cass swiveled her nose until it was almost level with her secretary's. "I know a motherfucking gringo when I see one." She turned her indefinite gaze to take in the others. "In-n that right?"

Sally bit her lip. She wasn't sure if it was to keep from laughing or from crying. It was ludicrous, Cass swaying, holding a dead dog wearing a designer sweater. Ludicrous and somehow terrible. The salt taste of blood was in her mouth. Oh, sweet Jesus. Why didn't she put him down?

Sir William said, "While there's a diversion, I suggest we move round to the kitchen as quickly as we can. Those with arms pair off with the unarmed. And the first inside shut those doors to the entry hall."

"Come on," said Tim Jefferson. Shouldering the SIG rifle, he went through the window, froze for a moment, then motioned for Sally to follow. With a quick breath, she stepped over the low sill. The chill night wind bit through the thin wool of her dress and whipped her skirt around her legs. Shivering, pressing close to the wall, she crept to the edge of the veranda and stepped off. The high heel of her sandal sank into the sand. She clutched at a low branch for support and looked in vain for Tim. Where was he?

She stared toward the corner of the house. There, thank God. Just ahead. A crepe myrtle stretched out bony branches and clawed her hair. Her eyes flicked from side to side as she threaded her way along the wall, but it was impossible to see much of anything. She imagined the terrorists watching her, watching through those awful goggles, laughing to themselves as they took aim. Don't think about it, she told herself. It didn't pay to think about things like that.

The fireplace wall was cold against her groping finger-tips. One step. Another. A tangled snare of ivy caught her heel and she fell, scraping her knee against the rough wall. Tim grasped her arm and steadied her. "We'll make it," he whispered.

A palmetto frond rattled against Tim's leg as he pushed past. Then, miraculously, she saw the faint gleam of the kitchen window. They ran the last few steps, clattering across the little porch, pushing open the door.

Relief flooded Bru's face when he saw them.

"Thank God," said Paige Cole. The surprised look on her face changed to alarm. "Where's Ashley? She was right behind us."

"And Nathan," said Tuck. "Where are they?"

Sally stared blankly at the two of them, then at Tim. She saw her questioning look reflected in his dark face. "I don't know," she said. "We didn't see them."

Chapter 29

THE ONLY LIGHT IN THE DINING ROOM CAME FROM THE ADJA-cent entry hall. The curtains, closed except for a narrow flap at the center window, rippled as the muzzle of the SIG automatic rifle slid toward the dark glass, paused, and moved slowly toward the north. The kitchen door swung open, throwing a yellow rectangle halfway across the room. Sir William glanced up from his post at the window as Bru came in. "Quiet so far," he said. "Are the lookouts in place?"

Bru nodded. Armed with one of the rifles, Tim Jeffer-son had just gone up to the third floor. From the Coles' room he could cover the road and a stretch of prairie. Tony Herrera, stationed on the tiny utility porch off the kitchen, was backup.

The ambassador glanced toward the kitchen. "Have they all got through?"

"Tony Herrera and Lillian just made it," said Bru. Lillian had insisted on staying in the Great Room until everyone else had gone.

"That's everyone, then."

Bru shook his head. "Still no sign of Nathan and the Borden girl." Slinging his rifle over his shoulder, he glanced at his watch and reached for the radiotelephone. Less than twenty minutes had passed since the canister was punctured, but it seemed at least twice that long.

A guarded male voice answered. "Booth here."

"This is Bruton Farrier. Get me the McIntosh Sheriff's Department."

"You've got the FBI here. What's your situation?"

"We've taken over the lodge. Iguana is wounded. Two other terrorists are dead."

Booth's voice rang with relief. "Good work."

"Maybe not," said Bru. "The canister—that plague broth—it's punctured. Iguana and one of our people were splashed with the stuff."

There was a long pause.

Bru went on: "The terrorists outside the building don't know what happened. So far it's quiet, but I don't know how long we can hold them off. The quicker you send in the marines, the better we'll like it."

"Right. I'll get back to you with instructions."

"Wait. Give me an operator."

Booth was gone. In half a minute a woman's voice came on the line. She sounded young and very tense. "Get me Wally Carruthers," said Bru. "McIntosh Sheriff's Department."

A minute more passed before the operator came back. "Trying another number," she said. Silence, then Wally's gruff voice came on.

"Wally, it's Bru. We've taken over the lodge."

"Thank God."

"The FBI knows. They're monitoring the line. But we've got big trouble. The plague canister took a bullet. It's ruptured."

There was a quick intake of breath. "Get everybody out of the area."

"We did that. We had to go outside and circle around to the kitchen. We wouldn't have made it except for the lawman on the island. One of the terrorists spotted him and called in the others. It gave us an opening."

"What man?"

"I don't know. The guy landed near the lighthouse. There was an explosion. It blew up the boat, but somebody made it to shore. They've been after him for hours. Now they're closing in."

A pause, longer than the first. This time Wally's voice was low—so low that Bru had trouble hearing him. "That's not a man they're after," he said. "It's a kid, a little boy. His name is Calvin."

Calvin's heart thumped in his throat. The man was at the end of the stable. Waiting. It seemed like hours since he had heard the last faint footstep. Scarcely daring to breathe, the boy began to creep across the hay toward the half door of the feed room. Why had he closed it? If it was open, maybe he could run.

He froze as a new sound came from the distance. A rustling. No. It was the crackle of the walkie-talkie. But it was coming from the wrong direction. It was coming from somewhere in the woods at the other end of the stable.

Two? There couldn't be two men, he thought frantically. Not two of them after him at once.

The low mutter of a voice . . . a footstep. No. Not a footstep at all, but the sound of a hoof glancing off splintered shell. Then he became aware of the low-pitched panting of Cajun, echoed by the even breathing of another horse just across the stable aisle.

The voice again. This time there was no mistaking the sound of a shoe scraping on coarse sand.

His heart was a drummer in his ear. He had to do something. Had to. Had to.

He remembered the metal scoops—two of them—hanging on the wall beside the feed cans. He slid his hand along the side wall. Fingers outstretched, he traced the inch-wide gaps between the planks. Something cold and metallic swung away at his touch. Then his hand closed over it.

The feed scoop was a puny weapon. Clutching it, he stared blindly into the dark.

Another step, this one closer.

Another.

Squeezing his eyes shut, Calvin flung the scoop with all his might.

A thud as the scoop struck flesh . . . an anguished whinny, then the clatter of metal on shell and the louder clatter of horses' hooves stampeding toward the fence.

The man's shout drove an electric shock through his chest. Then he was climbing, hand over hand, up the rough plank wall toward the vaulting roof.

The wall ended abruptly. His hand scrabbled out in the darkness. The rafter was nearly a yard away and splintered. Half turning, he grasped it; teetering, he reached out with his other hand, grabbed hold, and swung free.

Sally looked around the storeroom. "I'm not much help, I guess." The room was no bigger than a walk-in closet, but its unfinished wooden shelves stretched to the ceiling, each crammed with supplies.

"Over there." Lillian nodded toward the back. "Next to the white box." She added a half-full carton of Lysol to the assortment of bags and boxes by the door.

Sally scanned the shelf and spotted the disposable kitchen gloves next to a large box of Pampers. "Diapers?" It was somehow incongruous to think of diapers here, now.

"You'd be surprised how often people show up with everything they need for their baby except enough didies.

We have to keep them on hand. There's no RevCo on the next block, you know.'' Lillian tugged at a heavy roll of plastic shelf liner. "We keep all sorts of drugstore things.''

"What about bandages?'' asked Sally. "Tape? That sort of thing?''

"Some,'' said Lillian. "But not in here. There's a first-aid kit in the cabinet by the back stairs.''

The door to the kitchen swung open. Dave Cole scooped up two of the cartons and glanced at the box of gloves Sally added to the stack. "Good,'' he said. "But we're going to need isolation gowns, too. Enough for several people. We're going to have to move Borden and Iguana into the entry hall near the bathroom, near a water source. They can't stay where they are now. Not for long . . .'' His voice trailed away.

He was right, Sally thought. He couldn't stay there. Not with three dead men in the room. Not unless help came soon.

"Can you use sheets for gowns?'' asked Lillian. "Lena's getting them now.''

"I don't know,'' he said doubtfully. "They're too easily contaminated. I'd give a front tooth for an autoclave right now.''

"Autoclave?''

"It's a sterilizer.'' Sally tried to remember what she knew about making do in emergencies. Most of it had been about home deliveries. "We could use the oven,'' she began. "No—'' No, they couldn't. They'd contaminate the kitchen. Then as a thought struck, "How about plastic garbage bags? We could use them once and then soak them in Lysol.''

"Maybe,'' said Dave, "if they're not too thin. If they tear we're in for it.'' He turned toward the kitchen. "Let's get the rest of this stuff laid out.''

The kitchen shades were drawn. In the hubbub of the brightly lighted room, it was almost possible to forget the armed men prowling the island outside. The long kitchen table had been transformed into a supply depot. Paige

Cole, emptying the boxes as quickly as she got them, added a stack of black garbage bags next to a thick pile of clean dish towels. "I'm just unpacking," she said to Sally. "You can shuffle the stacks."

Sally stared at the table. The makeshift isolation supplies had to be separated from the rest of it. They were going to need more space. She glanced across the room at the worktable, but Tuck Perry had taken it over, slicing ham and turkey for sandwiches, pulling out a giant wedge of pale cheese from a round wooden box.

The thought of food made Sally slightly nauseated. Her head was pounding. Someone had put on coffee, and the smell of it was filling the room. Maybe a cup would help her headache. "We need to pool all the medicine," she said to Lillian. "Aspirin, codeine, anything we have. I've got a bottle of Tylenol in my room and some Benadryl."

"There's no telling what's up in my apartment. I'm afraid I never toss out old prescriptions like they tell us to." Lillian pulled a set of master keys from a hook near the door. "I'll clean out my medicine chest and pick up your supply." She headed for the dining room door.

"No," said Dave Cole. "Don't go that way. We can't use the main stairs."

Lillian turned. "Why?"

"Most of the second floor is open to the balcony. When that culture dries, it's going to be airborne. Anyone without protective clothes is going to be contaminated."

Miranda Gervin was pouring Zinfandel into a water glass. The wine bottle clunked down onto the counter. "You mean we can't use our rooms?" She handed the glass to Cass Tompkins, who huddled in a chair near the stove.

"Not if they're on the second floor. The third floor is okay, I think, but we'll have to use the back stairs."

As Lillian disappeared up the kitchen stairs, Cass took a gulp of the Zinfandel. Some of the red wine sloshed out of the glass, speckling the fur of the dead dog in her lap. Blinking, Cass dabbed at the drops that streaked her fingers like blood. "I'm sorry. I'm sorry, baby." Fat tears greasy with mascara began to glide down her face.

"I've got to get her to bed," said Miranda. "She's been through more than she can handle."

"I haven't been through more'n a few drinks," protested Cass.

Miranda and Sally exchanged a glance.

Cass's face twisted. " 'S true." Purple eye shadow streaked the creases of her lids. Somehow she reminded Sally of a child, a little girl caught trying on her mamma's makeup. "It's all right," she whispered. "It's going to be all right." She ran warm water over a dish towel, wrung it out, and gently wiped Cass's face. Then reaching into a slim pocket in her skirt, Sally pulled out her key and handed it to Miranda. "You can take her up to my room. It's on the third floor." She glanced up as Lena Jefferson, black arms wrapped around a stack of white sheets, came down the back stairs. "But, please," Sally added quickly, "don't take the dog up there."

Paige Cole pulled a black garbage bag from the stack on the table and held it out to Cass. "You can put him in here."

Cass stared at the bag without comprehension. Then her eyes widened and she jerked back and shook her head. One hand crept toward Miranda's arm, the other clutched the dead Caligula.

Lena set the linens on the counter and stared at Cass for a long moment. Then turning, she took the empty cheese box from the worktable and pressed a folded sheet inside it, her dark fingers tucking the corners, following the curves of the round wooden box. She set it down by Cass's chair. "It's time, Miz Tompkins. Time to put him to bed now."

Cass looked at her uncertainly.

"Time for bed," Lena repeated. "I'll help you." Slowly she lifted the little dog from Cass's lap and laid him in the box. With a gnarled finger she freed a snagged loop of his sweater from a splinter. "There. Now, isn't that a fine bed?"

Cass's gaze slid toward the box, then back to Lena. She nodded faintly.

Lena stood. "Time for your bed, too, Miz Tompkins. Let's us go on up now." Nodding again, Cass rose unsteadily to her feet, and flanked by Lena and Miranda started up the back stairs.

Sally stared down at the cheese box, at the little dog curled inside it. When she was sure Cass was gone, she slid the lid in place and it settled down with a faint whooshing sound. A sense of unreality struck her. As if to validate herself, she ran her fingers over the pale, splintery wood of the lid. Three dead men in the other room, she thought, and Caligula gets the casket. She felt a wild impulse to laugh.

A shadow fell over the box and she looked up quickly. It was Bru. "Caligula brand cheddar?" he asked.

The laugh came burbling up, shaking her, choking her.

"Sorry. That was in bad taste."

She felt her throat close over the lump there. For a moment no sound came, and then the sobs began: harsh, ripping, as if they tore through flesh. His arms closed around her and he drew her up, held her close. "Get it out," he whispered. "Get it all out."

She clung to him; she did not know for how long. Then faintly, as if from a great distance away, she heard the voices of Tuck and Paige blending in a close, sweet harmony as they sang:

Michael, row the boat ashore,
  Al-la-lu-ya,
Michael, row the boat ashore,
  Al-la-lu-oo-ya. . . .

Digging her fingers into the muscles of his back, she clung to Bru as if to let go would be to die. And slowly, very slowly, she felt the warmth and strength of his body creep into hers.

> *Jordan's River is chilly and cold,*
> *Al-la-lu-ya,*
> *Kills the body, but not the soul,*
> *Al-la-lu-oo-ya. . . .*

Chapter 30

CALVIN THREW A LEG OVER THE RAFTER AND SWUNG UP. A long splinter drove into the flesh of his palm. Gasping, he lost his balance for a moment and swayed like a drunken thing on the timber.

His heart pounded in his ears like storm surf, half drowning out the shouts of the men. He could hear them coming; he could hear their feet scrabbling on the gravel. He had to hurry . . . had to hurry. . . .

It was pitch-black under the roof. Hand over hand, he crept along the rafter. Its rough edge cut into his knees. If he could make it across, he'd be all right. At the other side of the stable several long boards had been stored crosswise on the rafters. He could go there. Hide there.

His toe dug into the rafter, then slid off, swung into space, caught on something curved. For a moment he panicked. Then he knew what it was: the wheel. The old wagon wheel had been wired to the bottom of the rafter in the center of the aisle. He was halfway across then. Halfway.

Footsteps. A voice—from just beneath him.

A light blazed—a brilliant yellow light swinging from a

single naked bulb. The boy's eyes squeezed shut. Don't let them look up . . . don't let them look up. . . .

Oh, please, oh, please . . . oh, please . . .

"First the gown goes on," Sally said to the small group assembled in the dining room. The isolation gown, jerry-rigged of snipped and taped plastic bags, rustled as she took it from the little stack on the dining room table. She pulled it over her head, layering the jeans and sweatshirt she had hurriedly changed into, settling the black plastic garbage bag over her torso. "Sleeves" made from smaller white plastic bags covered her arms.

At one end of the table, Paige Cole, snuffling from another allergy attack—this one from Lysol fumes—was taping the white bags to the hastily cut black ones, the stack of "gowns" growing as she worked. At the other end, Lillian tucked more white plastic bags next to a pile of thin bird's-eye dish towels, a roll of masking tape, and a large box of disposable kitchen gloves.

Dave Cole, wearing a makeshift gown and gloves, tied a split-tailed dish towel over his nose and mouth. It made a passable mask.

Sally handed a rain slicker to him. The rain cape was sturdier than the flimsy plastic bags, and Leroy needed the extra protection.

"I'll get it to him right now." Dave Cole's voice was muffled by the mask. Poking the slicker into a bag along with gloves, peroxide, dish towels, and extra plastic bags, he turned to Sally. "As soon as the lesson's over and everyone's gowned up, come on in. I'm going to need all the help I can get." At her nod, he went into the entry hall and closed the door behind him.

Sally took two white bags from the table and held them up. "Next, shoe covers." As if they'd never seen a plastic bag before, she thought. She felt faintly ridiculous, the way she imagined airline stewardesses did when they demonstrated seat belts to passengers. She slid a sneakered foot into one bag, then the other, and secured the tops around her ankles with twists of masking tape.

Tuck Perry retrieved the tape, tore off two pieces, and taped a grocery bag on the door to the entry hall. The bag was crudely lettered with a black Magic Marker:

!!KEEP OUT!!
UNLESS YOU'RE WEARING MASK & GLOVES

At the bottom someone had written in a different hand, ALSO GOWN AND SHOE COVERS.

"Now the mask," Sally held up a dish towel folded the long way. It had been torn at both ends. Two strips dangled from each side, leaving only the area in the center intact. "Cover your mouth and nose with it, and tie it twice," Demonstrating, she caught a strip in each hand, knotted it at the back of her head, and repeated the process with the other two strips.

Bru and Miranda Gervin mimicked her actions. As the cloth tightened over her face, Miranda muttered something about "smothering." She said it lightly, but her eyes, pale gray above the mask, looked uneasy as she glanced toward the door that led to the entry hall.

"Don't worry about getting enough air," she said, knowing Miranda wasn't concerned about that, knowing that what really frightened her was the idea of going through that door with only a flimsy piece of cloth between her and contamination. The masks wouldn't be safe for long, either; as soon as they were moist they'd have to be discarded. Sally glanced at the little pile of dish towels, calculating how long they would last. When they ran out, they'd have to start tearing up sheets.

Sally pulled on a pair of disposable gloves and topped them with a second pair, hoping everything she was demonstrating would sink in. Their safety depended on it. She wished no one had to go back in there, but somebody had to take care of Iguana.

She held up her gloved hands. "Wear two pairs."

While you can, she was thinking. The gloves were more critical than the masks. When they were gone, there would be no replacing them. "The outside of everything you've got on is considered contaminated. So don't touch your face, no matter what."

Sally went through a mental checklist as she looked at Bru and Miranda. "Okay," she said slowly. "I guess we're ready." Grabbing up a dozen bath towels, she opened the door to the foyer. "Can you guys get that?" She nodded toward the garbage can near the Franklin stove. "It's heavy." The can was filled with several gallons of strong Lysol solution.

Bru grabbed one side and Miranda the other. Balancing the garbage can between them, they carried it into the entry hall. The double doors to the Great Room beyond were closed.

Their plastic shoe covers whispered over the glossy parquet floor. Moving carefully to keep from slipping, Sally laid the stack of towels in front of the dining room door. The towels were her own innovation; it seemed to her that by discarding one layer of soiled towels after another, the doorway might be kept cleaner. The garbage can, sloshing with fluid, went just beyond. "When you go back out, put everything in the can except the inner pair of gloves," she said. "Take off the gown and mask first, then the shoe covers. You can turn them inside out, but don't shake them; they'll be loaded with bacteria. Just drop them in the Lysol. After that, step on the pile of towels and throw the outer pair of gloves into the can. And don't poke your fingers inside the gloves when you take them off. Remember, the outside is contaminated. Pull them off like this—" Holding up her hands, she pantomimed a tug at the tip of each finger.

"Don't touch the doorknob with the outer gloves—just the inside pair. When you go back into the dining room, close the door behind you and drop the inner gloves in the plastic bag by the door." She stared at Bru and Miranda intently, hoping she hadn't forgotten something vital; the crash course in isolation technique was half-assed at best. "Got it?"

The double doors to the Great Room slid open and Dave Cole stuck his head out. "We've got problems."

Bru's eyes widened innocently above his mask. "No shit?"

Ignoring the remark, Dave scanned the entry hall and shook his head. "I wanted to move him in here, but I don't see how . . . now that I've had a look at him." He glanced over his shoulder at Iguana, who lay sprawled where he had fallen. Only half conscious, the terrorist threw a hand to his face and moaned. "He's got a compound fracture of his femur. He needs traction." He stared around the entry hall again. "We can probably use the draperies."

"Draperies!" Miranda snorted at the idea.

"The cords and pulleys off them," Dave said defensively. "But there's no way we can set up in here. Nothing to hook on to."

Sally glanced at the wide stairway. "How about the banister? We could hang weights from there." They could use those empty lard buckets she had seen in the storage room. Fill them with cans or pickle jars. Surely there was something in the kitchen that would do.

Dave followed her gaze. "The stair rail occurred to me, too, but I don't think it'll work. We'll need countertraction, and there's just not enough space."

Leroy Jefferson, wearing the slicker now and a mask, pulled on a pair of gloves, crossed the Great Room, and picked up Iguana's handgun. "I be glad to see it gone," he said to Sally. "I been thinkin' on him waking up—an' it right there where he be lying."

Although he had stayed away from the gun, Sally saw in alarm that Leroy had covered the dead Cuclillo with rugs gathered from around the room. Too close to the canister, she thought. He shouldn't have gone near him without protection.

As if in answer, he said, "It wasn't right he be lyin'

there, staring out like that. It wasn't right, him with
nothin' over his eyes." The old man's dark hand looked
gray under the white, translucent glove.

Sally stared at the weapon he held. The splattered bacterial culture had begun to dry, mottling the barrel with pale,
dusty streaks. Recoiling, she pointed toward the garbage
can in the entry hall. "Drop it in there. Please."

Shuffling awkwardly in the bags hastily tied over his
shoes, Leroy nodded and moved past. The gun disappeared inside the garbage can with a splash.

At the sound, Alex Borden, slumped on a leather couch
near the fireplace, raised his hand and stared, bewildered,
at the others. He had put as much distance as possible
between himself and the ruptured canister. And he had
appropriated the mobile bar, pulling it protectively toward
the couch, his toe locked around its leg, his grip tightening
on a nearly empty bottle of Gilbey's.

Sally gave a little shrug that crinkled the plastic gown,
but she was thinking, Why not? Wouldn't she? . . . under
the circumstances. "He needs a mask," she said to Dave
Cole.

He shot a glance at Borden. "I tried. He won't keep it
on."

Then she saw the dish towel wadded in Borden's lap.
She took a step toward him, then stopped, remembering
the glistening streaks of bacterial broth on Borden's hands
when the canister ruptured. What good would a mask do
him now? she thought. But from a crevice of her brain
came the accented voice of Dr. Heidelmann, her old micro
professor: ". . . the larger the number of bacteria, the
worse the infection—and the sooner the manifestation of
disease. . . ." Strange. She hadn't thought of Heidelmann
in years. Uncertain, she looked at Dave. It seemed to her
that he was avoiding her gaze.

Borden tipped his head. "Godda cigarette?"

She shook her head. They had to do something for him.
At least get him washed up.

"Shee-it." He tipped the Gilbey's into focus, stared at

it for a moment, and raised it to his lips. Twin trickles of gin ran down the corners of his mouth.

Like saliva, Sally thought. Like a baby drooling. The sharp memory of a child she had nursed came to her then: Laird Farrier, three years old. Bru's little boy. He had died in her arms.

Dave Cole stared at Iguana, and then at Hoby's and Cuclillo's rug-covered bodies. "If we can't move him, we've got to move them. But where?"

Bru turned to him. "The wine cellar. We could put them down there." He glanced toward the balcony at the sprawling body of El Poeta. "That one, too. The cellar's under the stairs. It's locked, though. It always is."

"I'll get the keys." Sally went to the dining room door, then stopped. If she opened it, she'd have to discard a pair of gloves and there just weren't enough. "Hey," she called. "Open the door."

A moment passed, then another. The door opened a crack and Tuck Perry, holding a dish towel to her face, peeped out. "What is it?" Her green eyes were wide with alarm.

"We need the keys to the wine cellar."

"Wait." The door closed. In less than a minute, it opened just long enough for Tuck to throw a key to Sally. As she caught it, the door clicked shut again.

Bru took the key from her and glanced at Miranda. "Maybe we ought to wait for one of the men to help. This is going to be heavy work."

Miranda drew herself up. "I'm sure I can manage."

He gave her a sharp look. "All right. Let's start with this one." He grabbed the dead terrorist under the armpits. Miranda, staring for a moment, reached for his feet and hoisted. As she did, congealing blood spattered the floor and she gagged.

"Take a deep breath," said Sally. "It'll help." She needed one herself. Turning toward the open window, she sucked at the air for a minute, feeling its chill penetrate the mask, and waited for them to leave before she turned to help Dave Cole.

Iguana's eyes fluttered open.

"He's coming around," said Dave.

The two bent over him. Although at times their eyes strayed nervously toward the punctured canister, the wound in his thigh took most of their attention. Neither one of them could see the blood-spattered FM transceiver beneath Iguana's uninjured leg; neither one of them saw his fingers splaying and his hand creeping toward it.

Nathan Katz stared into the woods. "Ashley?" The wind and the rustling cedars swept away his harsh whisper. He bit his lip. She had been right there. Not more than a yard away. "Ashley?" he said again, louder this time. His grip tightened on the gun.

"Help me."

"Where? Where are you?"

"Here. I found the gate."

A shadow moved, jet against gray. He followed it and felt her hand graze his arm.

"I can't get it open," she whispered.

Hoping to God the safety was on, he shoved the gun into his belt and groped in the thick darkness for the gate. The iron railing was cold beneath his fingers. He found the latch and tugged. Nothing moved. The gate to the Sniveley family cemetery was old. He tried the latch again. This time he felt the long shaft of a horizontal bolt that ended in a metal loop. He slid it to the right, lifted, and the gate creaked open.

The small mausoleum, elevated against storm tides, sat in the center of a low knoll beneath the spreading branches of an old live oak. He caught Ashley's hand and felt his way up the steps. The wooden door was a dark blot against the pale marble. Let it be open, he thought, yet a part of him recoiled, and he hesitated, hand on the door. God. How could he be such an incredible jerk? There were men with guns crawling all over the island. At least, nobody in here was going to shoot at them.

The hinges groaned. A puff of musty air struck his

nostrils as the heavy door sighed open and they stepped inside.

"Don't close it," came Ashley's urgent whisper.

"Wait. I've got a light." Careful not to latch the door, Nathan pushed it shut and drew out a bent package of matches from his blazer pocket. The first match sparked and guttered out. The second flared, touching their lips with pale light, darkening their eyes with hollow shadows. "Dark as a tomb," he said, and wished he hadn't. His voice sounded strange to him inside the closet of marble. He held out the match.

"What's that?"

"Where?" As he turned, the match seared his fingers. He shook it out and fumbled in the dark for another.

"There?"

The match flame reflected on the curved surface of a small blue glass. The votive candle inside was half gone, its drowned wick congealed in pale wax like a bug in amber.

Ashley scratched at the wax and lifted the blackened wick with a fingernail. "Light it. Quick."

It took two matches from his dwindling supply, but finally the little candle caught. Its light flickered through the cobalt glass and, stretching like thin blue fingers across the pallid marble, touched the dark bronze plaques of the crypts. "We'll be safe here," he said, wishing he could be sure, wishing the trembling candlelight didn't remind him of fingers—of Alex Borden's hands. Coming here had seemed like a good idea, the only thing to do, really. When he found Ashley in the dark outside the lodge, it had made sense not to go back. It was only a matter of time before the other terrorists found out what had happened. He didn't want to think about the other thing—the plague. But his mind crept toward it as inexorably as the candle-light crept across the stone.

"I'm cold," said Ashley.

He felt her body tremble as he held her close, and for a moment it seemed as ephemeral as the candle flame. "Here.

Take my jacket." He started to pull away, but she clung to him. "No, don't . . . so cold. I'm so cold."

They sank to the stone floor and he cradled her against him, covering her as well as he could with arms and jacket. "We're all right," he told her. But the thought nagged at him: For how long? For how long without water, without food?

"Go to sleep if you can," he whispered. The half inch of wax was dwindling quickly. He stared at the candle, trying to draw warmth from it, trying not to think about how soon its flame would go out.

Dizzy with fright, Calvin clung to the narrow rafter. He could hear the men moving in the stable aisle below him. Only the narrow timber and the wagon wheel shielded him from the blazing light bulb that swayed beneath him.

Please . . . please . . . don't look up. . . .

One of the men turned sharply toward the feed room, rifle arcing, shadows bulging at his feet. The other swiveled, and then slowly raised the dark barrel of his rifle until its muzzle stopped only inches from the light.

The muzzle was huge; it was aimed at his eyes.

The boy's heart flipped inside his chest; his mouth slid open in a silent scream. Breath cut off, he shut his eyes and waited for the explosion.

Silence.

He opened his eyes a tiny crack and looked down at the terrorist drenched in light from the naked bulb.

Eyes squeezed nearly shut, the man blinked and stared past the wheel, past the narrow rafter, directly at the boy.

Slowly the rifle moved and slid away. It was only then that Calvin realized the man, staring with eyes long-accustomed to the dark, could not see him, could not penetrate the shadows, could not focus beyond the hot-white brilliance of the circling, blinding light.

*   *   *

Balancing on a leather easy chair, Sally teetered for a second as the heavy drapery cord popped loose from the traverse rod.

With a final tug, Dave Cole wrenched the brass curtain pulley from the wall. "First designer traction I ever set up." He examined it for a moment, cupping it in his gloved palm. "I hope it's sturdy enough." He glanced over his shoulder toward Iguana. "I hope he appreciates . . . Oh, my God!"

Whirling, Sally nearly fell. Clutching the wall for support, she stared at the terrorist.

The FM transceiver was pressed to his lips. And in the stark silence that followed, she could hear the low-pitched stream of Spanish and the repeated word that ended it:

". . . *venganza* . . . *venganza* . . . *venganza*. . . ."

Barely three minutes passed before the shooting started.

Chapter 31

DR. DANIEL ELTON WOKE ABRUPTLY AND TRIED TO FOCUS his eyes. It was cold in the bedroom—cold enough to hang meat, he thought—and the predawn grayness did nothing to give the illusion of warmth. Ginny, never one to tolerate much heat, had kept the thermostat locked on 68° all summer. Now that cold weather had set in and her pregnancy was more advanced, she had repeatedly flipped the heat cycle to off, or worse, fan only.

Shivering, he pulled a corner of the quilt over his bare shoulder and threw a resentful glance at the somnolent mound beside him. During the night, Ginny had contrived to steal most of the covers. He had never understood how she could enjoy a frostbitten nose and forty pounds of bedclothes, but the key word according to her was "heavy." By Ginny's standards it was impossible to be warm without heavy, and in order to tolerate heavy you had to have cold. Unassailable logic. And when the baby came, what then? Maybe if they gave him a little fur-lined hood and a bit of blubber to gum, he would acclimate.

He tried to doze off again, but within minutes he knew there was no sense in trying. Usually a heavy sleeper, he had tossed most of the night. When sleep finally came, it was disturbed with strange dreams that shattered and vanished when he opened his eyes. He tried to put last night's newscast out of his mind, but like the man who was told not to think of purple giraffes, he could think of nothing else.

It still did not seem real. How could it be real when everything had been so normal two days ago?

When he heard the news, he had reached for the phone three times. He had intended to call Bru's father, to offer what little consolation he could, but each time, not knowing what to say, he had put the receiver back on the hook. And what could he have said? Something banal, like "these things happen"? Or how about the meaningless "I'm sorry"? What good were they to a man whose son was a captive of terrorists? And yet, even as the thought came he knew he was rationalizing. "I'm sorry" meant just that. It meant that someone cared, that someone was there. The words had stuck in his throat, because behind them, overriding them, was the sharp knowledge that it could have been him, could have been them.

What was left was the guilt. Except for the caprice of fate and bureaucracy, he, Ginny, and an in-hock Cessna would have been there now. And all because of a can't-wait scenario about a trumped-up plague.

Ginny rolled over in her sleep. One hand cradled her swollen belly, the other pulled at the covers as she turned. He reached out, caressed her. It could have been us, he thought. Thank God, it wasn't.

In the dimness Elton held his watch to his nose, stabbed at its light, and peered myopically at the time. He groaned. It was too damned early for a rooster to crow, even if the rooster was compulsive about it. Fumbling for his glasses, he found them, slid them on, and reached for his robe.

He flipped on the kitchen light and switched the Mr. Coffee from automatic to manual before he headed into the bathroom. On the way, after a surreptitious glance toward the bedroom, he turned on the heat pump. The forecast called for a high of only 42° in Atlanta today, and God only knew what it was right now.

After his shower, he took his coffee to the window and peered out at the lawn for the *Constitution*. He saw nothing but scattered oak leaves turning from gray to brown in first light. The paper boy was probably still in bed, he thought ruefully. But there wouldn't be anything about St. Cyrils Island in it anyway. It had happened too late to make the morning paper.

He turned to the TV. CNN would have something. But as he reached for the switch, the phone rang. It was Jonah Schwartz, one of the epidemiologists who worked closely with the infectious disease specialists.

"What's happening?" asked Elton.

"Something's come up. You need to get down here."

"What? What's up?"

"I'll fill you in when you get here."

"See you," Elton muttered ungraciously. He hung up wondering why Schwartz was so evasive. It wasn't like him.

Grumbling to himself, Elton pulled on his clothes. Not even time for a goddamned doughnut, he thought. But in truth, he was glad of the diversion; it gave him something else to think about besides Bru.

Outside, the air was crisp and still after yesterday's blustery winds. He tossed a pile of papers and unmailed letters onto the passenger seat and slid into the car. The old Camaro, balking after the night's chill, coughed and cleared its throat before deigning to start. Picking up speed, it suddenly lurched and lost power.

"Well, shit."

Properly rebuked, the Camaro coughed again and crawled back up to forty-five.

There were few vehicles on Decatur's streets this early. Give it a couple of hours, he thought; it was the day after Thanksgiving, the biggest shopping day of the year. Without the stimulus of traffic-generated adrenaline, Elton felt drowsy. At a red light, he clicked on the radio and twisted the dial. Yuppie rock, he thought with distaste, upwardly mobile dreck. The next station down was dentist-office stuff. The third caught his attention at once:

". . . Our demands will be met. If they are not, we unleash a biological weapon on the prisoners of St. Cyrils Island. A second biological aerosol will then detonate within the United States mainland.

"The bomb will spread pneumonic plague, genetically altered, throughout North America. No vaccine can protect you; no medicine can cure you.

"Defy us, and the Black Death will come again to the world. . . ."

The light turned from green to red again before Elton focused on it. All he could think about was a scenario of pneumonic plague—a scenario his office had begun eighteen hours before the terrorists struck.

Jack Hubert parked the dark blue rental Pontiac a block away from the house. He had given Hertz a Maryland driver's license and a MasterCard in the name of Herbert M. Morrison. If anyone were to check, they would learn that Herbert M. Morrison, a government employee temporarily attached to the State Department, had hurried to Brunswick, Georgia, to the bedside of his elderly grandfather who had been stricken with a heart attack while vacationing on St. Simons Island.

Hunched behind the wheel, Hubert listened intently to the newscast. When it was over, he lit one cigarette from the end of another, crumpled the empty Winston pack, and got out of the car. The radio had carried no word of the hostage takeover on St. Cyrils Island.

Uneasily he thought of the DCI. He would be waiting. But there was no help for it. The only telephone line to the island was monitored by the FBI. Until he could back up his credentials, he couldn't risk phoning the lodge.

The morning sky was pale ash streaked with pink on the horizon. The air was crisp and clear and brought a scent of woodsmoke from the chimney of the white frame house he passed. A single light glowed yellow from one of its windows. The kitchen, he guessed.

The windows of the duplex beyond it were dark. Hubert dropped the half-smoked Winston, ground it out with his heel, and walked up the three steps to the porch. A black plastic B with an irregular surface designed to look like wrought iron marked the door to the right. He pressed the buzzer.

After half a minute, a yellow porch light came on and the door opened to the length of its safety chain.

"Amelia Fletcher?" he asked.

There was a pause. "Who wants to know?"

He pulled out a I.D. folder and held it up to the door. The folder identified him as Special Agent Kenneth B. Tournquist, FBI.

He heard a swift intake of breath, then the door closed, a chain rattled, and it opened again. The pale-eyed woman in the doorway drew her pink chenille bathrobe together. "What's this about?"

"Just a few questions, ma'am." He glanced significantly over her shoulder.

Taking the cue, she said, "I guess you want to come in."

The gas space heater by the narrow stairway cycled on and blew a draft of overheated air in his direction. The woman flicked on the overhead light and he followed her into a small living room. She nodded toward a faded tweed easy chair and perched across from it on the edge of the couch. The fake-marble coffee table between them held a dozen miniature owls. The largest, made of ceramic, stared at him with round, yellow glass eyes. Its curved beak was cracked at the base and stippled with amber dots as if it had been glued back on.

"You're employed as a maid at the St. Cyrils Island Lodge?"

She blinked, then nodded.

"You left the island by boat at approximately five-thirty last night. Is that correct?"

She nodded again. Her eyes skittered away, then back, never quite meeting his. He wondered if there was something more here than ordinary nervousness. "On the trip back, did you see anything unusual? Another boat?"

"No." she shook her head—a little, trembling motion. Her eyes slid away again and she fixed her gaze on the coffee table.

"The boat docks at the landing on St. Simons," he said. "Do you park your car there?" At her nod, he framed his next question. He was planning to ask what she had seen. Instead, on impulse, he said, "Who did you see after the boat landed?"

"I didn't meet anyone."

Meet? What was she hiding? "But you *did* meet someone there before, didn't you?"

She was on her feet. "I didn't have anything to do with what happened last night."

His voice took on an edge. "Who was it you met?"

She pulled the robe tighter over her chest, her hand tightening on the lapels. "Nobody."

"You're headed for big problems, Amelia. Do you know that?" He leveled a hard gaze at her and waited. A little longer, he thought, enough to screw up her mind.

She sank down on the end of the couch and fumbled in her pocket for a cigarette. Her hands trembled as she lit it. "I didn't do anything wrong."

"Who did you meet?"

"This Spanish guy. He said he was from *The National*

Enquirer.'' Her pale eyes met his defensively for a moment, then slid away. ''It made sense. I mean, we get a lot of celebrities over there, you know. People you want to read about. Only, he just asked about the guy from the U.N.''

''Sir William Talbott? The ambassador?''

''Yeah. Him.''

''The guy who paid you off, what did he look like?''

''He was young. And real skinny. I thought maybe he was a student at first, but there was something about his eyes. I think maybe he was older.''

''I don't suppose you got his name,'' he said sarcastically.

''It was a funny one—the same as a city, or maybe a car.'' She blinked. ''I forget. But I wrote it down.'' She crossed the room and rummaged through a brown vinyl handbag thrust on a shelf. Smoothing a crumpled piece of paper, she handed it to him.

The paper was flecked with tobacco crumbs. The name was scribbled in pencil: Orlando Salazar.

''I thought I ought to write it down,'' she said. ''I mean, he was a contact, you know?''

There was dead silence in the situation room as the Crisis Committee listened.

Andrew Hagen rose. ''It would seem that they've called our hand, gentlemen.''

A dozen people began to speak at once. Only the DCI was silent, staring at his close-cropped nails, scraping them across his palm. His fatigue was overlaid with a sharp edge of adrenaline. When it hit the fan, he thought, it came in chunks. First the fucking bug bomb gets shot open. Now this. And why in hell hadn't he heard from Jack Hubert yet?

The DCI was uneasy. It was not that Hubert wasn't trustworthy; he had been checked, fluttered, rechecked, and fluttered again like all the rest, but lie detectors and security clearances weren't enough. What bothered him was less definable. It wasn't a matter of loyalty or special skills or tradecraft. It was the feeling that the younger ones—the operations officers trained in the late sixties and thereafter—were cut from a different cloth. Denim, he thought, playing with the analogy. Blue-jean denim. Prewashed, and soft and gray at the fiber. It was the fiber that bothered him. It was not like his own; of that, he was sure.

"The voice was Iguana's." Cordell Holt stubbed out his cigarette. "We know Iguana is wounded and still on the island; ergo, the message was taped in advance of the strike. It's obvious they anticipated a news blackout."

The DCI distrusted people who used words like "ergo." He had a notion that people spoke in Latin because they couldn't think in English. The chief of staff's pronunciation—"air-go"—set his teeth on edge. At least, he had put out his fucking cigarette. The air was blue with smoke and the DCI's sinuses were clogging.

Harold Walheimer looked grim. "NSA has narrowed down the transmission site to a four-block area in Alexandria. They'll nail it, but there's no way we can put these worms back in the can." The deputy national security adviser edged forward in his chair. "We're going to see widespread panic. And there's no way of putting a lid on it now."

"The President wants to hold back on any corroboration of the newscast pending further investigation," said Holt. "Corroboration would mean a mandatory evacuation of St. Simons Island and its surrounds. The President feels this would be premature. An evacuation now would probably be seen as an admission of weakness."

"Probably?" General George Everett glared. "If you start evacuating strategic military installations on the coast, our enemies will have a field day."

Isaac Benjamin, the science adviser, reseated his glasses with a jab of his index finger. "If evacuation of the south Georgia coast were carried out, all it would take is a rumor that the fail-safe was in a specific urban location—say, Manhattan—and we'd have chaos."

Carter Booth clicked a Tic Tac against his teeth. "And how can we be sure the terrorists aren't bluffing? We don't have any proof that this so-called bacteria really exists."

The DCI flicked an unbelieving gaze toward the press secretary. A born-again optimist. He bit his tongue to keep from answering.

"We'll know the answer to that soon enough," said Benjamin. "If the plague is real, it's going to show up on St. Cyrils Island. According to the initial CDC evaluation—this is a best-guess analysis, you understand—the incubation period could be as short as eight to ten hours. In the case of direct inoculation into an open wound, the time frame drops to six to eight hours."

The DCI glanced at his watch involuntarily. Time was running out, and not just for the island; Jack Hubert had to find out, and find out fast, if that second canister was on St. Cyrils. If it was, they could contain the thing. If not . . . He scarcely felt his nails bite into his palm.

"What about their manifesto?" put in Harold Walheimer. "They demanded that satellite broadcast by noon today. With Iguana wounded—and who knows what shape he's in?—who in hell do we negotiate with?"

"Someone on the mainland was responsible for disseminating that tape," said Carter Booth. "We can hope that contact will be made from that quarter and—"

"We can hope!" Everett popped upright in his chair. His eyes narrowed in outrage. "You're suggesting we can *hope*! I want to emphasize—and I want this read into the record—that without immediate military intervention, I predict the result will be a disaster of nationwide, perhaps global, proportions. I do not want the military to be held responsible because this committee decided to 'hope' instead of act." He scrabbled in a breast pocket and extracted another cigarillo.

Cordell Holt flashed him a look. "The ATOM team is mobilized. We have full strike capacity within fifteen minutes." The chief of staff swiveled toward the general. "The President understands the position of the military completely, but this tape proves without doubt that the terrorists have confederates on the mainland. A counterstrike now might well guarantee that the fail-safe aerosol will blow." He lowered his voice. "Are you willing to risk that, General?"

The general fixed him with a cold gaze. "I say to you again, all we need is one terrorist, just one, and he *will* lead us to that mainland bomb."

Just one, thought the DCI. One man. But only if he was the right one.

Chapter 32

A BILLION FRAGMENTS OF LIGHT GLITTERED FROM THE SURF and danced on the mullioned upper windows of St. Cyrils Lodge. As the sun rose higher above the wooded dunes, its rays crept downward, sending a narrow yellow shaft between the gap in the dining room curtains.

The long shadow of a rifle barrel bisected the light playing on the polished table. The curtain moved an inch, then dropped back. Bru lowered the rifle and shook his head.

"They're still there. Aren't they?" Tuck Perry moved closer to the window, and the sun streaked her pale hair with gold lights. Her slanting green eyes were wide with apprehension.

"I'm afraid they are," said Sir William.

"When are we going to get help?" Her voice rose. "When?"

"Soon." Bru answered quietly, but a hard lump ticked at the angle of his jaw. "You'd better get away from the window," he said to the girl.

Tuck dropped back and slid into a chair. She began to play with a black plastic bag from a stack on the table, crinkling a corner, releasing it, twisting it again, as if to conceal the fine tremor that touched her fingers.

She's near the edge, thought Sally. But who wasn't? She glanced uneasily toward the window. There had been no gunfire for nearly fifteen minutes. She realized that she had been straining to hear. Waiting for the other shoe to drop. She thought of Nathan and Ashley. What had happened? She did not want to think of Calvin Borden out there alone.

Across the table, Lillian Sniveley cleared her throat. "Since it's quiet, for now, I'd like to say a few words about Hoby." She paused, then added almost apologetically. "It seemed to me that we ought to have a service. We ought to say something." Her gaze moved from one to the other, and then focused on the narrow shaft of light, on the slow dance of tiny dust motes flashing in the sun.

"Hobarth Donnelly was a good man," she began. "He came to this island when I was twelve years old. He was a young man then—no more than a boy, really. St. Cyrils was his home. He grew old here, and somehow I feel sure he would have wanted to die here, when his time came.

"He didn't have a formal education, but he was a wise man, a gentleman in the truest sense of the word. He didn't go to church much, but Hoby believed in God, and so I would like to say these words for him. . . ." She paused then, raising her chin as if to defy the others to challenge her. ". . . And for the other two who lost their lives here, even though we knew them as our enemy:

"The Lord is my shepherd. I shall not want. . . ."

She spoke the familiar words of the Twenty-third Psalm from memory in a voice touched with the lowland accent of the South, and when she was finished no one spoke for a moment.

Tuck Perry blinked as if to hide the sudden brimming in her eyes. "There ought to be music." Then she was moving toward the kitchen, snapping open her flute case, fitting the instrument together.

Paige Cole gave a frightened glance toward the window. "No, don't. They'll hear."

"Then let them," said Tuck. When she raised the instrument to her lips, the breathy notes and the slow, plaintive tones of "Amazing Grace" filled the room.

As she listened, Sally tried to hold off the emotions the music had unlocked. Biting her lip, she began to count the bird's-eye dish towels in their regimented stacks on the table. Twenty-two, twenty-three. Twenty-three dish towels. Twenty-three masks . . . She needed them all.

The telephone shrilled in nervous counterpoint to the last dying notes.

Sally was closest. Heart pounding, she lifted the receiver. "Yes?"

A man's voice said, "Go ahead." A pause, then another man's voice: "Who am I talking to?"

"Sally Strickland."

"This is Dr. Millard Abramson, Public Health Service. I need some information from you people. We know about the plague canister that ruptured. We need to know if the other one is intact."

"The other one?"

"The, uh, second canister. We have reports that there were two on the island. Is the second one intact?"

"I don't know. We only saw one."

"You sure about that?"

"Yes, but"—Sally shot a glance toward the window— "we didn't see all of them, all of the terrorists. There're more of them outside."

A pause. "Uh, this leader—Iguana, is that his name? —you need to check him, be sure about that second canister."

She frowned. "We couldn't do that quickly. We have him in isolation. But I'm sure he didn't have two canisters."

"You can't know that without a search. The second one could be ruptured, too."

"The shot that punctured the canister broke his femur. We would have seen—"

He interrupted. "You might *not* have seen; it could be hidden in a backpack—anywhere. I want you to search him again. Do you understand?"

A backpack! She held the receiver for a moment, staring at it in disbelief. Then she beckoned to Dave Cole before she put it to her lips again and said, "I think there's someone else you ought to talk to."

Dave Cole shook his head. "He wasn't even close."

"I couldn't believe it," said Sally. "When I told him Iguana had been shot in the femur—the *femur*, for God's sake—he started talking about backpacks."

"So you might say our 'doctor' didn't know Iguana's ass from his elbow," said Bru.

"If he wasn't a doctor," said Lillian, "then who was he?"

"And why was he so concerned about a second canister?" asked Sally. "Even if there was one, even if it was ruptured, how could it make a difference to us?"

Bru stared at her for a moment. "It wouldn't make a difference to us. Only to him."

"What do you mean?"

"When Iguana broadcast his demands, he talked about a second aerosol—a bomb on the mainland. I think that's the one our man was checking up on. If it was here, then it couldn't be there."

Lillian frowned. "In other words, he was trying to find out if Iguana was bluffing."

Bru nodded. "I think so."

"But why not say so?" she asked. "Why didn't he come right out and say so?"

Sir William turned toward her. "That *is* the question, isn't it?"

"That's one of the questions." There was an odd look on Bru's face as he looked down at the rifle he held.

"So you've thought of that part of it, too," said Sir William.

A faint smile tracked across Bru's lips. "The rifles, you mean."

The ambassador nodded. "A bit off, don't you think?"

Sally looked from one to the other. "What are you talking about?"

Bru looked down at the rifle again. "It's a SIG—all of them are—and brand-new. So is the rest of their gear, the transceivers, the goggles, everything. Not the usual for a little band of revolutionaries. You'd expect a hodge podge of secondhand weapons: French, U.S., Soviet surplus. That's what you'd expect, if they're who they say they are."

"And they're professionals. I've no doubt of it," said Sir William. "Contract soldiers." He glanced toward the window. "Have you noticed how they've handled this siege? They've shot at us just often enough to draw our fire and waste our ammunition, haven't they? I don't think they're interested in Iguana's *venganza*. It isn't vengeance they want. What they want is to keep us inside."

"Away from them." Sally stared at the sign taped to the door. Keep out, she thought, keep away, keep out. "They're afraid of us. They're afraid of the plague."

Sir William nodded slowly. "I'd say so. Yes."

Calvin Borden crept from his hiding place under the eaves and peered down at the dim stable floor. At his movement the boards straddling the rafters shifted with a low rattle.

When the two men, responding to the bleating of the transceiver, had run toward the lodge, he crawled hurriedly to the stack of boards, cowering there while intermittent gunfire exploded in the distance.

It was quiet now. It had been quiet for a long time. A sharp hunger pang cramped his stomach. He stared down, scanning the gloomy stable. No one there. He grabbed the beam and kicked off. Poking a toe between a gap in the wide wall boards, he climbed down hand over hand until he felt the shell floor under his feet.

He had to get something to eat. But first he had to pee—really bad. Facing the wall, he unzipped. He tried to be quiet, but it seemed to him that the low hiss was especially loud. They could probably hear it way off, he thought. Maybe all the way to the creek. Even the sound of the zipper sliding shut seemed ominous. He peered through a crack in the wall and scanned the clearing for signs of the men. It was empty except for the horses clustered in a patch of sunlight near the fence. One was lipping specks of grain from the empty feed trough. The others cropped at the sparse grass along the fence line.

Hunger drove him into the feed room. One of the metal garbage cans held grain; the other, a mixture of cracked corn, oats, and molasses that Hoby had called sweet feed. The lid, tight-fitting to keep out rats, stubbornly clung to the can. Working his fingers around the edge, he pried, and the lid came loose with a shocking clatter.

The smell was pungent in the closeness of the room. He slid the lid partway off and scooped up a handful. The corn was hard as rocks in his mouth. He spat it out, but the thick sweet taste of molasses was tantalizing. He was picking out the softer oats when he heard the sound: the horses, responding to the rattle of their feed can, were running toward the stable. In moments they were jostling together in the narrow aisle.

"No," he whispered. "Go away."

The big bay gelding called Buddy shouldered past a black filly and pushed into the feed room. Calvin flapped his arms to shoo the horse away, but the animal, driven by hunger, extended his neck and nosed the lid. It fell with a horrible clang and landed between the two cans.

He stared at it in horror. They'd know. They'd have to know.

The horse opened his lips and began to feed while the

others, drawn by the odor like a magnet, pushed toward the open can.

He had to get out before somebody came. He shoved the filly with all his strength. When she took a skittering step sideways, he squeezed through the door and began to run.

At the end of the stable he stopped short. After the dimness inside, the sunlight was dazzling.

No one was in sight. He sprinted across the corral, grabbed the fence rail, and threw himself over. Landing on hands and knees, he rolled into a clump of palmettos. The dead brown lower fronds rattled like wooden swords.

He lay sprawled on the ground for a long time, peering through the stiff, pleated fronds until a disturbed colony of ants swarmed over his sock and invaded his pants leg. Scrambling away, he rubbed at the bites. His palm was swollen and red; a long wood splinter bisected it with a dark, jagged streak. Sucking the heel of his hand, he managed to catch the end of it between his teeth. Most of it came out, but the rest was buried too deeply.

He could see the road from his hiding place. He did not dare follow it, but he couldn't stay here. He thought of the Jeffersons' house near the old lodge. He could go through the woods. And there would be food there. Leroy and Lena wouldn't mind, he told himself. He wouldn't eat all that much. Besides, he was supposed to get meals. Daddy said they came with the room.

Blinking, pushing away the thoughts of his father and Ashley that crowded into his mind, he set out cross-country toward the old frame house near Oyster Creek.

At a break in the woods in a place where the dunes flattened to a grassy stretch dotted with oaks, he saw the footpath. Leroy's house was just across. Beyond it the marsh, awash with the high tide, stretched out for miles. He had to be careful. The old lodge was within sight now, and if he could see it, then anyone there could see him.

He took a deep breath and ran toward the sagging porch. The house stood on low pilings. He ducked down by the steps. The dim, cavelike space beneath the house smelled of mold and humus. A slant of sunlight crept below the sills and glittered on a piece of broken glass.

Shifting his gaze, he stared across the clearing at the old lodge. The two trucks were still in front. Through the distant branches of an oak he could see the widow's walk on the roof.

Something—someone—was up there.

A man was moving slowly on the roof. He didn't dare go up the steps now and cross the porch. The man would see him for sure. He stared in despair at the front door that had seemed so close.

But there was another way in, wasn't there? He was sure he remembered a door in the back. Ducking under the sill, he crawled on his hands and knees over the dark earth beneath the house. Nose and eyes stinging from the mold he had stirred up, he pushed through a low sprawl of bushes and came out by the back steps.

The kitchen doorknob turned, and with a faint groan the door slid inward. Ducking so that no one would see him through the open curtains, he made his way to the front of the house and peeked out a window. At this angle no branches obscured his view of the widow's walk. He could clearly see the man as he paused, slowly turned, and faced in his direction.

On the widow's walk El Ojo scanned the woods, squinting as he turned toward the sun. Fatigue dragged at his coarse features, making his eyes seem more deeply set beneath the thick brows, his heavy jaw more square.

There were only six men left now, one at each of the three lookouts, the others circling the lodge. It was enough, he thought. Their job would end at noon. But until then, their presence on the island was insurance that the manifesto would be broadcast. The manifesto was no more than an overture, but an essential one. From that point on, the orchestration would be automatic; the concert would begin, would play to its inevitable conclusion, and no one could stop it.

The hostage takeover and the puncture of the canister had crippled them. He knew that two of his men, and perhaps a third, would desert, would run like rats in the face of the plague that was sure to come. Only his assurance that there was no immediate danger from hostages confined to the lodge had kept them here this long. He contemplated the odd quirks of human nature: the way a soldier could show enormous courage in war and yet be paralyzed by a teaspoon of bacteria. It was the helplessness, he decided, the loss of control, the feeling that there was no defense against an enemy who lay in wait, ready to strike from any quarter with no warning.

They had wanted to destroy the lodge and the people in it with explosives. Fools. Nothing would quicker ensure their own destruction. Within minutes of such an attack the U.S. military would retaliate. But to desert the island would guarantee an invasion, too—one that might force their wounded and weakened leader to talk, to reveal the location of the aerosol.

At noon they would attack the lodge and recapture at least one hostage. Nothing else would guarantee them safe passage off the island. Iguana had to be sacrificed, of course. But not until then. El Ojo felt no compunction about this. Iguana was a dead man. Noon would be time enough for the grenades—when the signal for the rendezvous had been sent.

The makeshift plastic gown crinkled as Sally bent over the couch and the wounded terrorist. When she came into the room, she had felt a moment's apprehension, but she brought it quickly under control. After all, the gun was gone, and Iguana certainly wasn't going anywhere. Neither was Alex Borden, she thought. Borden was asleep on a couch near the fireplace, the empty bottle of Gilbey's cuddled next to him. It had taken four of them to get him to the bathroom under the stairs, four of them to scrub him down.

As Iguana moved, cord slid through the traction pulleys

suspended from the overhead wagon-wheel lamp, and the weighted lard buckets dipped and rose. She took a quick look at his dressing. It was dry so far, with no trace of blood, but the irregular line of his thigh told her that the traction had a long way to go before his fracture was reduced. She winced involuntarily. That had to hurt.

"Swallow this. It's for pain." She held out a glass of water and a yellowish Percodan tablet culled from Lillian's stock of medicine.

His lips were dry and beginning to crack at the corners. He was getting dehydrated. "Drink it all," she prompted.

He drank greedily, but when he tried to swallow the pill, it rolled out of his mouth and slid between two cushions. She bent to retrieve it. Not too sanitary, she thought, but they couldn't afford to waste anything. She held it out. "Let's try again."

This time, his lips clamped shut and he shook his head.

"Try to take it," she said. "It'll make you feel better."

He shook his head again. His belly rippled and suddenly he vomited convulsively. She stared down at the watery stream of yellow bile dripping from her gloved hands. Blinking, she grabbed a towel and sopped up most of it. She dipped a washcloth in the basin of water she had placed on the end table. As she squeezed it out, the traction apparatus began to quiver. She whirled toward him.

Iguana was shivering violently. The jars weighting the lard buckets jittered and clicked; overhead, the light fixture swayed on its chain.

She reached automatically for his forehead. The heat of him burned through the thin gloves. Fighting a growing apprehension, she felt for his pulse. It was thin and rapid— far too rapid.

At that moment everything in the room seemed hyper-real: the damp stain spreading over his shirt; the luminous, fever-bright eyes; the tap of his pulse against her fingertips.

He vomited again through cracking lips and chattering teeth.

"No," she whispered.

He answered her with the faint whimper of a child.

This is the way the world ends, this is the way the world ends. . . .

It was ending with the feverish twitch of curtain cords and the ridiculous jittering dance of a two-pound jar of Orville Redenbacher popcorn weighting a lard bucket. It was ending with Alex Borden's slurred voice from across the room saying over and over, "What's up? Huh? What's up?" It was ending with a sing-song bit of nonsense in her head:

> Ring around a rosy . . .
> Pocket full of posy . . .
> Ashes. Ashes.

Dave Cole's eyes were bleak above his mask. His gaze darted toward Iguana, then back. Shaking his head, he turned away.

Sally followed him to the door. "Is it—" Her voice dropped. "What do you think it is?"

"I don't know. I just don't know."

"But the fever—" She had found a thermometer after a hasty search in Lillian's first-aid kit, but she had been afraid to place it between Iguana's chattering teeth. Instead she held it in his armpit, all the while praying that it would register close to normal. It had read 103.4.

Dave's eyes did not quite meet hers. "I'm a pediatric resident, Sally, not an internist. I just can't be sure."

Her gaze flicked toward the sick man, then back again. "But we're all he's got," she said.

"God help him." He turned away, but not quickly enough to hide the pain in his eyes. "God help us all," he whispered under his breath. He began to pace back and forth, as if it helped him think. "No cough. Nausea and vomiting, but no cough. Rigor . . ." He stopped and looked sharply at Sally. "Does he have a headache?"

"I don't know. I think so. He kept holding his temples, but when I asked him, he didn't seem to understand."

Dave started the pacing again, feet shuffling in their plastic coverings. "No cough. God, I wish I had a stethoscope." Frowning, he stared at the terrorist for a long time. "If it's plague, and he's not coughing, it's an ominous sign."

"What do you mean?"

"Septicemia. Septicemic plague. If it's in his bloodstream—and it could be—he could be dead before there were any lung symptoms." He swung toward her. "What kind of medication did you turn up? Any antibiotics?"

She thought of the cardboard box full of pill bottles that Lillian had brought down. "I didn't have a chance to make a count, but there's some penicillin—maybe two dozen of those—and some old tetracycline."

"How much tetracycline?"

"Not much. Ten or twelve."

"Damn." He shook his head. "The penicillin won't do us any good. Tetracycline might, but a dozen won't go very far." He shot a glance across the room at Alex Borden. "We have to think about him, too." He turned to her suddenly. "Is there a lock at the top of the stairs?"

"What?"

"On the third floor. The double doors at the end of the hall."

Sally tried to visualize the doors. She remembered white porcelain knobs with brass surrounds, but a lock? "Maybe," she said doubtfully. " I don't know."

He glanced at Borden. "The second floor is theoretically contaminated, but he's got to be safer in a room up there." He paused. "I just don't know if he'll stay there by himself."

She blinked. Borden was drunk. If they left him alone, how could they be sure he couldn't wander into the uncontaminated part of the house? "What about Leroy?"

"We need to get him out of here, if we can. We got rid of the gun; he doesn't need to watch Iguana now."

"We can lock the dining room doors," she began, "but I'm not sure about the second-floor door to the back stairs. I'll find out. Lillian will know." She turned toward the entry hall.

"If they don't lock," he said, "we'll have to nail them shut. And tape, too, around the cracks."

She nodded and went to the door.

"The meds—"

"I'll get them," she said, wondering whether Iguana would be able to keep the tetracycline down. She tried to remember if there was anything for nausea in Lillian's box. *Hang on, Sally,* she told herself sharply, fighting against the dissociation that came with stress and fatigue. *You can cope; you're coping.*

But the part of her mind that was watching said, *Only for so long. Only as long as you keep busy.*

Ignoring it, she thought of the contents of the box: aspirin—a whole bottle of that; a few Percodan; half a dozen aspirin and codeine tablets left over from Lillian's dental work; eye drops . . .

The sudden thunder of rifle fire.

". . . Eye drops," she whispered, staring at the window. Two kinds of eye drops; over-the-counter stuff. Got to stay busy.

Shock etched Lillian's eyes. "Are they sure?" Not plague, she thought. Not here.

Bru shook his head. "They can't be sure without lab tests." He reached for the telephone.

"What else could it be? " said Tuck Per y. "You don't get sick like that from a broken leg." She whirled from one to the other. "Do you?" Her voice rose. "Do you?" Then her shoulders sagged and she began to cry softly into trembling, cupped hands.

The entry hall door opened and Leroy Jefferson came into the dining room. Awkwardly pulling off his inner gloves, he dropped them into the plastic bag tied to the doorknob. "They tol' me to go," he said. "They say it be too big a risk fo' me to stay." He said the words in a low voice as if he were ashamed, as if he had failed in some way.

Bru stared at him for a long moment. Then he lifted the telephone receiver. "This is Bruton Farrier. Where in hell is the help we need?"

Lillian saw him set his jaw, the way he did when things weren't going well.

"That won't do, my friend. I want to talk to your director, and I want to talk to him now. . . ." Bru's eyes narrowed at the man's answer. "I don't care what kind of conference he's in. Get him." A pause. "Then put me through to the Crisis Committee."

Lillian stared. Bru's fist curled, tightened, uncurled as he waited. What was wrong?

"Goddamn it," Bru exploded. "Get a message to him, then. I want you to tell him that we're running out of rope. We need help and we need it now." At a volley of gunshots, he held the receiver toward the window. "Do you hear that?" he demanded. "We're under fire. And Iguana is sick with a high fever. It may be plague. . . ."

Plague. Lillian pushed away the thought. This was her home. It could not happen here. It could *not*.

"How kind of you to offer to convey my request." Sarcasm dripped from Bru's voice. "Now, put me through to Wally Carruthers's office. . . ."

He blinked. "Say again . . . say that again. . . ."

As he listened, Bru's lips twisted into a thin, tight smile. "So the cheese stands alone."

He slammed the receiver onto its hook and stared at the wall beyond it for a moment before he turned to the others. "They won't let us call out. To anybody," he said. "They've cut us off."

As the hollow echo of rifle fire reverberated inside the mausoleum, Ashley clutched Nathan's neck. "Make them stop," she whispered. "Please. Make them stop."

"Maybe it's our own people," he said, wishing he could believe it. "It may even be the police." He held her tighter. A dusty stripe of sunlight that brought no warmth penetrated the narrow fixed glass near the ceiling and crept across the pale marble floor. Shivering, he drew her into the light. "Better now?"

Her breath was warm against his throat. "I think so." But when the next volley of gunshots came, she trembled violently. "I can't stop thinking about Calvin, alone out there all night, and Daddy—what's going to happen to them?"

Nathan shook his head. He wished he could see out, see what was going on. Maybe he ought to open the door and take a quick look. He tried not to think about how hungry he was. Thinking about it just made it worse. He looked down at Ashley. The angling light made red-gold glints on her hair. She was probably hungry, too, he thought.

God! Of course she was. "Your insulin," he whispered. "You've got to have it."

"I'll be all right," she said. "As long as I don't eat. I can go a long time without eating. But I'm so thirsty. I wish we had some water." She struggled up to a sitting position and looked around the little marble room as if she were searching for something.

"What's wrong?"

"Nothing. I've just got to pee."

"Go ahead," he said. "I won't watch."

"Not in here. I couldn't." She glanced toward the door.

"Being thirsty and having to pee a lot," he said uneasily. "Isn't that all part of diabetes?"

She stared at him in amazement. "It's been all night. Don't you have to go? Aren't you thirsty?"

He gave her a sheepish look. "Well, yeah." Then suddenly they began to chuckle. Like village idiots, he thought, but he couldn't stop the grin spreading over his face.

"Don't make me laugh," she gasped. "I can't hold it if I laugh."

The smile danced in her eyes. God, she was beautiful.

He caught her chin in his hand and whispered, "I love you, Ashley."

"Yeah," she said. "Me, too."

Her lips were curved and warm; his tongue parted them, and he pressed his body against hers.

"Careful," she whispered. "We'll have a flood." Then suddenly her eyes widened and she pulled away. "Listen."

He stared over her shoulder. "I don't hear anything."

"I don't, either. They've stopped. They're not shooting anymore."

Just like before, he thought. They had stopped for over half an hour. He got to his feet.

"What are you doing?"

"I'm going to take a look." He cracked the door open and stared out. Leaf shadows shivered in the cold morning light. An inch more and he could see the wrought-iron gate standing ajar. We didn't close it, he thought. We should have closed it. "I'm going back to the lodge," he said. "I can get us some water and something to eat. I'll get your insulin."

"No." Alarm sharpened her voice. "You can't. They're still out there."

"I've got to." His eyes met hers. "If I don't, you'll be sick."

"Don't you blame this on me, you fucker. I told you, I'm fine."

He hesitated a moment, then shook his head. "I have to go now. While I can. I'll be back soon."

"No." She struggled to her feet; fright etched her eyes. "They'll kill you."

"I'll be okay." He shot her a final glance. "I love you. I'll be back."

"Don't. Don't leave me here." But the door slid shut and he was gone.

"Fucker. Goddamn fucker." Ashley's lips twisted and she sank to her knees on the stone floor. "Come back," she moaned, "come back. Don't you know they'll kill you?"

*   *   *

Sir William held the receiver for a moment before he replaced it. Then he turned to Bru. "Apparently our friend from the FBI did relay your message. They've sent word from Washington. But I'm afraid it isn't much good." He hesitated. "They've put us—the whole island—under quarantine."

"Quarantine!" Bru exploded. "Where in hell do they think we're going?"

"That's it?" asked Dave Cole. "That's all of the message?"

Sir William nodded. "Nothing more except the vague possibility of some sort of airlift later today. They've promised some medicine: tetracycline and something else, chloro—chloro something."

"Chloramphenicol?" asked Dave.

"Yes. That was it, I think."

Sally sat huddled on the floor near the dining room wall, arms wrapped around her knees. As their words sank in, she shivered and drew closer to the heat register, though the room was not particularly cold. Just tired, she thought. She always felt shivery when she was this tired. A numbness had clamped down that made everything seem not quite real. Fading out, she thought. Her eyes slid shut.

Something made her look up suddenly. Lillian was bending over her, wrapping an afghan around her shoulders. "You looked like you were cold," she said. "Maybe this will help."

She muttered her thanks.

"I'm afraid it's going to get colder," Lillian said. "We won't have power for much longer. The generators are nearly out of fuel. Hoby always fills them—filled them," she amended, "on Friday mornings from the barge tanks. We'll have to do without central heat. Fortunately we've got the Franklin stove, and most of the kitchen uses bottled gas. We're all right on that, I think. When the power goes, we'll still have the phone for a while. It has its own battery pack."

Sally nodded and inched closer to the register. The warm air against her face was making her drowsy. She stared at the louvered aluminum warm-air vent until she felt her eyes drag shut. Then with a start, she opened them.

Central heat.

They had been blowing warm, bacteria-laden air from the Great Room all over the lodge.

Chapter 33

THE DCI WIPED HIS FOREHEAD. IT WAS TOO HOT IN THE ROOM to suit him, and his sinuses were clogging up again. Though the air filters were working valiantly, they could not eradicate the thin blue clouds of cigarette smoke that erupted with dismal regularity.

The committee chairman was reading from the NSA report projected on the wall screen. The security agency had located the terrorists' computer in a duplex in Alexandria. It was still cycling though its calls to the news media when they found it; still sending the damning message to the public.

They knew we'd find it, thought the DCI. He was sure they had set up other computers; Iguana's second phone call last night told them to expect the text of their manifesto, but the IBM PC they'd found had been programmed only with the single message to the media. The terrorists' plan seemed to be progressing in spite of the hostage takeover. That meant someone was acting—was meant to act—independently of Iguana and the others.

He chewed a stale cheese Danish and stared at the

report. The computer had been rigged with a battery-powered electrical backup system to guard against power failure, and it was hooked to a modem. It could have been set up weeks ago.

He ran Jack Hubert's report through his mind again. Hubert had posed as a doctor and questioned the hostages by phone. The DCI was convinced: There was only one plague canister on the island. The trick was to find number two.

Orlando Salazar was the key. He had to be the man on the mainland. There might be more than one man. But one was enough, if he had laid a network of computers to do the work for him. One man, he thought—working alone, isolated from his confederates on the island. And yet, there was no way to be completely sure.

Catch-22. The DCI had told the President as much an hour ago. Military strike teams had been mobilized, and a CIA antiterrorist contract force had been on alert since last night. They stood ready to invade St. Cyrils at a moment's notice. But in the face of the evidence the President had not dared to give the order to attack. If they attacked, if the island terrorists alerted Salazar, the aerosol would blow.

Orlando Salazar had to be an alias. A sketchy description and a phony name added up to a needle in a field of haystacks. But Salazar was all they had. Over two hundred operatives were looking for him now, combing the Alexandria area, checking phone bills, airports, bus terminals—looking for the man who could lead them to Pestis 18.

Head pillowed on his thick down jacket, backpack wedged against the airport bench, the young man slept. With each slow breath, his ribs splayed out, stretching the navy turtleneck tighter over his narrow chest. He was oblivious to Miami International's morning rush, the loudspeaker announcements in English and Spanish, the clank of coins in vending machines, but at the faint, warning beep of his wristwatch, he awoke instantly.

A teenager on the next bench was fishing quarters from the pockets of his stone-washed jeans. Swinging the TV set close to his eyes, he deposited the money and clicked the dial to *Family Feud*.

The young man glanced at his watch, checking it against the wall clock. At the bank of telephones beneath it, a woman with an assortment of oversized straw market hand-bags clattered the receiver onto the hook and left. He took her place and dialed a local number.

In a deserted walkup apartment over a pawnshop in Miami's Little Havana, a computer answered the incoming call with a high-frequency tone. At the sharp series of electronic beeps that came over the wire, it sent another high-frequency signal and disconnected.

A red light came on as the computer searched its disk drive. Then the machine, connected by a thick tangle of cables to a backup power source and an electic array of telephone equipment, began its programmed phone call to the White House.

Dr. Jonah Schwartz clamped his pipe in his teeth and leaned back. The desk chair gave a dangerous creak and settled on its haunches. "I'll admit it's an odd coincidence."

"Coincidence? Is that what you call it?" Daniel Elton stared at his colleague. Schwartz looked like his bony body had grown to the chair. Something for the cleaning woman to dust around, along with the stacks of papers and ashtrays filled with half-burnt tobacco and pipe cleaners. "You think it's coincidence that we start working on a hypothetical plague that shows up for real eighteen hours later?"

"I'd call it that."

"Yeah? Well, I'd call it damn strange." There had been a shade too much emphasis on this one. Too much push. Elton thumbed through a stack of papers, extracted a dog-eared document, and began to read: "Foreign terror-ists threaten the U.S. mainland with an artificially mutated culture of *Yersinia pestis* which they claim to be resistant to all known antibiotics. . . ." He looked up at Schwartz. "*Yersinia*, Jonah. Not Legionnaires, not hemorrhagic fever. *Yersinia*. Why?"

"Why not?" Schwartz said mildly. "Do you think we can ignore the possibility that someone, somewhere, might be monkeying around with plague?"

"I'm not arguing that. I'm talking about timing." He rattled the paper. "It even calls for an aerosol in a metropolitan area."

"How else would you spread it? Poisoned toothpicks? Sabotaged Big Macs?" A slow smile quirked his lips. "How about a guy in a black cape? Vector Man. He could sneeze on public telephone receivers."

Elton grinned in spite of himself. "Thank you for using AT&T?"

"Reach out and fuck someone."

"Pretend you can think, Jonah. You can't really believe this is coincidence."

"I can believe in a lot of unbelievable things: the virgin birth of clones, the national debt, that necktie you had on yesterday."

"Shit."

Schwartz sucked his pipe and a cloud of smoke blued the air in the tiny office. "I think you're digging the wrong ditch."

"What do you mean?"

"No, friend. What do *you* mean? Just what in hell are you trying to say? That we knew about this in advance? That we're in league with the terrorists?"

Elton blinked. Put that way, it sounded pretty ridiculous.

"Come to think of it, that's not such a bad idea. We hook up with those guys, put in for a cut of the ransom, and who knows?" Schwartz rolled his eyes. "Maybe we could get new filing cabinets all around, or a photocopy machine that doesn't need a German shepherd and a white cane."

"Maybe."

"At any rate," Schwartz said, "coincidence or not, our

scenario is more than a defense exercise now, isn't it? Have you got the atmospheric factors worked out? Washington is beginning to push hard. They tell me a weather front—a low-pressure area—is headed for the south Georgia coast.''

"Give me another hour."

When Elton was gone, Dr. Jonah Schwartz sucked on his pipe and stared at the closed door for a long time.

General George Everett curled his lip. "How in hell can we expect to negotiate with people who won't talk to us?"

How indeed? thought the DCI. Except for the two phone calls from St. Cyrils last night, the computerized message to the media had been the only communication. According to the brochure, the terrorists weren't going to negotiate. He suspected they had never intended to.

Andrew Hagen's usually mild expression hardened. "You have a point, General, but I'm sure you'll agree that we're doing everything on our end to keep the lines of communication open."

"These people only understand one thing, Mr. Chairman, and that is force." The general stabbed out his cigarillo, grinding the stub into the ashtray as if it were an adversary. "I don't like the direction we're headed in. I don't want to see the military stuck with this committee's dirty laundry when it's too late to act."

It wouldn't be the first time they were screwed, thought the DCI. The military was no virgin. He glanced at his watch. The deputy director was due to relieve him soon. Another half hour of this and maybe he could get a hot shower and some sleep.

"There's another avenue we need to explore," said the chairman. "The matter of the man mentioned in Iguana's first communiqué. 'Where is Wiley?' he said. I'd like to ask the same thing. What do we know about this guy, Burt?"

The FBI director unfolded his hands from across his bulky stomach. "Not much, Andrew. We're running all the usual checks. We can't overlook the fact that 'Wiley' may be a code name.''

The DCI caught his breath. He had to steer them away from this.

Andrew Hagen jumped on it. "Code name?"

The DCI broke in. "Foreign agents often work under a code name. Iguana, for instance. But I'm afraid we're looking for the proverbial needle in the haystack here—''

"Can we let Burt go on?"

The DCI glared. Hagen was waggling his hands again. Another fucking benediction from St. Andrew.

"There's really nothing to add at this point," said the FBI director.

"In that case, I'd think we're going to have to admit the possibility that the quarantine area might need to be extended if this weather front materializes." The science adviser peered over his glasses at the map. "That would include Little St. Simons Island, Sea Island, and the northern portions, at least, of St. Simons Island. The front is due early afternoon Saturday. That's just a little over twenty-six hours from now. If we're going to move people out of the area before then, we'd better get things under way."

"Is the medical environmental report in yet?" Andrew Hagen asked.

"No, not yet, but I think we have enough here to order evacuation of the areas in question."

Carter Booth looked up. "How long will it take to evacuate St. Simons?"

"I don't have any figures on that. All I have here is a rough estimate based on the island's own hurricane evacuation plan, but I believe"—he consulted the map again—"I believe that plan predates the four-laning of the mainland access causeway." Benjamin turned to an aide. "Can we get those figures from Civil Defense?"

"Evacuation is a serious step." Harold Walheimer hunched forward and glanced at the press secretary. "We could have complete panic in that area."

Carter Booth nodded. "The public doesn't know about the plague on St. Cyrils. Are we going to tell them about it now? Are we going to tell them that Black Death has broken out next door?"

Andrew Hagen shot him a startled glance. "We can't use that term, certainly."

"It doesn't matter if we do or not. The media will."

"If the evacuation is limited to the north end of St. Simons, we could give out the word that the terrorists planted an explosive charge," said Walheimer. "A bomb scare would cause panic, but nothing like the threat of plague."

Isaac Benjamin frowned. "I want to emphasize that we can't rule out an island-wide evacuation. Depending on medical and meteorological updates, we just can't make that kind of decision right now. What I would suggest is that we set in motion plans for a partial evacuation. We can extend that if it becomes necessary. . . ." He glanced up as the door opened and a White House aide hurried toward Andrew Hagen.

The chairman read the paper the man handed him. "Excuse me. The White House has just received the text of the terrorists' manifesto. It seems to be another one of Iguana's prerecorded messages." He turned to the aide, questioned him in a low voice, and then went on: "We'll be getting that voice tape in just a few minutes, but the gist of it is the same. They're still demanding that worldwide broadcast at noon. That doesn't give us much time, but we have a TV crew on standby."

"I don't like this," said Walheimer. "Knuckling under to these people—it's bad strategy."

Hagen looked up sharply. "'I believe that decision has already been made."

Made last night, thought the DCI, and reconfirmed an hour ago by the President. No one liked it. But it was a way of buying a little more time.

"While we're waiting for that voice tape," the science adviser began, "I'd like to go back to the quarantine situation for a moment. We'll be using a Black Hawk helicopter to make the medicine drop to the hostages."

"A Black Hawk, Isaac?" came a skeptical voice. "Isn't that overkill?"

"Not when the enemy is armed with automatic weapons and grenades," put in General Everett. "And since military aircraft are already involved, I am asking for full authorization to use force, if necessary, to uphold that quarantine. If people start jumping the island, I don't want the military to take the blame for plague spreading to the mainland."

The security adviser set his coffee cup down with a rattle. "The President has indicated that the quarantine has priority." Walheimer glanced at the aide by the door. "I believe that authorization will be coming through shortly."

"If I can go on . . ." Isaac Benjamin cleared his throat. "Due to the possibility of bacterial resistance, the CDC is recommending treatment with a combination of streptomycin and either tetracycline or chloramphenicol. . . ."

The DCI ignored the discussion of the antibiotics. He knew that the medicine would not work. Not against *Yersinia Pestis 18*. He had reluctantly but irrevocably written off the little group of hostages. They were, after all, only a tiny minority.

It was a matter of priorities, he told himself. The nation's fate—and the fate of the Company—hung in the balance.

Chapter 34

TONY HERRERA CROUCHED ON THE KITCHEN PORCH AND peered through a break in the thick tangle of honeysuckle that wound through the railing. The shooting had stopped again—for nearly ten minutes now—and just in time; the Walther PPK was out of ammunition. He had exchanged it for Bru Farrier's rifle and a quick lesson in the care and feeding of automatic weapons, but the SIG made him nervous.

His father had taught him how to use a handgun when he was fourteen—the day after their home had been burglarized for the second time. It was locking the barn door, he thought, but when you grew up in a place like Miami, maybe it made sense. Automatic weapons were something else; you left those to the Colombians or the Marielitas. You had to be carrying more than a two-thousand-dollar guitar in your little black bag before you got into machine guns, even in Miami.

He glanced at the fire selector again; it was set to "1." To conserve ammunition, he told himself. In truth, he hoped the single-shot setting would give him more control.

He rubbed his burning eyes with the back of his hand and then reached for the thermos jar. What was left of the coffee Lena had given him was cold. So was the air; the sun would not work its way around to this side of the lodge until afternoon. He huddled against the railing and stared up at the baskets hanging from the eaves, twisting on their hooks with each faint puff of wind. Guard duty was a lot like auditions, he thought: hours of boredom interspersed with a few minutes of sheer terror. The difference was, when you were shot down by a conservatory, you lived to be shot down another day.

He caught his breath at the sudden rustle near the parking shed. Probably a deer. He stared at the palmetto thicket. It was still now, so still that he could hear the distant sound of the surf pulsing in his head like the flow of blood.

The rustle came again, closer. With it, an explosion of rifle fire splintered the sagging shed door. Two of them, he thought wildly. One shooting, distracting him, so the other could slip around the back. His finger curled on the trigger.

A man burst from the thicket.

Tony's single shot was high and to the right. The man spun and staggered. Then he was running in a strange loping gait straight toward the porch.

And he was yelling, "Don't shoot. . . . It's me . . . Nathan . . . it's me. . . ."

Tony shoved Nathan into the kitchen ahead of him just as gunfire sprayed the porch. The volley was answered by a series of short bursts from Tim Jefferson's third-floor post.

With one look at Tony's white face, Bru grabbed the rifle. At the kitchen window, he nudged the shade aside with the muzzle and stared out. "Take care of Nathan," he said over his shoulder, but Sally was already reaching for the first-aid kit.

Another burst of gunfire raked the porch. Lena Jefferson clutched an egg. Eyes fixed on the window, gnarled hand poised over her mixing bowl, she stood, staring as if she could see through the lowered buff shade. Her dark face was unreadable. In the quiet that suddenly fell, her hand smashed down on the rim, and the egg ran like glue into the bowl.

Nathan slumped against the kitchen counter and looked down stupidly at the bright blood dripping from his coat sleeve and pooling on the white Formica.

Tony licked dry lips and shook his head. "God, I'm sorry," he whispered. "I thought—God, I'm sorry."

"Let's get his jacket off." Paige Cole slid a chair under Nathan and reached for his collar.

"Wait." Sally pulled out a pair of scissors. "That might make it worse. We need to cut it off."

"I've got to go," Nathan protested.

"You're not going anywhere."

"But I've got to." Sweat broke out on his forehead. "Got to get back. Ashley's out there."

"Where?" asked Bru.

"In the cemetery. I've got to get back." He tried to get up, but Sally pushed him down.

"Be still. You can't help her like this."

As she clipped along the seam of the sleeve, she swayed with fatigue. With relief she stared at Nathan's wound. It was no more than a nick. "There's a lot of blood," she said, "but it looks worse than it is." She doused his upper arm with peroxide and the white foam bubbled red. Folding two sterile gauze 4x4s, she applied them to the wound. "Press here till I get him taped," she said to Paige. "Where's Dave? He needs to take a look at this."

Blood seeped through the 4x4's and stained Paige's fingers. "He's still screwing with that goddamned filter."

They had turned off the lodge's central heat, but Dave had been worried about the air return under the entry hall stairs. Sure that the fiberglass filter was loaded with bacteria, he had gowned up again, and armed with plastic bags and Lysol, went in to remove it. Paige's eyes redder than her allergy seemed to warrant. Sally wondered if she had been crying. "Are you all right?"

"Oh, sure. How could things be better?" Her lips trembled. "He's the one. He's going to kill himself screwing around with that shit." She shook her head. "Some honeymoon, huh? Why did we have to pick St. Cyrils Island?"

"All in all," said Bru, "I'd rather be in Philadelphia." Though he kept his voice light, his eyes narrowed as he nudged the window shade aside and scanned the shed and the silent, deserted road.

"He'll be careful," Sally began, but her voice sounded strange to her. It was all a sick joke—their little plastic gowns, their gloves and masks, Leroy's rain slicker—all of it. How could they have forgotten the central heat? How could they have been so stupid?

The louvered hot-air register by the back stairs was covered with a faint film of dust. They needed to wash it off, Sally thought. Scrub it down with Lysol. But what about the air that had already blown through it? She remembered a film from her nursing fundamentals class: an animation that showed a dirty yellow cloud of bacteria streaming through a house. It was a silly, ludicrous film— how could she have forgotten it? Right now, she knew she would give anything, do anything, if only she could see what had crept through the ducts.

She imagined it moving in invisible, wispy curls like a poison gas, coiling near her nostrils, slithering into her lungs. It could be anywhere. Or nowhere, she told herself sharply. Nowhere but in the strands of the air filter. But in her mind she could see bacteria dancing in a slant of sunlight like dust motes, falling in a deadly rain on a coffee cup, a sandwich, settling on the countertop to hide and wait for an unwary hand. She could see it dusting the shiny pots and pans hanging from the open wrought-iron racks, peppering a blue-striped crockery bowl of broken eggs, coating a freshly opened bandage labeled *sterile*. She stared at Nathan. "Better now?" Her voice was faint.

He nodded. "I think my leg was the worst, anyway."

"Your leg? Where?"

He stuck out his left foot and pulled up his pants leg, wincing as he did. A piece of shell was sticking out just above his ankle.

"How did you do that?"

"I don't know." He stared down at it. "I thought I was shot."

Sally knelt and slid down his sock. She stared at the

jagged, bleached shell in surprise. "There's concrete on it."

Lillian Sniveley took a look. "Tabby."

"What?"

"The cement and shell foundation of the buildings. It's called tabby."

"But how?"

Bru looked over his shoulder. "One of the bullets must have knocked it off the foundation. It could have ricocheted into his leg."

Sally frowned. Several shell fragments were embedded in the angry reddened wound. The adjacent skin felt doughy. If they didn't get the pieces out soon, the swelling was going to make it impossible without an incision. She stood abruptly and reached for the first-aid kit. The moment she did, black rags swam at the edge of her vision. Oh, damn, she thought. Don't faint. She clutched at the table top, and as the blinding rags floated over her eyes, she felt herself begin to fall.

Someone caught her.

Vision crept back and she looked up at a half-dozen blurred faces. "I'm okay," she mumbled in embarrassment. Shaking her head, she struggled to a sitting position and looked up.

Fear etched each face.

Her eyes widened. "What's wrong?"

No one answered.

"My blood pressure dropped for a minute," she said quickly. "Orthostatic hypotension. I just stood up too fast. It's happened before—when I get too tired." She scrambled to her feet.

As if orchestrated, the group fell back and split into a widening aisle. Like Moses parting the Red Sea, she thought uneasily. "I'm okay," she said again, and her voice took on an edge. Her gaze flicked from one to the other.

They were staring back at her in horror, staring as if they saw a rabid dog—or worse.

"I'm not sick," she said in a voice she knew was too loud. "I don't have the plague."

"Of course you don't." Bru's arm slipped around her shoulder. "She needs some rest." He stared defiantly at the others. "She's wiped out."

Shame crept slowly over Lillian's face. "Of course she is." She stepped forward and took Sally's arm. "Let's get you upstairs and into bed."

"But Nathan. . . ."

"We'll manage," Lillian said firmly.

"I'll fix his leg," said Paige. "If I'm going to be a vet, I can use the practice." Then her eyes widened and she said to Nathan, "No offense."

"It's his hind leg, Doctor," Bru said soberly. "The right one."

Paige giggled in embarrassment. And suddenly they all were laughing with a relief that was almost palpable.

As they went up the narrow back stairs, Sally said, "You don't need to come with me. I'm all right."

Lillian stopped. "I know you are. I wanted to talk to you." The dim light on the landing touched her white hair with yellow lights. "It's going to get worse, isn't it?"

Sally looked at her; she didn't speak.

"I thought help would come before now, before anyone got sick." Her chin went up. "We have to help each other. Otherwise . . ." Her voice trailed away for a moment. "Otherwise, we're not going to make it."

What was she trying to say?

"I have an unfortunate way of jumping to conclusions—the way I did a few minutes ago." Lillian touched the banister lightly and stared down at her hand. It was trembling, or was that a trick of the light? "I'm not afraid to die. But I'm afraid of giving up. Do you know what I'm talking about?"

"It's me. You think I am."

Lillian blinked as if she had been struck. "You?" She gave a nervous little laugh. "I was born here, Sally. This is my home. And I live on an island. Do you know what that means? My life has edges to it. Boundaries. It's five miles long and not quite three miles wide.'' She began to move up the stairs again, slowly, as if she were climbing an endless hill. ''When you live on an island, it's easy to forget about the rest of it—about what's outside.''

Until it's violated, Sally thought. Until you feel raped by the dirty, penetrating stare of a terrorist. Her eyes met Lillian's, and when they did, she saw a look there that she had seen before. A look she had seen in the eyes of patients whose bodies had been invaded by glittering, sterile knives and cell-destroying drugs. The place where you live, she thought. The center of yourself. Bad as it was, it had to be worse for Lillian. She had defined herself by a bit of earth five miles long and three miles wide. Now she was watching what she was shrink down to a few rooms in a beleaguered house.

They reached the second floor. The door was locked, and someone had taped it shut with dull silver AC tape. ''Another boundary,'' Sally whispered.

Lillian's eyes met hers again. Then they slid shut and she nodded.

Their hands touched, gripped hard, squeezed tight. She's afraid, thought Sally. She's afraid of losing control. And losing control wasn't a matter of tears or nerves or silly fainting spells; it was a matter of holding on to the edges of yourself and not letting go, not giving up, because if you did, if you once let go that way, it would be like losing focus, like taking off the polarized glasses in a 3-D movie. Nothing would be left but the drifting blur of chaos.

They stood, clasping each other's hand. Then Lillian said, ''Get some rest. I'll try to take care of your patient. Dave can tell me what to do.'' She headed down the stairs.

Sally watched her for a moment. Then turning, she went up the last flight and opened the door into the library.

The double doors that led from the alcove to the main stairs were locked. Tuck Perry was sealing the crack beneath the doors with the rest of the AC tape. At Sally's footstep, her head jerked around, pale hair falling across her face. "You scared me."

"Sorry." Fatigue dragging at her legs, she turned down the wide hallway that bisected the library. When she reached her room, the door was open. Miranda Gervin looked up sharply as she came in. "Sh-sh-sh. You'll wake her."

Cass Tompkins rolled over, dragging blanket and quilt with her. "No, she won't."

Sally stared at the two women. She had forgotten they were here. It was too much to deal with right now; she was just too tired. Mumbling a faint apology, she turned abruptly and went back down the hall.

She opened the door to the linen closet. Maybe she could get a blanket and curl up on one of the library chairs. But when she thought of Tuck still at work in the alcove, when she thought of having to say even a few words to her, the effort seemed too great. Instead, she pulled down a pillow from the long shelf against the wall, wrapped herself in a thick blue quilt, and lay down on the floor. When the distant roar of gunfire came again, she pressed the muffling pillow over her head and said to herself, it's only thunder. Only thunder.

Miranda Gervin started at the burst of rifle fire. The last shots had come from the south. These were from the northeast. They were circling the lodge. Like wolves, she thought, holding a wounded animal at bay, confusing it.

Across the room, Cass sat up abruptly and stared at the window. "They're all around us," she whispered. She struggled up and stood barefoot on a tangle of fallen bedclothes.

Miranda could hear Tim Jefferson moving in the next room. He had cracked open a window and cold air was seeping down the hall and into the room. She closed the door and passed a hand over the air vent. No heat. The fire in the little wood-burning stove had died down long ago, but a few small coals were left. The log bin was only half full. Wadding a sheet of newspaper she found there, Miranda poked it on top of the coals, and when a slender flame streamed out, she tented it with slivers of kindling.

Cass pressed her temples. "God."

"Headache?"

She nodded, wincing as she did. Her eyes were red and puffy.

"Iguana's sick," Miranda said in a low voice. "Plague. I found out while you were asleep."

"Good. I hope he dies."

"How can you say that? Don't you know what it means? We're all in danger now."

"In danger! Tell me about danger." She waved at the window. "What the hell do you call being shot at?"

Miranda set her square jaw and thrust another stick on the fire. Cass was trying to pick a fight. Well, let her. She glanced across the room. Cass had turned away. She sat hunched at the side of the bed; her shoulders began to shake. Miranda stared for a moment, then went to her side and slipped an arm around her shoulder. "You're upset."

Cass turned on her. "And you're just the one to comfort me, aren't you? You're a real sweetheart."

"What do you mean?"

"Don't think I don't know what you want. It shows. It always shows in cow eyes."

Miranda stiffened; her arm dropped to her side.

"You'd like it, wouldn't you? You'd like to touch me. That's what you've been wanting, isn't it?"

Her mouth felt dry. "You've had too much to drink."

"Not nearly enough, sweetheart. I've known about you for years." Cass gave a low, mocking laugh. "Hope springs eternal, doesn't it? Even if you never had the power of your convictions."

Miranda jerked her chin away. Her face was burning, but something cold and heavy grew inside her body.

"Don't turn away, sugar. Not at your moment of epiphany." The corner of her lip twitched. "You know why I put up with you? It's never a bad idea to have a secretary who's in love with her boss. It keeps her from stealing too much.''

Miranda whirled toward her. ''You wouldn't know about love, would you? Even when you chase it. Even when you try to buy it.''

''I don't know what you mean.''

''You know damn well what I mean.'' She tried to keep her voice from shaking. ''What is he? Half your age? How interested do you think he'd be without the money you send him?'' Her fingers curled into her palms. ''. . . You're wonderful, Cass,'' she mimicked. ''You don't know how much your check means to a starving artist. . . .'' That one had been postmarked Belgium.

Cass looked stunned. ''You read my letters.''

Her eyes narrowed. ''It's my job. Remember? I answer your mail, too. All of it—the bills, the tacky little notes from your readers—all of it.'' She caught her breath. ''Yes, I read them.'' Heart pounding, she stared at the floor, at the deep red band that tracked along the edge of the Oriental rug and disappeared under the bed. Her voice dropped. ''I had to.''

''And that's what you're thinking?''

What did she think? That thirteen years meant something? That one day Cass would look at her for once as if she were something more than a piece of office equipment? And why did she care? Why did it hurt so damned much? ''He's making a fool of you. You're keeping him.''

Cass's eyes were unreadable. She looked away. ''I wanted to.''

''That's what people are to you, aren't they? Something to pay for on the installment plan. Buy two; they're cheap.''

Cass stared at the window, at the dazzling play of sunlight on a patch of ocean in the distance. ''I wanted to keep him. But I couldn't.'' Her eyes slid slowly toward Miranda and fixed there, but with a strange blank look as if she did not see her at all. ''David—'' she said. ''He's my son.''

Miranda felt the breath rush into her lungs; she felt the

pressure of it swell against her ribs. Why did it feel as if she had no air? *Dear Ms. Temple*, the letters began. *Dear Ms. Temple* . . . It was only later that he called her Cass. Her voice was a whisper. "He doesn't know."

"They let me hold him." Her gaze slid toward the ceiling, slid back and forth as if she saw something etched on the rough white slant of plaster, something playing out among the leaf shadows. "His hair was like silk," she said. "When he cuddled up his knees, he fit into my two hands." Her fingers played across a wad of bedclothes and found a pillow. She pulled it to her.

For a long time she sat there, staring at a featureless stretch of wall. Then she turned wide, stricken eyes to Miranda. "They killed Caligula, you know."

"I know."

Her fingers curled and dug into the pillow; her face sagged. "I want my little dog." A tear left a shining snail track on her cheek, and she began to sob, clutching the pillow, cuddling it as if it were a live thing. "I want my puppy."

Miranda stood there for a moment, her eyes darkening with pain. Then she reached out and gathered Cass in her arms, hugging her, stroking her hair as if she were a child. "I know you do. I know."

"There." Paige Cole smoothed a strip of tape over Nathan's gauze-wrapped ankle and looked up anxiously. "Did I get it too tight?"

He shook his head and stared at the door that led to the kitchen porch. "It's all right."

From across the room, Bru followed his gaze. Leroy Jefferson, armed with a handgun, had taken over Tony Herrera's watch out there a few minutes ago.

Nathan's eyes jerked back to Paige. "Ashley's a diabetic. I've got to go up and get her insulin."

"I don't know," she began doubtfully. She turned to Lillian. "Weren't the Bordens staying on the second floor?"

At her nod she frowned. "It's closed off, Nathan. The second floor's contaminated."

"But the insulin isn't up there." Lillian opened the door to the large refrigerator and scanned the shelves. "Here it is." A plastic bag crammed with orange-capped syringes and two vials of milky fluid sat next to a wedge of cheese and a tray of Saran-Wrapped sandwiches.

Bru glanced at Nathan. "Forget it. The rules say you're only allowed one turn as a target." It was crazy for the boy to go out there again. "Somebody else can bring her back."

"No." Nathan's chin went up. "I don't want her back here. It's not safe."

"It's a hell of a lot safer here than out there," Bru said sharply. "We'll go as soon as the helicopter makes the medicine drop." At the worried look on Nathan's face, he added, "Don't worry. She'll be all right." He wished he could believe it. It was risky enough to go outside once; it was nothing but lunacy to do it twice. Bru twisted the knob of the little AM-FM radio Lillian had brought down. Album rock gave way to a bellowed "Juh-*ay*-sus wants *you* to spread the good *news*, brothers and sisters. . . ." He edged the dial to the right an eighth of an inch and got a Mozart string quartet. "Nothing," he said. "Not even on Public Radio."

Lillian glanced at the white-faced clock above the stove. "There'll be news on at noon."

Bru glanced at his watch. It was 11:35 now. And where was the chopper? It was overdue. He went to the window, edged the shade aside, and looked up at the hard blue sky.

Tony Herrera came up to him and said in a low voice, "I'll go."

Bru shook his head.

White lines traced the edges of Tony's mouth. "It's my fault Nathan's hurt. I've got to do it."

Bru gave him a close look. No good, he thought. Right now, Tony was too shaken to be reliable, and guilt over Nathan wasn't the antidote. Couple that with a little macho face-saving and he was likely to take unnecessary risks. "Sorry," he said. "The job's taken."

"You? You're going?"

He nodded.

"You won't make it alone." Tony glanced outside. "You can't grab the package and shoot at the same time."

"Tim can cover me."

"If he can cover you, he can cover me."

"Get some rest, Tony," he said evenly. "This one's a long haul."

Tony's lips compressed into a pale line. He stared at Bru for a moment. Then he turned and stalked away.

"Listen," said Lillian.

A faint throbbing rumble from the northeast grew rapidly in volume.

Sir William's voice came from the next room: "Here it is."

Bru ran to the dining room bay window and the rest followed. The helicopter was coming in fast from the Atlantic. In moments the pulse of its rotors shook the oak limbs at the crest of the dune. The engine roar almost masked the sharp click of the kitchen latch turning.

Bru spun toward the sound just in time to see Nathan slipping through the open door. "Shit." He ran to the porch as the Black Hawk streaked overhead. Leroy Jefferson's startled gaze met his and darted toward the shed. Head low, Nathan disappeared behind it, just as a canvas airlift bag thudded to the ground, bounced once, and slid to a stop in a shallow depression a dozen yards away.

"Look." Lillian pointed to the refrigerator. The door stood open. Half a dozen sandwiches and the bag of insulin were gone.

A burst of rifle fire split the air.

"Get inside," Bru yelled at Leroy. As the door slammed shut behind them, another burst raked the porch. "The chopper—they think it's an attack."

Lillian's hand fluttered toward the window. "Nathan—"

Bru spun toward Tony. "Get on the radio. Tell them it's medicine. Tell them Iguana has the plague."

With a quick, shocked glance at Bru, Tony grabbed the transceiver and switched it on.

Let it work, thought Bru. It had to work; it was Nathan's only hope.

La Culebra stared through the smeared glass of the lighthouse as the helicopter roared in low from the Atlantic. In the distance he could hear the echo of fire. Madness, he thought. El Ojo was crazy to wait until noon. Every minute they stayed increased the risk.

Below him, the Cigarette bobbed at anchor in the lowering tide. He narrowed his eyes against the glare and looked out to sea. The aquamarine bands that marked the sandbars gave way to the blue-black of deep water. The submarine would be there now, waiting. But until the black box in the Cigarette squawked its electronic signal, it would not surface.

El Ojo was a fool, he thought. *Tonto*. La Culebra spat in contempt. It was Iguana he had agreed to follow, not this paper soldier who blindly pursued a doomed plan because he could think of no other. If they had answered Iguana's call for *venganza* and destroyed the lodge, they would be safe by now.

He glanced toward the southeast. He could not see the lodge from here; it was too far, and masked by wooded dunes. He thought of it turning into a pest house, and a chill coursed along his spine. Their only hope now was to keep the hostages inside. If they didn't, if plague broke out, it would spread across the island.

It had made him nervous to see the silver cylinder intact, even though he knew the *microbio* was safely locked away. Now it was shot open. He imagined the bacteria oozing out, creeping through the house, infecting everyone—everyone on the island. A part of his mind shut out the thought, but another part felt the dark pang of mortality, and he shivered.

The transceiver at his belt crackled—the musician, Herrera, transmitting from the lodge.

He listened without breathing. Iguana was stricken.

It begins, he thought. And though he had expected it, though he had known that it would happen, his mouth turned to cotton. The rifle fire died and an unnatural stillness hung over the island. And from the depths of his mind, La Culebra heard the whisper of death.

His hand trembled against the windowpane as he stared down at the Cigarette tugging against its anchoring line. His gaze darted out to the horizon and skimmed along the pale line where sky met water. Do it, the thought urged. Do it. The Cigarette was their only way off the island. Without it they were stranded here. Doomed.

His voice sounded hoarse to him as he spoke over the radio. "I'm taking the boat," he said in Spanish, "I'll wait five minutes. No more."

He shut off the transceiver then. He did not want to hear El Ojo's curses; he did not want them to intrude on his resolve. While the seconds crept inexorably into minutes, he clutched his rifle and stared at the empty road that stretched across the prairie to the dunes. And when there was still one minute left of the five, he clattered down the spiraling stairs of the lighthouse and raced for the boat.

As the helicopter thundered above the dune, Ashley Borden caught her breath and stared out from the thicket at the edge of the cemetery. Across the empty clearing, she could see the door to the little mausoleum standing ajar. The lodge was just beyond the low crest of the dune, but it might as well be miles. She had never felt so alone in her life.

At the sudden explosion of gunfire, she clamped her hands over her ears. "Please," she whispered. "Make it stop. Make it stop."

The shooting had started just after Nathan left. When it had stopped, the silence that followed was somehow worse to bear. She had waited alone in the tiny marble cell until

she could stand it no longer. Then she crept out and
dashed to cover in the little tangle of holly and palmetto.
Giving in to the pressure in her bladder, she pulled down
her panties and squatted over the sand for what seemed
like an eternity while a narrow little river puddled and
pooled between her feet and disappeared into a pile of
brown leaves.

She had been too afraid to go back. And now with the
sound of gunfire in her ears again she hated Nathan for
going away, for making her go through this alone.

It was suddenly quiet. She could hear nothing but the
low breakers drumming the shore. As she shifted her
position, dry leaves rustled and a spine of holly scratched
her cheek. Her mouth felt dry and sticky as if she had
swallowed glue. The sound of the salt surf mocked her
thirst.

She saw the rifle before she saw the man. She saw the
dark glint of sunlight on the barrel as it moved from the
shadows halfway up the dune.

Just over the top of the dune branches rattled. Someone
was coming. Running.

At the sound the terrorist slid behind the wide bole of an
oak.

Adrenaline coursed through her chest like an electric
shock. It was Nathan, cresting the dune, skidding, sliding
down the narrow path. She stared white-faced as the rifle
slid toward him.

Then she was bursting out from the thicket, screaming,
"No! Don't! No!"

The terrorist spun toward her. For a moment he froze
and horror grew in his eyes as if he saw the face of death.

She dived as gunfire shredded the branches over her
head. He swung the rifle toward Nathan. The burst went
high. Spinning, he swung again, wildly, as if he were
surrounded.

Then he was running through the woods, feet shattering
dead-brown leaves, branches cracking in his wake—running
as if all the demons of hell were after him.

*   *   *

The transceiver squawked at the fleeing terrorist's waist: "*Cinco . . . Cinco minutos . . .*"

Five minutes. Five minutes.

Running, he fumbled for the radio, switched it on, yelled, "*Parada!*" Stop.

He had to hurry. Had to get away. He streaked past the shed and broke out in the clearing near the lodge. One car was there: the Bronco. Panting, he raced to it, flung open the door. No keys. No keys.

He spun, stared. Then he was running toward the lighthouse, toward the anchored boat. And as he ran he screamed in Spanish, "Wait for me. Wait for me."

Before he could reach the prairie, he heard a faint rumble in the distance. He ran faster, his heart pounding in his ears, his breath exploding from his lungs. Eyes wild, feet pounding the shell path, he ran. And he could not stop even after the Cigarette's engines roared to life and the boat veered away from the shore toward the open sea.

The Cigarette! The only way off the island. El Ojo thought of La Culebra, and hate blazed from his eyes. La Culebra. Traitor. Racing to the rendezvous he had planned for all of them at noon. His fingers tightened around the transceiver. "Kill him!" he barked to his man in the boardwalk tower. "Use grenades."

In moments the answer came back: "Too far . . . Out of range."

Trapped. They were trapped. And all of them knew it. If he did not regain control of his men now, he never would.

Desperation in his eyes, El Ojo raised the transceiver to his lips.

Tony Herrera's head jerked up from the transceiver. "The guy at the lighthouse—he's taking the boat. He gave the others five minutes."

Bru spun toward him. "Is he the leader?"

Tony shook his head. "No. The top man's El Ojo—The Eye. He was at the old lodge. I think he's still there."

Mutiny, thought Bru. If the terrorists panicked and fled the island, it would all be over. The transceiver squawked. "What are they saying?"

Tony held up his hand for silence and cocked his head. "Another one's following. He's yelling for him to wait. Hold it—" He listened intently for a few moments. "It's El Ojo. He's threatening to shoot anyone who follows."

"He's running scared," said Bru.

"He's telling them to report," said Tony. "By the numbers." A pause. Then a different voice came over the transceiver. "Number one's coming in now from the board-walk." Another pause. "Two. Two now."

They've created their own diversion, thought Bru. He swung toward Paige Cole. "Go upstairs. And hurry. Tell Tim to cover me. I'm going after the medicine."

She shot a startled glance at Bru and disappeared up the stairs.

He cracked open the back door and slipped outside. Crouching on the porch, he told Leroy to cover him.

Bru scanned the road through a thick growth of honey-suckle. The canvas bag lay in a tangle of leaves and roots no more than forty feet away near the far corner of the shed. His gaze slid along the edge of the woods. A few leaves moved in response to the faint wind. At the edge of the shed, the path veered off toward the incinerator. Again nothing. He took a deep breath and let it out. Then he was running, head low, in a zigzagging path toward the bag.

Arm outstretched, he grabbed it and slid to the ground. His gaze shot from bush to bush. Nothing. The sound of his breath rushed in his ears.

The bag was surprisingly light. He came to a crouch and pushed off. In moments he was back at the lodge, rushing the porch.

The door fell open and Lillian pulled him inside.

He plopped the bag on the kitchen table. As he caught his breath, Lillian got it open. She was pulling out the contents when a shout came from upstairs.

Bru ran up the back stairs and the others clattered after

him. On the third floor he swung through the alcove and raced down the hall.

Paige and Dave Cole were already in the room, staring at what Tim Jefferson pointed to from the jutting dormer window. Cass and Miranda crowded in behind them.

At first, Bru could see nothing but a patch of ocean. Then just beyond a spit of sandbar that curved into the Atlantic like a flattened C, he saw the white boat, small as a toy in the distance, skimming the surf.

"It's the Cigarette," said Tim.

A half-dozen people crowded the window and stared as the ocean racer spewed out a fantailed wake and veered toward the open ocean. "They're getting away," said Cass in disbelief. "The fuckers are getting away."

For the beat of a heart there was no sound. Then the rumbling that began in the distance grew to a roar and the Black Hawk thundered overhead, its shadow blotting out the sun, stretching, climbing the dune toward the sea like the umbra of a giant predator.

"Get 'em," someone yelled. But as Bru stared, slivers of ice grew in his belly.

The missile that burst from the helicopter vaporized the boat into a churning plume of steam and surf.

"All right!" shouted Dave in jubilation. "All right!" He grabbed Paige and spun her around as a fierce yell of triumph went up. But Lillian clutched the windowsill and stared around at the others. At the look in her eyes, grins faded, and the silence grew tense.

"They didn't know who was out there," she said.

Bru watched the quick, blank realization grow on every face before he said, "It could have been anyone. It could have been us."

Chapter 35

THE LITTLE BLOND KID WAS NIBBLING HIS FRIES THE SAME WAY Jamie did, crooking his elbow over his head, dangling the end in front of his mouth, nipping bits of it off with even little teeth. He doesn't mind an audience, either, Jack Hubert thought, watching the child tip his head and give him a flirty look. Cute.

He was suddenly acutely aware of how much he missed his family. Ought to be used to it by now, he thought; some months he was away more than he was home. It had taken Marta a long time to adjust, but lately she seemed to mind his absences less and less. "My 'Company' manners," she had said lightly. And at the time, it had seemed innocent enough, but now and then in his darker moments, he wondered if she was playing around.

He wadded up the thought along with his Big Mac wrapper and lit a Winston. The first drag felt dry and scratchy and he followed it with a swallow of coffee. When all this was over, he was going to quit. Maybe give up the coffee, too. He glanced at his watch: 12:04. In twenty minutes he was going to have something for the DCI or else it was back to square one.

He sucked deeply on the Winston and waited for the time to pass. It was the waiting that got to him. He stared out the plate-glass window at the pay phone next to a browning cabbage palm. Funny how he used to think that his work would be a hot ride on the fast track. He had never imagined that so much of it would be fast foods and podunks like Brunswick, Georgia. All the glamour of a

245

vacuum cleaner salesman, he thought, but without the commissions.

Beyond the pay phone, a patch of salt marsh stretched out in the distance, Unbidden, an image came to him: a dark mist rolling in across the marshes, a fog, damp as breath, that carried with it swarms of bacteria. The thought made him uneasy and he pushed it away, but it was replaced almost at once with a picture of the ape, saliva dribbling from one corner of her mouth, pleading eyes fixed on his as if she knew that the one antibiotic that could save her was locked up a dozen yards away like the emperor's gold.

The empty foam coffee cup split under the pressure of his fingers. For Christ's sake, he told himself, stop all this shit. But his gaze slid toward the salt marsh again, toward the island. Those were people over there, he thought without wanting to. Human beings.

He blinked and looked away. The little boy was sucking up the last of his drink, making slurping sounds with his straw. There was a kid on St. Cyrils. He wondered if he was blond like this one. Nine years old, they had said.

Jamie was three. Three plump fingers held in the air: "dis many." One day he would be nine. One day—if Orlando Salazar fell into their hands twenty minutes from now.

One day, please God.

The young man with the backpack pressed a button on the little black box he held, and at the signal the computer on the other end of the telephone line disconnected. His work was nearly done now. In twenty minutes he would be boarding a plane to Guatemala City. The last phone call would come from there. Tomorrow. To an empty apartment in Atlanta next to Grant Field.

As he hung up the receiver, he slid a finger into the coin-return slot, then turning, headed toward the Pan Am counter. On the way he passed a row of benches filled with waiting passengers and glanced down as a gray-haired woman swiveled a coin-operated television set. He paused and stared over her shoulder. She was watching the noon news. At the top of the screen a logo displayed a rifle and the word TERRORISTS. Beneath it, a computer-generated map of St. Cyrils Island flashed a red X that pinpointed the lodge. The voice-over was accented and he recognized the words at once: the manifesto. He watched only a few seconds more before he moved on. He did not need to listen further; he knew what was being said.

The area near the Pan Am section was crowded. Maneuvering his way past a pair of nuns dressed in drab gray, he looked up at the bank of monitors. A startled look came into his eyes: Flight 209 was canceled. Why? His gaze flicked toward the counter. Three lines of baggage-laden passengers clogged an area roughly delineated by portable stanchions.

He slid into the shortest line and scrutinized the area. Behind the counter two men and a woman in uniform contended with the press of passengers and baggage. As the line grew shorter, he pulled out his ticket, smoothing it with a nervous little gesture.

In the next line a dark-haired man was handing over a ticket to the woman behind the counter. There was something in her eyes that set off a warning surge of adrenaline. The woman's movements were stiff and self-conscious as if she were being observed. He watched as she scanned the man's ticket, his eyes narrowing at the look of relief that crossed her face.

His gaze shifted to the other passengers. Just ahead to the right, a man wearing a gray suit clutched a briefcase in his left hand. His jacket was open. And on the left, another man, this one in a blue suit, carried a briefcase too—in his left hand. Two of them? Two of them with no other luggage on a trip to Guatemala? Two of them, with their right hands free to reach into a breast pocket—or a concealed shoulder holster.

There were only two people ahead of him now. He caught a few words over the hubbub of the crowd: ". . .

rescheduled . . . sorry for the delay. . . ." His eyes slid toward the right. Two uniformed airport security guards stood there, apparently talking casually with each other, but their gaze slid back and forth over the crowd of passengers—a crowd carefully hemmed in by stanchions.

His thumb and forefinger played over the ticket that bore the name Orlando Salazar. He had been careful not to use the I.D. twice in a row; the flight from Atlanta had been under another name. He had used Orlando Salazar only once before—in Brunswick, when he bought the guest list from the maid. *Estúpido*. How could he have been such a fool? He had left a neon trail and they had followed it.

His expression was carefully bland as he slid the ticket into his pocket. Then a startled look tracked over his face and he slapped at his side. "Shit! My camera . . ." Mumbling to himself, he stepped out of line and headed purposefully toward the lockers just beyond the pay telephones.

It was only when he insinuated himself into a thick cluster of passengers that he changed direction and moved quickly toward the exit.

In a small rented office tucked back in the hill country of Austin, Texas, a disk drive whirred as a computer searched its files. A telephone number flashed on the screen; a modem dialed. When a secretary in the governor's office in Atlanta answered, the computer began to speak in a strangely accented synthesized voice. Its mispronunciations might have been comic were it not for what was said:

This urgent message is to be relayed to the governor: An explosive deviss is concealed in Atlanta. The deviss will spread pneumonic play-gew throughout your city. Seventy percent of your citizens will die. There is no help for them. There is no cure. . . .

After a pause of three seconds the message repeated. Then the computer disconnected. The disk drive whirred again, searching its data base, making substitutions. Another number flashed on the monitor; another call:

This urgent message is to be relayed to the mayor: An explosive deviss is concealed in New York City. The deviss will spread pneumonic play-gew thoughout your city. Seventy percent of your citizens will die. There is no help for them. There is no cure. . . .

Again the computer dialed. Again:

. . . explosive deviss is concealed in Denver.

. . . in San Francisco.

. . . in Houston . . . Boston . . . Miami . . . Los Angeles . . . Chicago . . . Little Rock . . . Phoenix . . . Salt Lake City . . . Washington . . . Las Vegas . . . Raleigh . . . Charleston . . . Oklahoma City . . . Louisville . . . Jacksonville . . . Philadelphia . . . Des Moines . . . Seattle . . . Minneapolis . . . New Orleans . . . Baltimore . . . Detroit . . .

Chapter 36

DANIEL ELTON LOOKED UP FROM HIS PAPERWORK AS SYLVIA stuck her head in the open door and scanned the office. "I'm looking for Dr. Schwartz. Have you seen him?"

"Jonah?" He shook his head. "Not since before lunch."

"Super, I've got somebody from the governor's office on the line. He seems to be in a real flap over something hush-hush. Will you talk to him?"

"Sure."

She disappeared, and moments later his phone buzzed. "Dr. Daniel Elton speaking." As he listened, his fingers tightened on the receiver and the color drained from his face. "Yes, please," he said, "let me hear the whole thing."

The governor's office had managed to tape a portion of the telephone message:. ". . . An explosive 'deviss,' " the computer transmission said. "Pneumonic 'play-gew.' "

In Atlanta.

"Uh, could you play that back for me again," he said, knowing he was trying to buy time to think.

Pneumonic play-gew. Dear God. His mind darted into one dead end after another and came back to wonder how it was possible that a machine could pronounce "pneumonic" correctly and do such a hatchet job on "plague." Brave new world.

The idea that they were being threatened by the disembodied voice of a machine was ludicrous. And somehow, that made it more horrible. He had an instant flash of an Atlanta utterly destroyed: a city of the dead defiled with electronic parodies of human speech peddling aluminum siding and ballroom dance lessons and pneumonic playgew to a hundred thousand passive answering machines. Be the first on your block.

"That isn't much to go on," he said tentatively.

"That's all we've got." The voice on the other end was tense. "Do you understand what I'm saying? There's a *bomb* somewhere in Atlanta. We have to know about this plague. How many people are going to be affected?"

"I'm afraid that's just not enough to give you any kind of definitive answer," Elton said. "It would depend on a lot of variables: the size of the device, the amount of bacteria, whether or not it was in a heavily populated area. . . . What's that?"

"The governor. How can we protect him?"

Elton thought for a moment before he said, "You might want to consider a temporary relocation of strategic officials. Say, to Macon, or possibly the north Georgia mountains."

An incoming call was flashing on line two. "Let me get right back to you," he said, grateful for the interruption.

He scribbled down the number and punched the phone button.

"Dr. Daniel Elton speaking." He blinked. "Who?"

It was the office of the mayor of San Francisco.

It was not until the third call—this one from the White House—that he began to suspect what was going on. The computer call had gone to everyone, to every major city in the country.

The White House aide was saying something. "What was that?"

"Prevailing winds. We've got to know how they would affect this thing."

Elton thumbed through a stack of files on his desk. "Excuse me just a moment." He pressed the mute button, and yelled at Sylvia, "Where's the aerobiology report?"

She stuck her head in the door. "I just ran it through Old Obliterans," she said. "I put it on Dr. Schwartz's desk. Want me to get it?"

"Yes." Then, as he saw her hands were full with another bleary stack of copies from the bowels of the recalcitrant copier, he said, "Never mind. I'll get it myself."

He put the White House on hold, realizing that it gave him a certain sense of power to do so, and went into Schwartz's office. The report was stacked neatly on the center of the desk, and it was obvious that Sylvia had had to relocate several stacks of papers to make room for it. Reaching for the phone, he went through the data.

"That's going to depend whether the aerosol is generated from dry or liquid material," he said.

A pause. "The science adviser tells us the time of day might affect it."

"That's right. If the bomb is set off during daylight, solar radiation is going to start destroying the bacteria, but you can't extrapolate that across the board. Air pollution can alter that. So can humidity, if it's high enough."

"Hang on for a minute, will you? I'm going to put you on hold."

Elton tore off a sheet from Jonah's memo pad and

pulled a pen out of his pocket and scribbled down a note to himself. Phone cocked to his ear, he absently began to outline the indentations in the memo sheet.

The indentation of the single word was heavy enough, as if the person who wrote on the overlying sheet had done so with a hard lead pencil. Still, it wasn't until Elton had outlined the depression with pen that he could read what it said:

NKWILY.

He glanced at it without comprehension, and when the White House aide came back on the line a moment later, he folded the paper and tucked it into his pocket.

"It's the GBI again," said Marge Tyson. "Line one."

Wally Carruthers picked up. He recognized Joe Murphy's voice immediately. "What's up?"

He drummed bony fingers against the steel desk top and listened for a half a minute. "Well, shit," he said slowly. Iron bands began to tighten around his chest again and he reached for the little pill bottle tucked in his shirt pocket. A minute later he hung up and summoned Pete Wiggins. "It's piling thicker and deeper," he said. "The task force is pulling half of the state troopers out of south Georgia because of that Atlanta bomb threat."

"Right in the middle of an evacuation?" said Wiggins in disbelief. "But it's got to be a hoax."

"Probably," said Wally. "But what if it isn't?" From early reports it looked like every city in the country with a population over half a million had received the computerized call. It was obviously a destabilizing tactic, and it was working. Every governor's office in the Union was in an uproar. "They want all the men we can spare over on St. Simons," he said.

Wiggins shook his head in disgust. "If they'd put local law enforcement in charge to begin with, they wouldn't be so far up shit creek."

Wally glanced at the clock: 3:08. The evacuation of St. Simons and Sea Island had started just before noon and it wasn't going well. Now the causeway was hopelessly snarled in traffic. Thanks to the FBI, he thought darkly. Hundreds of agents in blue windbreakers labeled with gold letters identifying them as FBI swarmed over St. Simons, panicking the people, alienating them. Some of the old-time residents could be mule-stubborn. The FBI was spitting against the wind, he thought. Any of the local law enforcement agencies could have done a better job of it. And a quieter one, too. At least a dozen TV crews were helping to clog traffic, and there was no telling how many more were on the way.

The south Georgia police and sheriff's departments had been dealing with evacuations in the face of hurricanes for years. The residents might listen to them, he thought, but they didn't think much of a bunch of boys from Washington telling them what to do.

"Wait'll the word gets out about the airports," said Wiggins.

Wally nodded grimly. The St. Simons airport had been quietly closed for anything but priority flights at 3:00. And Glynco Jetport was going to shut down all commercial flights at 5:00 P.M. The St. Simons residents knew nothing about the plague outbreak on St. Cyrils. They had been told they had to evacuate because of a bomb threat on the north end. When they found out about the airport shutdowns, all hell was going to break loose. They'd be ready to believe an H-bomb was planted on the island.

Wiggins lit a Tareyton and blew a cloud of blue smoke into the room. "What about the phone line to St. Cyrils? Did you ever get through?"

Wally swiveled his chair away and focused on the window. "We're just the flunkies, Pete," he said in a low voice. He turned back then and leveled his gaze at Wiggins. "Do you think the FBI gives a shit about local jurisdiction?" They knew how to lop off your balls, he thought. Clean as a Sears Roebuck hog ringer.

But what did he expect?"

His fist tightened in his palm and his eyes grew dark

with pain as he thought of a little boy named Calvin, and of the two dead deputies who tried to rescue him.

The phone was ringing. It had not stopped all day.

"It's the doctor's office again," said Marge Tyson.

"Tell 'em I'm out," Wally said abruptly. "Tell 'em I'm gone for the day."

Chapter 37

THE SETTING SUN WAS A FIREBALL FLAMING THE MARSH, BUT on the higher ground, deep shadows crept through the woods and darkened the lodge. A chill was settling over the Great Room.

Shivering under her plastic isolation gown, Sally reached for the light switch. As the lamp threw a circle of yellow light into the room, Iguana's eyes opened. They were bright with fever. His face was flushed.

"It's time for another shot," she said.

He stared at her with open hostility.

Still not going to talk, are you? she thought. Iguana had not spoken to her or anyone else. Bru had tried to question him again and again, first to get answers for the FBI, and later, for his own information. He finally brought in Tony, gowned and gloved, to talk to him in Spanish. Their only answer had been the chatter of teeth as another shaking chill seized the terrorist's body.

She checked the supplies she had laid out. The end table was covered with vials of sterile water, syringes, medication, and alcohol wipes. She swiped the top of the vial with alcohol, drew up the reconstituted chloramphenicol in a large syringe, and reached for a makeshift tourniquet made from strips of a rubber glove knotted together. As she snapped it around his upper arm, a knot came loose. "Damn," she muttered, and tied it again, wondering if she would have remembered to include tourniquets if she had been in charge of the airlift pack.

She tapped the vein at the crook of his arm and tried to make it rise. It was flaccid. A quick glance at his shriveled lips showed how dehydrated he was. Dry as a bone, she thought. And he wasn't putting out much, either; the plastic pitcher she had handed him showed barely an inch of dark urine. Less than 150 ccs. He was going to go into shock unless they got more fluids into him. They should have sent IV fluids, she thought. A bag of D5W would do a better job than fluids by mouth dumped into a stomach tortured with nausea. She slapped the bluish vein and felt again. This time a faint pulse ticked rapidly against her fingertips.

She touched the beveled point of the needle to skin glistening with alcohol and felt the sudden lack of resistance as it slid into the vein. He had had his first injection six hours ago. So far, it hadn't touched him, but at least the vomiting had stopped, thanks to some Phenergan that Lillian had in her stockpile. He still had tachycardia; his pulse hovered at 130. And his temp was 103.6. She was afraid to give him aspirin to bring it down for fear of setting off the terrible nausea again.

She was slowly pushing the medication into his vein when suddenly the lights flickered off. In a moment they came back on, flickered again, then steadied. The generators, she thought, remembering what Lillian had said. They must be nearly empty. The diesel fuel was still on the barge.

It was going to be dark soon. She shivered. At least Nathan and Ashley were together. Calvin was out there alone, and night was coming.

She held a glass of water to Iguana's lips and urged him to drink. He managed to swallow barely half of it before he shook his head and clamped his lips together.

When the lights flickered again, she hurried up to the second floor to a room off the balcony and looked in. Alex Borden was sprawled on the bed asleep. The empty bottle of gin lay on the floor. The tray of sandwiches and juice she had brought him earlier sat untouched on the dark oak night table. The sour odor of his breath filled the room and she felt her stomach lurch. Thankful that she did not have to contend with Borden just then, she closed the door softly and went down the stairs.

Flicking off the lamp, she stripped off gown and mask in the entry hall and tapped on the dining room door.

"Who's there?" came Tuck Perry's cautious voice.

"It's me."

The lock turned and the door swung open. She dropped her inner gloves into the black plastic bag and turned to Tuck. "Where's Bru?"

The girl jiggled the lock to make sure it would hold, and nodded toward the kitchen. "They're getting something over the radio."

Bru and Sir William were huddled over the little portable Sony, but it was switched off now, and the two men were deep in conversation. Bru looked up sharply as Sally came in. "Will he talk yet?"

She shook her head and glanced toward the kitchen sink. She wanted desperately to scrub her hands, but Lena Jefferson was there, running water into a large blue enameled pot. Three others, filled to the rim, sat on the wide white drainboard at her side. Sally wondered how Lena stayed so calm. She had to know that Leroy was at risk. But so was everybody else now. Their only hope was to keep exposure down.

Across the room, Lillian trimmed the wick of an oil lamp while Cass Tompkins filled another from a plastic jug of yellow lemon-scented oil. Three more oil lamps, a Coleman lantern, and a box of flashlights and batteries sat on the worktable. Preparations for a power failure, thought Sally. She looked at Bru. "Any news?"

Bru glanced at the FM transceiver. "Nothing in English. And Tony's asleep. I can't make much sense of what they're saying."

"I meant the radio."

Bru exchanged a look with the ambassador before he said, "The six o'clock news says we're still being held hostage. There's not a word about our takeover." Sarcasm tinged his voice. "But you'll be glad to know that everything is just fine here. According to official sources, 'rumors of a plague outbreak on St. Cyrils Island are entirely false.' "

"They said that?"

He nodded grimly. And as the lights flickered out again, a hard smile tracked across his lips. "This just in from our Washington bureau: The St. Cyrils Island hostages have been thrown to the wolves."

El Ojo looked out toward the west from the widow's walk. The sun was sinking over the marsh, streaking the sky with red-golds and pinks. He turned slowly, scanning the clustered outbuildings to the northwest, the road to the northeast.

He had only a handful of men now. Only three he could count on: one at the boardwalk tower, another near the lodge, the third replacing the bastard La Culebra at the lighthouse. The fourth was crazy—*loco*—wandering through the woods with a mind as twisted as a mad dog's. The man's transmissions had stopped an hour ago, but what he had babbled then might be of use: He had seen two of the hostages loose on the island. El Ojo swung toward the southeast toward the curving spit of higher ground that wrapped around a bay of marsh. In the distance he could see the narrow island of trees that marked the Guale Indian mounds.

He scanned the twisting curves of Oyster Creek. The white motor launch tugged at its mooring as the tide came in. The floating dock was rising now, its angle less steep. The Cigarette was gone. This slow boat was their only way of escaping the island now. Hopeless—unless they

could retake hostages. There were too many defending the
lodge, too many weapons, but two people out there—alone—
that was another thing.

And when night came, when their goggles faded the
dark to shades of gray, they would have the advantage.

The helicopter had destroyed the Cigarette, had blown
La Culebra to a richly deserved hell. If they were to have a
chance with the launch, they must have hostages. But
hostages alone were not enough; the government must
know it, know that if they destroyed the launch they would
destroy their own people.

He looked back at the little house that sat on the edge of
the marsh. The black couple's house. It held the only other
radiotelephone on the island.

It was going to be their line to escape.

Calvin Borden pushed aside the curtain and looked out
toward the old lodge. The man with the gun was still
there. Blinking, he slid away from the window and crept
back down the hall to the kitchen in the back.

The kitchen was shadowy. It was going to be dark soon,
he thought. It had to be time for supper. He scooped more
peanut butter out of a half-empty Peter Pan jar and spread
it on a heel of bread. He had drunk all the milk, but there
was still a half-empty carton of orange juice in the
refrigerator.

He reached for the refrigerator door and opened it. As
he did, the motor of the old Frigidaire shuddered to a
stop. The light inside was off. He shut the door quickly
and opened it a crack. The light was still off. He bit his
lip. All he did was open the old door. Lena and Leroy
were really going to be mad.

He wolfed down the peanut butter and followed it with a
half-dozen Oreos he found in the cupboard. In search of
something else to eat, he opened cabinets and drawers.
There was a penlight in one, next to the phone book. He
switched it on and a narrow beam played on the black
radiotelephone on the countertop. He put it in his pocket.

It was all right to take it, he told himself. He was going to give it back later.

He crept down the hall to the dim room where Tim Jefferson stayed, and slipped inside. The windows here faced toward the east, away from the old lodge. He felt safer here.

The old iron bed squatted against one wall. Lifting the blue chenille spread, he crept underneath and reached for the pile of magazines near the head of the bed. Taking one, he pillowed his head on the rest, switched on the penlight, and opened the magazine. And deep in his cave, eyes widening, he began to turn the pages of the May issue of *Heavy Metal*.

The surface of the rain pond glowed bloodred in the sunset. As Ashley knelt to drink, something splashed at the edge of the water beneath a cluster of cattails. She stared. A frog. It was only a frog. Black ripples rode the scarlet surface of the pond in the wake of the creature.

The cattails trembled. She caught her breath as a thick snake glided silently into the water, its dark sinuous body undulating as it followed its prey. Ashley gave a little shriek and scrambled to her feet.

"Sh-sh-sh." Nathan pulled her down into the saw grass ringing the pond and stared anxiously around the shadowy clearing.

"Cottonmouth," she whispered. Her horrified gaze tracked the moccasin, then darted toward the edge of the pond. Snakes always came in pairs. "Give me the gun."

He looked at her without comprehension.

"Give me the gun."

He shook his head. "You can't shoot."

"Yes, I can. Daddy taught me."

'No." His eyes slid toward the woods. "Somebody'll hear."

"Come on, then. We've got to get out of here." She scrambled to her feet and, head low, ran toward a grove of trees at the dark edge of the woods. Limping, cradling his injured arm against his side, Nathan followed.

They huddled together under the whispering branches of a giant cedar and stared out at the dying light. Like Neanderthals in a cave, she thought. But there weren't any caves on the island; there weren't any safe places. And it was going to be dark soon. She could hear the night sounds beginning, and from a hidden place an owl called. Another night to get through.

Yesterday at sunset she had dressed for dinner and everything had been ordinary and normal and boring. She had dressed and combed her hair, and then she had had a fight with her brother. Over something that didn't really matter, she thought. Her words had been sharp and belittling. Hateful. But she didn't mean it. He had to know she didn't mean it, didn't he? She tried to picture him, tried to imagine him smiling at her, but with a start she realized that she couldn't remember the color of his eyes or the shape of his mouth. His face was blurred like a watercolor in the rain. She pressed her lips against Nathan's throat and began to cry.

"What's wrong?" he whispered.

Everything. Everything was wrong. "Calvin," she said. "I can't remember what he looks like."

He wrapped his good arm around her and they clung together as night crept in from the sea and the purpling twilight drew strange silhouettes and monstrous shapes that shuddered in the wind.

A swarm of mosquitoes rose from the marsh like a curl of smoke, and soon they were covered with hundreds of the insects.

They ran, slapping at the mosquitoes, darting to higher ground. By the time they reached the crest of a wooded sand hill and slid down the other side, they had left most of the swarm behind. Collapsing in a pile of leaves, Ashley rubbed her neck, and a streak of blood, charcoal in the fading light, came away on her hand. She moaned with the stinging pain. "I never saw mosquitoes like that. Not even in August."

"I know." Nathan rubbed an eyelid swelling with a dozen bites. "Lillian said they hang around until December sometimes."

A rustle in the underbrush. Nathan's hand flew to the gun tucked in his belt. It came again skirting them, moving into a thicket of young pine.

Ashley's gaze froze on the moving branches.

A low, muffled snort.

God.

Another.

What was it?

Nathan let out a breath. "A pig. I think it's a pig," he whispered.

Ashley stared. She knew there were wild pigs on the island, but she had never seen one. "Do they have tusks?

"I don't think so," he began, then broke off as she got to her feet. "Where are you going?"

"Anywhere. Out of here."

Moving as silently as they could, they made their way through the darkening woods until the trees thinned and the prairie began. There was more light here. Just ahead, an armadillo rooted at the dim edge of the mowed section of grass that marked the landing strip. Beyond the prairie the ocean drummed the shore, and to the northeast, the sea oats that covered the high dunes like pale fur rippled in the last of the light.

"Let's get back to the mausoleum," whispered Nathan. "Before it gets too dark."

She shook her head. "No." She couldn't. She couldn't go back to that dead place again no matter what happened.

"But we can't stay here."

"We can go to the dunes," she said. The high sand hills would be safe, she thought. They could see off in all directions and nothing could creep up behind them. She ran ahead toward the narrow shell road that led toward the Atlantic. Limping, Nathan followed.

Neither noticed the faint rustling of a clump of sparkle-berry behind them. Neither saw the dim outline of the armed man who watched.

For hours the terrorist had been quite mad. That morning he had run for miles toward the lighthouse, pleading, begging La Culebra to wait for him. But the boat was gone, and with it the last tags of rationality. The voice had begun to speak to him then, whispering in his ear, urging, insinuating. He recognized the sound of it. It was his mother's.

Stumbling back to the woods, he had waited for darkness and for the voice to return. And when the bark of El Ojo's commands had registered in his brain, he'd switched off the transceiver.

He parted the low branches and looked out across the prairie. The boy and the girl were no more than dim outlines in the purpling light.

Two of them, said the voice. *Looking for you.*

El Ojo had sent them. He was sure of it. El Ojo wanted him dead and he had sent them. He switched on the transceiver and holding it to his lips, laughed softly. "You have failed," he said. "The boy and the girl. They cannot see me."

There was a pause, and then the transceiver's hiss became El Ojo's voice, low, cautious. "W...re are you?"

He narrowed his eyes; he would not be tricked so easily. "Where they will never find me."

A pause. "They must be punished, then."

Yes, he thought, and stared across the prairie. The two had crossed the landing strip now. Beyond them the high dunes faded to purple in the last light.

"Where did they go?"

"Where the wild oats hear the sea," he answered slyly. Then flicking off the transceiver, he scratched a hole in the sand beneath a clump of rustling bamboo and buried it. With a final look toward the prairie, he began to move quietly in the opposite direction.

He stopped when the voice came again:

How many more? How many more with the face of death are waiting for you in the woods?

He knew that she was right. If they came close, he would die. He could feel his body swelling, his skin splitting open like the skin of rotting fruit. His gorge rose and he shivered.

It had been that way when he was a child. He was eight years old when plague had decimated his village: blackwater fever that followed the clouds of mosquitoes swarming from the lowland. For days he shook with chills and burned with fever. At first his mother had been there, holding a cup to his lips, cradling him in her arms. Then no one came. And when finally he woke, when he was able to stand on legs of sand, it was the trail of ants and the low humming of the flies that led him to his mother.

He vomited silently into a shallow bowl of earth between two snaking roots and clutched at the rough trunk of a tree until his strength came back. Then he began to lope through the woods toward the west.

The marsh lay in full twilight now. The tide had begun to turn over an hour ago, but it still ran low. At the sandy edge of the marsh grass, a living tide of fiddler crabs washed away at his step. He stared at the dark salt marsh stretching for miles to the west.

The only way, said the voice. *The only way.*

Catching his breath, he stepped out onto the sea of grass.

With the pressure of his boot the muck grabbed hold, and when his foot broke suction, it gurgled like a drowning thing. Staring wildly, he took another step. Another. Dark marsh grass brushed his knees. Cold water seeped into his boots and he felt his feet begin to numb. As the twilight dimmed, he picked up his speed, pacing himself to the beat of his heart and the rush of air in and out of his lungs.

The slogging rhythm of his steps masked the sound that came from his left—a slapping sound, followed by a splash, as if something broad and heavy struck the water.

At the low-pitched grunt he froze, his chin jerking toward the sound, his eyes dilating.

At first he thought it was a half-submerged log. Then it moved. And in the thick gray remnants of light it opened terrible jaws.

He gasped. Jets of brine spurting with each step, he ran. He ran without daring to look back, sure that his pounding, splashing footsteps were echoed by the giant alligator's.

He dashed headlong until his foot plunged into a narrow, twisting rivulet sequestered in the grass. His boot lodged shin-deep in the mud, and as he fell forward, sprawling facedown in the chilly water, he heard the unmistakable sound of bone snapping.

The pain in his shin was knives and ice. He grabbed at his leg, digging, clawing, shredding his hands on the razored shells of oysters, but each desperate thrash of arms and body drove his leg deeper into the muck.

Panting with pain and exhaustion, he finally lay still. He could feel the heat of his body draining away in the water and the sucking chill of the mud.

The cold numbed his leg, dimming the pain, replacing it with an awful clarity of mind. The voice was suddenly gone and he knew he was alone. He began to howl then— great shuddering howls—the anguished, wordless wail of a wild thing in a trap. And he did not stop until the deep black tide rolling in with the night crept up his throat and pulsed into his open mouth.

He surrendered then to the dark sea, his arms bobbing gently, his hair flowing like grass in the salt current. And at full tide, when the moon came out and flooded the drowned marsh with silver, it reflected from his eyes with a flat, cold glow.

The yellow light of the oil lamp crept up the bookshelves of the third-floor alcove and reflected dully from the silver tape that sealed the double doors. Sally switched off the dimming flashlight and looked around the room. "Can't anybody sleep? It's nearly midnight."

Bru looked up from his conversation with Sir William and patted the couch. "Sit down. You look bushed."

She sank down next to him. Across from her, Tim Jefferson sprawled in a leather recliner, his hand shading his eyes from the flickering light. He ought to get some rest, she thought, while it was quiet. He had been on watch until Miranda Gervin had taken his place down the hall at sunset. They had heard no more gunshots since then, and once or twice Sally had even been able to forget the terrorists waiting outside in the dark.

"He still won't talk, will he?" asked Bru. He meant Iguana.

She shook her head. "No. But I haven't seen him for a while. I've been keeping Lillian company in the kitchen." She dreaded going back into the Great Room. She dreaded the faint sick smell that crept through the mask and into her nose and lungs. She had felt the same way about patients dying from AIDS and fulminant hepatitis. You did what you had to do, she thought. Then you got out. You got out and you scrubbed your hands until they were raw. And afterward you dealt with the pangs of guilt that told you those were human beings in there, with human needs. "He was asleep the last time I checked him."

"Most of us haven't thought much of sleep, I'm afraid," said Sir William.

"Maybe it's the idea that there's nothing between us and disaster except Cass Tompkins," said Tuck Perry. Cass had taken over the dining room watch from Sir William, while Lillian, armed with a handgun, guarded the kitchen. "Call it a vote of no confidence." She pushed a round of Brie and a tin of rice crackers toward Sally. "Have some cheese."

Paige Cole opened her eyes and stretched. "That sounds like a good idea." She was lying on the floor next to the couch, drowsy after another of Sally's Benadryls. Exhausted, Dave Cole was asleep down the hall.

Paige sat up and pulled the thick patchwork quilt around her shoulders. "It's cold in here."

"I thought you were sleeping," said Tuck.

"Not for a while now. I had a dream."

Tuck twisted a lock of pale hair. "You might as well go back to sleep. It's all a nightmare, anyway, so what's the difference?"

Paige cut off a wedge of cheese before she said, "Dreams are worse. In a way they are, anyway. When you're sleeping, you're alone." She took a bite of cheese and stared around the room. "We ought to do something together. Read out loud. something . . ." She struggled to her feet and, dragging the quilt behind her, went to the bookshelf.

Tim Jefferson spoke without moving. "There're some games over there. On the bottom shelf."

Swathed in patchwork, Paige squatted down and took a look. "Checkers. Whoopee." She rummaged through a stack of boxes. "Here we go. Trivial Pursuit. Who's on?"

Tuck took the dark blue box from Paige's outstretched hand. "How about the men against the women?"

Sally stared at her blankly. Trivial Pursuit? What could be more appropriate when plague breaks out and you're under siege? she thought. Maybe a brisk game of Hangman? The idea was ludicrous, and yet at the same time somehow it wasn't. She remembered playing Monopoly with her sister the night their grandmother died: she and Barb, laughing hard, playing as if their life depended on it.

It was a way to forget for a little while, she thought. But she knew that wasn't really true. It was only a way to postpone—no, not even that. It was aspirin for a toothache; it still hurt, but you didn't mind as much.

Bru looked at her closely for a moment, and his hand closed over hers. Then he said lightly to the others, "Sure. We'll take you on."

Sally stared at the open box of colorful tokens and cards. "Sure." Then she smiled slowly. "And you guys had better watch your step."

Tuck held up the dice. "We need to roll, to see which team starts."

"We'll let you ladies go first," said Bru.

Paige plopped next to the coffee table and adjusted her quilt. "Don't do us any favors."

"That's all right," said Sally. "They'll be sorry for their chauvinist remarks." She tipped her head and gave Bru a smile. "We're going to love it when you lose."

He grinned. "Ah, there she is. A lady after Charles Dickens's heart—'affection beaming in one eye and calculation out of the other.' "

Raising an eyebrow, Sally selected a player disk. "Pink. Unless you boys want that color," she added quickly.

"I guess it's blue," Bru said, "for us puppy dog's tails."

Tuck rolled the die. "Let's try geography."

"Geography it is." Bru pulled a card out of the box. "In what city was the first subway excavated?"

Sally looked at the others. "New York?"

"Sounds good to me," said Tuck.

Bru clucked and shook his head. "Provincialism. Trips them up every time."

"London, wasn't it?" said Sir William.

At Bru's nod Paige said, "Nobody gave me a chance to answer. I might have said London."

Tim Jefferson leaned forward and the leather recliner popped upright. "Sure you would," he said with a grin, and grabbed up the die and tossed. "Six for a wedge. We'll go for history."

"Don't count your wedges before they're hatched," said Tuck.

Squinting in the dim light, Sally stared at the card. "Is history blue?"

"Yellow."

"Okay, Mr. Wizard. What was the headline of the *New York Daily Mirror* on December 6, 1933?"

"I know that one," said Bru. " 'Prohibition' something." He frowned, then his brow smoothed. " 'Prohibition Ends At Last.' "

Sally looked up in surprise. "That's right."

"How in the world did you know that?" asked Paige.

"He's played it before," said Tuck. "He remembered."

"I am truly shocked at your insinuation," said Bru. "Actually, I learned it from Miss Hattie Mae Henderson, my eighth-grade civics teacher. As I recall, Miss Hattie was particularly scornful about the 'at last' part. It was a black moment for her—and for the nation." He rolled his eyes toward the ceiling. "A day of infamy.

"She was one of those wonders of southern womanhood." Then leaning forward, Bru dropped his voice to a low, confiding tone and said, "Hattie Mae Henderson was not naked under her clothes."

Paige snorted.

"It's true. She was born with a swaddling cloth. And when they unwrapped her, they found a tiny little corset with bones, and linen drawers."

"Linen drawers," Sally repeated solemnly.

"It was only proper," Bru said with equal solemnity.

"Sounds rather like my old nanny," Sir William observed. "One morning I found her knickers hanging out the window. Frozen hard. The wind had puffed them up, you see, and they were shaped rather like Miss Pettibone herself. I thought they really were—a part of her, that is."

When the laughter died, Tim said, "We go again."

Bru tossed the die. "Geography."

Sally pulled out a card. "What was the nickname of Alcatraz Prison?"

"St. Cyrils Island," said Tuck.

No one laughed.

"It's our turn, I believe," Bru said lightly. But though they kept on playing, the steam had gone out of the game.

Tim was reaching for a blue wedge to tuck into the player disc when they heard the sound. It came from somewhere outside the locked doors that connected the wing to the rest of the third floor—a faint creaking. He froze with the little plastic wedge between his fingers. "Hear that?"

Tuck's green eyes grew alert as a cat's. "What is it?"

"The house," said Sally. Houses always made sounds in the night. "It's just the timbers."

Silence. Then another creak.

Paige Cole caught her breath. "The terrorists," she whispered. "They got in."

"No," said Bru quickly.

"They did. I know they did."

Sally shook her head—a little nervous shake. "They couldn't." But no one was guarding the Great Room, she thought, or the entry hall. Her eyes sought Bru's, but his were locked on the door.

A sharp scrabbling brought him to his feet and he grabbed for the rifle.

A scratching sound, as if something metal played against the brass lock. The doors shuddered, held, shuddered again. "Let me in."

A nervous laugh caught in Sally's throat. "It's Alex Borden."

"Drunk," said Tim. "He's drunk."

The pounding started then—a rhythmic pounding of flesh against wood that echoed through the room like thunder.

Tim's eyes cut toward the door. "It'll hold. It's got a dead bolt."

The doors boomed. The dead bolt ticked in its socket.

Paige clamped her hands over her ears. "Make him stop." Her frantic gaze darted wildly from face to face. "Make him stop." Tripping over the quilt, nearly falling, she scrambled to her feet and ran to the door. "Stop it, damn you. Stop it!"

A thick silence came. A silence so deep they could hear the rasp of Borden's breath on the other side of the door—hear it quicken and catch and shatter in an explosion of strangled coughing.

The relief skittering over Paige's face changed to horror. "Oh, god," she whispered. "He's got it."

They stared at the door as if they could see through it,

as if they could see his fingers scrabbling at the thick wood, see his face growing dusky with air hunger.

They stared and held their breath because the terrible spasm of his throat and lungs felt like their own.

The cough drew away to guttural rasps, then nothing.

They looked at each other in shocked silence as the door to the back stairs swung open and a white-faced Lillian came in. She clutched a handgun in one hand and a flashlight in the other. "I heard a noise."

From the hallway another voice said, "So did I." Miranda Gervin came in carrying a rifle.

"It was Alex Borden," said Bru. He looked from one to the other before he said, "We think he's sick."

Lillian closed her eyes for a long moment. They were etched in deep shadows, and when she opened them again, she looked suddenly very old. "We thought this might happen," she said slowly. "But the doors are heavy. They ought to hold." She turned abruptly, saying. "I have to go back down," and the door closed behind her.

After a moment's silence, Miranda went back down the hall.

Paige glanced toward the silent double door. "I guess he needs a doctor. Do you want me to wake up Dave?"

Sally bit a nail. Dave was exhausted. And now it looked like they would need him worse later. She shook her head. "Let him sleep."

Paige brushed a curly strand of hair out of her eyes and stared at Sally. "But he needs medicine, doesn't he? Antibiotics, like Iguana's getting."

Sally could not meet her eyes. Her gaze slid toward Bru and Sir William, then away, and finally came to rest on the rug. "We did that," she finally said. "He was contaminated, so we started him on antibiotics nearly twelve hours ago." She looked up at Bru then, and her eyes were bleak. "We thought it would prevent the plague."

"Oh, shit," Paige whispered.

"Iguana's threat wasn't an idle one, was it?" said Sir William slowly. "No prevention. No cure."

Tuck Perry stared around the room with eyes that looked like a cornered animal's. "I'm getting out of here." She ran toward the back stairs and grabbed the doorknob.

"No." Bru's hand closed over hers. His voice was low and intense. "You can't do that. It's suicide."

"Suicide?" Her green eyes blazed. "You're full of shit. What do you think this place is?" She twisted and stared at the others. "What have we got? Medicine that doesn't work. Two guys coughing shit over half the house. Maybe you think the marines are going to land just like in a John Wayne movie, huh?" Her chin jerked up and she stared at Bru, contempt burning in her eyes. "Big government man, aren't you? Lots of pull. I'm going to tell you something. Your government sucks. It fucking sucks."

"We've got a chance here. That's more than we'd have out there."

"You don't know that. Nathan's out there. And Ashley and the kid."

Sally slipped an arm around her shoulder. "Tuck," she said gently, "they may not be alive."

"Oh, Christ." Tuck's hand flew to her mouth. "Oh, Christ." The girl crumpled in Sally's arms and began to sob.

Patting her, whispering against Tuck's silky hair, Sally led her back to the couch and sat down beside her.

The sharp intake of Paige Cole's breath made Sally stare. The girl was pointing toward the double door. Her hand trembled.

At first, Sally saw only the dull silver AC tape tracking around each door seam like a child's crayoned outline. Then she saw the glint of lamplight on bright metal and she heard the sound of splitting fabric as a slim knife blade worked through the tape and slid upward toward the lock.

Tim jumped to his feet. "Shit. He's got a pocket knife."

Somehow Sally was on her feet, too, walking toward the door, saying in a firm, commanding voice, "Mr. Borden. go to bed now. You need to go to bed."

The blade slowed, paused.

"I'm a nurse, Mr. Borden. I'm going to take care of you. But first you have to go to your room and go to bed." Her voice grew louder. "Go to bed."

The voice on the other side of the door was muffled. "Dark. It's dark in here."

"I'll come soon, Mr. Borden. I'll bring a light." She took a breath. "I promise." Nails biting into her palm, she stared at the knife blade. Slowly it withdrew and disappeared. "That's right, Mr. Borden." She emphasized each word. "Now go to bed."

At first there was no sound. Then a floorboard creaked and she heard a footstep. A pause. Another—fainter, this time. Then nothing.

Knees trembling, Sally sank to the floor as Paige threw down the patchwork quilt and ran for the AC tape. Staring, not quite comprehending, Sally watched as the girl taped and retaped the door with the dwindling roll, watched as she reinforced the tape with card after card from the Trivial Pursuit game until finally the tape was gone and the doors were studded with hundreds of multicolored cards crisscrossed with silver.

She stared at the dark heavy doors as if they were a gate to another time, as if the only thing holding them shut was a zigzag, ragtag wreath of cardboard. It needs a cross in the center, she thought. A cross made of rowan twigs. And fennel seed to stuff in the keyhole and sprigs of rosemary knotted with string.

The stunned silence ended as the empty roll of tape clattered to the floor. Tuck's wide gaze slid toward Sally. "Can he get a knife blade through all that?"

Sally shook her head. "I don't know." Slowly she got to her feet, picked up the flashlight, and moved toward the back stairs.

Bru looked up sharply. "Where are you going?"

"It's time for their medicine," she said. "It's been six hours since the last dose. I have to go down."

"You can't," he said. "He's got a knife."

"He must have had it in his pocket all along," she said.

"He won't hurt me," She turned and reached for the doorknob.

"I'll go with you, then."

"No," she said quickly. "They're both contagious. Nobody should go in there unless it's necessary."

His hand closed over her arm. "I think it's necessary."

She looked into his eyes., "Thanks, but no." When he started to protest, she laid a finger lightly across his lips. "Sorry. But you flunked that crash course of mine in isolation techniques." She looked around the room. "All of you did, I'm afraid. I'm a lousy teacher." And then before he could say anything more, she opened the door and started down the stairs.

The narrow stairwell was dark. Overhead, a naked light bulb blinked in the pale circle of her flashlight like a dead white eye. She turned the light downward toward the wooden steps and felt the blackness close around her body like a physical thing.

Footsteps echoing, she moved slowly down the stairs. At the second-floor landing, dull silver tape crept around the edges of the door. Another strip, anchored on the dark floor planks, sealed the crack at the bottom. Staring, she caught her breath. The tape was split along the top of the door and down the side. So he'd been there, too. She felt her heart beating in her throat. They'd have to tape it. Tape it again.

Clutching her dimming light, she hurried past the door. The stairs turned here at the landing. She swung the flashlight down the final flight and froze.

Behind her, just behind, she heard a sharp click and the unmistakable sound of tape ripping away from the floor.

Whirling, almost tripping, she spun toward the sound and stared in horror as the door slowly opened. A scream ripped from her throat as Alex Borden, knife blade pressed against the lock, stepped through.

Dully she heard the rush of footsteps overhead and the door to the kitchen opening below. She thought she heard Bru's voice. Then someone was running down the stairs.

And from the kitchen came a flicker of light as Lillian hurried up.

She stared at Alex Borden's face. A tiny line of spittle ran from the corner of his cracking lips. Numbly she felt his sour breath blow against her face.

He swayed and reached for the doorjamb. "Sorry," he said unsteadily. "I don't feel very good." His eyes glittered and danced with fever and when they slid toward hers they widened with the bright edge of sudden fear. "Don't make me go back in there," he said, and his voice ebbed to a child's pleading whimper. "It's dark in there. It's very dark."

She could not move at all for a moment. When she could, she reached out with a hand as cold as winter and took his arm. "I said I'd bring you a light, Mr. Borden. Now it's time to go to bed."

SATURDAY

CRISIS

Chapter 38

THE SITUATION ROOM WAS BLUE WITH SMOKE. THE SINUS PILL
the DCI had taken was not only ineffective, it was making
him groggy. He glanced at his watch. It was after midnight. He had had only six hours of disturbed sleep in the
last thirty-six, and that in the middle of the day. The quart
of coffee he had drunk since he woke was stretching his
nerves to the limit.

The loss of Orlando Salazar had been a heavy blow. He
had eluded their Miami airport net, and now they had the
entire city for a fishing hole. The DCI was sure the man
was still in Miami. Miami was the gateway to South and
Central America and the Caribbean. He was in Miami, he
thought—if he was in the country at all. But south Florida
was a land with a thousand little bays and islands, a
thousand harbors for as many illicit smuggling boats. If
someone wanted to leave the country, there were many
ways to arrange it if you had the fee.

The national security adviser had begun to talk again
about reprisals against the government of Guatemala.

"With all due respect," Harold Walheimer began, "I'd
like to remind everyone that we've been over all this. We
agreed last night that we had nothing to gain from that sort
of action. Guatemala has offered us her complete cooperation, and she has consistently denied any connection with
these terrorists. We have no reason to think otherwise."

"On the other hand," the chairman began, "swift reprisal can act as an object lesson here. The—"

The DCI scowled. There was a fucking time bomb on

the mainland and this clown was talking reprisal. "Excuse me, Andrew, but it seems to me that we're setting the wrong priorities. This country is threatened with a disease that antibiotics won't touch—if we can believe the CDC, that is," he added quickly. "Where is our contingency plan in case this gets out on the mainland?"

Andrew Hagen raised an eyebrow. "It's my understanding that that's exactly what we're formulating here."

The DCI frowned. *Formulating*. Something for Mommy to do with baby's bottle, he thought. He fixed Hagen with a look. "I'm not hearing specifics."

"Perhaps you can give us those now," said the chairman with a thin smile.

"When cancer strikes an organism," he began, "radical treatment is necessary. We have to be prepared no matter where that cancer strikes. If plague shows up in a major city and it's not contained, there'll be no stopping it." He looked from one to the other. "I'm talking about stringent quarantine."

Carter Booth looked up. "Exactly what do you mean by 'stringent'?" The press secretary reached for another Tic Tac.

General Everett leaned forward. "The area would have to be cordoned," he said, "just as we've done with St. Cyrils Island."

"The threat will be to a densely populated area," added the DCI. "These terrorists aren't going to set off their aerosol in Small Town, U.S.A. We're talking about the quarantine of millions of people. And not one of them can be allowed to break that quarantine. Enforcement is going to take a lot of manpower; we're going to need state troopers, army, the National Guard—possibly the FBI," he added grudgingly. "And antiquated Civil Defense plans aren't going to help us here. I suggest we put the governor of every state on immediate standby alert."

"But there's another aspect," said Isaac Benjamin. "I'm thinking about animal vectors. You can't cordon off a bird population."

The DCI glared. Birds? Jesus Christ. What did it take to keep these people on the track? "I suggest that the animal vectors we need to worry about are the human variety. If this thing isn't isolated, we're going to see the United States go right down the drain."

The general nodded grimly. "Ripe for an enemy takeover."

"Are you suggesting we condemn an entire city to plague?" asked Carter Booth.

"If necessary, yes."

Andrew Hagen eyed the DCI. "Rather than see this nation destroy itself with the kind of surgery you're suggesting, I think we would better serve the country by a little prevention. An invasion force on St. Cyrils Island might well be the answer. I say the time for equivocation has passed."

A vein at George Everett's temple began to bulge. He drew himself up and stared at the chairman. "You're right about that," he said. "You are fucking well right that time has passed. It has passed to hell and gone. And now—*now*—you're suggesting that we invade the island. Well, sir, you are suggesting a suicide mission."

"I am suggesting a remedy—"

"You are suggesting a suicide mission," blazed the general. "To a plague island. Since this situation began, I have been advocating a timely invasion." Sarcasm tinged his voice. "Now, when it's too late, you think it's a good idea."

"I'd like to point out that it's not too late to question a captured terrorist."

"No? Well, I'd like to point out something to you. You seem to have forgotten that there was an attempt to leave St. Cyrils Island by sea today." The general's lips tightened. "We destroyed that boat. Do any of you know who was on board? Can any of you guarantee that there *are* any terrorists left to question?" His gaze pinned one after another, then his lips thinned and twisted into a smile that was devoid of humor. "I didn't think so." He stood abruptly. "And now if you'll excuse me, gentlemen, I'm going to take a crap."

They stared in silence as the general stalked from the room.

"Uh, I'd like to go further into the vector situation," pressed the science adviser. "Sylvatic plague is endemic in parts of the Southeast. I think it's necessary to examine the possibility of rodent or bird populations spreading this thing from St. Cyrils Island."

"How about from Washington, or New York City?" asked Carter Booth.

"Call Orkin," someone said. The laugh that followed was strained.

Harold Walheimer leaned forward. "I'd like to remind everyone of the number of government installations close to St. Cyrils Island." The security adviser looked grave. "If we have contamination of the South Georgia coast, we lose Fort Stewart and the Rapid Deployment Force. We'd have to evacuate. Hunter would be next. If it extends to Jacksonville, we lose three navy installations and the submarine grid. And what about King's Bay? Instead of a Trident base, we'll end up with a two-and-a-half-billion-dollar home for sick owls. If birds can carry this thing, the nation's entire security system is at risk."

The DCI stared at the man. Of course the nation's security system was at risk. The fucking *nation* was at risk. He bit his lip and tried to remember what, if anything, he had ever heard about animal vectors and Pestis 18.

The dying ape lay with its eyes closed, its hands folded across its chest. It was barely conscious now. He could hear its heartbeat echoed in the electronic bleat of the machines that recorded its dying.

". . . a matter of national security," said the priest. "A matter for the SPCA."

"It's the principal's office, for you, young man," said Miss Marstead. "This is a serious offense. Isn't that right?"

The ape turned its face blindly toward him and opened

bright blue eyes. Its mouth gaped; its tongue moved over
shriveled lips: "Daddy . . . help me . . . . Daddy . . ."

Jack Hubert woke to the thundering of his heart. A red
light shimmered in the dark. The EKG machine? Blinking,
he focused on it.

In relief, he saw that it was only the light on the motel
alarm clock. Nothing else. Just the clock.

Gradually the adrenaline spent itself and his heart slowed
to normal. But as it did, a dozen questions that he had
never allowed himself before crowded into his mind.

It was a very long time before he could go back to sleep.

Chapter 39

"DON'T DO IT!" BRU WAS RUNNING DOWN THE BACK STAIRS
toward the landing. "Don't go in there."

But Sally snatched the key from the lock, and pushing
Alex Borden ahead, stepped through the door and pulled it
shut. It closed behind her with a solid chunk. Like a log on
a fire, she thought. A bonfire.

Bonefire.

She aimed her light at the lock and turned the key.
Metal clacked on metal as the key withdrew.

"Sally!" The door shuddered with the hammer of his
fist.

"Everything is fine," she said, and her voice wavered
in her throat. Another thump. A pause. Then muffled
footsteps scuffed away down the stairs like rats scrabbling
in a wall.

Shadows stalked the yellow flashlight beam, circling it,
closing in at every flicker of its dying batteries. Each

sound, each stimulus, was heightened: the rat's wool of Alex Borden's jacket sleeve against her fingertips; the harsh rush of his breath; the hollow tap of their footsteps on the wooden floor.

They came to his room and the light crept up the wall, moved, found the bed, the table at its side. The light glinted on the pocket knife he held.

Gently she took it from him. "Lie down, Mr. Borden," she said.

Obedient as a child, he crawled into the bed.

She pulled off his shoes, and with hands that trembled, held a glass of lukewarm apple juice from the bedside tray and held it to his lips. "Drink this now."

His throat worked as he drank. When he was done, a fit of coughing racked his body and droplets of amber juice sputtered from his lips. He lay back shivering, in spite of the wool jacket he wore. The bed shook with the rigors of his chill.

"Try to sleep," she said, and drew a blue blanket over him. And when his eyes widened in fear, she pressed the flashlight into his hand. "I'll leave you this."

His fingers closed around it. The light threw a dim halo on the wall and bled its yellow watercolor onto a seascape, pale as glass and framed in driftwood.

She backed to the door, turned, opened it.

The hall was ink and shadow. She found the balcony rail and followed it until it became a banister plunging downward toward the black of the entry hall. At the foot of the stairs she huddled against the wall and shivered. Don't think about it, she told herself. Don't think. If she didn't think about it, the screaming in her mind would go away.

A bolt on the dining room door slid. "Sally."

It was Bru.

"No," Came a voice from the next room. "Not without a mask."

"Stop!" another yelled.

A pause. A scuffling sound. A click.

Sharp light dazzled her eyes.

"Oh, God. Sally." Bru's flashlight swung away as his arm closed around her shoulder. The tails of the bird's-eye mask he held to his face brushed her cheek as he pulled her toward the dining room.

When she realized what he was doing, she drew back. "No."

But he pushed her through the door and pulled it shut behind them.

Lamplight gleamed on the dining table and flickered on the dark tile floor. A half-dozen people stood in the room, their eyes locked on hers. The look in them was wary as if they saw a predator.

For a moment there was no sound, and then Paige Cole gave a single cry and buried her face against her husband's chest.

Dave Cole's eyes locked on Sally's.

"Sorry to wake you," Sally said. Then her mouth fell open and she blinked at the inane sound of her words.

"Oh, God," Paige whimpered. "Ohgod, ohgod."

Tuck Perry swung toward Bru. Her face was white. "You've killed us all. We're going to die." Her voice climbed to a howl. "We're gong to die."

Lillian took Tuck's arm. "Stop it. We were all exposed the minute Alex Borden opened that door."

"Maybe before that," said Dave slowly. "Through the heat vents." His gaze moved from one to another. "This makes it worse. A lot worse. But we can't stop taking precautions. It's all we've got now. We've got to try to keep the exposure to a minimum." His eyes slid toward the radiotelephone. He hesitated a moment, then reached for it. When the response came, he said, "This is Dr. David Cole. Get me somebody at the CDC."

A pause. "The Centers for Disease Control. In Atlanta."

Another pause. "We need their help. We need yours." He listened for a moment longer. Then his voice dropped, yet it had an intensity that carried through the room. "Damn you. God damn your soul to hell." The receiver banged onto its base and chattered to a stop with a nervous ticking sound.

Paige stared at it for a moment. Then she grabbed it up. "Please. Help us. Please." Her throat worked. "Please . . . please." She began to sob.

Dave shook his head, took the receiver away, and put it back down without a word.

Sally refused to go to bed. If she went to bed, the silence would let the thoughts come crowding out and she could not handle that just yet. She scrubbed her hands with Octagon soap until they were red and tender. Then, wrapped in Lillian's afghan, she huddled in a kitchen chair and sipped from a steaming mug of tea. The scent of the tea and the lemon filled her nose and she sniffed deeply, but she could not erase the lingering memory of Alex Borden's sour breath on her face or the look that glittered in his eyes.

Lillian was doling out vitamin C to everybody. One after another, they washed the thick tablets down with water from red and white paper cups. It won't do any harm, Sally thought, obediently swallowing hers when Lillian offered it. Maybe they should write a sequel to Linus Pauling's work, she thought. *Vitamin C and the Common Plague.*

Yet just below the surface of her deprecation lay the wild hope that the tablets would do some good. It was possible, wasn't it? Couldn't it be possible? If the vitamin C didn't work, what was left? Acupuncture with Lillian's knitting needles? Cupping? Plenty of cups and glasses in the cupboard, she thought. How about leeches?

Or a pocket full of posy.

We've got the antibiotics, she told herself, but as she did, her eyes narrowed. They had not worked; they were not going to work. She knew it—and so did Dave Cole. Even so, he had gone to give the midnight dose to Iguana and Alex Borden. He had nothing else to offer them.

Eye of newt, she thought, drawn up in a sterile syringe.

She stared around the shadowy kitchen. The power was gone, and with it the refrigeration, the water, the heat. A thin plume of smoke twisted from the chimney of the oil lamp, and as she focused on it, she knew that very little separated them now from a darker time when plague ran wild through London Town.

She stared at the flickering light until the dining room phone began to ring. It took a few moments for the sound to register and a few more before anyone moved to answer it.

We have that, she thought in relief. We have the phone. At least they had the radiotelephone for as long as its batteries lasted. Suddenly she saw it as a link. A bridge to clean white hospital beds and science and rationality. This was the twentieth century. People didn't die of the plague anymore. It was the twentieth century, not the eleventh, and they could do all sorts of things now. They could cure tuberculosis and leukemia. They could prevent polio.

And they could manipulate the genetic material of a bacteria and turn it into a killer no medicine could touch. . . .

Her hand flew to her throat as if she could slow the sudden choking beat of her heart. Fool, she thought. Superstitious idiot. She had been trying to turn an old black radiotelephone into a talisman. An amulet. A magic charm to keep away another dark age. She let out a little strangled sound that was meant to be a laugh. Instead, it came out sounding like a whimper.

Dave hung up the radiotelephone. "Change of heart."

"So our friendly phone operator came through, after all." Bru's voice was light, but he watched Dave Cole closely.

"He told me his career would be on the line for making that call to the CDC." He slid into a chair at the end of the dining table next to Sir William and Bru. "And I'm afraid it didn't do much good. The CDC is fresh out of magic bullets. They're operating in the dark just like we are."

Sir William gave Dave a sharp look. "What have they to say about the exposure?"

Dave gave a quick glance toward Cass Tompkins at the other end of the room, and lowered his voice. "We can't be sure about the central heat vents. We changed the filter and scrubbed down the grates, but there's better than an even chance that some bacteria got through. And now, with Alex Borden—" He hesitated. "We have to go on the assumption that the entire lodge is contaminated."

Bru searched his face. "Are you saying we're all going to get it?"

"I wish I could give you a definite answer. There are a lot of variables: general health, age, the number of bacteria in a given exposure, the virulence of the bacteria." His eyes slid away, then back. "We know it's virulent. Alex Borden came down hard with it in less than twenty-four hours. But that could be a fluke," he added quickly. "The man may be an alcoholic. If he is, it would make him more susceptible. But no matter how you cut it, he's contagious. Contagious as hell. And the antibiotics haven't helped too much."

Dave dropped his gaze to the table top and stared at the polished teak for a moment before he met Bru's eyes again. "That's a lie. The truth is, the antibiotics haven't helped at all. I don't think Iguana will make it through the night."

"What can we do?" probed Sir William.

"Not much. We can keep the exposure down and keep everyone's resistance as high as possible. That means we've got to watch fatigue, chilling, diet. Things like that. The stress doesn't help."

"In other words, 'nothing,' " said Bru. "There's nothing we can do at all."

"I wouldn't call it 'nothing,' " said Dave. "Leroy was exposed shortly after Alex Borden, and so far, he's all right." He looked toward the Franklin stove, where Paige was coaxing the beginnings of a fire from a handful of pine kindling. "I guess you already know that Sally is high risk. So is Lillian. They were both on the stairs when Alex came out. They were directly exposed. He looked at Bru. "So were you. But they're higher risk."

"Why?"

"Lillian's exposure was roughly equal to yours. But she's not a young woman anymore. She seems to be in good health, but she must be at least sixty and that's a factor. And Sally—" He broke off for a moment and stared at the kitchen door as Tony Herrera came in.

Bru followed his gaze. "Sally's young. She's got a chance."

Dave did not answer.

"Doesn't she?"

"We, uh, have to think about the central heat," said Dave. "Sally was sitting on the floor by one of the vents before we realized. She was breathing in anything that got through."

The fire crackling in the stove was the only sound for a moment. Bru narrowed his eyes. For a few moments he was deep in thought. Then he looked up suddenly. "I think Iguana's been lying about the plague."

Dave gave him a cautious look. "What do you mean?"

"How do we know he meant what he said? How do we know there's no cure?"

"The antibiotics—" Dave began.

Bru interrupted. "Would you take the chance of turning plague loose in the world if you knew there wasn't any cure?"

"Of course not."

"Then why do we think they would?"

"Because they're terrorists," Tony put in. "Extremists."

"That doesn't make them suicidal. And it doesn't mean they're planning genocide, either."

"What are you saying?"

Bru stood, took two steps, and turned. "I'm saying that they're mercenaries. They're not the type to go off the deep end. I don't think they'd take that kind of chance."

Sir William stared at Bru intently. "You think there might be a cure. Is that it?"

"Or a prevention. Think about it. It doesn't make sense otherwise."

"But they're afraid of us," said Dave. "They're afraid of infection."

"That's right. But that doesn't mean there isn't a cure. It just means they didn't bring it with them." He grabbed up a mask and a pair of gloves.

Dave jumped up. "What are you going to do?"

"I'm going to ask that son of a bitch a few more questions. And this time I'm going to get some answers." Bru grabbed up a flashlight and reached for the door. Just as he did, a yell from across the room stopped him.

"Out there." Cass Tompkins's eyes were riveted to something she saw through the window.

A dim yellow light bobbed in the darkness, paused, then zigzagged toward the trees. Bru threw open the window and aimed his flashlight.

It was Alex Borden.

"Good God," said Tony. "How did he get out? Why didn't we hear him?"

Bru glanced toward the Franklin stove. Flames leaped from a hissing pine knot with a sharp snap. "The fire. It must have covered the sound of the latch."

Tony stared at the others. "He'll die out there. We've got to get him back in."

"Wait," said Dave. "He's contagious. If we bring him back, he'll kill us all."

"But, out there he hasn't got a chance."

"No, he doesn't," Dave admitted. "Not there. Not here. Not anywhere."

The dim light from the dying flashlight glimmered in the night like a will-o'-the-wisp. Alex Borden followed the light, turning as each erratic tremor of his hand thrust it in another direction, pausing as its beam twitched downward or bobbed high among the shadowy treetops, until, confused, legs turning to water, he clutched at a low tree limb for balance.

At first he could not remember why he had gone outside the lodge. Then the sobering rush of cold salt air on his face brought relief from the terrible burning of his body. That was why. That was why he was here. Cool. It was so cool.

He sank to his knees and felt the delicious coldness of the ground begin to seep into them. So good. He stretched out on the ground with his fevered cheek against a patch of grass. His head hurt . . . hurt so bad. . . .

The cold night air eased the torture of his aching joints and numbed the pain in his temples. Then the next chill struck and his muscles contracted with the violence of it. For a few minutes he could do nothing but draw his twitching arms and his knees to his chest. He tried to speak through the chatter of his teeth, to call out for help, but the only sound he made was a low moan that might have come from an animal. He began to vomit then, emptying his stomach onto the black earth beneath a water oak, retching until only bile remained, and then not even that.

When the cramps in his belly subsided and the awful weakness ebbed a little, he got to his knees again and scrabbled for the flashlight he had dropped when the chill seized him. Swaying, he grabbed for a steadying branch and pulled himself up. He had to get to bed . . . go up to bed. . . . He could crawl into bed and get under the blanket and quilt.

He stumbled after the bobbing light that was no more than a dull glow now. Squinting, trying to focus eyes that would not quite track, he made out the dim horizontal line of a rising step. Get into bed, he thought. Go up to bed. And clutching at the rough railing of the cedar boardwalk, he began to climb.

Chapter 40

BLACK CLOUDS GNAWED AT THE MOON AND A RISING WIND chopped the sea into ink and froth. High above the beach, Ashley huddled on a sand dune swept by night winds. She wrapped her arms across her chest and shivered. Below her, a dark line of flotsam left by an ebbing tide followed the pale curving beach like a snake.

The rush of the surf merged with the whisper of sea oats and the even sounds of Nathan's breathing. She held her watch to her face and pressed a button on the dial. The dim light showed the time: 1:42. Nathan had been asleep for nearly an hour, lying on his side in the shallow depression they had dug in the sand.

Her stomach was suddenly, hollowly, empty. She had been hoarding half a cheese sandwich. For a time she had forgotten it, but now she could think of nothing else. Better not, she told herself. She might need it worse in the morning. But the insulin she had taken was near its peak now. If she didn't have something, she was going to be sick. Pulling it out of her pocket, she pinched off tiny pieces to make it last. The rye bread was stale and the cheese hardening, but nothing had ever tasted so good to her. When she finished, she lay back. But when she tried to sleep, each sound intensified in the night. Her eyes started open again and again, and when an intermittent but persistent rustling came, she sat up and stared.

From her position at the top of the dune, the prairie was a dark plane marbled with ashen streaks of sand. Turning her head, she looked down at the beach. Nothing.

The rustling came again, closer this time. Something was moving through the sea oats. Staring with eyes that burned from the salt wind, she tried to make it out. "Nathan," she whispered. Her fingers worked his shoulder and he moaned. "Nathan," she said again.

"Wha—?" He sat up and clutched at his injured arm. "What is it?"

"Over there."

Tensing, he reached for the gun in his belt and stared toward the sound. After a few moments he relaxed. "Just a rabbit," he said. "That's all." He sank back again. And in a few moments his breathing became regular again.

Don't let him go to sleep, she thought. She pressed her body as close to his as she could and closed her eyes, but as each new night sound came over the rhythmic wash of the surf, her heart quickened. Eyes wide, she stared into the dark, and with a sudden feeling of dread, imagined a thousand eyes staring back. She thought of the cottonmouth at the rain pond. There might be snakes here, too. There were supposed to be rattlesnakes in the dunes, weren't there? A dry stem slithered against another and she heard the slither of scales; a wind pulsed through the sea oats and she heard the hollow pulse of leather wings. And when something began to root less than a dozen feet away, she heard the sound of human feet. Jiggling Nathan's shoulder, she willed him to wake up.

Groaning, he struggled awake.

"Somebody's coming," she said.

His breath touched her ear. "Where?"

Her hand brushed across his mouth. "Sh-sh. Don't move." He can see us, she thought. He could see in the dark. She imagined the terrorist watching them through the single lens of his goggles, and the dread grew until it verged on panic. She wanted to run, wanted desperately to run, to plunge headlong down the dune toward the ocean, but she did not dare.

Her breath came in silent, shallow waves that did not fill her lungs. An eternity passed and suddenly she saw the

familiar shape of an armadillo outlined in the moonlight.
The relief that passed over her threatened to make her
faint. "Guess I was being silly," she whispered weakly.

Nathan answered with a faint snore.

Staring in disbelief, she pinched him awake.

"What's wrong?" he whispered.

She did not answer. Instead, she scrambled to her feet,
and half sliding, half falling, began to run down the soft
sand face of the dune.

He caught up to her on the beach and grabbed her arm.

"I can't stay here," she sobbed. "I won't. Not another
minute." Twisting out of his grasp, she plunged down the
beach, lost her footing in the loose sand, and sprawled
across a pile of drying seaweed.

He slid down beside her and catching her in his arms,
patted her shoulder awkwardly. "We'll go wherever you
want. Okay?"

"Okay," she said in a small voice.

"So where?"

"I don't know." Her voice wavered. "I don't know."

"Do you want to go back to the graveyard, like before?"

She shook her head. But, she thought, at least there were
walls there. Walls and a roof. Nothing could get in. . . .
"Yes. Anywhere."

Hands locked together, they followed the curving line of
the ocean back toward the lodge. When they came to the
older dunes at the edge of the woods, they left the beach.
Scrambling up the low, sandspur-studded hills, they threaded
their way through a labyrinth of black palmettos pricking
through the sand and murky shrubs that crouched like
grotesque animals. After a dozen twisting turns they were
completely lost.

"Which way?" she whispered.

He shook his head. "I'm not sure."

Straining to see, she made out a narrow patch of gray.
"Over there. It looks like a path."

She pressed ahead. Limping, Nathan followed.

The narrow sand trail wound through head-high bushes

that rustled in the wind at the top of the dune. Ashley's
feet sank in the loose sand and her shoes filled with splinters of shell that grated against her heels like sandpaper.
She stared at the ground. Just ahead, the path widened and
curved. The sand was pale ash in the moonlight.

She took a step. Another. Suddenly her toe caught on
something hard, and she fell. Pain blazed in her hands and
knees. Then she was feeling the surface, feeling with a
horrible sense of doom the rough-cut boards just below the
thin dusting of sand.

The boardwalk.

Too far! They'd gone too far.

The tower was just to the left, then. The tower—and the
man who guarded it. She scrambled to her feet. "Turn
around. Quick. Go back."

They had time to take one stop, one rushing breath,
before the voice came:

"*Parada!* Stop. Stop or I kill you."

Bru stared down at the dying terrorist leader with a
certain grim admiration. It had taken delirium to loosen
those clamped, cracking lips. And when he finally began
to speak, it was only in the language of his childhood.

The lamplight accentuated the hollows in Iguana's cheeks.
His eyes were sunken now. Dehydration, Sally had said.
Bru glanced at Tony. "What did he say?"

"He's calling on the Blessed Virgin." Tony's voice was
muffled by the bird's-eye mask. "He's got her and his
mother confused, I think."

"Did he say anything else about the submarine? The
rogue?"

Tony shook his head.

The traction cords twitched as Iguana began to thrash
against them. Wincing Sally squeezed out a washcloth
and wiped his lips. "He's got to be having a lot of pain."

She's exhausted, he thought. He had urged her to lie
down and get some rest. But with a quick shake of her
head, she had refused. Now a pale line traced her lips and

the cloth trembled in her hand. Bru looked at Tony. "Try again."

Nodding, he leaned closer. "*Tiene usted frío?*"

Through chattering teeth, Iguana spoke. "*Escalofrío.*"

"Another chill." Tony waited while Sally pulled a blanket over Iguana's shoulders. "*Mireme usted.*" As the terrorist's eyes focused slowly on his, he said in a low voice, "*Haga usted exactamente como le digo y esto mejorara.*"

Iguana's lips opened. "*No.*" His gaze whipped away to follow a shadow that crept along the ceiling. He began to shake his head and mutter rapidly.

"What is it?" Bru's eyes sought Tony's. "What's he saying?"

"He says he's dying." Tony glanced around the Great Room uneasily. "He says death is in the room, watching him."

"Tell him that we have to get medicine for him. Ask him where it is?"

Tony nodded, but when Iguana's answer came, he frowned. "*Su madre?*"

"What is it?"

"I'm not sure. He's talking about his mother again." He listened for a moment more. "*Y su padre?*"

As Iguana spoke, Tony put up a hand to ward off Bru's question and leaned over the terrorist again. "And the others?" he said in Spanish. "What about the others?"

A stream of Spanish followed. When it was over, Tony straightened and looked at Bru, puzzled. "I don't understand it," he began. "He's not from Guatemala. But the others are. All of them, except for The Eye—El Ojo." He looked down at Iguana. "He's Cuban."

Sally's eyes widened. "Then both the leaders—" Her gaze darted toward Bru.

He was staring intently at the terrorist. "The medicine," he prompted. "Ask him again."

Tony nodded. But this time, Iguana's mouth fell open and he stared, transfixed, at the flickering light and shadow show playing on the old wagon wheel fixed on the ceiling above his head. "*Muerte . . . muerte . . .*"

He said it again and again, his shriveled tongue moving like a worm in his mouth: *death . . . death angel . . . death. . . .* His lips formed the words—and something else: *en . . . kay . . . en . . . kay . . .*

. . . NKWILY . . .

At the voice of the terrorist the hair rose on the back of Nathan's neck. For a second or two he heard only the sound of the sea and the quick rush of his breath. Then a low laugh came from the man in the tower.

"Do you know how long we look for you? Hours." The mocking laugh came again. "The dunes, they hid you well. Someone is still looking for you there—'where the wild oats meet the sea.' But now you come to us."

His heart raced. Looking for them? Why? "What are you going to do?" he said in a voice not much louder than a whisper.

"Turn around. The girl, too."

Nathan turned slowly and stared up at the tower. It was almost invisible against the night sky and the thick cluster of head-high bushes camouflaged the pilings at its base.

Nathan could scarcely see the man. He can see us, he thought. He felt naked. Suddenly, he was acutely aware of the gun tucked into his belt. Could the guy see that, too? Or did his jacket cover it? He wanted to look down, to see for himself, but he did not dare.

The man was going to kill them. He was sure of it. The gun at his belt felt heavy. He could grab it, blow the guy away with it. His breath quickened at the thought. All he had to do was grab it, aim, pull the trigger. Do it. He could do it.

But his hands would not work. They hung like dead things at his side, and it was only then that he realized he did not have the nerve.

Ashley pressed close to his side as if he offered her protection.

His hands felt cold and numb as if they had been immersed in freezing water. Some protection, he thought in despair. Some hero. His lungs felt empty. He couldn't get his breath, couldn't get enough air.

"The gun," she whispered in a voice so faint he could have imagined it.

He could not move. His body seemed to belong to someone else. The man was coming down from the tower now, each slow-motion footstep echoing on the planks of the steps. Nathan could make out the faint line of his rifle.

"The gun," she whispered again.

Please, God. He had to. Had to. Needles crawled in the flesh of his hands. His lips tingled.

The man was near the foot of the tower now, no more than a dozen feet away.

Ashley pressed closer. He could feel her breath on his face. Then with a motion so quick he could barely register it, she snatched the gun from his belt and swung toward the terrorist.

A sharp metallic click.

Ashley's two hands stretched out toward the man, and for a split second he thought it was an act of supplication. Then the explosion came.

She was killed. He knew she was killed.

But it was the terrorist who spun, one hand clawing out, clutching at the railing. He fell with drumlike thumps down the last three steps and sprawled like a crumpled dummy on the ground.

"Oh, God," she whispered. The gun fell from her hands and landed with a thud in the sand. For a few seconds they did not move or make a sound. Then Ashley clutched his arm. "Is he dead? Did I kill him?"

Somehow Nathan's legs started to move. A pool of blood, dark and shiny as tar, seeped raggedly into the sand. So much blood. The faint, metallic smell of it was sharp in his nose. The man's eyes were open and flat. Like fish eyes, he thought. Like a fish left by the tide.

"Is he dead?"

"I think so." He was not sure why he equivocated; there was no doubt the man was dead. He thought he knew how it felt: It was not being able to move, not being able to feel anything but numbness, not being able to breathe. The man was dead and it could have been him, it could have been both of them, except for Ashley.

Her voice was very small. "I really killed him. I killed a person."

He looked back at her. She had crumpled to her knees in the sand. "You had to," he said. Because he was too damned yellow to do it, to do anything except cringe like an animal.

"What am I going to do?" She was crying softly now, holding her hands to her face, rocking back and forth on her knees. "What am I going to do?"

He tugged at her shoulder. "Come on. We can't stay here. Somebody might come."

She shook her head. "I can't do this anymore. I can't."

He pulled her to her feet. "Come on," he said. "It isn't far. We can make it to the mausoleum." Where he belonged. Where people belonged who couldn't move, who couldn't feel.

"Not there. Not again." She clutched at his arm. "Take me back to the lodge, Nathan. Please, I want to go back. I want to see my daddy."

He started to protest, to say, "It isn't safe." Then he looked away. He was the one who had brought her out here. *I'll take care of you,* he had said. *I've got a gun.*

"Please take me back."

He could feel her body trembling against his. "They won't know it's us," he said. If they went back to the lodge, they might get shot by their own people.

"Please."

"All right." Pulling away, he turned back to the dead terrorist and bent over him.

"What are you doing?"

"Getting this." He held up the man's transceiver. They had been monitoring the messages back at the lodge.

Maybe they still were. "When we're close, we can use it. We can tell them we're coming."

"Hold me, Nathan. I'm so cold."

He put his arm around her and felt the pain bite into his injured shoulder. Strangely, he welcomed it as he welcomed the stabbing ache in his ankle. There was only so much pain, he thought. Just so much a person could feel at one time.

"So cold," she whispered.

He could do that. He could make her warm. Drawing Ashley close, he turned his back on the dark sea, and together they began to walk toward the lodge.

The gunshot echoed throughout the fevered layers of sleep and registered as thunder in Alex Borden's brain. Moaning softly, he stirred. The dark, moist smell of earth and decaying leaves filled his nostrils, and for a moment he was eleven years old again, lying in his sleeping bag by the creek at Barton's mill, listening to Uncle Athol's ghost stories. Then the pain in his joints pulsed into consciousness and he moaned again.

His head was pounding, but in spite of the pain, it seemed clear to him, as if the cold night breeze rustling through the limbs of the oaks had swept through his brain as well and blown away the dust clogging his mind. Strange, he thought. Strange how a brain trapped in a cage of exquisitely throbbing bone and flesh could work at all, could think of anything at all except the pain.

He sucked at air, thinking that a deep breath would help, but it ended in a gasp and a fit of coughing that tore at his ribs. Mucus rattled in his throat, and when the coughing was over, he spat it out and lay back exhausted with his back against the narrow bole of a young cedar.

Plague, he thought. He had gotten it on his hands and now it was everywhere—in his chest, his head. Got to wash. He had to wash his hands. Scrabbling in the dirt, he scrubbed them with a handful of sandy soil thick with leaf mold. No. No good, he thought, as the wind swept through his head again. But the washing movements went on as if his hands had a will of their own.

His spiking fever drove the pain from joint to joint. Lingering for a time in the bend of his knees, it crept up his thighs and drew his hamstrings tight as the strings of a bow. He felt it crawling along his body, burrowing into his hips, the small of his back, gnawing at his spine. Involuntarily he whimpered.

The sound ricocheted in his head and grew into a sob that was not his, a voice that was not his. His lids blinked over dry, burning eyes. The voice came again, and then another. Straining to hear, he filtered them through the whisper of leaves and the mutter of surf.

Ashley.

Somehow, incredibly, it was Ashley, coming closer, moving down the stairs. No. Not the stairs, he told himself. Not the stairs. He cocked his head at the other voice. A man. She must have called the ambulance. Ashley would ride with him, stay with him.

He wanted to call out to her, but something held him back. Calvin. He mustn't wake Calvin. No point in scaring the boy. Just an ulcer, like before. Just another goddamned ulcer.

"No," said another voice. And this one came familiarly from inside his brain: *No*.

He felt his head clear again. Plague. It was plague and there was no cure, no help, no cure at all. When he thought of Ashley this time, it was with alarm. Stay away, little girl, he thought. She had to stay away.

But if she heard him, if she saw him, he knew she wouldn't.

Only for a moment, he thought. A moment wouldn't hurt, would it? He wanted desperately to hug her, hold her one more time. Please, God, just once. He wanted to talk to her, explain things to her. He wanted to tell . . .

No.

He crept beneath the rustling fronds of a dark palmetto and pressed his fist in his mouth to stifle the cough welling in his chest. And when he heard her footsteps gritting against sand and wood, passing him in the dark, he bit down, partly to keep back the cough, partly to keep from crying out, until the blood ran salt in his mouth and mingled with thick, silent tears.

When she was gone, he waited for a long time before he drew his aching legs under him and crept to his knees. The faint glimmer of a moving lantern came from inside the lodge. Safe there, he thought. She'd be safe there. Safe as long as he stayed away.

Plucking at a steadying tree limb, he got to his feet, and drawn by the flickering light, moved toward the lodge. He stopped near the veranda. Crouching beneath the limbs of a giant old oak, he scraped the leaves away from a patch of soil, and with a piece of broken shell scratched something on the ground. And as he did, he repeated the words over and over to himself as if they were a litany: "Daddy loves you. Daddy loves you, baby. . . ." Then not trusting himself to stay so close, he crept away in the night and followed the dusty road that twisted like a pale gray ribbon through the black dunes.

For a time, the dimming moon shone on the words he had left. And then dark, ragged clouds began to erase them and a sharp chill wind buried the rest under a rustling blanket of dying leaves.

Chapter 41

TONY HERRERA STOOD IN THE DEEP SHADOWS BY THE BAY WINdow, his rifle aimed at the road beyond the veranda. He had been alert since the single gunshot came from the boardwalk two minutes ago. Behind him, the fire in the Franklin stove was burning low. Its flickering orange light crept through the dining room and touched the faces of the men at the table.

Sir William looked at Bru in surprise. "Rogue subs? So he said that, did he?" A thoughtful expression came into his eyes. "I haven't heard that term in a good many years." His gaze strayed from Bru toward the ceiling as he remembered. "They're part of the myths left over from World War II. Several German submarines, complete with crew, disappeared. Unverified rumor has it that they exist to this day. They're supposed to be used by a group of neo-Nazi expatriates in Paraguay. The story goes that the subs are for hire—for a substantial sum."

Bru raised an eyebrow. "You think the terrorists planned a getaway in a forty-year-old U-boat?"

The ambassador shook his head. "As I said, the German rogues are probably myth. I suspect Iguana's allusion to a rogue is generic—a name for an independent submarine without ties to any country or ideology."

"That fits in with the weapons," said Bru. All of them brand-new, he thought, and a sub that couldn't be traced. But how could a sub, even a new one, get through the country's defense net without being detected?

Or did it?

He looked up sharply. "How do we know there is a sub?"

"Interesting." Sir William thought for a moment. "Iguana thinks he's got one out there. If he's wrong, it puts a new light on the subject, doesn't it?" He gave Bru a careful look. "There could be other things here that may not be as they seem."

In the silence that followed, Bru remembered the words Iguana had repeated over and over in his delirium—the only words that were in English: *N. K. Wiley.*

Who was Wiley? And why did that name ring a faint bell deep in his brain? He associated it with science somehow. Physics, or maybe biology. A biologist, he thought. Wiley could be the one who engineered the plague mutation. But even if he was, why would his name be on the lips of a dying terrorist? And that was the second time. Iguana had mentioned Wiley in his first ultimatum to the press.

But there was something else. Something nagging at his mind. There was another part—a missing name, he was sure, like Watson and Crick, or Laurel and Hardy. What was it? He tried to remember the exact words that Iguana had used in his message to the press. "Who is Wiley . . ." No. "*Where* is Wiley, amigos?"

Where is Wiley? It was as if he could see the shape of the missing piece of puzzle, but he couldn't lay his hands on it.

N. K. Wiley . . .

Things may not be as they seem. . . .

The thought struck as hard as a blow: Naomi. NAOMI.

Wiley wasn't a man. Those weren't initials; they were a prefix. And the word was "wily," he thought, like a fox. NK. NKWILY.

NK was a prefix for a CIA operation. Technical Services Division. NKNAOMI was the code name for the agency's biological and chemical warfare program in the sixties, back in the days of nerve gas stockpiles, back when chemical and bacteriological warfare figured into every defense plan. The program had been killed off. But CBW was in the ascendant again—nerve gas stockpiling was discussed openly in the newspapers, and new biologicals were on the horizon. It never goes away, he thought.

Maybe it had never gone away.

He blinked. NKNAOMI had simply gone underground. Suddenly an image came into his mind of a body clawing at the ground, rising from a grave, spewing plague from dead lips. The late Naomi, he thought, and his mouth twisted. But she didn't die. Instead she had been carefully kept alive, fed with the latest genetic broths, nurtured, renamed. "NKWILY is a CIA code," he said abruptly. "The plague. It's ours."

"CIA?" It was Sir William's turn to raise an eyebrow. Several seconds passed before he spoke again. "I'd say it's yours then, not 'ours.' "

Bru's hand closed slowly into a fist, opened, closed. "If there's a cure," he said, "the CIA is where we'll find it."

Sir William's brow furrowed for a long moment. "That could explain why Iguana was so anxious for his manifesto to be broadcast all over the world."

Startled, Bru looked up. He was silent for several seconds. Then he said, "There's no submarine out there."

Their eyes met and locked. They stared at each other until Bru voiced their common thought: "The fail-safe. It's going to blow. It was always meant to blow."

The oil lamp in the Great Room was turned low. Dave Cole twisted the wick higher. Yellow light flickered over the couch and the motionless traction gear.

Bru closed the door to the entry hall. "Talk to him," he said to Tony. "We've got to find out where that fail-safe is."

Tony went to the couch and looked down at Iguana. Then his eyes widened above his mask and slid toward Dave.

Two quick steps brought the doctor to the couch. He stared at the terrorist for a moment, then he pressed his fingertips into Iguana's neck below the angle of his jaw.

Iguana's pupils were the size of dimes. No light reflected from his eyes.

"He's dead," said Dave, his fingers still pressing deep against the doughy flesh of Iguana's throat as if he could resurrect a pulse with the laying on of hands.

The man's skin had a yellowish cast. Like tallow, Bru thought. Like one of Madame Tussaud's waxwork figures. He needed a plaque: *The notorious St. Cyrils Island terrorist, Iguana. The first to die of mutated plague.*

He stared down at the terrorist. One corner of Iguana's lips quirked in a blasphemy of a smile. Son of a bitch. He had died with that mocking smile frozen on his face like a mask. Frozen until the lips rotted away and the skull grinned through. Something to remember him by.

Irrationally, he thought of the "death" masks. They had cast them on a lazy spring day in college, anointing each other with plaster of Paris in the interest of posterity—he and Daniel Elton, faces smeared with Vaseline, red and white plastic soda straws sticking out of their nostrils. He remembered the finished mask: pale closed eyes in a damp, gray-white face that was eerily familiar, yet disconcertingly alien. It was the first time he had ever really thought about his own death.

A sudden crackle came from the FM transceiver. Without thinking, Tony started to reach under the plastic isolation gown for it.

"No," said Dave. "Not in here. You'll contaminate it." He waved toward the dining room. "Don't touch it until you get those gloves off."

Tony nodded and left.

When Bru and Dave followed a few minutes later, they found a group assembled in the dining room. Paige Cole looked up as they came in. "Nathan and Ashley. They're alive. They're coming back."

Tony grinned. "They wiped the guy at the tower."

Bru gave him a sharp look. "They said that over the radio?"

"Sure did. They blew him away."

Bru frowned. El Ojo knew it, too, then. With the tower lookout dead the subleader was likely to consolidate his few remaining men back at the old lodge. That was going to make things more difficult. A moment later he took Sir William aside.

"Iguana's dead," the ambassador said. "Tony told us."

Bru nodded grimly. "That leaves us just one chance." There was only one terrorist left who knew where the fail-safe was.

"The other Cuban," said Sir William. "El Ojo."

One chance, thought Bru. If they could capture El Ojo, if they could make him talk, it would be collateral. Something to bargain with. It was the last chance for them—and the last desperate chance for the country.

Chapter 42

THE DREAM ABOUT THE APE HAD NOT RECURRED. JACK Hubert had fallen into a sleep so profound that it took five rings of the bedside phone before he heard it, and two more before he fumbled at the unfamiliar light switch and dragged the receiver to his ear. He listened for a moment, muttered a reply, and hung up. The red LED on the plastic clock said 2:18. Blinking, he stared at it for a moment, then he flung back the covers and struggled out of bed.

After a few minutes' application of icy tap water to his face, he unwrapped a glass and brushed his teeth. The water tasted of chlorine and rusty pipes. He spat it out quickly. You needed water to wash down the water around here, he thought in disgust. He pulled on his clothes and reached for his jacket.

The street was dead. Fog blurred the light in front of the motel parking lot and misted the blinking red vacancy sign. It was not as cold tonight—or so the thermometer said—but the chilly dampness felt like it was seeping into his bones. Passing the telephone on the corner, he crossed the street and headed south to a pay phone he had spotted earlier. It was six blocks away, but what were the options? It was risky enough making the contact by telephone, he thought. There was no point in goosing luck on top of it.

The receiver felt like ice. He dialed a long-distance number, spoke quickly, and hung up. After five minutes he had to pace back and forth to keep warm. Twenty more passed before the return call came from the contract man.

"We need to know about animal vectors on 18," said Hubert. "Birds, rats, and mice. Can they spread it?"

There was a pause. "What we know is in the prelim."

Christ. He was talking about a preliminary report over three hundred pages long and full of medical jargon. "Just capsule it for me, Doc. Okay?"

"The studies aren't finished. I couldn't give you anything definitive."

"Forget definitive. Give me some maybes." He hated dealing with medical types. None of them knew how to get off the pot.

"All we've got is early studies. Infected blood was fed to Oriental and European rat fleas. Although the bacillus was cultured later from the crushed bodies of the fleas, there were no incidents of infection in laboratory rats exposed to living insects. But we're not sure why," he added quickly. "It's going to take a lot more work to figure that one out."

"You're saying animal vectors can't spread it?"

There was a pause. "I wouldn't go on record as saying that at all."

"You're not going on record. Can they spread it?"

"I couldn't give you a definitive, uh, definite yes or no about that."

"We're dealing in maybes, remember?"

"The answer to your question is maybe yes, maybe no. It could take months—"

"Look," he said abruptly. "We don't have months. You're going to have to extrapolate from the data you've got."

There was a pause. "You're asking me questions I can't answer. I'm not an entomologist."

And I'm not a goddamned dentist, thought Hubert. So why was he having to pull teeth to get some kind of an answer? His voice took on an edge. "Can they spread it?"

He hesitated. "If you've got to have a yes or a no, then I'd have to say no. Probably not."

Hubert was unable to keep the faint tinge of sarcasm out of his voice. "Thanks, Doc. You're a big help." He hung up and stared at the receiver for a moment. Maybe in his next life he could be a shoe salesman. It beat standing out in the cold in the middle of the night. Better yet, he could be a contract doctor and get paid like royalty to equivocate. Just like Jonah Schwartz, he thought. Just like Jonah "sit on the pot and fart" Schwartz.

The Crisis Committee chairman gave the signal. The report from the Centers for Disease Control in Atlanta flashed onto the projection screen:

RE YERSINIA PESTIS OUTBREAK,
ST. CYRILS ISLAND, GEORGIA:
    In view of the demonstrated lack of response to the treatment modality begun at approximately noon, Friday, by on-site detainee Dr. David Cole, and in view of the occurrence of a second case of suspected plague in spite of prophylactic antibiotics, the situation on St. Cyrils Island can be described as grave. The incubation period is apparently of shorter duration than the usual *Yersinia pestis* infection. This, coupled with the early

onset of what appears to be the pneumonic form
in the second victim, is seen as particularly
ominous. . . .

There was more, but the DCI was thinking about the
message just in from Jack Hubert: *The vet says the live-
stock is okay.*

One less headache, he thought. Then he blinked at his
choice of metaphors. His head felt stuffed with glue. The
area below his left eye had begun to throb and his irritation
was rising with the pain. He wanted to tell off every
smoker in the room. Instead, rather than display his weakness, he surreptitiously washed down another sinus pill
with black coffee. He had never bothered to analyze his
Spartan behavior around other men—it did not extend to
hearth and home, as his wife was quick to point out—but,
then, the DCI had never been interested in self-analysis. A
catalog of the obvious, he called it. A waste of time. It
was far more important to psych out the other guy. Then
you knew where you stood.

The CDC report slid off the screen and a satellite map of
the south Georgia coast took its place. The DCI stared at it
perfunctorily. When there's nothing to say, say it louder,
he thought. The weather updates had been coming at
thirty-minute intervals for hours as the front crept closer.
This one added nothing to the earlier predictions. It was
still due in a little after noon.

"What's the status on the evacuation?" someone asked.

"Still about a hundred and fifty who refuse to leave, I
believe." Andrew Hagen glanced at the FBI director for
confirmation.

As Burt Kittredge manipulated his massive bulk, his
chair creaked ominously. "According to the latest reports,
we've been able to reduce that number to around eighty or
ninety holdouts."

And lucky at that, thought the DCI. The residents had
been told to evacuate because of a bomb threat on the
north end of St. Simons Island. When the airports were

closed to commercial traffic, the rumor mill began to grind and hundreds believed that a bomb was planted at the Glynn Co. Jetport. The idea of a bomb on the mainland, and the fear that their homes would be looted, caused dozens of residents to refuse to leave the island.

"We think we can cut that figure by at least one third," added Kittredge.

"That's not good enough," said Isaac Benjamin. "We've not only got to get everyone off those islands, we've got to keep them off." The science adviser peered over his bifocals at first one, then another. "Unless we address the problem of animal vectors, St. Simons and the entire south Georgia coast is likely to be contaminated—permanently."

"Short of destroying the wildlife on St. Cyrils Island, how do you propose to do that?" asked Carter Booth. The press secretary raised an eyebrow as if he had said something extremely clever.

"There are a number of ways," began Benjamin. "Motion detectors, trenches filled with phenol solution—"

General Everett snorted. "How about little boys with BB guns. They could take potshots at every bird that flies past your motion detectors. Or maybe you expect your owls and hawks to wade through a trench." His lip curled. "The 'phenol solution' to the vector problem."

"Have you got a better plan?" snapped the science adviser.

The general's eyes narrowed. "Napalm."

Benjamin stared.

"Napalm," repeated the general. "Turn up the heat to twenty-five hundred degrees and any bird that gets off St. Cyrils will have to rise from its own ashes."

"There are people on that island," said Andrew Hagen. "Do you realize what the public outcry would be if we used napalm?"

"It would be considerable," Everett said slowly. His voice dropped. "If the public thought the hostages were still alive."

A sudden quiet fell over the room.

Carter Booth's gaze darted from face to face. "You can't do this. You can't really go along with this." As he registered the look in one pair of eyes after another, his own widened. "Jesus Christ," he whispered. "Jesus Christ."

Chapter 43

As Bru walked into the kitchen, Sally looked up from the transceiver. "It's Ashley and Nathan. They're okay. They're at the shed now." She glanced toward the window. Lillian was clutching the edge of the curtain, staring out through the inch-wide gap, tension in every line of her body.

"I told them to stay away, but they won't." Sally turned stricken eyes to Bru. "Why won't they listen to me?"

"It's their choice, Sally."

"They'll get sick. They'll catch it, too." Her final word trembled away to nothing.

Bru searched her face anxiously. Pale lines traced her lips and there were dark circles beneath her eyes. She was worn out physically, but this was something more. It was the bone-weary numbness that came on with mental stress, the kind that stripped away all your defenses. The idea that she might get sick was chilling. Sweet thing, he thought. Don't do it. Hang in there.

"It's their choice," he said again. "You told them. That's all anybody could do." She was still taking responsibility for the world. And who was looking after her? He wanted to gather her up and cuddle her like a little girl, but something in her eyes held him back. Not the time, not the place, he told himself. But underneath the thought, he realized uneasily that he had seen the shadowed look before—in the eyes of his dying son.

Footsteps clattered across the porch. Lillian threw open the door and pulled Ashley and Nathan inside. She took one glance at the girl and shook her head. "Oh, child. Look at you." Ashley's eyes were enormous against her white face and she was shivering. Lillian hugged her and after a quick look at Nathan, encompassed them both in her arms. "It's going to be all right," she said. "It's all right."

"Daddy—" Ashley caught her breath. "I want to see him."

A guarded look came into Lillian's eyes. "Not just now, honey. Let's get you something to eat and some warmer clothes."

"What's happened?" Suspicion darkened her eyes. "Where's my daddy?"

Lillian exchanged a glance with Bru.

Ashley's gaze darted from one to the other. "He's dead, isn't he?" Her accusing glance fell on Sally. "He's dead and you didn't want me to know."

Sally shook her head.

"He is. I know he is. That's why you didn't want us to come back."

"No," said Bru. "He's outside. He went out about an hour ago."

"Outside? Why?"

"He's sick, honey," said Lillian. "He wasn't himself."

"And you let him? You let him go out there alone?" Shock and outrage flashed in her eyes. "I can't believe you. Don't you know what it's like out there?" Her face crumpled and she turned helplessly to Nathan. "What kind of animals would do that?"

Lillian reached out to the girl again, but Ashley pulled away. "He was gone before we knew it, honey."

Bru stared at Lillian, but he was remembering a crazy,

flickering light darting through the trees in front of the lodge. They could have brought Alex Borden back, but it was a matter of survival. He would have infected everybody. From the time Borden shot open the canister, any moral question was academic. Ashley was crying now, clinging to Nathan's neck. It wasn't resentment, he told himself. They had no choice. It was pure and simple survival.

Just the way it is with wolves and jackals, said a mocking voice in his head. *Fall on the sick one and drive it away before it can infect the rest of the pack.* They would have done it to Sally even though she wasn't sick, he thought, if he hadn't stopped them.

And wasn't that noble of him?

A lump of muscle began to tic at the angle of his jaw. Where was his goddamned nobility when it came to Alex Borden? Had he thought one time of what it would be like to be sick, to be dying, out there alone in the dark? And if he had, would it have mattered?

Incongruously, he remembered a silly unicorn nightlight: frosted plastic and fifteen watts, holding off the night for a little boy—a little boy who had died in a nurse's arms instead of his father's—and he closed his fist and clamped his lips together at the sudden taste of bile in his mouth.

The trees were thinner near the marsh. The tide was coming in and the pungent smell of salt and decaying shellfish stung Alex Borden's nostrils. The damp breeze chattering through a dead palmetto frond felt good, but the relief it brought was fleeting. The freshening wind harbored a swarm of mosquitoes that clung to his face and neck and to the crevices between his fingers. He slapped at the insects until his palms were smeared with blood, but more took their place and soon their tiny darts of poison had swelled his eyelids to twice normal size.

He opened cracked lips and slid his tongue drily over them. He had to have a drink. He could hear the hiss of the sea creeping inward across the flats. A faint warning sounded in his mind, but the seductive tide drew him closer.

He found himself swaying unsteadily in ankle-deep muck at the edge of the marsh. Knees buckling, he pitched forward, and the flashlight flipped out of his hand and sank into the mud. He watched stupidly as it gave a final wink and disappeared. Then he was crawling through the marsh grass on his hands and knees, and when the ooze between his fingers gave way to brine, he lowered his face and began to lap like a dog.

He drank until an icy gust of wind knifed through his wet clothes and into his bones. Teeth chattering like dry pods, he crawled blindly back to higher ground and crept beneath the low branches of a cedar.

The force of the chill shuddered through him like an electric shock, knotting his muscles, convulsing his limbs. His stomach heaved and brine and bile gushed out of his mouth and nose. A strangling cough erupted, draining him of the little strength he had left.

When it was over, he lay prone on the dark ground, his pulse rushing in his head like the mocking whisper of surf, his breath rustling like the night wind through the saw grass at the edge of the freshwater rain pond only a dozen yards away.

They had missed their chance to catch El Ojo alone. Five minutes ago, Tony had heard the subleader call back his remaining men. Now they were converging on the old lodge. Bru thought of the motor launch anchored there. El Ojo would be a fool to use the launch for a getaway, but if he was desperate enough, he might try.

A low whistle, barely audible over the crackle of the transceiver, came from the back of the lodge. "He's back," said Nathan.

The whistle was followed by faint footsteps scraping across the kitchen porch. Bru opened the door and Tim Jefferson darted inside. He was out of breath from excitement as much as exertion, and laden with spoils from the dead terrorist on the boardwalk.

Bru caught the ammo belt Tim tossed to him. "Good." Their ammunition had dwindled sharply during the terrorists' siege. This would help.

Obviously pleased with himself, Tim pulled off the Oldelft night goggles and twirled them. "These things are pretty good," he said admiringly. "They don't exactly turn night into day, but they're better than carrots. You get a sense of power—like you're invisible." A disarming grin crossed his dark face. "Me and Lamont Cranston." He threw down the terrorist's rifle and tossed a pale coil on top. "He had that hanging from his belt."

Nathan looked down at the coil. "What is it?"

"Primacord," said Bru, picking it up.

"This, too." Tim dropped a pack onto the floor.

Bru opened it. It was crammed with fuses, blasting caps, and igniters. He glanced at Sir William. "Would you say this was meant for us?"

"Possibly," said the ambassador.

Tony Herrera looked up from the transceiver he held. "What do you mean?"

"From the way that boat of theirs went up," said Bru, "I'd guess it was full of explosives. Now we find this. I think they planned to blow up the lodge—and us with it—before they left the island."

"If you're right, it's proof they never intended to negotiate, isn't it?" said Sir William.

He nodded and glanced uneasily at his watch. It was after three. "We may not have much time."

"Then let's get it on," said Tim. He tossed rifles to Tony and Sir William.

Bru crossed to the kitchen table and grabbed up a pair of night goggles.

Nathan followed him. "I want to go with you," he said in a low voice.

Bru shook his head.

The young musician set his jaw. "I said, I want to go."

"Impossible." Nathan's ankle was streaked with red and badly swollen, and the wound in his shoulder made his arm almost useless. "You can barely walk."

"Yes, I can."

"No." Bru suspected the boy had never fired a gun in his life; he wondered what he was trying to prove. He glanced across the room. The door to the dining room was ajar. Miranda Gervin stood in the shadows at the corner of the bay window; she held a handgun. The lodge's defenses were going to be thin when they left. Miranda and Leroy were the only ones standing watch, and they were short of ammunition. "You're needed here," he said to Nathan, hoping it was a lie. The tone of his voice precluded further argument.

White-lipped, Nathan fell back and watched the four men leave one by one through the kitchen door. When they were gone, he stood at the window and stared into the darkness for a long time before he turned and limped slowly up the stairs.

Concealed by the thick trunk of a water oak, Bru scanned the marsh through night goggles that transformed it into a desert of sculptured ash. Ahead, the Jeffersons' house squatted on dark pilings at the edge of the grass flats. Bru broke into a crouching run. Ducking behind a sprawling bush at the corner of the house, he slid to the ground and crawled on his belly toward the sagging porch. He could see the old lodge now. No one was in sight.

Sir William was next. He was breathing hard. Bru hoped he had not overestimated the man's endurance. In seconds Tony Herrera and Tim Jefferson followed.

"There." Tim pointed to the dock.

Bru narrowed his eyes and faint gray lines became shadowy stick figures. "The launch. They're taking it."

Tim scanned the creek. "If we cut the barge loose, we can block them. Slow 'em down, anyway."

A low rumble came from the launch's inboards. Tony stared. "It's too late."

"No, it's not." Tim scrambled to his feet and began a zigzagging dash to the creek.

Bru was on his feet, running toward the old lodge. "Cover us."

A harsh crackle; a rapid stream of Spanish. Tony's hand jerked to the transceiver. "They've seen us."

Gunfire splintered the porch rail above his head.

"Up there." Sir William's rifle swung toward the roof of the lodge and the dim figure crouched on the widow's walk.

"It's El Ojo," Tony hissed. "Don't kill him."

The ambassador veered and the burst went wide. The terrorist scrambled to cover as an answering volley blazed from the motor launch.

Shadowed by the lodge's overhang, Bru swung onto the porch and ducked behind the railing.

Tim was at the creek now. Feet clattering across the floating dock, he raced to the barge. A man scrambled onto the deck of the launch. Bru had only a moment to fire. The terrorist spun, his rifle arcing into the water just as Tim jumped.

A shot exploded from the roof of the lodge, and an outbuilding went up in flames. Grenades. Bru saw Tony darting toward him through the cloud of smoke. Whirling, Bru kicked open the door and ran inside. Tony behind him, he took the stairs two at a time. At the top a narrow second flight led to the widow's walk.

As they burst through to the roof, El Ojo raised his rifle and aimed at the barge.

"Drop it," yelled Bru. Too late, he spotted the grenade bulging from the muzzle of the SIG. He leaped.

El Ojo's finger closed on the trigger, squeezed.

Swinging the rifle, Bru slammed the butt into the terrorist's ribs. He felt them snap.

Too late, too late.

Tim!

For an instant the barge was dark. The concussion thrust her from the water and she convulsed, diesel fuel spewing from her ruptured storage tanks in a wall of fire that turned the sky to blood. In midstream a flaming canoe spun and hissed, and scudded down a salt creek blazing with the torchlight from a clump of burning cabbage palms.

At the first sound of gunshots, Calvin Borden woke abruptly and stared into the darkness. Disoriented, he struggled up and cracked his head against the underside of the bed. In panic he rolled over and the stack of magazines he had used for a pillow slid beneath the edge of the bedspread and cascaded into the room.

Heart beating in his ears, he pressed his body to the floor. Something hard dug into his ribs. The penlight. His fingers curled around it.

A wisp of a feather lost from an aging pillow skittered across the floor and touched his cheek. Gasping, he jerked away and scrambled out from under the bed. The room was black as tar. He could feel the penlight's switch under his thumb, but he did not dare turn it on.

He felt his way to the door and into the hall. In the front room he crept to the window. Fingers clinging to the sill, he raised his head and looked out. At first he could see nothing. Then rifle fire blazed from the old lodge. When a return volley came from almost under his nose, he dropped to the floor with an involuntary cry.

They're coming, he thought frantically. They knew where he was.

He crouched in the darkness and tried not to cry, but in the thick silence that followed, hot tears stung his eyes. Trembling, he waited for the blaze of lights that he knew would come. They'd kill him then, he thought. An awful cold trembled in his belly and he grabbed his crotch to keep from wetting his pants. He couldn't do that. He wouldn't. He wasn't a baby. They could kill him, but he wouldn't let them laugh.

He huddled in the blackness, silence thickening around him until he could not breathe.

Another volley.

A moment later thunder split the air. Orange light blazed. Heart shuddering beneath his ribs, Calvin scrambled to his knees and stared as a wall of flames leaped from the barge and engulfed the dock.

Outside the window something moved. The armed man stood motionless for a moment, silhouetted by the flames. Then he was running—toward the dock.

Calvin's nails dug into the wood of the windowsill. A second passed, then another, before comprehension came: The man was leaving. Going away.

He took a quick, shuddering breath and scrambled to his feet. Plunging into the hall, he fled to the back of the house. He had to hurry. The back door, swollen with humidity, refused to budge. At his second frantic tug it flew open with such force that his knuckles slammed against the side of the refrigerator. Scarcely feeling the pain, he darted onto the porch, grabbed the railing, and jumped. The moment his feet hit the ground he was running.

Not daring to look over his shoulder, he raced along the edge of the marsh to the only place he could think of that might be safe: the Guale Indian mounds, just beyond the rain pond.

He ran until hot bands constricted his lungs and set them on fire. Collapsing in a heap, he sucked air through dry lips until some of the pain went away. Then he scrambled to his feet and began to run again.

Sir William's breath came in harsh, painful rasps as he ran toward the wall of fire that had been the dock.

Swinging a rifle that felt like lead, he veered to the right. He could see the creek now. Orange flames danced on the black water. The launch swung crazily at the end of its tether; the wounded terrorist sprawled on its deck like a broken toy soldier.

The slight movement at the corner of his eye triggered a sluggish reflex. Gasping, he hit the ground. Gunfire shredded a palmetto; splinters of shell peppered his head and arms. And something hot, then agonizingly cold, slammed through his chest and belly.

The force of it knocked him into the drowned cord grass at the edge of the creek. Water flooded his nostrils and mouth and mingled with a warm salt taste that gurgled up from his throat. Struggling for air, he raised his head and looked up in wonder at the man who had shot him. He was young. Only a boy, really. He stared, fascinated, as if he were trying to memorize the narrow face, the scraggly attempt at a moustache, the thin finger tightening on the trigger.

So this is the way of it, then, he thought.

There was time for only a tiny flash of regret before the bullets split his skull. Searing light exploded in his retinas. Then nothing.

The terrorist stared down at the man he had killed. Then his gaze jumped to the old lodge as the door wheezed and swung open.

Crouching, he froze. Then sliding into the shadows, he turned and loped away into the woods.

El Ojo between them, Bru and Tony dragged the wounded subleader toward the pickup truck outside. The pull of his muscles twisted his broken ribs and the terrorist grunted in pain.

Bru's lip curled. You'll live, he thought.

Leaving Tony to guard the man, Bru circled cautiously to the creek. Skirting the burning dock, he followed the scuffed path that led down to the rowboats. His foot skidded on something greasy near the water's edge. It wasn't until he saw the ambassador's half-submerged body that he knew what he had slipped on. He drew a slow, shuddering breath. Smoke from the burning diesel fuel filled his nose and mingled with the smell of blood. Clamping his lips, he suppressed a gag.

The launch tugged at its blackened tether. The wounded terrorist on the deck twitched, his hand scrabbling through a black pool of blood. Alive, Bru thought. But barely. The other man was gone.

A pair of rowboats bobbed next to the bank. He grabbed the gunwale of the closest and reached for an oar to snag the line anchoring the launch. Water slapped at the rowboat's bow.

A sudden echoing splash came from beneath the burning dock. Bru whirled toward the sound.

For a moment he thought it was Sir William. For a flashing instant he thought he saw him rising from the creek, draining brine, staring through dead eyes. Bru's finger curled reflexively on the trigger.

Another splash. The man stumbled out of the water and fell to his knees.

Tim! It was Tim.

Bru stared as Tim raised his head. His goggles were off, bulging at his throat like a dark goiter. His hands clamped his head.

Bru ran to him.

Water rained from his body. He raised his eyes to Bru; a bewildered, drunken look flickered in them.

"Are you hurt?"

The whites of his eyes rolled up. Then Tim's dark pupils focused again and skittered away. His low answering moan was drowned by the rumble of a jet.

Bru's head jerked upward. The surveillance helicopter was coming in low and fast, drawn like a moth to the flames. He raised his voice above the noise. "Where are you hurt?"

Elbows out, Tim clutched his head; his upper body swayed. The Black Hawk thundered overhead, roared past; he gave no sign that he had heard it.

Wind gusted the burning dock. The flames leaped. In their light Bru could see the thin streams of blood draining from Tim's ears, running between his fingers. The explosion, he thought. It had burst his eardrums.

Tim was deaf. Stone deaf.

Chapter 44

"IT'S FOR PAIN." SALLY HELD OUT ASPIRIN AND A TINY codeine tablet to Tim. She hoped it would help. The Percodan was gone.

The codeine had come from the jumble of Lillian's out-of-date prescriptions. "I think it was for the flu," she had said.

The great pandemic of 1918, Sally thought darkly. The date on the yellowing label was obliterated, but the pills looked all right. At least they were still white and in one piece. There were only three left. She capped the brown prescription container, plopped it back onto the kitchen table, and wondered again why the airlift pack had been crammed with all sorts of antibiotics, but nothing for pain. Care from the air, she thought, and not even a Darvocet. Her lips compressed. Not even a goddamned Darvocet.

Tim tipped his head and stared at the pills with a bewildered look.

"For pain." She exaggerated the words, hoping he could read her lips.

He nodded and threw back his head to swallow. The motion made him wince. Blood trickled from his ears, staining the blue blanket around his shoulders with rusty streaks.

She thought she saw his pupils jitter. Nystagmus? Narrowing her eyes, she stared. There. No. She couldn't be sure. Picking up a stubby pencil, she glanced at her watch and scribbled on a kitchen pad she had appropriated for notes:

4:47 AM: ASA gr. 10 c̄ Codeine gr. ½, p.o.
Slight nystag?
Hearing loss, bleeding continue.

Her headache had come back with a vengeance. As she wrote, she rubbed her temples. Tension, she told herself. That was all it was. That was *all*. She stole another bleary glance at Tim, but she still couldn't decide if she had imagined the nystagmus. Dave could decide, she thought.

Dave Cole had taken a brief look at Tim, but there had not been time for more. Bru had hustled him into the pickup with Tony to bring back the wounded terrorist from the motor launch. When they were gone, Bru went back to the shed where Leroy was guarding El Ojo.

So far, El Ojo had not said a word. And he won't, Sally thought. She had caught only a glimpse of the terrorist in the headlights of the pickup. They were marching him to the shed, hands tied behind his back. As they passed the kitchen porch he turned his head and looked at the window where she stood. It was only for an instant, but the black hate in his eyes had blazed into her, and she knew she would never forget it.

Tuck Perry stood near the back door. Head tipped, pale hair masking her face, she stared out the window. Beyond the porch the shed was dark with only the faint light from a kerosene lantern flickering from its single window. "What are they doing out there?"

Sally shook her head and dabbed Tim's ears with a piece of gauze that quickly darkened with blood. She held the soiled 4x4 for a long moment, staring stupidly at it as if she could not remember what it was. Then blinking, she dropped it into the yellow plastic wastebasket by the worktable.

He needed a dressing. She tore open more 4x4s and, folding them in half, secured them to his ears with a length of gauze wrapped around his head. Tucking in the end, she reached for the tape.

Tim grabbed her hand. "Will I stay this way?"

She looked at him blankly.

His voice was louder than normal. "Am I going to be deaf?"

Lena Jefferson paused at the foot of the back stairs and gave a sharp look to her grandson. "You gone be fine." She was carrying a bundle of clothes and Sally recognized the sweater Bru had worn Thanksgiving afternoon. Setting the clothes on the table, Lena grasped Tim's shoulders and fixed him with a dark gaze. "You gone be fine," she repeated.

Hunching forward, he stared at her lips. Slowly a faint grin began to twitch at the corner of his lips. "Or else, huh?"

Lena peeled back the damp blanket. Her gnarled hands working buttons and zipper, she stripped off his wet clothes and began to replace them with Bru's dry ones.

Sally moved to the back door to give him some privacy.

"It's starting to rain," said Tuck without looking up.

Tiny drops gathered on the windowpane, coalesced, ran down. Like doll's tears, thought Sally. Her fingertips grazed the glass. It was cold. The chill communicated itself to her body and she shivered.

A sound on the stairs. Yellow light puddled into the room and Cass Tompkins came in. The oil lamp she carried emphasized the shadows under her eyes. Her face was bare of makeup. Without mascara and the dark streaks of rouge that had hollowed her cheeks, she had the wide-eyed look of a frightened child. "I know it's my turn to be sleeping, but I can't. Do you want your bed back?"

Sally shook her head.

Cass set the lamp on the counter, fingered it. "I tried to write for a while, but it all turned to shit. But maybe you think that's all it is, anyway." Her round blue eyes met Sally's anxiously.

Sally blinked. Cass seemed to want her approval. Why?

"People think it's all glamour. Writing books. But it isn't. It's good hard work." She pronounced it "hod." *Hod work.*

Like laying bricks. Sally imagined a business card: *Cassandra Temple. Hot romances and antique brick patios. A damned good lay, either way.* She wanted desperately to giggle, but she knew if she did, she would not be able to stop.

"It is, you know," said Cass quickly, misinterpreting Sally's look. She moved closer and the faint odor of liquor on her breath mingled with the smell of Opium. She's got my perfume on, Sally thought, wondering if she had gargled with it to cover up the smell of whiskey like Scarlett O'Hara had.

"I was going to be a nurse once," said Cass. She looked away. "I would have been a good one, too. But Mamma was against it. She used to say, 'I'd rather see you wash dishes than dirty bodies.' " Cass's gaze swiveled back to Sally and she leaned closer. "What she really meant was men. Naked ones. She never could say that word; she called it 'nekkid.' I guess she thought the sight of a 'bare nekkid' cock would make me lose control." She laughed thickly and the odor of her breath made Sally feel suddenly dizzy and weak.

"Mamma only read one of my books," Cass said abruptly. "It was my first, and I was so proud of it." Her eyes slid away as she remembered. "I wrapped it up in pink foil and I put a pink silk rose on top. It was for her birthday. I couldn't wait for her to read it, to talk to me about it.

"She took it out to the sun porch and started to read, and I was a wreck. I sat in the living room and thumbed through *House Beautiful* a dozen times until I just couldn't stand it anymore. Then I got up and peeked through the curtain for a long time and watched her. She knew I was there, because after a while, she put the book down—she wasn't even halfway through it—and she looked up at me. Do you know what she said? She said, 'I'm glad you chose to write under a pseudonym. I would not want to see our family name attached to something like this. And I'm quite sure Mr. Tompkins would have felt the same.'

"That's what she always called my daddy—Mr. Tomp-

kins. She called him that all her life, even at the end. They
thought she was unconscious, but she wasn't. I was sitting
by the bed when she opened her eyes. She cocked her head
and looked up at the bottle of sugar water they had running
into her vein and said, 'Why, yes, Mr. Tompkins. . . .'
And then she died.''

Sally tried to murmur a quick "I'm sorry," but the
words died in a wave of overwhelming fatigue. She felt
suddenly chilly.

"I could have been a nurse," said Cass. She was silent
a moment, then her chin went up. "Lucky for me I
wasn't. I like what I do. It's important to give people a
little happiness, a little romance." Her eyes sought Sally's. "Isn't it?" Without waiting for an answer she turned
away, and crossing to the kitchen counter, poured the last
of a bottle of Zinfandel into a paper cup. "There's never
been enough fucking happiness in the world."

A thin plume of smoke curling from the oil lamp hung
in the brighter glare from the Coleman lantern on the worktable. Sally blinked to ease the burning in her eyes. Too
much smoke; it was making her head pound. She wanted
to say something to Cass, tell her, "Yes, your work is
important," but somehow she couldn't. All the things that
had mattered so much a few days ago seemed almost silly
now. She stared at the lamp, watching it gutter and dim,
watching the smoke curl and thicken in its chimney. The
elemental things were what mattered now: food and water,
light. Suddenly she knew that the most important thing she
could do was to fill the lamps, trim the wicks, hold off the
dark. "The lamp is going out," she said. "I'll fill it."

Oil. It needed oil. She crossed the room, passed the
table, swayed, reached out. "Oil," she said under her breath.
The handle of the metal door was cold in her hand; she
clicked it open.

"What are you doing?" said Tuck. Alarm entered her
voice. "What's she doing?"

The door swung open. The light from the Coleman
lantern gleamed on wire racks. Blinking, Sally stared at

the shelves of food—of meat and cheese, of warming, curdling milk. What was it she wanted? Something important, she thought. What was it?

Fingers clinging to the damp edge of a rack, she stared bewildered into the refrigerator. Something. What was it? The shelves seemed to tilt. Puzzled, she tipped her head. Pain stabbed her eyes and she gasped. And as she began to fall, her fingers tightened on the shelf.

"My God!" cried Tuck. Then she was running to Sally, dodging the containers of food cascading from the rack, the eggs, the butter spattering the floor.

She reached out, touched Sally's face, recoiled. "She's burning up." Scrambling, crouching, she backed away, collided with the table. Began to scream.

The pain in her head stole Sally's breath. She gasped again and tried to draw in air. A vise gripped her lungs. Panting, she looked up, tried to focus. Cass was standing over her, looking down, eyes widening.

Sally's hand twitched open. "Help me."

Cass stared. She did not speak.

A breath, a rattling chill. "Please . . ."

Cass stared, shook her head. "I can't." Her head trembled left to right, left to right, as if it were on wires. "I can't," she whispered. "Oh, my God, I can't. I can't, I can't."

Tuck's scream propelled Bru to the house. Hand on the trigger of the SIG, he leaped onto the darkened porch and burst through the door.

Shocked faces met him. "It's Sally," said Cass. Lena and Tim knelt by her side.

He ran to her. "What happened?" But he already knew: he felt it in the sudden clenching of his gut. Her lips were shriveled and outlined with a deathly pallor; her cheeks were flushed as if someone had obscenely streaked her face with clown-spots of rouge. "Sally?"

Her eyes fluttered open and the look in them chilled him. They glittered darkly with fever—and there was no recognition there, none at all. "Sally," he said again, but this time it was an anguished whisper. He reached out, touched her throat, felt the quick thrum of her pulse against his fingertips. It was that, the faint birdlike tap of her pulse, that somehow filled him with dread; it was as if the life it carried was too fragile to withstand his touch.

He pulled his hand away, spun, ran to the door. A mist of rain blew against his face and he felt its damp chill deep inside his body. He closed his eyes, saw hers again, and saw his little son: Laird, pale as sand, eyes bright-dark with pain and fever. Utter helplessness washed through him. Bru focused on the road that led to Oyster Creek and willed Dave Cole to come back. He knew that Dave's medicines could not help her, yet at the same time, he wanted him there the way a primitive wanted a shaman; he needed someone to act, to go through the motions, to take responsibility.

He turned his face to the dark shed where El Ojo was, to the light flickering from its single window, and a cold rage began to grow.

Footsteps clattered on the back stairs and Paige Cole hurried into the kitchen. Lillian followed, clutching a rifle. The puddle of light from Paige's lantern faded in the white glare of approaching headlights. Bru was outside before the truck had stopped.

Tony slammed on the brakes and scrambled out. Dave Cole was in the back, crouching on the bed of the pickup beside the prone terrorist. As Bru ran up, Dave shook his head. "The guy's dead. He convulsed, then nothing. He—" The look on Bru's face stopped him. "What's up?"

"Sally. She's sick." Bru grabbed Dave's arm. "Help her."

Dave nodded and ran to the house.

Tony stared at Bru for a long moment. Then turning, he grabbed the dead terrorist under the arms and pulled him off the pickup. The man's legs slid across the slick, rain-misted truck bed and thudded onto the ground. Panting, Tony began to drag the body to the shed.

"No," said Bru abruptly. "Leave him here."

Tony straightened. "Why?"

"El Ojo." A strange, hard look settled on Bru's face as he turned toward the shed. "We're going to make that fucking son of a bitch talk."

Tuck Perry huddled by the back door and stared wildly at the scene in the kitchen. Dave Cole was bending over Sally, injecting something into her arm. The dim yellow light from the lantern glinted on the needle. It isn't real, she told herself. None of it was real.

Someone moved out of the way.

"Get a blanket," said someone else.

Sally moaned and began to cough—a racking, body-wrenching cough that twitched her head and thrashed her limbs as if she were a rag doll. A dark stain spread across her thighs and began to seep onto the floor.

Tuck pressed her body closer to the wall and twisted a lock of hair into pale rope, pulling it, twining it, until hot pain stung her eyes. "Oh, God," she whispered. Ohgod, ohgod, it couldn't be real.

The fit of coughing passed and Sally fell limp and still. Then a long gasping breath came, and the terrible cough shuddered through her body again. It's going to kill her, Tuck thought. It was going to kill her just like it killed Iguana.

Tuck had seen Iguana not long before he died. Drawn by a shocking curiosity that made her feel unclean and ashamed, she had opened the door a narrow crack and peeked through. Somehow he had known she was watching. He raised his head, fixed his mocking eyes on her, and grinned a death's-head grin that chilled her blood.

Maybe they all looked like that now—Hoby, the dead terrorists—all of them. She shivered and squeezed her eyes shut. The dead men in the wine cellar stared back. Their jaws hung open; their lips were split in terrible frozen grins. Whimpering, she shook her head. Suddenly, she could see herself, her flesh dark with rot, strings of tissue clinging to jaws that gaped and grimaced in the dark.

She pressed her face to the wall. The rough plaster scraped her cheek; flecks of blood dotted the white paint. "No," she whimpered. No, no, no, no, no.

Clutching at the wall, she scrambled to her feet. She had no idea where she would go, what she would do, but any place was better than this. Anywhere.

A battered black flashlight lay on the countertop a few feet away. Her fingers closed over it. She looked around the room furtively. No one had noticed. Turning, she slipped through the back door and pulled it shut behind her.

At the edge of the porch she turned on the flashlight. Its yellow glow emphasized the darkness that pressed in around her like a live thing. The only other light came from the window of the shed where Bru and the others were holding El Ojo. She strained for any sound. One of the terrorists had gotten away. He was out there somewhere. Suddenly she realized that he could be here, watching the house.

Her light was a beacon! He could see it, follow it, find her. Horrified, she switched it off and stared wide-eyed into the night.

A misting rain beaded her face and hair. Sliding a tentative foot forward, she clutched at the wet rail and felt for the top step. Her eyes began to adjust to the dark, and the driveway became an ash-gray curving line bisected by the dark blotch that was the pickup truck. She could follow the road for a way, then take the shortcut back to the old lodge.

She felt her way down the steps and across the grass. when she came to the hood of the pickup, she moved faster, trailing her hand along the body of the truck. Beyond it she could make out the pale curve of the road, its edges ragged with inky trees.

Shell crunched under her feet. She took a hesitant step, then another. All she had to do was take her time. After all, she'd been here nearly a month now; she knew all the trails. Her eyes strained to make out the road.

A screech came from just above her head and she jumped, heart pounding. Just an owl, she told herself. Lots of owls around. Uneasily she thought of it watching her, watching every move she made. Just an owl. Right now, she wished she could see in the dark, too. She took another step and suddenly froze, paralyzed by a thought: The terrorist *could* see in the dark. He could be watching her now through night goggles.

Her breath came fast and she heard it as his. He was here. She was sure of it. He was following her, stalking like a predator, waiting until she was away from the lodge so the others wouldn't hear when he attacked.

Her fingers tightened on the flashlight. If she turned it on, shined it through the trees, she knew she would see him. Her teeth closed on her lower lip and brought the faint salt taste of blood to her mouth. The truck, she thought. It was only a few yards away. She could crawl inside, lock the door.

Whirling, she ran toward the dark pickup. The keys were in it; they had to be. She could start the truck, run him down.

Heart hammering in her throat, she dodged around the tailgate. Suddenly her foot plunged into something thick—something horribly thick and soft that sent her sprawling to the ground. Gasping, she triggered the flashlight and stared.

The glazed dead eyes of the terrorist stared back. A dribble of blood oozed from the corner of his mouth.

She had no breath to scream. Clawing at the ground, she tried to scramble away.

Cooling fingers caught at her thigh; thick clots of blood slid beneath her knees.

Propelled by a terror as black as night, she scrabbled, rose, stumbled to the steps. Arms flailing, she tripped, fell across the porch, crawled to the door on hands and knees. It wasn't real, it wasn't real, it wasn't happening.

She would not let it be real, because if it was, then there was nowhere left to run, nowhere left to hide.

Her icy fingers splayed across the kitchen door. She

desperately wanted it to open; she was gripped with a chilling terror that it might.

A low animal moan came from her throat, but she did not hear it. She heard only the sharp, metallic click of a lock. Light splashed from the kitchen onto the porch, but deep within her brain, another door opened. And curling, slowly, drawing bent arms to her face, drawing knees tightly to her chest, she crawled inside and pulled it firmly shut behind her.

The dark wood of the shed absorbed most of the meager light from the kerosene lantern. The three-car jeep tram hugged one wall; Leroy stood near another. His head went up as Bru and Tony came in.

Bru narrowed his eyes when he saw El Ojo. The terrorist lay trussed to the bench seat of the last car, his arms tied behind his back. Bru swung onto the tram and leaned over the man.

El Ojo raised his chin.

Bru's voice was intense. "You're going to tell me what I want to know. You can do it now, or you can do it the hard way."

The terrorist's black stare was unreadable.

"The bomb on the mainland—where is it?"

He shrugged.

"I said, 'Where is it?' "

A mocking look came into his eyes. *"No comprende."*

"You'll have to do better than that." A humorless smile tightened Bru's lips. "We've been talking to your friend. He tells us you *comprende* English just fine."

The startled look that crossed El Ojo's face was replaced at once with one that was carefully blank.

"You didn't know about him, did you? You thought he got away."

The terrorist jerked his chin away and stared at the wall.

Bru cracked El Ojo across the face with a hard backhand. He swung again and a dribble of blood streaked the corner of the terrorist's mouth. "Now that I have your attention, *comprende* this: You and your buddy are going to talk to me." His voice intensified. "And you are going to tell me exactly what I want to know."

Bru fixed El Ojo with a long stare. Then wheeling abruptly, he grabbed a coil of rope, gestured for Tony to follow, and stalked out of the shed.

Outside, Tony grabbed Bru's arm. "What's up?" He glanced toward the dead terrorist. "Why did you tell him that guy was alive?"

"Because he's no good to us dead."

A low rumble, and a Black Hawk streaked overhead. They were overflying the island more frequently now, and Bru didn't like the implications. Something was up. He did not know what, but one thing was sure: Time was running out.

The plan that Bru had hatched was a gamble; if it did not work, he had no other. He dispatched Tony to the kitchen. Then feeling his way in the dark, counting steps, he followed the road to the top of the dune and estimated the distance: about thirty yards from the lodge. He went back down to the dead terrorist, grabbed him under the armpits, and began to drag him toward the road.

The kitchen door wheezed open and a flashlight glimmered on the steps. A woman called out hesitantly, "Bru?" He recognized Paige Cole's voice.

"Over here."

"Tony asked me to bring you a light. He said he'd be back out in a few min—" Paige stopped short at the sight of the blood-spattered body and turned her face away. "God," she whispered.

"Sorry." He took the flashlight and clipped it to his belt.

"Tuck must have seen him, too," she said, studiously avoiding the dead man. "She flipped out. We found her curled up by the door. She won't talk to us or anything. Dave says it's an acute psychotic break."

Bru looked away, and for a second or two only the

distant rush of surf and the patter of rain on leaves broke
the silence. "How's Sally?"

Paige shook her head. "I don't know. Not good." The
rain had pasted thick curls to her forehead; she brushed
them loose with the back of her hand. "We're going to put
her to bed in the entry hall and try to keep up isolation."
She bit her lip. "I guess it'll keep us off the streets,
anyway."

Bru stared at her for a moment. Then he dragged the
dead man onto the road. His heels left twin trails in the
shell.

"Where are you taking him?"

He nodded to the top of the dune. "Up there."

A startled look crossed her face. "It's uphill." She
paused, then abruptly said, "I'll help you." Hesitating for
a moment, Paige gingerly grabbed his boots and taking
care not to touch his legs, hoisted.

Panting, they carried the terrorist to the top of the sand
hill. The road curved to the west here, then plunged down
the other side.

"I can make it now," said Bru. He dragged the body to
a pine at the bend in the road and propped it in a sitting
position. With quick twists of the rope, he tied the dead
man to the tree.

Paige's eyes widened. "What are you doing?" Then
quickly, "No. Don't tell me. I don't want to know."

The kitchen door swung open. At Bru's short whistle,
Tony switched on a flashlight and ran up the hill. He was
carrying a bundle.

"Go back to the lodge, Paige." Bru unclipped the
flashlight. "And take this. Tony's bringing one."

She reached out for the light, but instead, grabbed his
arm, squeezed. "Get us out of this, Bru. Please." Without waiting for a reply she took the flashlight, turned, and
ran back to the lodge, passing Tony without a word.

They watched her go in silence. Then taking Tony's
flashlight, Bru dropped back a few yards downhill and
shined it on the pine. The terrorist's arms hung like sticks;

his head slumped forward. Shit. Even from a distance he looked dead. Bru flicked the light toward Tony. ''Give me your belt.'' It was black and about two inches wide. It would have to do.

Using his own belt, Bru pulled the dead man's hands behind the tree and lashed them together. He looped Tony's belt over the terrorist's eyes blindfold fashion and, tugging his head upright against the trunk, secured the belt to the pine with a twist of rope. This time, when he backed off and shined the light, he thought it might work. But not for long, he thought. It wouldn't bear close inspection.

''Hold the light,'' he said to Tony. A misty rain swirled in the glow of the flashlight. Bru took out a pocket knife and knelt beside the terrorist. Opening the bundle, he set to work. In a few minutes he was done.

He scooped up the bundle, straightened, and looked at Tony. The flashlight cast dark shadows on the young musician's eyes. Not a boy anymore, Bru thought, and he said aloud, ''Sometimes, we have to do things we don't want to do.''

Tony nodded slowly.

''Now,'' said Bru, ''we get El Ojo.''

They marched El Ojo out of the shed onto the dark swale below the kitchen porch. Leroy had moved the pickup. Now it was aimed toward the road and the top of the dune.

Bru played a light on the terrorist. Tiny drops of rain glittered on his hair. ''Are you ready to talk?''

El Ojo's heavy features were set, his lips clamped together. In a moment they splayed open and he panted with the pain in his broken ribs.

Bru's chin jerked toward Leroy. ''Hit the lights.''

The pickup's lights blazed, outlining the terrorist staked to the pine. Tony stood next to him.

''Now,'' yelled Bru.

Tony leaned forward and reached for a cylinder dangling from the neck of the terrorist. He yanked the ring pin on the end, then sprinted down the hill.

Bru heard the sharp intake of El Ojo's breath as the time fuse ignited and the bright point of light on the dune began to burn toward the coil of primacord looped around the dead terrorist's neck. Bru's voice was low. "He didn't talk fast enough. That was his mistake. He didn't realize how impatient I can be."

El Ojo's eyes were fixed on the dune.

Bru watched El Ojo sharply. He was buying it. But the time fuse was set for two minutes—too long to let him stare. He whipped out a length of primacord and held it up. A blasting cap lay along one end; a meter of fuse hung from it. El Ojo's eyes flicked toward the primacord. His pupils widened.

"I'm an impatient man," Bru repeated. "I don't like people who won't talk. It makes me nervous." With a swift movement he looped the primacord around El Ojo's neck, looped it again, drew it tight.

El Ojo's eyes met his, then slid toward the creeping point of light.

"The bomb. Where is it?"

A faint shrug.

Bru tightened the cord. "Talk. Or I'll blow your fucking head off."

El Ojo's lips parted, closed.

Bru spun him toward the dune. "Then take notes, you bastard. You're next."

The man stared.

Thirty yards away, the burning fuse glowed for a split second more like a fiery jewel at the throat of the terrorist.

A tongue of fire leaped to the top of the pine. A shower of blazing bark and pine needles sizzled in the rain. Bits of bone and tissue spattered the pickup.

El Ojo stared. He did not move.

Bru set his jaw. "Too bad about the tree. We'll have to find another one for you." He looked at the others. "This one wants to be next." Grabbing the primacord looped around El Ojo's neck, he steered the terrorist to the top of the dune as the Black Hawk flew in low in response to the explosion.

Smoking branches littered the ground. A nearby cedar, obscured by a thick pall of pungent smoke, hissed and smoldered in the rain. Bru shoved El Ojo to the ground against it. With the last of the rope he lashed him to the tree. "No blindfold for you." He held up the end of the fuse. "You get to watch it burn."

Bru pulled out an igniter and began to attach it to the end of the time fuse. "That is, unless you've decided to talk."

The terrorist stared at him in silence. Bru could hear the quick shallow rush of his breath.

"Where is the bomb?"

No answer.

Bru pulled out the cotter pin on the igniter. "Last chance."

"For both of us," said El Ojo slowly. "I lose. You lose."

Cold rage swept through Bru. "That's the chance we take," he said. Slowly, deliberately, he reached for the ring pin, yanked it, and turning his back on the terrorist, walked away.

At the bottom of the hill he spun around. El Ojo was straining against the ropes that held him. Not going to talk? "We will fucking well see," he whispered.

The fuse was half gone now; less than a minute left.

Bru watched the sizzling point of light creep toward the terrorist's throat. He thought of Sally, and for a moment he could see the blank and awful look in her eyes again.

No more than forty seconds now.

Time to move. Then he was running up the dune, feet pounding, hand closing on the pocket knife.

Less than twenty seconds. The terrorist's eyes bugged. The fuse sputtered inches from his throat.

Then Bru was on him, hacking at the fuse, flinging the burning end into the woods. "No, you bastard. It's too quick." And cutting away the ropes, he yanked him to his feet and shoved him toward the lodge.

Chapter 45

AT THE SOUND OF HEAVY FOOTSTEPS, MIRANDA GERVIN swung her rifle toward the kitchen door.

It burst open and Bru walked in. There was a set to his jaw that had not been there before. El Ojo followed at the point of Leroy's rifle. The terrorist's knees suddenly buckled and Tony Herrera grabbed him from behind to keep him from falling.

The stack of bird's-eye masks on the dining room table had dwindled to half a dozen. Bru took one, put it on, and slowly pulled on gloves and a plastic gown. His eyes never left El Ojo. "Gown up," he said to the others.

Taking Leroy's SIG, Bru trained it on the terrorist while Tony and Leroy put on masks and gloves. Miranda stared in silence from her post at the bay window. Her eyes were dark with stress and fatigue, and flickering shadows hollowed the square planes of her face into gauntness.

The door to the entry hall still had its crudely lettered grocery bag with the warning KEEP OUT UNLESS YOU'RE WEARING MASK & GLOVES. In the humidity the tape had curled away from the door, and the sagging right corner of the bag quivered with each current of air. El Ojo's eyes slid from the door to Bru. His lips were dry. He had read it; he knew what it meant.

Bru dangled a mask in front of the terrorist. "We're a little short on these. I'm afraid you'll have to do without." He tossed it back on the table.

Leroy swung the door open.

"After you." Bru prodded El Ojo with the rifle.

The tip of El Ojo's tongue protruded from his mouth and skittered across his lips. Behind his back, his bound hands moved; his fingers curled, released, curled again.

"In there. Move it."

Hesitating, half stumbling, the terrorist moved.

The entry hall was chilly and dark. A small red-glass oil lamp that had been meant more for decoration than light glowed from a table near the staircase. Tony switched on his flashlight and shut the door.

Bru stopped short. Dave and Paige Cole were huddled over Sally. She lay at the foot of the stairs on a hastily improvised bed of leather couch cushions from the Great Room. "How is she?"

"We're trying to get her temp down," said Dave. "It's nearly 104." His eyes did not meet Bru's.

At the voices Sally struggled up on her elbows and stared wildly around the entry hall. "What?" The exertion led to a fit of strangled coughing.

"It's all right." Paige's mask muffled her voice. Her plastic gown crackled as she gently pressed Sally back against the cushions.

Pain darkened Bru's eyes, but when he turned to El Ojo, they narrowed in rage. "Inside." He jabbed the rifle into the terrorist's injured ribs and herded him into the Great Room.

A damp chill permeated the darkened room. Leroy followed the beam of Tony's light to a table between two tall windows. An unlit ceramic oil lamp stood next to a plastic cigarette lighter. He picked up the lamp and sloshed it. Satisfied that it contained fuel, he pulled off the soot-smudged chimney. On the second try the lighter flared and he touched it to the wick. With the chimney back in place, the flame brightened and giant black shadows leaped on the walls.

The pool of light played across a coffee table covered with empty syringes and wadded paper wrappings. A coil of nylon drapery cord tied to two lard cans cascaded onto the floor like a pale thin snake.

Bru prodded El Ojo close to a long couch flanked by end tables. A stained white sheet covered it. With one hand he yanked it off and the fetid odor of clotted blood and feces puffed into the room.

Iguana's skin was the color of tallow. His glazed eyes stared as if they could still see the terrible death angel that haunted him; his lips were skinned back in a grinning rictus that exposed yellowing teeth and blackened, oozing gums.

El Ojo sucked in his breath.

"Shine the light over here," said Bru.

Tony aimed the flashlight at Iguana's leg. His pants leg had been cut away and a clean gauze dressing covered the wound in his thigh. The light glinted on something else: a shiny chain that circled Iguana's waist and disappeared between two thick cushions. Bru grasped it and pulled. The punctured canister popped out and dangled at the end. "Something of yours, I believe."

The canister swiveled slowly, catching the lamplight. Curls of metal bloomed and twisted like a silver flower at the place where Alex Borden's bullet had exited. The slim cylinder was clotted with blood and streaked with the pale glue of dried bacterial broth.

"I'd like for you to have it back," said Bru. "But Iguana seems quite attached to it." The look in his eyes hardened. "I'm afraid you'll have to share." He spun toward Leroy and Tony. "Tie them together."

Tony blinked.

"Use that." The muzzle of Bru's gun jabbed toward the drapery cord that had been used for Iguana's traction. Leroy's eyes met Bru's for a long moment. Then he turned and began to untie the knots that fastened the heavy cord to the lard cans.

El Ojo's head jerked toward Bru. His mouth worked. "The plague. Eet ees yours—your Central Intelligence Agency."

Bru stared at him.

"They can help. You get them to help."

Just like that. *Dial our 800 number now; operatives are standing by to take your call.* Face dark with rage, Bru threw down the rifle and grabbed the rope that bound El Ojo's hands. Planting a knee against the man's broken ribs, he yanked sharply upward. The terrorist gasped in pain and bent forward, his face inches from Iguana's. "Get a good look." He yanked again and El Ojo's face grazed the dead man's. Half from pain, half from revulsion, he gagged, and vomit spewed into Iguana's open mouth and trickled down his cheeks.

Gagging, Tony turned to the wall.

Eyes wild, El Ojo threw back his head.

"Tie them," Bru said again.

Leroy looped the cord under Iguana's shoulders. Bru shoved El Ojo down onto the dead man, grabbed the ends of the cord, and twisted them. "Today, amigo, is the first day of the rest of your life."

Shuddering, El Ojo thrust his chin as far away from Iguana's face as he could get it. He shook his head again, jerking it back and forth in little palsied thrusts like a carnival toy on a spring.

Bru knotted the ends of the cord to the rope that bound El Ojo's hands and stepped back.

In a frantic struggle to free himself, El Ojo kicked and, thrashing against the dead man in an obscene embrace, began to roll. For a moment the two men clung together like lovers at the edge of the couch. Then sliding, they plunged to the floor with Iguana on top, stiffened fingers clawing at the rug, bile dribbling from dead white lips.

Bru's stomach clenched. He forced himself to watch.

El Ojo began to tremble, his muscles tensing, releasing, tensing again in terrible rhythmic spasms. "Mercy." Beads of sweat on his forehead coalesced and dribbled down his face. "Mother of God, have mercy."

Mercy. The word seemed to have no meaning.

El Ojo was blubbering now, his eyes black with terror. "I tell you. I tell you everytheeng."

Bru caught his breath. "The bomb. Where is it?"

"Atlanta."

"Atlanta! Where?"

"A building." El Ojo's voice was a hoarse whisper. "Apartment building. Next to your Grant Field."

Grant Field. Georgia Tech's stadium. And the game was today. Bru's mouth felt like cotton. "When will it go off? What time?"

"After one. Five minutes after one."

Five minutes after kickoff. The color drained from Bru's face. He could see the stadium crammed with thousands of fans. Sixty thousand of them. Sixty thousand plague carriers. He stared at El Ojo as if he saw an animal snared in a trap. The terrorist was groveling like a whipped dog, terror in his eyes.

A cold stone lay in Bru's stomach. He turned away, and in a low voice laced with overwhelming fatigue, he said, "Cut him loose."

Lillian looked up sharply from the portable radio as Bru came in.

"What's wrong?" he asked. Dave Cole had stuck his head into the Great Room moments ago saying Lillian needed him at once. It was urgent. Leaving Tony and Leroy to question El Ojo, Bru had stripped off gown and gloves and hurried to the kitchen.

She held a finger to her lips and turned up the volume. The tinny speaker of the radio buzzed with each word of the newscast:

"*. . . early this morning on St. Cyrils Island. All are believed dead. Authorities can offer no explanation for the slaughter. Wakened early this morning with the news, the President was said to have expressed grief and outrage. A formal statement is expected within the hour. We will be bringing you updates as we receive them. Now this. . . .*"

A Toyota commercial came on and Lillian switched off the radio.

"Slaughter? What was he talking about?"

"Us," she said. "He means us. He said, 'Terrorist

inside the St. Cyrils Lodge gunned down their captives an hour ago.' ''

"He said that? That we were dead?"

Lillian nodded faintly. "He called it a massacre." She stood and clasped one hand with the other, stroking and kneading her fingers as if to warm them. "Bru, what does it mean?"

Bru shook his head and stared at the silent radio as if he could read some secret from it. Why? he thought. When they recaptured the lodge from the terrorists, the public had not been told. So far, understandable. If word had gotten out, the press would have demanded a telephone statement from the hostages. And that was clearly impossible in the government's view; it would have led to a plague panic. But, why this? Why the false story that they were all dead?

A rumble. Bru looked up as another Black Hawk streaked overhead. The overflights had increased in the last hour. Something was up and he didn't like the smell of it: they had been pronounced dead for a reason. And whatever that reason was, it was irrevocable. You didn't announce someone's death if you thought he was going to show up later and prove you a liar.

The newscast was self-fulfilling prophecy, he thought bitterly. But, it would be plague that killed them, not terrorists' bullets. And when it did, no one would know. The news would be suppressed—for the greater good. Dropped into the covert tar pit to disappear without a ripple.

Any thoughts he had had about revealing the bomb location to the government were wiped out now. If he told the FBI where it was in exchange for an alleged plague cure from the CIA, who would buy it? The FBI? Even if they did, the CIA would deny it, and he had no proof.

And their only line of communication was a battered radio telephone with an FBI agent on the other end.

Bru clenched his fist until his nails dug into his palm

and the tips of his fingers grew numb with the pressure. There had to be a way.

Lillian watched him for a moment. Then she said, "Do you want me to turn the radio back on?"

The radio.

He spun toward her. The CB radio.

With the power out, the base station was dead. But there were units in every truck and Jeep on the island. Their range was short and erratic, but if conditions were right, they would be powerful enough to reach the mainland.

And Wally Carruthers monitored emergency channel 9.

The layers of sleep fell away, and Wally's eyes popped open. He stared into the darkness and tried to remember the dream, but it was gone. Only the sharp sense of loss remained—and the image of Martha's face.

It was too early to get up. And too late to go back to sleep, he thought. Yet he tried, clutching the clean faded quilt to his chest, punching the pillow, making a hollow that cradled his head as snugly as a cowbird's egg in a sparrow's nest.

He lay there for a long time. But the twilight state that preceded sleep eluded him. Finally, he threw back the quilt and sat on the side of the bed. The house was chilly. His bony fee searched for slippers. Ought to make the bed, he thought. Instead, he pulled on a red plaid robe over his pajamas and went into the kitchen to make coffee.

The tag end of night pressed thick and dark against the kitchen windows as if it were cornered there by the dawn that was coming. The coffee maker belched and a brown stream began to trickle into the Pyrex pot. Pulling the pot off the burner, he deftly substituted a Blue Willow mug. When it filled, he snatched it off and slid the pot back in place without spilling a drop. Matter of timing, he thought. He called these first stolen cups Coffee Interruptus. They were stronger than the rest and they carried a sharp black jolt that gave him pleasure. "Cut out the caffeine," the doctor had said. But the habit of almost fifty years was too strong to break.

Cradling the mug in one hand, he sat down at the enameled kitchen table and switched on the radio.

He listened absently at first. Then at the mention of St. Cyrils Island, he swiveled his sharp chin toward the radio. His first reaction was shock.

Dead? All of them?

He shook his head. It wasn't possible. It had to be a lie; he had talked to Bru just after Iguana was disarmed. They weren't "captives"; there were no "armed terrorists" in the lodge. His eyes narrowed, but when he thought of the punctured canister of bacteria, a dark fear came into them. Maybe it *was* true. Maybe they were all dead of plague and this was only a way to explain their deaths without causing panic.

It wasn't likely that the FBI would tell him what was going on. County sheriffs were pretty low on their priority list, he thought bitterly. But he had to find out. Joe Murphy would know something. Since the governor's task force had linked the GBI and the state patrol with the FBI, they were working pretty closely together.

He picked up the phone, then hesitated, wondering if it was too early to call Joe at home. A moment later the CB radio hissed and came to life.

The words came in over a crackle of static. "Channel 9. Break channel 9."

Even with the poor reception, the voice was familiar. Wally picked up the microphone.

"Break channel 9. This is Pip," the voice said again. "Pip, calling the convict."

Bru. It was Bru.

Wally stared at the radio. It was a code.

White noise hissed from the CB. "Calling the convict. This is Pip."

Suddenly Wally remembered a warm July night long ago and two boys, ears perked with excitement, listening as he began to read chapter one of Dickens's *Great Expec-*

tations. He thumbed the mike switch. "You've got the convict."

"I have your vittles, sir. Should I bring them to the usual place."

Bru wanted to meet him. But where? Frowning, Wally tried to decipher his meaning: Pip had crossed a marsh; he had met the convict in a graveyard.

A graveyard. A cemetery. Where?

He tried to remember where Bru and Jimmy had played when they were children. Could he mean Egg Island? It wasn't too far from St. Cyrils; it would be possible to get there if he stuck to the marsh most of the way. "Did you put an . . . egg . . . with the vittles?" He emphasized the word.

"No. No egg. I don't like the sound—I don't like the sound at all."

Altamaha Sound. Bru wanted to stay away from the main channel. And no wonder. It would be crawling with Coast Guard. But if it wasn't Egg Island, it had to be someplace close to it. Someplace where he could take the police boat.

"I'd like to see ter your vittles, sir," said Bru.

"Repeat that. Say that again."

"I'd really like to see ter it," Bru repeated.

See ter it.

Cedar it. Cedar Island.

Cedar Island was tiny, no bigger than a postage stamp, and tucked in a backwater off the sound. Not one native in a hundred even knew its name, yet Bru remembered it. "We could do that," Wally said carefully. "We could Cedar it."

"Yes, *sir!* Seven hundred thirty."

Seven hundred thirty. Wally glanced at his watch. It was 6:18 now. Bru would have to make it on foot across the marsh, and much of the trip would be in near darkness. Then there would be a final swim. And it was cold out there and raining. "Are you sure about this?"

There was a pause. "There's no choice."

He heard a click and the radio went dead.

No choice.

Wally set his jaw. The whole operation had carried the stink of something dead from the beginning. Now it was worse. He raised his eyes to the dark window and tried to fathom what was going on. It was then that he remembered the sea gull.

It had been years ago. He had been fishing with the boys and they had put in to little Cedar Island for a lunch of baloney and cheese, warm Coke, and soggy potato chips. As they waded ashore, they found a dead sea gull caught in a tangle of half-drowned silver branches. With pomp and circumstance and crocodile tears, the boys buried it in a shallow hole in the mud and laid a gnarled cross of driftwood on top. The bird had been dead a long time, and Wally had made them scrub their hands with sand and salt water to get rid of the stink before he let them eat.

Pip's graveyard, he thought.

Wally went to the bedroom and began to throw on his clothes. Then he stopped. He would have to take the Chris-Craft down Altamaha Sound to reach Cedar Island, and the sound was off limits now. Anyone caught in the area would be arrested—or worse. He'd have to get clearance.

It took six rings for the task force switchboard to answer.

"This is Carruthers, McIntosh County sheriff. We've got word of a cocaine drop up one of the creeks off Altamaha Sound. We'll be entering the area by boat—a department Chris-Craft—in about one hour."

There was a pause. Then the man on the other end said, "Stand by on that." A minute passed, then two, before he came back on. "Give me your coordinates."

Wally had located Cedar Island on a chart of the channel. Skewing the coordinates a little, he gave them.

"Stand by, please."

He frowned as another minute went by.

"That area is restricted."

"I know that." Sarcasm stretched each word. "Why the

hell do you think I'm calling?" Without waiting for an answer he said, "The area is in McIntosh County. That's my jurisdiction. Or have you people forgotten that?"

Another pause. "How long do you expect to be in the area."

"How long can you hold your breath?"

"Just give me the answer."

"If I knew that, I would."

"Stand by."

Half a minute later, another voice came on. "Sheriff Wallace Carruthers?"

"Yes."

"You have permission to enter the designated area. You will proceed no closer to St. Cyrils Island than that. And you will vacate the area no later than 1130 hours."

"Vacate! You're talking about my jurisdiction."

"I'll tell you what I'm talking about." The man's voice took on a sharp edge. "If you or your men are found in the area after 1130 hours, you will be subject to arrest. Is that understood."

Wally stared at the phone for a moment. "I guess it is."

He hung up. A moment later he dialed Joe Murphy.

"Yeah." Murphy's voice was nasal; he sounded like he was catching a cold. "What's up?"

Wally snorted. "I was hoping you had the answer to that." He told him about the 11:30 deadline. "What in hell is going on, Joe?"

Murphy gave a short laugh. "Well, the right hand doesn't know what the left is doing, and the left hand doesn't have a clue. But I can let you in on the rumor. . . ."

As Wally listened, he felt cold fingers squeeze his gut. He hung up, grabbed the CB mike, thumbed it on. "This is the convict calling Pip. Come back." His voice grew urgent. "Come back, Pip."

But all he heard was the wind rustle of static. Nothing more. Nothing more at all.

*   *   *

Dawn was a gray ghost creeping in from the east. The Bronco, its headlights off, was no more than a dark shadow moving along the road.

It would have to be cross-country now, Lillian thought. She dropped into four-wheel drive and swung to the right. The Bronco began to creep up the face of a dune studded with overhanging oaks. Even with night goggles it was hard for her to see.

"Watch it," said Bru. "Log ahead."

She veered, but not in time. The Bronco bucked sharply as it climbed over the fallen tree. The wheel jerked in her hands. "Sorry." She swung her chin toward Leroy. "Are you all right?"

The old man nodded. The goggles he wore made the motion grotesque. Leroy held a rifle across his lap. Riding shotgun, thought Lillian, like someone out of the Wild West. But there was a terrorist still out there. And he had a gun, too.

They crested the dune and the Bronco veered again and straddled a foot path. Palmettos scraped its sides and belly and a wet branch slapped the windshield. Suddenly Bru said, "Stop." His voice was a hiss.

She jammed on the brakes and the Bronco idled.

He thrust his head out of the window and listened.

"What is it?"

"Thought I heard a helicopter," he said. "There."

The distant drone of rotors grew. A few seconds later, the copter passed overhead just to the north.

"They can't see us with the headlights off," she said.

"I hope you're right."

She dropped into first and the Bronco began to move again, more slowly now as the underbrush pressed in around them. A faint dawn light broke through the pine branches overhead. "Scrub," she said. "We did some timbering here a few years ago. It gets clearer up ahead." They were heading west toward the edge of the marsh that connected with Cedar Island. "I thought we ought to stick to the woods as long as we could."

She changed the subject abruptly. "Are you going to be warm enough, Bru?"

"Sure."

She frowned, partly from the headache that was coming on, partly from worry. Dave Cole had been worried about Bru, too. He talked about hypothermia. Immersion in water as warm as 68° could cause a serious drop in body temperature. Even 72° could be dangerous if you were in it long enough. It was going to be a lot colder than that out there.

"Don't worry," said Bru, reading her thoughts. "I've got my layer of goose grease on."

"Lard," she said, and tried to grin. Bru was covered from head to foot with a slick coating of the stuff. Dave had insisted on it. On top of that, he wore jeans, two pairs of wool socks, and two wool sweaters.

"What's a little salt marsh? I'm ready for the English Channel."

Lillian suddenly put on the brakes.

"What's wrong?"

"Nothing. Eye strain, that's all." She pulled off the goggles and pressed her fingers to her temples. The pressure seemed to help the sudden pain. Squinting, she looked through the rain-streaked windshield. A low knoll covered in bushes stretched out ahead. Which way? Left or right? She couldn't remember.

Bru touched her arm. "Are you all right?"

"Fine," she said. "I'm fine. Just getting my bearings."

Leroy's dark hand swung to the left. "The best way be over that rise."

She nodded, pulled the night goggles back on, and swung the wheel. A few minutes later the salt marsh stretched out in front of them like a rumpled gray rug.

Lillian turned off the key. "Tide's up." She pulled off the goggles. Coiling fog slid like a ghostly serpent through the marsh grass; first light was a thick cold gray. There was no sound but the whisper of rain on the leaves and the faint hum of insects.

Bru got out and went to the driver's side. When Lillian slid to the ground to meet him, he took her aside. "I want you to monitor the CB. Channel 9. When you answer, don't give your name or location. If I make it, I'll call in every thirty minutes, on the half hour, until I reach you. If I don't, try to reach Wally."

"Bru—"

He shook his head and gave her a sudden, crushing hug. The goggles hanging from his neck pressed painfully against her chest and took away her breath. Half frightened, she pulled away and looked up at him. She could not read his eyes. It was as if the fog had crept into them, had veiled them with a look she could not fathom.

"Take care of my girl for me," he said.

At her nod he gave her a long, searching look. "Take care of both my girls."

She tried to smile. "I'll be all right."

Bru gave her a slow, answering grin. "I'm going to hold you to it." He circled the Bronco, grasped Leroy's hand, pressed it hard. Then he pulled on the goggles, wheeled abruptly, and walked away.

The fog turned him into a shadowy specter and then into nothing at all. And at that moment Lillian knew she would never see him again.

She started to call out to him, to say, "Don't go." Instead, she stood motionless while the misting rain beaded her hair and cold stole into her bones. Finally, she slid into the Bronco and reached for the key, but something kept her from turning it. It would be like an abandonment, she thought, to let him hear us drive away, to leave him out there utterly alone. Instead, she switched on the CB and stared at the silent speaker as if somehow it linked her to him.

Leroy stirred on the seat beside her, turned, looked toward the woods.

He wants to go back, she thought. At least she wouldn't need the goggles now. There was just enough light to see. "We'll go," she said aloud.

"Sh-sh!"

Startled, she turned.

Leroy's rifle was aimed at a thicket of palmettos. The fronds were moving, a slow rhythmic movement that bent them to the ground like stiff fingers.

Something was there—someone—crawling through the underbrush.

The SIG tracked the moving fronds.

"No," she whispered.

He did not look up. "Be like killin' a varmint, Miss Lillian. That's all."

It could be anyone. "Maybe it's Calvin." But as soon as she said it, she knew it was not. Calvin would have come to them.

Leroy's finger tightened on the trigger. "Ain't no boy."

"No!" She grabbed the key, turned it, gunned the engine. The Bronco leaped forward, snarled, dug in. Then she was battling the wheel, swinging the truck to the west in a wide arc.

Leroy stared at her in stunned silence.

The Bronco assaulted a dune, plunged down the other side, crawled up an overgrown firebreak in the pines. "There's been enough." Her voice shook. "Enough killing." Adrenaline raced through the muscle fibers of her heart and boiled in her veins. Her pulse fluttered in her throat. "No more."

Her head exploded in pain. Gasping, she tried to hold on to a wheel that suddenly she could not feel beneath her fingers.

She slumped forward. The Bronco swerved, snapped a young pine, shuddered to a stop.

She tried to say, "You'd better drive." But the words scrambled themselves into nonsense. The pungent odor of pine resin filled her nostrils. She felt Leroy's hands on her shoulders; she thought she heard him say, "Lord God, Lord God." And then rags of darkness passed over her eyes and she lost consciousness.

It took Leroy nearly ten minutes to get back to the

lodge. Stumbling with her weight, he carried her up the porch steps and kicked the kitchen door until someone opened it. He stood just inside, clutching her, calling out, "Dr. Cole, Dr. Cole." Tears brimmed in his eyes, magnifying the yellowish whites of them, and when Dave and Paige came running in, the tears spilled over and oozed down his dark lined cheeks. "She be on fire," he whispered.

Together, they lowered her to the floor.

Paige caught her breath. "It's plague." Her voice broke. "It's plague, isn't it?"

"Maybe. I don't know. She's got a fever." Dave's fingers teased Lillian's eyelids open. He stared at the disparate pupils. "Shit."

Alarm flickered on Leroy's face. "She be all right," he insisted. "She gone be all right."

Dave's finger traced the corner of Lillian's mouth. The right side was drawn sharply down. A thin line of saliva glistened like a snail track at the corner. "It may be plague," he said. "But that's not all. She's had a CVA."

Dave's eyes slowly met Leroy's frightened, uncomprehending ones. "A stroke," he said. "She's had a stroke."

Calvin Borden shivered. He had been asleep only a few minutes when rain began to mist through the canopy of trees overhanging the Guale Indian mound.

That had been a long time ago. Now he was wet to the skin.

He pressed his body close to the wall of the excavation that stretched beyond his feet like a shallow grave, and looked up. A graying length of nylon cord, one of several that dissected the dig into measured squares, stretched over his head. He reached up and touched it, sliding his index finger along the cord for as far as he could reach. Far above, a faint dawn light glowed through the treetops.

He slid his tongue out and tried again to catch the rain that rolled slowly off the leaves and spattered down onto his face, but each drop accentuated his thirst. He sucked a drop of water from his thumb. He could probably drink a gallon. Maybe a whole bucket. He tried to pretend he was an Indian. Indians didn't mind being thirsty. And the Guales were really brave, Sir William said. But the more he tried to deny his thirst, the worse it got.

In desperation he crawled out and stood, shivering, at the edge of the excavation. He switched on the little penlight and tried to find the path. It went close to the rain pond, he thought. He could get a drink there.

Something crackled under his foot. For a blazing instant he was sure it was the bad guys' walkie-talkie. But it was only a crumpled piece of cellophane from a cigarette pack.

Somehow the knowledge that he was completely alone made everything worse. Even the bad guys were somebody, he thought. Somebody to hang around, to talk to. A loneliness worse than any he had ever known crept into his soul and turned to fear. What if nobody was left anywhere? What if he was the only person left in the whole world?

The thought made him shiver and turn wide eyes toward the dark woods that pressed close to the path.

There was Wally, he told himself. He'd still be around. Suddenly Calvin wanted to hear Wally's gravelly voice more than anything. All he had to do was go back to the truck and call him on the CB. He could get him to send another boat.

The image of the lighthouse came back and he saw the explosion all over again. The horrible thought came to him that Wally might not have another boat.

But he did. He had to.

Calvin began to run, his feet pounding down the dark path, his heart pounding in his throat. A cedar branch slapped his face and showered him with stinging drops. He spun, tripped, fell to his knees. The cold rain mingled with hot tears, and he bit his lip. There *was* another boat, he told himself. There *was*. It was going to take him home. And when that old boat came, he was going to make them find Ashley and Daddy and take them, too.

He left the tiny patch of higher ground and followed the

narrow elevated path through the salt marsh. The dark tide lapped at either side. Startled by the grunt of an alligator a few feet away, he ran faster until he made out the stand of cedars that flanked the rain pond.

He dropped to the ground in a clump of saw grass at the edge of the pond and began to drink, scooping up the cold water, lapping at his cupped palms with an outstretched tongue. Then from the corner of his eye, he saw the snake.

The thick-bodied moccasin was coiled by his right elbow. He saw the white of its mouth, the bared fangs blurring. He jerked away as the terrible head struck and missed.

Rolling away, Calvin scrambled to his feet. His terrified screams split the air as he stumbled, ran, stumbled again.

And from a thicket of young cedars, a dying man lifted his head and heard the screaming of his son.

Alex Borden opened eyes streaked with matter and registered a blur that slowly resolved itself into a child running toward him. Something was wrong.

"Calvin?"

Dehydration had shriveled Borden's lips. When they formed the name, they cracked like burnt paper. He struggled up to his elbows and called again. The effort brought on a tortured spasm of coughing. White froth dotted with flecks of dark red blood bubbled from his mouth.

"Dark," he muttered to himself. His right hand scrabbled at a wet branch as if it were a light switch.

He stared out in the gloom. "Son?"

The boy stopped short, froze.

"Calvin."

"Daddy?" Then the boy was running, sobbing, reaching out, tumbling to the ground. He threw his arms around his father and buried his face in his chest. "Daddy, daddy." His words broke into gasping sobs and his small body shook as if it would fly to pieces. When his voice came back, all he could say, over and over, was, "Daddy, daddy, daddy."

"All right. It's all right." He caressed the boy with feeble little pats that robbed what little strength he had left. When that was gone, his head lolled back and he began to cough again, his ribs retracting sharply, his throat raw with pain. " 'S awright."

Those were the last words he ever spoke. His throat filled with the sudden gush of blood that welled from his lungs and ran from dusky lips in a dark stream that in the dawn light looked gray on gray.

Calvin pulled back. Horror filled his eyes. "Daddy!" The word rose in a wail that sounded like a tortured wild thing. He tugged his father's arm, jerking it again and again with grubby hands. And in response the blood-streaked arm flailed back and forth and slack fingers clawed the air.

The boy shook his head in disbelief and beat small fists on the still chest as if to hammer life back into it. Exhausted, he fell back and raised his face to the weeping sky. His voice was a whimper. "My daddy, my daddy."

He scrambled to his feet. A cold tremor passed through his body and threatened to knock him down again. He stood for a moment, tears streaking his face, and stared down at his father. A terrible howl broke from his throat. His legs trembled, buckled. Then he was running as fast as he could.

And he ran until the flickering oil lamps of the lodge beckoned through the wet gray morning.

Chapter 46

THE MARSH WAS A COLD GRAY LIMBO THAT STRETCHED TO the ends of the world. With an effort Bru controlled the shiver that rippled down his spine. He couldn't give into it.

The tide rolled high through the cord grass and sluiced around his calves. Like walking in deep snow, he thought.

As gray light began to creep across the marsh, he threw away the goggles. Tiny raindrops beaded his face, and a freshening wind bent the misty cedars in the distance. Bru hugged his arms to his chest. A litany played again and again in his mind: keep going . . . keep going.

But underneath the thought, another crept in, dark and seductive as a woman. He shook his head and tried to submerge it, but suddenly he saw the pain shadowed in a little boy's eyes—and he heard the old familiar whisper in his mind: *get away . . . don't come back . . . don't come back. . . .*

His foot plunged into a drowned gully studded with oysters. Gray shell knives slashed his knee. Stinging salt water washed away the seeping blood. One step at a time. Keep going.

The tiny island was just ahead—on the far side of a tributary swollen with the tide. He'd have to swim. At the edge of the creek he pulled off running shoes thick with mud.

The sound of rotors.

Bru dropped to his belly and marsh water washed over his body.

The helicopter was a giant dragonfly in the mist. The

cord grass rippled and flattened with its passing. When it was gone, he slid into the black creek and began to swim.

The cold turned his arms to lead. Water ran into his nose and mouth.

Nearly there.

A stroke. Another.

He grabbed a tangle of silver branches, and dragged himself onto the tiny mud beach of Cedar Island.

He took shelter under a cluster of young trees and tried to keep from shivering. A few minutes later he heard the pulse of an outboard engine. It died abruptly.

The Chris-Craft was a pale ghost gliding toward the little island. Wally poled the boat silently. His oar struck bottom.

Bru watched from the trees. "Don't come ashore."

Wally looked up sharply. "Bru! Where are you?"

Bru stepped out; his hand went up in warning. "Stay there. I'm contaminated. I've been exposed."

Water lapped at the shore, crept inland, drained into a dozen tiny crab holes. "Here." Wally reached down, grabbed a thermos bottle, threw it.

The bottle rolled to a stop at Bru's feet. He twisted the top off. The steaming coffee inside was laced with brandy. He took a swallow, then another before he told Wally what had happened.

The old sheriff listened in silence. Finally, he said, "The bomb. What time will it go off?"

"1:05," said Bru. "Five minutes after kickoff."

Wally's fist tightened on the oar. "Not much time."

"Who can you trust in the state patrol? On the bomb squad?"

"We can't risk that. The state boys are part of the task force now. They're under FBI control." Wally did not speak for a moment. "I guess you're stuck with me."

Bru shook his head. "I can't let you do that."

"I don't think I gave you a choice." Wally scanned the marsh. "Feel that breeze? The wind's beginning to shift. There's a low front moving in from the south and it's got the feds worried. They're afraid it's going to blow whatever hatched out of that canister toward the mainland. They're planning to sterilize the island.''

Bru took a slow breath.

"They're going to napalm St. Cyrils," said Wally. "At noon.''

White lines traced the corners of Bru's lips. "We've got to stop them.''

They stared at each other in silence. Then Wally said, "Time's running out. Get in.''

"No. Not in the boat. I may be contagious. Throw me a rope and that oar.''

Wally narrowed his eyes. "You're crazy.''

"If I am, I got it from you. You taught me about Poor Man's water skis when I was ten years old. There's no choice," Bru added abruptly. "Altamaha Sound is patrolled. I've got to stay out of sight.''

Wally hesitated.

"For God's sake, man. If you've got a better way, let's hear it. I'm freezing.''

Turning, Wally threw a coil of rope to Bru. The oar skittered across the mud after it.

Bru lashed one end of the rope just below the blade of the oar and tested the knot. He drained the rest of the coffee and tossed the thermos into the trees. "Let's haul it.''

The Chris-Craft's engine fired to quarter throttle and the boat slid away from shore. When the rope at its stern stretched to full length, Bru waded into the water. The bottom dropped quickly. A few feet more and he was floating.

Wally swung around. "Ready?"

Bru grabbed the blade of the oar with both hands; his legs straddled the shaft and locked on. "Ready.''

The engine roared and the Chris-Craft sped toward the channel.

The oar bucked. Then its blade broke the surface and began to plane. Only Bru's head was above water now.

The boat veered. Its icy wake nearly strangled him, but he hung on, fists clamped to the blade. The dark water sucked warmth from his body. His vision blurred. Concentrate. Got to hold on. Hold on.

There was no feeling in his hands. He willed them not to let go. If he let go now, he knew he could not make it to shore.

An eternity passed. Then the Chris-Craft swerved and slowed. Its engine coughed to a stop. The rope went slack; the oar sank.

Gasping, Bru went under, touched bottom. He pushed off, bobbed to the surface, sucked air.

Wally was standing in the boat.

"Get out," yelled Bru. "Get away." He went under again. With the last of his strength he surfaced, grabbed the rope, and pulled himself to shore.

Water streamed from his body and he fell to his knees on the grassy slope that led to Wally's house.

Wally had retreated across the lawn to the back porch. One hand was on the doorknob. "Hold on," he yelled, and ran inside. A few seconds later he came back with a rolled-up navy blanket. He pitched it to Bru.

Bru doubled the blanket around his shoulders. It cut the wind. "Are you sure about the state patrol?"

He nodded.

"You'll have to get a flight to Atlanta."

Wally shook his head. "Not so easy. They've closed the airports."

Both of them? Bru struggled to overcome the terrible numbness that slowed his thinking. Wally couldn't go by car. It would take six hours. He'd have to fly. "The Savannah airport, then. Or Jacksonville."

"I can try. But we've got hundreds of media people flying in and out of the area. And we've got several thousand evacuees from St. Simons on top of that. There's a waiting list for every seat." Wally turned to go inside.

"Wait."

Wally swung back.

There might be time if they hurried. Bru shot a glance at his watch. The display was blank; the water had ruined it. "A friend of mine in Atlanta has a Cessna. Call him. His name is Daniel Elton."

Daniel Elton was wakened by a hand on his shoulder. He reached for his glasses.

Ginny was crying.

"What's wrong?" He threw back the quilt. "Honey, what's wrong?"

She shook her head and turned away.

"What is it? Is it the baby?" He jumped to his feet, and a pillow slid to the floor. "The baby's coming."

"No. It's Bru. And Sally. They're dead."

"Dead?"

"I just heard it on the radio."

He blinked.

"They're all dead," she said. "All of them."

Disbelief.

"They were shot." Her voice broke. "Oh, Danny—they shot them down like animals."

The bedside phone began to ring. At first, neither seemed to hear it. Then reflexively Elton picked it up.

A gravelly voice came over the line. "Daniel Elton?"

"Yes."

"This is Wally Carruthers, McIntosh County sheriff. I'm a friend of Bru Farrier."

It was true, then. Bru was dead.

"We need your help. We need it bad."

"What? What's that?"

"Bru says you have a Cessna."

Says?

"We need you to fly down here as quick as you can. If you tell them you have priority medical clearance, they'll let you land at St. Simons."

"Fly down?" He tried to make sense of it. "Why?"

"I can't tell you over the phone. But it may be the most

important thing you'll ever do. Bru says if you hurry, you can get here in two hours.''

Outrage came into Elton's voice. "What is this? Bru's dead.''

A pause. "No. He's not.''

His face twisted in pain. "Look, we just heard it.''

"You heard wrong. Bru's alive. He's here.''

Suspicion darkened Elton's voice. "Then put him on.''

"I can't do that.''

"Christ,'' he exploded. "What is it with you? What in hell do you want?''

"Listen to me,'' said Wally. "Your phone's unlisted. Bru gave me your number.''

No more than fifteen people knew that number. Elton shook his head; he wasn't sure what to believe. "That's not much proof.''

"It's all I've got. You're going to have to take the rest on faith.'' Wally's voice sharpened. "Bru's alive. So are the others. But they may not stay that way without your help. If you get your airplane down here right away, there may still be time. Will you do it?''

For the stretch of five seconds, Elton did not speak.

Later, as he threw on his clothes and brushed off Ginny's questions, he wondered why he had said yes. Just what in hell had he agreed to?

He was still wondering when he cranked the Camaro and headed toward Peachtree-Dekalb airport.

Though Wally had been in the house no more than five minutes, Bru could not judge the time. The icy water had brought an awful lethargy and it was difficult to concentrate. Dave Cole's warning crept sluggishly into his mind: hypothermia. Got to move, he thought. Got to keep moving. He began to jog in place. With each step, needles stabbed his feet and legs. As circulation slowly returned, violent shivers racked his body.

The kitchen door swung open. "I got Elton,'' Wally said. "He's coming.''

"The CIA," said Bru through chattering teeth. "Call them. Talk to the DCI. Tell him you made contact with a go-between for the terrorists. Tell him the guy won't talk to anybody but CIA." He drew a shaky breath. "If you can get somebody from the CIA here, I'll do the rest."

"They won't buy it. Not if I call from home. I'll go to town. Set it up on the department radio." Wally frowned. "As soon as I'm gone, you get in the house."

"If I go inside, you can't come back."

"I know that." Wally turned. "I'll phone you."

"Wait," said Bru. "Do you still have the shotgun?"

Wally nodded. "Same place. Now, get the hell inside before you freeze." He turned abruptly and was gone.

Bru waited until he heard Wally drive away before he went into the house. The warmth of the kitchen set off another round of shivering. He focused on the wall clock. 8:35. Five minutes too late to radio the island.

He tried anyway, clicking the CB microphone on, speaking quickly. "Break channel 9. Calling Lily. Calling Lily of the Field."

Nothing.

He'd have to try later. Lillian would be monitoring the Bronco's radio at 9:00.

Bru peeled off his soaked clothes and put on Wally's wool robe. He threw the soggy pile into the dryer and set the dial to high. The old Kenmore began to clatter. He pulled the robe's sash tight and went into the back bedroom. The shotgun was hidden inside an old golf bag at the back of the closet. He found the box of shells on the shelf under a pile of Wally's sweaters.

Back in the kitchen he poured coffee and stared at the CB while he drank. No point in trying until 9:00, he thought. He did not want to think about the napalm.

At 8:54 he pulled his clothes out of the dryer. The jeans were dry; the wool sweaters had shrunk to child size. He found the largest of Wally's sweatshirts and pulled it on. It tightened over his arms and chest. When the clock crept to 9:00, he went to the CB and called again.

No answer.

What was wrong? What the hell was wrong?

An old image suddenly flared in his mind—and a jungle thousands of miles away exploded in orange flames. A fire so hot that every living thing shriveled in its path.

He had to get word to the island. The lodge would go up like a torch. They had to get out, go somewhere safe. Maybe the edge of the marsh. But Sally—how could they move her?

They'd have to, he thought. They'd have to try.

Bru thumbed the CB microphone again. "Break channel 9. Calling Lily of the Field. Calling Lily. . . ."

Wally was waiting for an answer from the DCI when Pete Wiggins came into his office.

"What's going on between you and the CIA?" Pete grinned. "You got the hots for gray suits and paper shredders? Or is this your fundamental unholy alliance?"

Wally did not answer the question. It made sense to send a younger man, he thought. Put Pete on that plane with Daniel Elton, send him to Atlanta. He'd trust Pete with anything, with his life.

The deputy slid a haunch onto Wally's desk, pulled out a Tareyton from a crumpled pack, lit it.

Pete could handle it, thought Wally. He had bomb squad training; he'd know what to do. It made sense to send him. But it had made sense to send Delton Sheppard and Joe Carter to St. Cyrils Island—and Shep and Joe were dead now. Both dead. His lips tightened.

Pete quirked a thick eyebrow. "What's up?"

Wally stared at him. Pete was his friend. For nearly seventeen years. He spoke abruptly. "In twenty-five words or less? Nothing. Nothing's up."

Pete gave him a carefully bland look.

Wally read it as an opening. Pete's invitation to level with him. "I've got a couple of things to do," he said. "I'll be out of pocket for the rest of the day."

A quick knock. They glanced at the door. Marge Tyson

came in and handed a note to Wally. He read it, then nodded to her.

When she went out, he said to Wiggins, "I've got a job for you. There'll be a man here within the hour. His name is Jack Hubert. I want you to drive him to my house. When you get there, let him out."

"Yeah?"

"You let him out, you turn around, you come back here. That's all."

Pete started to say something.

Wally turned away and reached for the phone. It was a dismissal. He waited until Pete had gone before he called Bru.

It was 9:22 by the kitchen clock when Wally phoned. Bru hung up and went into the little living room. He loaded the shotgun and sat back on the couch to wait for Jack Hubert.

The image of orange flames came flooding back, and from some primitive part of his brain the smells came with it—napalm and the sick-sweet stench of burning flesh.

Bru threw down the shotgun and ran to the kitchen.

"Break channel 9. Calling Lily. Calling Lily of the Field. . . ."

Outside the lodge the Bronco's CB radio crackled as Bru's voice urgently repeated the message again and again.

No one heard.

Tony Herrera, guarding a bound El Ojo in the shed, turned his face toward the Bronco, but the sound of the radio did not register.

Leroy Jefferson was too far away. He sat upstairs with his grandson, Tim, who could hear nothing at all. Neither could Tuck Perry, who lay curled in a tight fetal ball on a bed in the next room.

Downstairs in the kitchen, Cass Tompkins cuddled an exhausted nine-year-old boy who clung to her neck and sobbed for his dead father. Nathan Katz stood next to them, his arms wrapped around a weeping dark-haired girl. Miranda Gervin watched in silence from her guard post by the dining room bay window.

In the entry hall, daylight penetrated the high windows, but the red oil lamp still burned. Lillian lay near the stairs on a makeshift bed next to Sally.

"What's she saying?" asked Dave Cole.

Lena Jefferson's dark eyes were unreadable above her mask. She put her ear close to Lillian's lips.

Lillian clawed the blanket. Again she tried to speak. Her words were unintelligible: "Ruhjoe. Nuh . . . nuhnn . . ." They ended in an explosive cough.

Paige Cole leaned closer. "She keeps saying it. Over and over."

Lena shook her head. "I can't make nothin' out of it."

"She's so frantic," said Paige. "It's like she has to make us understand."

Dave nodded. "Aphasia. It's very frustrating." Suddenly he coughed, and his mask puffed out, sucked in over his nose and lips, puffed out again.

Paige's eyes widened in horror.

"I'm all right, honey," he said quickly. "I'm okay."

Her hand flew out to him.

"I got something down the wrong pipe," he said. "That's all."

"Are you sure?"

"Sure, I'm sure. I'm a doctor. Remember?"

Paige gave a little laugh, but despair flickered in her eyes. "I keep wondering who's going to be next. You know? I keep wondering if it's going to be me. I almost wish I could do what Tuck did. Go away. Turn it all off." She began to tremble. "Sometimes I know it's going to be me." Her hand fluttered toward the two sick women. "I don't want it to be like this. I've even thought about wiping myself out. Before it gets me." Her voice broke. "I guess I'm crazy."

"No, you're not," he said. "It's just a reaction."

"Yeah. Real normal, huh?"

"You're not crazy. Back in the Dark Ages, people even jumped off cliffs when they knew the plague was coming."

"Oh, God." Paige began to cry.

Lena took hold of her shoulder. "You go on out, Miz Cole. You go on out an' get some rest now."

Something in her tone made Paige obey.

When she was gone, Lena drew herself up. "You got no call to be talkin' like that," she said to Dave. "Talking 'bout jumping off cliffs." Her voice was low but indignant. "You got no call to be talkin' like that in front of sick folks."

"You're right," he said slowly. "I'm sorry."

Lena looked him up and down. "Go on out, now. Go on out and see about Miz Paige." She nodded toward the two sick women. "I'll see to them."

When Dave left, Lena bent over the bed.

Lillian's frantic eyes whipped back and forth. Her lips moved.

"Sh-sh. Don't you go tryin' to talk. You'll just wear yourself out." The old black woman picked up a damp cloth. Her gnarled hands were gentle as she wiped Lillian's face. "You gone be all right. It just gone take a little rest."

On the next bed Sally stirred. Her hand groped to her temple. "Hurts."

Lena turned to a tray of medicines and picked up the bottle of codeine tablets. They were nearly gone. She hesitated. Tim would be needing one soon. She did not know how long his pain would last. Her eyes slid shut for a moment as she thought of her grandson. Doctor Dave had said his hearing would come back in a few days. Maybe that was the truth. Maybe not.

Sally gave a low moan.

With stiffened fingers Lena resolutely worked open the bottle cap, shook out a tiny tablet, and held it to Sally's lips. "Swallow this, honey. It take away the pain." She followed the pill with a spoonful of water.

Sally ran her moist tongue over cracking lips. " 'S good."

"Try some more, now." Lena gave her another spoonful.

When Sally lay back, Lena picked up the worn old Bible that she had placed by the tray. She thumbed to the back. Maneuvering the fine print into focus, she traced a passage with her fingertip. Then, finding comfort in the verses, she began to read aloud:

"And I saw another sign in heaven, great and marvelous, seven angels having the seven last plagues; for in them is filled up the wrath of God.

"And I saw as it were a sea of glass mingled with fire: and them that had gotten the victory over the beast, and over his image, and over his mark, and over the number of his name, stand on the sea of glass, having the harps of God."

Sally's fever had responded to aspirin at first, but now it soared. Throwing a hand, palm out, across her burning eyes, she fell into a restless sleep.

The dream was a jumble of stop-frame images:

A fire . . . Children . . . Ragged children . . .

She was running along a nigh, stony path. A cold wind whistled through her thin shawl. Hurry. Hurry.

The hoop was just ahead now. A huge ring of bloodred roses, woven in a thorny circle at the edge of the cliff.

She leaped through and began to fall.

The water yawned below.

As she tumbled head over heels, she knew she had seen the ocean before: It was a miniature sea made of fiberglass, surf frozen in a rigid froth—and looping endlessly in front of it was a tiny model train.

She was riding the engine now, feeling its rhythm. As it swayed and clattered on the track, she heard its ceaseless singsong: sea of glass . . . sea of glass . . . sea of glass. . . .

Chapter 47

SHELL CRUNCHED UNDER THE TIRES AS PETE WIGGINS TURNED onto an oak-lined road bordering the water.

Jack Hubert studied him closely. Wiggins wasn't much on conversation. He wondered how much the deputy knew. "Where did you, uh, say this guy called from? Phone booth?"

"I didn't say." Wiggins defused the remark with a grin. "You'll have to ask the sheriff about that. I'm just the chauffeur."

Hubert stared out of the window and tried to hide his annoyance. He had been told next to nothing: only that the terrorists' middleman had agreed to talk to the CIA. That was it—and that much had come from the DCI.

Hubert hoped the sheriff had wit enough to get a telephone trace on the contact, but the hope was a faint one. McIntosh County was more rural than he had imagined; it wasn't likely to harbor a lawman with uptown methods. But even if it meant dealing with Andy of Mayberry, this was a breakthrough—the first since they had lost Orlando Salazar.

Hubert considered the possibility that Salazar might be the middleman. All the evidence pointed to a single confederate on the mainland—one man who controlled a network of computers. He didn't think the terrorists would water the soup by bringing somebody else in this late in the game, but he had to be sure. Let it be Orlando Salazar, he thought. Salazar knew where the bomb was.

The car turned off under an arch of live oaks and came

to a stop in front of an old frame house. "End of the road," said Wiggins.

Hubert stared at the building. It was supposed to be a DIA safe house—a contact place well away from hovering reporters and indiscreet switchboard operators. Certainly remote enough, he thought.

Wiggins nodded toward the house. "Sheriff's waiting inside."

Hubert got out in a fine mist of rain. When he closed the car door, the dark green latticework under the porch bulged and an old basset hound waddled out through a gap in the boards. The dog obviously lived here.

A pet? At a safe house? Not bloody likely. He shot a glance at Wiggins.

The deputy took it as a cue. The car sped away in a shower of gravel.

Hubert swung toward the house. The curtains were drawn, but inside the screened porch, the front door was ajar. It didn't feel right. With a quick movement he unbuttoned his jacket. The shoulder holster concealed under it did not yield to the slight pressure of his elbow.

The screen door creaked and Hubert's footsteps echoed across the wooden porch. He hesitated.

From somewhere in the house a voice called, "Come in."

The door slid open at his touch. He waited a moment, then stepped inside.

The small living room was dim. No one was there.

"In here."

As Hubert turned toward the sound, a man stepped out from the next room. "Freeze."

The shotgun was aimed at Hubert's heart.

"Hands behind your head. Make it slow."

Hubert did as he was told.

"You'll have to check your handgun. House rules." The man pulled the gun out of Hubert's holster.

"Who are you?"

Backing away, he flicked a wall switch. A floor lamp

threw a pool of light into the room. "Sit down." He jabbed the shotgun toward an armchair.

Hubert slid into the chair and stared. The man looked familiar. "Who are you?"

A tight, humorless smile.

It was enough. Suddenly it all fell into place. A photograph—the smiling picture of a man who had been on every TV newscast since Thanksgiving night. "God," he whispered.

"So you figured it out."

Bruton Laird Farrier. The congressman.

"I hated to leave the island," said Bru. He sat down on the couch and balanced the shotgun over his knees. It was aimed at Hubert's belly. "The sun, the surf—the plague. But I had business on the mainland."

"What do you want?"

"What do I want?" Bru gave a mirthless laugh. "What do you think I want, you son of a bitch? People are dying over there."

Then it was true.

"I want the cure. From Mr. N. K. Wily. I want the cure to your fucking disease."

"Ours? We don't—"

"We don't give a shit about the truth, do we?" Bru's mocking tone fell away and his voice took on a chilling intensity. "It would behoove you to come up with it pretty quick. You've been exposed."

Exposed? Jack Hubert stared blindly at Bru, but all he could see were the glazed eyes of a dying ape.

"I want the cure."

Hubert's mouth was dry. "We don't have it. It's Guatemalan. The plague is Guatemalan."

"You're going to spout the Company line, aren't you? All the way to your grave."

"It's Guatemalan. Eighteen is Guatemalan."

"Eighteen? So, that's what you call it." Bru's lips tightened. "Your tax dollars at work."

Sweat drained from Hubert's armpits.

"Where's the cure? Fort Detrick?"

He shook his head. "There's nothing at Detrick."

"But there *is* a cure."

Hubert felt sick. For a moment he could not speak. "There's an antibiotic. Experimental. R & D quantity."

"And you boys just didn't feel right about trying an experimental drug on dying human beings, did you, now?"

"I didn't have anything to do with that."

"But you knew about it. You knew there was a cure."

"For God's sake, man. It was triage."

Bru stared at him.

"The Russians have been playing with *Yersinia pestis*. We've known it for years." Hubert looked away, then back. "Sure, Pestis 18 is ours. What choice did we have?" He thought of Sanders lying dead on the autopsy table and his stomach clenched in a cold knot. "One guy," he said. "One guy sells out to a handful of terrorists and it all goes to hell."

"You could say that." Bru's lip curled. "A case of self-preservation. CIA versus citizens."

Hubert's jaw tightened. "Do you know what would happen if the agency went under? Do you have any idea? I'm talking about security. Our work was the nation's only defense against the Soviet plague." He thought of the ape again and his eyes slid away. When they finally met Bru's, they were full of pain. "It was triage."

Ten full seconds passed before Bru spoke. "You really don't understand, do you? You don't have a clue. Did you know that two of the 'Guatemalans' were Cuban?"

Hubert's tongue skittered over his lips.

"Nobody was supposed to find that out." Bru's fingers tightened on the shotgun. "The terrorists planned to blow the hostages to hell, and then rendezvous with a submarine—a rogue. It didn't show up in the navy sub net, did it?"

Hubert shook his head. "No."

"That's because it wasn't there. Are you beginning to understand?" Without waiting for an answer Bru said,

"The terrorists were set up. They were supposed to wind up as target practice. Presto, no witnesses." He glanced down at the shotgun. "Funny thing. Two Cubans tucked in with the Guatemalans—but their weapons were Swiss. And brand-new. Does that tell you anything? Does that sound like a third-world terrorist operation to you?" His eyes narrowed. "None of the weapons were Soviet. They couldn't risk it."

Hubert stared at him without comprehension.

"You knew the Soviets were tinkering with plague. So did Iguana. He was a KGB agent. An expendable one. But Iguana wasn't their only agent." Bru's lips stretched in a tight smile. "Wasn't it convenient for the CIA to be kept so abreast of Soviet genetic research?"

A startled look crossed Hubert's face.

"They were feeding you with a spoon," said Bru. "They planted intelligence reports to keep you up to date every step of the way. The Soviets were counting on you to duplicate their research."

"Sanders—"

"Sanders? Good work. You've caught your mole. How long was he with you? Eight years? Ten? Surely long before the KGB started to plant the reports. Your man Sanders was their double check. Their way to make sure your plague project was going the way they wanted it to. They'll probably give him a medal."

"They killed him," said Hubert in a low voice. "He took the two canisters of Pestis 18 from the lab. We thought it was a sellout."

Bru snorted. "It was. Only it was Sanders who was sold out. It makes sense. They didn't need him anymore; they must have killed him to throw off suspicion." His eyes darkened. "You were fed plenty of data about the plague. How much did you get about a cure?"

Hubert's mouth felt like cotton. Nothing. They had learned nothing at all.

"The Soviets must have been stockpiling a vaccine for years," said Bru. "They've been waiting for you to catch up, waiting for Pestis 18 to hit the assembly line. Then a bomb full of it goes off on the U.S. mainland.'' He gave a short laugh. ''Now you see the reason for the Swiss weapons. The Russians couldn't risk a link to the terrorists. We'd be sure to retaliate.

''Ingenious, isn't it? First Iguana broadcasts his demands on satellite and the plague threat is picked up all over the world. Then the bomb goes off—and it's revealed that Pestis 18 is ours, developed by the CIA.

''Now incurable plague threatens every nation on the globe. But help is on the way—from the Russians.'' Sarcasm sharpened Bru's voice. ''They'll tell us the truth, the gospel according to Big Brother. They'll tell us that once Soviet intelligence got wind of the imperialist plot, they began parallel development to protect the rest of the world from America's Black Death. Real heroes.''

Bru's eyes burned into Hubert. ''For a price there'll be enough Soviet vaccine for everybody—except for us. It's too late for America. But who cares? Everybody's down on the U.S.A.; didn't we bring this on ourselves?'' Bru closed his eyes for a moment. When he opened them, utter fatigue showed through. ''Very ingenious. World War III—and not a single Russian casualty.'' His head went up. ''What time is it?''

Stunned, Hubert stared at him.

''I said, what time is it?''

He looked at his watch. ''10:42. Why?''

Bru stood up. ''You and I are going on a little trip. But first you're going to get the DCI on the phone. Now, move it.''

When the DCI hung up, his sweat glistened on the telephone receiver. The faint voices from the Situation Room next door were lost on him. Bruton Farrier's ultimatum echoed in his head: ''. . . abort the napalm strike . . . full medical evacuation . . . the antibiotic. Then you'll get your bomb.''

He took a long, slow breath. Clear out the brain, he thought. Get control.

Another breath shuddered into his lungs. It wasn't the first time his tail was caught in a crack. Wouldn't be the last. His gaze flicked through the empty room and settled on a bare patch of plaster. Options. Figure the options. It was a matter of strategy. A chess game.

The antibiotic for the bomb. Farrier had spelled it out: He was going back to the island, and he was taking Jack Hubert with him. When he saw the antibiotic administered, when a medical evacuation was under way, he'd give the location. Only then. That meant isolation units and an airlift to Detrick.

The DCI glanced toward the Situation Room. Pull it out of the fire, he thought. He could tell the committee one of the terrorists was ready to talk to the CIA; tell them he had a man on the way by boat. No. Two men. Clearance for two men.

The radiotelephone was the link. It was the only way he could talk to Farrier once he was back on the island. But the FBI controlled the switchboard. He'd have to take it over, put his own man on.

Farrier had him by the short hairs. Fuck him, he thought savagely. But he had no choice; he had to play the congressman's game. It was the only way to stop the bomb.

And what then?

The DCI's jaw tightened. He had spent his life with one finger in the dike to keep the country from drowning. Now the fucking public was going to preside over his crucifixion.

He glanced at his watch. He had to call off the napalm strike. It was due at noon—and there was no way an evacuation plane could make it to St. Cyrils before 12:30. No time, he thought. No move left.

Or was there?

As he stared at the dial, his eyes turned to steel. A half hour more. That was all he needed. Thirty fucking minutes. His lips stretched into a hard, thin line. The game wasn't over. Not yet. . . .

Chapter 48

THE DRIZZLE ABATED TO A FOGGY MIST WHEN THE CHRIS-Craft reached the last stretch of Oyster Creek. Bru killed the engine and the boat glided toward the fire-blackened dock. The smell of smoke still hung in the air.

The tide was going out fast. The boat's wake lapped at a muddy stretch of shore, and a mass of fiddler crabs skittered away from something at the edge of the water. Bru winced when he saw it was Sir William's body.

White lines bracketed Jack Hubert's lips. "Looks like a war zone."

It is, thought Bru. The floating dock ramp angled steeply down to the water. He looped a line over a half-submerged post, stepped out, and signaled Hubert to follow. Though Bru still carried the handgun, he felt no need of it. Hubert wasn't going anywhere. If he were to try, he would be hopelessly lost in no time.

The two men had fallen into an uneasy truce. Foxhole mentality, thought Bru. Yet he had been almost grateful for Hubert's company. It made coming back a little easier. He tried to dislodge the picture stuck in his mind: Sally—eyes blank, not seeing him, not knowing him. A sudden feeling of helplessness threatened to overwhelm him, and he swallowed hard to get control. "What time is it?" he asked sharply.

Hubert glanced at his watch. "It's nearly noon. Five of."

Wally and Daniel would be landing in Atlanta soon. He had to get them help. Too much was at stake for them to go it alone. The DCI could get a bomb squad to the site within minutes, but Bru didn't trust him. The man had promised a rescue plane by 12:30. Bru intended to see it for himself before he told him where the bomb was. He frowned. It was cutting it close—too close. But there wasn't any choice.

So far, the DCI had kept his word. There had been no warnings to turn back, no hostilities. But they had been followed. A reconnoitering Black Hawk had tracked the Chris-Craft all the way to the mouth of Oyster Creek.

Bru knew he would breathe easier when it was past noon and the napalm threat was over. But so far, so good. Right now it looked like there was no need to evacuate the lodge. Still, he was bothered by the radio silence. Why hadn't Lillian answered his calls?

He squinted at the gray empty sky when a sudden tickle in his nose made him sneeze noisily.

Alarm registered in Hubert's eyes.

"No need to panic." Bru gave a short laugh. "You'd sneeze, too, if you'd been swimming this morning." He glanced up at the sky again and suddenly realized that he had been watching for aircraft ever since the Black Hawk had turned off.

No use to buy trouble, he thought.

The CJ5 was parked near the dock. Bru headed for it and glanced inside. The keys dangled from the ignition. Motioning for Hubert to get in, he slid behind the wheel, turned the key abruptly, and the Jeep spat shell from under its tires and swung toward the lodge.

Wally Carruthers cautiously looked down at the green patchwork farmland dotted with ponds, but when the Cessna banked suddenly, he gripped his knees and darted a sidelong look at Daniel Elton. "Uh, putting down soon?"

"What? Oh—" A grin twitched at the corner of Elton's lips. It seemed ludicrous that a sheriff with a .357 Magnum at his hip would get tight-jawed over a little altitude. "We'll be landing in about thirty minutes."

Elton's grin faded as his thoughts took hold again. Wally had filled in a lot of gaps, but there were still more questions than answers. Hanging over it all was the unanswered question of the scenario. "This terrorist," he said abruptly. "What, exactly, did he say to Bru? I mean, about the CIA."

"Iguana was sick by then. Out of his head. Everything he said was in Spanish. Well, nearly everything."

Elton glanced over. "Yeah?"

"Bru recognized a CIA code. He said—"

The Cessna dropped like a stone.

"Whoa!" Elton yelled. "Hang on." The plane leveled. "Air pocket. You okay?"

Wally's lips made a thin line. He swallowed. "Fine."

"Sorry. You said there was a code."

"It was NK. NKWILY."

Elton blinked. Several seconds passed before he spoke. "Are you sure?"

"I'm sure."

Blinking again, Elton dug into the pocket of his jacket and fished out half a dozen scraps of paper. Discarding a Doublemint gum wrapper, he plucked out a folded note. "Take a look at this."

Wally raised an eyebrow. It was a receipt from Video City. "You rented *The African Queen*."

"Shit." Elton scanned the papers again. "It's this one."

Wally unfolded the second note and stared at it in silence. Across the top was the penciled tracing: NKWILY. "Where did you get this?"

"From a guy at the office." From a doctor. A goddamned *doctor*.

Elton felt queasy. He thought about Bru, about Sally— sick, maybe dying. His lips compressed. NKWILY was the disease. The plague was only a symptom.

Leroy Jefferson gripped his rifle and stared out of the dining room window at the mist drifting through the oaks. He had taken over guard duty from Miranda Gervin at ten, but for the last half hour, little that he saw registered in his brain.

The old man stifled a cough. The effort tightened the muscles in his belly and chest, and the veins in his neck stood out like cords. The pain in his head was suddenly blinding.

The first chill had come an hour ago. Now his fever was raging. He braced his trembling body against the wall and clutched the rifle.

He glanced at the door to the entry hall. Lena and Dave Cole were still in there. With the sick folks. Leroy made a careful distinction between the sick and himself. He'd be all right. Long as he stayed up and around.

When another cough racked his body, he silenced it with a wadded handkerchief pressed to his mouth. It came away stained with a thin streak that looked like rust. He stared at it in dismay. No good, he thought. Doing no good. Without wanting to, he remembered his father. Leroy was no more than seven or eight when his daddy's final hemorrhage had come. He could still smell the blood-streaked rags burning in the oil drum in the backyard. "Keeps from catching the TB," his mamma had said.

He glanced anxiously toward the entry hall. Something was bad wrong with Miss Lillian. Lena's tone had alarmed him. She had called for the doctor nearly twenty minutes ago, and there had been an edge to her voice that Leroy associated with catastrophe.

The KEEP OUT sign on the door shimmied, and Dave Cole came in. His eyes were shadowed. He stripped off his mask and gloves before he spoke. When he did, his voice was low. "She's dead. Lillian's dead." He wheeled abruptly and went into the kitchen.

Bleakly, Leroy turned back to the window, but instead of the mist and the trees, he saw a knobby-kneed, pigtailed girl running through the woods with a fawn at her side. Lillian was only eleven when Leroy first came to St. Cyrils. He had planned to work for a season; he had stayed for nearly fifty years.

The next chill shivered through his bones like a brittle wind, and his strength drained away to nothing. The rifle slid through his fingers and clattered to the floor. He stared dumbly at it. Then, leaning heavily against the wall, he made his way to the entry hall door and opened it.

The air in the room was cold. He stared at the two pallets near the staircase. On one, Sally muttered and tossed in a tangle of blankets; on the other, Lillian lay still, her face covered with a pale blue sheet.

Lena gasped when she saw him. "What you doing in here with no mask on your face?"

He tried to answer, but the effort was too great. Instead, he took a tottering step and slid to a half crouch against the wall. His head dropped forward as if its weight were too much to be borne.

Lena scrambled to her feet and went to him. Her hands closed on his shoulders, tightened. Slowly he raised his head.

She searched his face. "Lord, oh, Lord." Her voice came through her thin mask like surf through a coiled shell.

He had always been a man of few words. None came to him now. His arms slid around her thin shoulders.

Lena's words trembled against his ear. "Lord, please. Don't take him. Don't take my man."

She fell silent then. Gently lowering him to the floor, she stretched out beside him, and for a long time they clung together like two lost children in the night.

Bru tied a hastily donned mask with gloved fingers and opened the entry hall door. Dave Cole followed.

Inside, Bru stopped abruptly. Leroy was huddled on the floor at his feet.

Lena struggled up from her husband's side. Her eyes were blank mirrors. "Leroy—he down with it, too."

Dave reached for a pulse. Head cocked, he seemed to be listening, as if the insistent tap against his fingertips were audible.

Leroy tried to sit up, but the effort brought on a spasm of coughing. Speckles of blood dotted the yellow-white sputum that frothed from his lips.

Bru's stomach lurched, but he kept his voice steady. "We're going to get you some help. There's a plane coming. Medicine."

Confusion glimmered in the old man's eyes. The wild hope in Lena's was more than Bru could bear. He pulled his gaze away, turned, and went to the pallets near the stair.

He looked down at the ice-blue sheet that shrouded Lillian's body. All that came into his head was the sound of the old banjo wall clock, each tick hollow as water dripping into a steel sink.

Sally stirred and gave a low moan.

He knelt beside her, touched her cheek. The heat of her burned through his thin gloves. "Honey?"

Her eyes flew open. For a moment they seemed to focus on his face. Then they skittered to the guttering red-glass lamp and widened in horror as if she saw a demon in its flame.

A whimper.

He stroked her temple. "It's all right. It's going to be all right."

Her gaze darted back. The fever had darkened her irises to a stormy sea green.

"It's all right," he said again. God, let it be all right. He reached for her hand, pressed it, felt underlying slender bones. "Sally?"

Her eyes glittered with dark sea glints. Doll's eyes, made of glass. No recognition. Nothing.

Sally struggled up onto an elbow. A cough exploded from bone-pale lips. Slim muscles tightened and quivered; a vein on her temple pulsed blue against whitewashed skin. Exhausted, she fell back, eyes fluttering shut, lashes like copper against the gunmetal hollows beneath them.

The clock dripped time in tiny discrete drops.

Bru felt a hand on his shoulder. It was Dave.

"Come on," he said, and nodded toward the door.

Bru followed him out.

Jack Hubert sat at the dining room table. His hunched shoulders straightened when Bru came into the room.

Nathan Katz was on watch. At Hubert's movement his grip tightened on the gun in his right hand; the left, almost useless now, hung by his side. The bandages on his upper arm were stained yellow with serum; reddened puffy flesh bulged from beneath them.

Dave pulled off his mask with one motion. "This plane. When's it due?"

A silencing hiss came through the open door to the kitchen. Cass Tompkins placed a warning finger against her lips. Calvin Borden had fallen asleep in her arms, his cheeks still traced with drying tears. The back of his thumb was pressed to the corner of his mouth. She drew him closer.

Bru pulled the door shut. "12:30. They know about the landing strip. We'll have to meet them with the pickup. They're bringing equipment."

"Vickers isolation units," said Hubert.

"I'll go," said Nathan. He turned haltingly toward the others, but his injured ankle brought him up short.

Dave frowned. "You're in no shape to drive." Then, to Bru, "I'll do it."

"No," said Bru shortly. One of the terrorists was still loose on the island. "No one goes alone."

"We'll both go," said Nathan.

Bru flashed a look at him, then nodded. "What time is it?"

Hubert looked at his watch. "12:22."

"Better do it, then."

Nathan jerked his chin toward the window. "Listen."

A distant rumble.

"It's the plane." Dave reached for the door. "Come on."

Nathan followed as quickly as his injuries would allow. The door wheezed shut behind them.

The rumble grew; the radiotelephone shrilled through it. Bru snatched it up. "Bru Farrier here."

A man's voice. "Stand by."

Another came on. The DCI. "Farrier, give me that bomb location."

Bru raised his voice over the growing noise of aircraft engines. "I hear your boys, but they're not here yet."

"You've got your plane." A breath. Urgency in the voice. "Give me the location."

The rumble grew to a roar. Loud. Too loud.

Jack Hubert ran to the window, looked up. "Shit."

Bru dropped the receiver, ran to his side, stared. The glass rattled.

C-130s. Six of them.

They swooped in from the Atlantic. Low. Dull wings spread like huge predators.

The transports roared overhead. The bays were open.

From upstairs a girl's scream wavered, rose.

Bru scrabbled for the phone. "Call them off." His stomach clenched. "Call them off, you stinking son of a bitch."

The terrorist ducked beneath a stand of palmettos and stared up at the planes. They were coming in low.

The first passed overhead, almost on top of him, and he flattened. He did not see the open bay; he did not see the drum of napalm rolling out.

Explosion.

Fronds jittered and burst into flame. White-hot jelly stuck to flesh, bored in. Screaming, he rolled away—into an inferno.

In moments his hair was shriveled, his scalp charred. He covered his face with burning hands, gasped, sucked fire.

He ran, zigzagging through streaming flames, until a blackened tendon in his leg burned through and pitched him to the ground. Air rushed from seared lungs; a final hoarse cry erupted through blistered lips.

Limbs twisted in spasm. A steaming eyeball gaped through

a ruined lid. Urine hissed against burning flesh. His body arched, convulsed, then curled reflexively as life shuddered out of it.

Two yards away, a dying garter snake whipped its length into a seething, tortuous curve. A yard beyond, a small owl opened a tiny curved beak and smothered in its burrow. And past a stretch of sizzling marsh grass, a frightened fawn crouched in a wash of tide and bleated for its mother.

Chapter 49

THE CONNECTION WITH THE DCI BROKE OFF ABRUPTLY. BRU slammed down the receiver and flung open the door to the kitchen. "Call Dave Cole," he yelled. "Use the Jeep radio."

Cass Tompkins jumped. Startled awake, Calvin Borden scrambled out of her lap.

"Move," said Bru.

Cass ran, slamming the door behind her.

Footsteps clattered down the back stairs. Paige Cole ran in. "Fire. The woods are on fire."

"Where?"

She pointed to the west. "That way."

"How close?"

"I don't know." She shook her head. "Near the edge of the marsh."

Bru's breath shuddered out. Dave and Nathan were all right, then. They were heading southeast.

Ashley Borden stumbled down the stairs. "Why are they doing this?" she sobbed. "Why?"

Calvin tugged at his sister's arm. "What's wrong?" His face twisted. "What's wrong?"

A shout from upstairs. A few seconds later Tim Jefferson ran into the kitchen. "Backfire. It's coming this way "

"Which side of the firebreak?"

Tim strained to hear, frowned, shook his head.

"The firebreak," yelled Bru. "Which side?"

Comprehension broke on Tim's face. "West. The far side." His voice was loud. "It might hold." He wheeled and ran back upstairs.

Bru's lips thinned. The C-130s had dumped their load on the inland side of the island, but they'd be back. Enraged, he whirled toward Jack Hubert. "What the hell are you people trying to pull?"

Hubert shook his head. "I don't know."

"You get your fucking boss on the phone." Bru's jaw clenched. "Do it. *Now*."

White-faced, Hubert reached for the radiotelephone, and froze.

An airplane engine.

Ashley darted to the window.

The rumble grew.

Spinning away, Ashley pushed Calvin to the floor and crouched on top of him. She screamed and pressed hands to her ears.

Bru ran to the window.

A C-130. Banking. Wings leaden against a flat gray sky.

Daniel Elton's grip tightened on the wheel. He swung the Camaro onto I-85 behind a cluster of cars in the right lane. In the left a BMW was tailgating an old man in a painfully slow black Ford pickup. The after-Thanksgiving sales were drawing record Atlanta crowds, and the traffic was heavy. Just keep it moving, he thought. The last thing he needed was a fender-bender tying up the interstate.

For the second time in as many minutes, he wondered how he had managed to get himself into this. He glanced at his watch, then over at Wally. "We'll make it. Plenty of time." He hoped it was true.

Wally nodded. He seemed cool enough, but a lump of muscle tightened at the angle of his jaw.

The pickup's right blinker came on, and the driver, looking for an opening, peered toward the right lane. Elton veered left. A semi was coming up fast in the rearview mirror. Elton slid into the hole just as the pickup moved right and the BMW darted ahead.

Wally reached into his pocket. Out of the corner of his eye, Elton saw him cup something in his hand. A prescription bottle? The lid popped open and a tiny white pill disappeared between Wally's fingers.

"Everything okay?"

Wally's voice was noncommittal. "Fine."

The BMW moved right into the exit lane, and the road was clear to the top of the hill. Elton floored it. The Camaro moved out briskly, but suddenly it lurched and lost power. He goosed the accelerator.

The Camaro slowed to forty. "Shit."

Thirty-five.

Elton bit his lip and cut to the right.

Thirty.

Twenty-eight.

He was on the shoulder now, creeping along at barely twenty-five miles an hour. "Happened the other day," he muttered. "It ought to clear out in a minute."

Wally shot him a look. "How long since you changed the fuel filter?"

"A while, I guess." He had no idea. The Camaro lurched again, made it up to thirty, then lost power. The Ford pickup passed at what seemed to be the speed of light. Elton licked his lips and goosed the accelerator again.

The Camaro coughed and leaped ahead.

Elton's held breath shuddered out. "It's okay. It's okay now."

But by the time he had edged back into the stream of

traffic, a solid phalanx of vehicles was between him and the old man's creeping pickup.

The back door to the lodge swung open and Cass Tompkins ran in. "The rescue plane. It's landed."

Bru's head went up. "Are you sure?"

"I got Dave on the radio." She was out of breath. "That's what he said. They're coming back."

Jack Hubert looked up from the phone. "They said to wait." His gaze suddenly whipped back to the receiver. "What? What's that?" He listened intently, then cupped his hand over the mouthpiece and said to Bru, "It's over. The napalm transports are headed back to Florida. Hurlburt Field." He turned back to the phone, listened again, then offered the receiver to Bru. "The DCI says it was a mistake. He wants to talk to you."

Bru smiled thinly. "Does he, now?" He made no move to pick up the phone. "Give him a message. Tell him he's damned right it was a mistake. Tell him he won't hear from me until these people are safe." He glanced down at his watch. The crystal was blank. "What time is it?"

"Twenty till one."

"Christ." He spun away. While Hubert turned back to the phone, Bru's fingers tapped against his thigh as if to mark each second.

Three minutes crept by.

Four.

A truck engine.

Bru threw open the back door and ran outside. In the distance a pall of smoke stained the sky.

The pickup truck careened around the last curve. In the shed Tony Herrera swung his rifle through the open door toward it.

"It's okay," yelled Bru. "It's the rescue team."

Tony backed up. Keeping the bound El Ojo in the corner of his eye, he watched.

The pickup truck skidded to a stop and seven men clinging to the side panels jumped off. They wore rebreathing

masks and heavy decontamination suits with the insignia
USAMRIID on the sleeves. Another, dressed the same, got
out of the cab. Nathan scrambled out and Dave followed.

When he saw Bru, Nathan hurried to him. "We saw the
fire. From the top of a dune. I think the firebreak is going
to hold it." His gaze jumped to the truck.

Two Stretcher Transit Isolators nearly filled the bed of
the pickup. Six of the men began to slide the first off the
truck bed. The other two, carrying medical packs, followed Dave into the lodge.

Nathan stared at the isolators. "They're heavy," he
said. "And that's just part. The main units are still on the
plane. They only have two of them, but two more are on
the way from someplace else. It's going to take all day to
get everybody out."

Relief flooded Bru's face. He glanced at his watch,
recoiled at the blank crystal, and wheeled toward the
lodge. Nathan followed.

In the kitchen Dave Cole was talking to the two men in
the decontam suits. He looked up when Bru and Nathan
came in. "Sally and Leroy go first. They can only take
two this trip. Nathan has to go next. He's got open wounds.
So does Tim, but—" He glanced at Calvin Borden. The
boy's hands and arms were deeply scratched. "Nathan and
Calvin next," Dave said decisively.

Shock crossed Nathan's face. "What about Tuck Perry?"

"Third," he said. "With Tim." At Nathan's frown he
said, "She'll be all right."

"She's catatonic. You said so yourself."

"But she doesn't have plague—or open wounds." He
lowered his voice. "She'll be okay in a week or two. I
promise you. It looks worse than it is."

"But—"

Bru interrupted. "Let it alone, Nathan. He's the doctor." He turned and went to the radiotelephone. Jack Hubert still held the receiver. "What time is it?" Bru asked.

"Nine of."

A heartbeat. "I'll talk to the DCI now," said Bru.

*   *   *

Bru spoke quickly into the phone, "Atlanta. The bomb's in Atlanta."

Jack Hubert winced. Only fourteen minutes left, he thought.

Bru retreated to the length of the cord as Cass Tompkins and Miranda Gervin pushed table and chairs against the window to make room for the isolation stretcher.

The door to the entry hall stood open. The paper bag KEEP OUT sign was on the floor, trampled underfoot. Dave Cole, not bothering with mask and gloves, had gone in with the two USAMRIID men.

Hubert could see Lena Jefferson bending over her husband. At the look on her face he clenched his fist. He wanted to reassure her, to tell her the army medical team was good—the best—but he did not know how to begin. Instead, he stood just inside the entry hall and watched as one of the isolation team snapped a tourniquet on Sally's arm and started an IV. The other drew up medication from a vial and injected it into the IV solution.

Moments later the evacuation crew carried the isolator into the entry hall. It barely cleared the door.

In less than a minute Sally was secured inside the unit, her IV hooked to a port. As they carried her out, the empty medication vial clattered against the side of a foot and rolled toward the wall, label side up.

A printed label.

Hubert stared at the vial and blinked. Then he crossed the room and picked it up.

Bru was hanging up the phone when Hubert ran back to the dining room. "Look at this." Hubert held out the empty vial.

Bru took it.

"It's not the experimental stuff. It's ordinary tetracycline," said Hubert. "We've been screwed."

Chapter 50

BRU SPUN TO THE PHONE, THEN STOPPED. NO USE. THE DCI's man controlled the radiotelephone now. He stared across the room without really seeing. Just inside the door, Calvin Borden was watching him intently, but Bru was barely aware of the boy. He turned to Jack Hubert. "The CIA's on the switchboard. We can't call out."

Hubert's eyes darkened and slid toward the USAMRIID team strapping Leroy into the isolator.

"Tell it to the army?" Bru's voice was low, but he spat out the words. "And then what? Another custom-tailored denial by your DCI?"

Hubert's jaw tightened. He looked away, then suddenly back. "There's one chance—but we've got to get a clear phone line."

A sharp tug on Bru's arm. He looked down.

Calvin Borden was clinging to his arm. "I know."

Distracted, Bru pulled away.

"I know." Another tug. "You can use the other phone."

Bru stared at the boy. "What phone?"

"There's one in Leroy's house. I saw."

Bru caught his breath. There were dozens of radiotelephones up and down the coast. They couldn't have cut off all of them. His eyes met Hubert's.

One chance.

"The Jeep," Bru said. "Let's go."

Five minutes later the CJ5 skidded to a stop in front of Leroy Jefferson's house.

*　　*　　*

In room 14 of the Coconut Palms Motel on S.W. Eighth Street, the young man known as Orlando Salazar picked up the phone. Squinting at the glare from the bright Miami sun, he pulled the heavy curtain shut and dialed a long-distance number.

When a stilted robot message began, he held a small black remote device to the mouthpiece and pressed a button.

A reciprocal electronic pulse. The recording broke off.

He listened.

A second passed. Then a synthesized female voice came on the line. "No messages."

There could have been only one: the words "Your dental appointment is canceled." The message to abort.

He tucked the remote device into the breast pocket of his shirt. In half an hour he would use it again; he would get his final instructions then.

Now it was time to call Atlanta.

When his watch showed 12:58, he began to dial. Dark eyes glittering, he stabbed the last four digits: 7796.

A ring. Five seconds. Another.

For protection against random wrong numbers and computer calls, he had set the device to answer on the twelfth ring. He knew it would not fail. He had personally checked each piece of electronic equipment he had been given.

All except one.

12:59. The last ring.

A sharp click as the Atlanta phone decoder activated. He hung up, a faint smile twisting his lips. The call had done its work. In six minutes the bulging Mylar bag would explode. Six minutes left.

Turning, he shouldered his backpack and went out. He walked briskly down S.W. Eighth toward a Cuban café he had spotted earlier. He was beginning to enjoy his stay. Too bad he had so little time left in Miami. By midnight he would be out of the country.

He was crossing against the light when the remote device in his breast pocket—the only piece of electronic equipment he had not bothered to check—gave a faint, almost inaudible, click. It had begun its five-minute count-down at the tone from the robot answering device.

The explosive charge it harbored was tiny. Not enough to kill. That was left to the little capsule of sodium cyanide nestled inside it.

He had one foot on the curb when the device detonated. Spinning once, hand clutched to his chest, he fell. There was time only for a drawn-out, shuddering gasp before the surprise in his eyes dulled to a glazed, wide-pupiled stare.

Bru's grip tightened on the receiver. A woman's voice came on. "Operator."

"Can anyone else hear us?"

A pause. "No."

"This is a CIA priority call. Don't disconnect after three minutes. Do you understand?"

"Yes."

"Stand by." Bru handed the receiver to Hubert, who gave her a number.

On the second ring a small child answered.

Hubert's hand tightened on the receiver. "Jamie, this is Daddy. Put Mommy on the phone."

A pause. Then Marta Hubert picked up. "Jack? Are you coming home? I didn't hear, and I—"

"Listen to me, Marta. This is important. I want you to record this call. Turn the recorder on now." He covered the mouthpiece and said to Bru, "Sometimes it's expedient to bug your own phone."

Bru's eyebrow rose.

A moment later Marta's voice came back. "The tape's rolling."

Hubert began to speak: "This is John Hubert, CIA, calling from St. Cyrils Island, Georgia." He gave the date and checked his watch. "The time is now 12:59 P.M." His voice dropped. "I want you to make a three-way call," he said to Marta. "You'll be the operator. You don't have a name. Do you know what I'm saying?"

A second's hesitation. "Yes."

"Call this number."

"Wait. I need a pencil." A moment later, "Okay."

Hubert gave the number. "That's direct to the Crisis Committee. Tell whoever answers that the call is for the director, Central Intelligence. Tell him I'm calling. And stay on the line."

"Got it. I'm putting you on hold."

Twenty seconds crept by.

Thirty.

A click. Marta's voice was crisp. "Ready on your call."

The DCI spoke without preamble. "Where are you?"

"St. Cyrils Island." Hubert's voice was cold. "The evacuation plane landed a few minutes ago. They showed up with a commercial antibiotic."

The DCI was silent.

"We've got two plague victims here. Two—and who knows how many more are in the chute."

A pause. "That's unfortunate."

"Believe it." Hubert's jaw tightened. "Where in hell is the goddamned antibiotic we need?"

"This line isn't secure."

"This line will fucking well have to do."

The DCI's voice was wary. "I'm sure Detrick sent the appropriate drug."

"Appropriate? Just who is it appropriate for?"

"I'm not a medical man, Hubert. Neither are you. You don't know what you're talking about here."

"I'm talking about an experimental antibiotic for a gerrymandered plague cooked up in a CIA proprietary lab."

Silence.

Hubert took a breath. "People are dying."

"I have to go along with Detrick."

"Are you refusing to release the antibiotic?"

"I don't know about any antibiotic. Detrick's got the medical experts. The army is running the show."

Hubert's eyes narrowed. "That's what I thought you'd

say." His tone changed abruptly. "Operator. Are you still on the line?"

Marta's voice was tense. "Yes."

"I want you to make copies of this tape. I want you to get them to the *Washington Post* and the *New York Times*. And the networks. Call the Washington News Bureau of—"

The DCI broke in abruptly. "Did you have reference to, uh, a small amount of R&D antibiotic? If, uh, that's what you mean, we would, of course, be sending that along to Detrick. We could, uh, have that in Maryland by the time the first victims arrive."

"Yes." Hubert's lips tightened in a thin smile. "That will do, sir. That will do just fine."

The color drained from the DCI's face as he listened to Jack Hubert. Thirty years, he thought. Thirty years.

But there was still the woman. The "operator." If he could find her, get to her in time.

Who was she? Hubert's wife? But the man wouldn't risk involving his wife. A sister, then. A sister. Or a mistress. But where? Where?

No time to trace the call. No time. . . .

It had all run out and now the game was over.

The DCI stared at the phone. Finally his lips moved and formed one last, silent word: "Checkmate."

Then he hung up.

The phone receiver rocked back into its cradle and Jack Hubert turned to Bru. For a second his face was blank. Then the beginning of a faint grin.

But Bru did not see it. He was staring at the old mechanical clock on the Jeffersons' kitchen wall.

A whir, and the minute hand jumped with an audible click.

1:03.

Chapter 51

THE CAMARO SWUNG OFF I-75 ONTO A ROAD NARROWED WITH parked cars. Band music blared from behind the curved walls of Grant Field. Street-corner vendors hawked red plush UGA Bulldogs, T-shirts, and chrome-yellow Georgia Tech pennants to the last of the sixty thousand fans streaming into the stadium.

Cursing, Daniel Elton swung around a double-parked van and turned down a side street clogged with cars.

He craned his neck to see over the cab of a Dodge pickup parked on the grass. "Where is this fucking place?"

Wally took a deep breath. The tightness in his chest had begun during the flight when the Cessna gained altitude. He had tried to ignore it. Now hot steel bands constricted his lungs. The nitro tablets he had taken—two within the last fifteen minutes—had done no good. Squinting, he spotted the faded sign. "Techwood," he said, raising his voice over the brassy notes of "Ramblin' Wreck." He pointed to a cluster of two-story buildings. "Over there."

Building C was just ahead on the right. The street curved left. Elton hit the brakes and the Camaro squealed to a stop in the middle of the road. "I can't get any closer."

Wally threw open the door and jumped out. Cold air struck his face. The pain leaped; fire and ice throbbed in his left jaw. He took a shuddering breath and ran. It was twenty yards to building C.

A roar erupted from the stadium. A chant: "Go-oh-oh-oh . . . Dawgs! Woof, woof, woof, woof."

Thirty thousand voices responded: "Bz-zz-zz-zz . . . Sting 'em!"

The heavy entrance door felt like lead. He pulled it open. Inside, a bare light bulb cut the dimness.

No time to get the building super. He'd have to shoot the lock.

Panting, he took the stairs two at a time. At the landing, searing pain jolted through his chest and traveled down his arm like an electric shock. He grabbed the railing with cramping fingers, swayed, sucked air.

Go on. He had to. No time.

In room 209 compressed air hissed into the paint tank. Inside the tank, *Yersinia pestis 18* bled from its ruptured canister and roiled within the stream of air.

The paint tank exhaled its lethal breath through transparent tubing into the silver Mylar bag against the window. The sac bulged—a giant, swollen cell veined with primacord. At its nucleus the igniter quivered against the outward thrust of swarming bacteria.

In one minute it would blow.

Wally hit the second floor and ran down the dim, echoing hall.

Room 205. 207.

He reached for his gun.

209.

The shot from his .357 Magnum rang in his ears; the lock shattered. No one responded; the hall was empty. He threw open the door and ran in.

The room was dim. Wally's hand shot to the light switch, hesitated. Too dark. He had to risk it.

The ceiling light flared on.

He stared. Caught his breath. Struggled for air.

The swollen Mylar bag bulged into the room. His gaze darted from the igniter to the paint tank. The timer. Where was it?

A vise tightened around his heart. Involuntarily he

clutched his chest, stumbled. Cold sweat popped out on his brow.

A breath. He gripped his left hand in his right as if to pluck out the gnawing pain.

Eleven seconds. Ten. Nine . . .

He blinked. Focused. Took in wires and tubes.

Eight. Seven. Six . . .

The air tank.

Five seconds. Four. Three . . .

A gauge. A single valve, cocked open. He grabbed it, pressed, throttled it off. Stared.

Two seconds.

He had to hold it. Had to.

Pain blazed in his chest. In despair he felt his grip weaken. The valve strained under it. Popped loose. He grabbed it again.

His left hand groped to his belt buckle, fumbled it open. Numbing fingers inched the belt from constraining loops. His sweat streaked the shiny leather.

Hang on.

A final tug. The belt swung free.

Cold nausea rippled through his belly. He fought it with a breath.

His fingers cramped on the valve trigger. Wedging his thumb against it, he lashed his hand to the gauge with loops of leather. With the last of his strength he pulled the belt tight, buckled it.

His heart fluttered against his ribs, paused, moved like a small child's flip-flop toy. He blinked at the sudden dimming of his vision.

No air, no air . . .

A fluttering in his chest: summer moth against a screen, fall leaf jittering on a branch . . .

Distant siren warbling . . . fading . . . blending into a single windy note inside his head . . .

A ragtag exhalation. A whisper. "Martha."

When the GBI bomb squad arrived fifty-eight seconds later, Wally was dead.

Chapter 52

At 10:00 P.M. Fort Detrick's isolation ward was dim with its nighttime lighting. With an eye out for the nurse, Bru stopped just inside a darkened room, then crossed to the bed.

Sally was asleep. Oxygen hissed through a cannula strapped to her face. Two IVs were running. He reached out and gently touched her cheek. Still feverish. She had been sleeping for hours now, oblivious to anything around her.

He was turning to go when she stirred. A frown furrowed her brow and she plucked at the IV. Bru covered her hand with his. "It's all right."

Her eyes fluttered open, startled, questioning.

He caught his breath. "Honey?"

"Wha—where?" She stared at the IV pole.

"You're in a hospital."

Her eyes slid toward his. "What?" Then suddenly she focused. "Bru? Oh, Bru—"

"It's all right. You're going to be all right." It was as if his words brought him a revelation. She was going to make it. His lips brushed her forehead and his hand tightened on hers. "I got you into all of this."

Her brow furrowed again; her lids fluttered shut.

He thought of Wally then. He had involved both of them. Now Wally was dead.

Suddenly Bru could almost hear a gravelly voice, dripping scorn, and he remembered something Wally had said long ago when Bru came back from Nam and Jimmy

Carruthers didn't: "There isn't any point to guilt. The point is to do something positive."

Sally stirred again, looked up.

"I love you," he whispered. He cradled her hand in his and felt the small bones that made it seem so vulnerable. He kissed her fingertips. "Poor naked little hand," he said. "It needs something to wear." He stroked her ring finger. "There, I think. Maybe something in gold. What do you say?"

"Love you," she said faintly, and slept again.

A shadow fell across his face. One of the nurses. Evans, this time. She came to the bed, checked Sally's IV, then turned to Bru and said pointedly, "You look tired, Mr. Farrier. Why don't you try and get a little rest?"

He grinned. "I give up."

Evans smiled back. At least, he thought so. Her mouth and nose were covered by her mask, but her eyes crinkled at the corners. He followed her back to his room.

He stared pointedly at her isolation jumpsuit and raised an eyebrow. "Do you ladies always wear green for plague?"

"Always. Now, *will* you go to bed?"

The phone in his room rang softly, and she moved to it, green booties whispering over the floor. "Evans speaking." She rolled her eyes. "But he talked to him less than an hour ago." She listened a moment longer, shrugged, and reluctantly handed the receiver to Bru. "It's the switchboard. Dr. Elton's on the line again."

Bru watched her leave the room before he said, "And what's new with the good doctor?"

Daniel Elton gave a low laugh. "The good doctor's getting pretty skilled at making phony high-priority calls," he said. "I think I missed my calling. Maybe I ought to give up medicine and go into the CIA."

"I know of an opening."

"I didn't wake you up, did I? I probably shouldn't have called back, but I was too wired not to." Elton laughed. "I may have to crawl in bed with my Old Granddad tonight. How's everybody doing?"

"The women are okay," said Bru. "Ashley's better."

"Then her acidosis is under control?"

"I think so." Bru glanced past the nurse's station at the center of the ward. Ashley Borden's door stood open and a dim light glittered on the IV bottle above her bed. By the time the girl arrived at Fort Detrick, she was in stress-induced diabetic acidosis. "She's still got the IV," he said.

"And will for a while. Till they get her washed out. But kids are like rubber bands," said Elton. "They snap right back. How's the boy?"

"He's a survivor." Calvin Borden lay in a rollaway bed next to Ashley. He was sound asleep in the center of a Gordian knot of sheets and blankets. Bru grinned. "He wouldn't go to bed until they let him make rounds with the doctor at eight. Calvin predicted that Nathan Katz's fever would be gone by morning, and it's down already. I think they're going to give the kid his own stethoscope."

"So everybody's okay?"

Bru hesitated. "Leroy's worse." Nathan was going to make it, but Leroy wasn't. The disease had struck him hard and fast, and now the doctors didn't think he'd live through the night. Bru stared at the wall. It was a drab institutional green. He thought of the low green island that Lillian had willed years ago to the Georgia Conservancy. That was where the old man would want to be buried, he thought. With her. Maybe someday.

"Bru?"

"Yeah. I'm still here." He cleared his throat.

"Sally—" Elton's voice dropped. "How is she?"

"Better, thank God. I just saw her." Bru's voice lightened. "She'll be up and around in a couple of weeks. She's going to be too busy to stay in bed," he paused, "with a wedding to plan for."

"All *right*," said Elton. "Hold on." He came back a few seconds later. "I had to tell Ginny. We've been watching the news. I guess we really gave those boys something to talk about. We've got a six-hour videotape half full already.''

"Yeah," said Bru, "but they left out the most important part.''

"What's that?"

"All right, my friend. Quit playing with my mind and give me a goddamn break," said Bru. "Who won the ball game?"

"Oh," laughed Elton. "We did."

BESTSELLING BOOKS FROM TOR

Buy them at your local bookstore or use this handy coupon:
Clip and mail this page with your order

TOR BOOKS—Reader Service Dept.
49 W. 24 Street, 9th Floor, New York, NY 10010

Please send me the book(s) I have checked above. I am enclosing
$_____ (please add $1.00 to cover postage and handling).
Send check or money order only—no cash or C.O.D.'s.

Mr./Mrs./Miss _____
Address _____.
City _____ State/Zip _____
Please allow six weeks for delivery. Prices subject to change without
notice.

MORE BESTSELLERS FROM TOR

RICHARD HOYT

"Richard Hoyt is an expert writer."
—*The New York Times*

THE BEST IN SUSPENSE